Also by Carole Walker Carter

Shadowy

Faces

Vol. II

Evers & McFarlan Detective Series

Carole Walker Carter

 WALKER CARTER PUBLISHING, LLC

Cover Design by Jennifer Coyle

Shadowy Faces / by Carole Walker Carter
Evers & McFarlan Detective Series / Volume 2

ISBN 978-1-947734-30-2

9 8 7 6 5 4 3 2 1 17 18 19 20 21

[1. Women Sleuths, 2. Mystery, 3. Detectives, 4. Mystery Suspense Thriller, 5. Paperback Mysteries, 6. Action Adventure Romance]

WALKER CARTER PUBLISHING, LLC

Please check out my website at <u>www.walkercarter.com</u>

To my girls Jennifer and Lisa, my grandson Nixon, my

granddaughter Alex and my husband, Don.

In memory of my mother and dad, Elda and Dean Walker.

I will always love you!!!

ACKNOWLEDGEMENTS

I wrote this book in cooperation with my best friend and husband, Donald E. Carter, author of _Concurrent Engineering, Product Development Environment_ business books. Don's inspiration helped to create characters for the Evers and McFarlan Series and researched all the technical information.

The first book in the Evers and McFarlan Series is _Final Alumni_. The second is _Shadowy Faces_, and the third is this book _Nine Points of a Circle._

Janis Lane supported me with my writing by cheering me on to tell my stories. Don and I worked diligently to edit this book over the past year.

My girls, Jennifer Hinger and Lisa Coyle, provided several useful resource books. Without their support and prodding, this book may still be in draft form. Jennifer, with a keen eye for graphics, helped with the cover art.

Janel Walker, my younger sister, provided encouragement by always asking for the next chapter while providing excellent suggestions. Without my mother, Elda Walker, and older sister Linda Sturgill, giving me love, support, and resources, I would not be able to write.

Special thanks to all those that donated to my GoFundMe page, Linda Sturgill, Elda Walker, Janel Walker, Judy Mathiesen, Linda Maddex, Afsaneh Fowler, and Carol Royce Davidson. These donations kick-started my venture by allowing me to acquire editing and review tools, ISBN numbers, audio equipment, and final publication costs.

Table of Contents

CHAPTER ONE

I headed toward Heather's safe house. I couldn't keep my mind from wandering. There was so much that happened the last year since Scott and I graduated from high school. My mind wanted to sort things out and put them in chronological order as best as I could.

Scott and I were now junior partners of a private investigation company run by the Jamiesons. It was only a matter of time before we would be old enough to have the business in our own names and buy the Jamiesons out. Much had changed in such a short time in our lives.

Classwork at the college, working part-time for three different people...the dojang where I taught self-defense to women and children, the police department work where I teach self-defense to rookie cops, and of course, the part-time work with the Jamiesons to learn their business. Scott, too, has firearms practice and his job with Aileen and Patrick, as well as classwork. All of this keeps us just a little bit more than busy.

This first year found us involved in several cases. The checks we are receiving from insurance companies are funding our down-payment on the private investigation business we are buying from the Jamiesons. Neither Scotty or I had any idea that cracking insurance fraud cases could be so rewarding. Patrick and Aileen Jamieson, our mentors and now business partners, have told us they were very lucrative. They also told us to stay away from divorce cases.

We sort of fell into some of our cases by being in the wrong place at the right time. Scotty was working as a night security guard at the mall, and his first bonus check of any size came when he and his co-worker stopped a jewelry store theft.

Checks from multiple insurance companies were unexpected as well. We were entering data into the computer for the Jamiesons' past cases when we realized a strange pattern which led us to investigate a family involved in fire insurance fraud.

The next case was, in fact, assigned to us by the Jamiesons. It also involved theft occurring at a modeling agency. A jewelry insurance scam was one of the latest cases we were actively engaged in for the Jamiesons. We are expecting additional checks from the insurance companies when their investigation is completed.

Looking in the rear-view mirror of my Harley, I stopped reminiscing. I thought there was a truck following me, but I must have been wrong. I kept driving, but I often checked to see if the forest green truck was still several cars behind me.

I pulled into the grocery store. I had a list of several items Heather asked me to bring. I told myself this would be the last day I would be her grocery delivery lady. I was determined to talk Heather into going to see Captain Jones so she could tell him all she knew about Jack.

I felt sorry for Heather. I understood her fear. She was totally convinced Jack, her husband, was trying to kill her. If I didn't believe her, I never would have secretly driven down to Stanton to help plan an escape to the safe house she now occupies here in Chicago.

That little plan backfired. I almost lost the love of my life and my partner over keeping that little secret. I knew deep down, I should have told Scotty immediately what I did and why, but I was too afraid of losing him.

Scotty was madly in love with Heather in high school, and I couldn't get that out of my mind. Our lives were too perfect together since high school, and I just couldn't risk losing him and our future. By being stupid and not trusting his love for me, I almost lost the most important person in my life.

I packed the few items Heather wanted into my saddlebags on my Harley and started the bike up once again. I scanned the parking lot and street to see if the green truck was anywhere to be seen. When I did not see the truck, I drove out of the grocery store parking lot and continued to Heather's house.

Heather was waiting for me at the front window. She peeked out between the slit in the drapes to make sure it was me. Heather was paranoid these days...not answering the door for anyone except me. Heather won't go out for a walk or to the grocery store or anywhere. Keeping herself sequestered in a dark, small house with no company except her television, I must admit I am worried about her.

I knocked once, and I heard the latch of the lock open. Heather opened the door a crack and expected me to slip inside.

"Aw, come on, Heather. Open the door wide enough for me to get in with these bags of groceries. Why do we need to go through this every time I come over?" I was feeling a bit grumpy after about the 100th time of trying to slip through a gap only an anorexic, tiny person could fit through.

Heather looked awful. "Heather, when is the last time you took a shower and washed your hair?" I asked bluntly.

"You know I am afraid to be naked and alone for that long. What if Jack should come into the house while I am in the shower. He could kill me with a kitchen knife just like in *Psycho*," Heather said, trembling.

"I told you not to watch scary movies while you are here alone. Can't you watch something upbeat? Watch *Seinfeld* or *Melrose Place*, but don't be watching such gruesome things. It only makes you more paranoid," I said with little sympathy showing in my voice.

"I'm not paranoid!" Heather said heatedly.

"Okay, it is time to prove to me you aren't all that paranoid. I am coming back in the car, and you and I are going to see Captain Jones. You need to tell him everything you told me about Jack's involvement with trying to kill all the alumni for the investment money," I dared her.

I knew she wouldn't agree to go, but I was hoping the dare would cause some backbone to grow. Heather was always a frilly, girlie-girl.

"I can't go. What if Jack is watching? He will follow us to the police station, and when he knows I am going to talk, he will shoot me. Jack has a gun, you know. Being a deputy sheriff, he can carry it anytime he wants. I am afraid; he is mean. Jack would have no qualms about killing me if he thought I was going to the police." Again, Heather was shaking.

I sat the food down on her counter. I unpacked the cans of baked beans and franks, canned peaches, potato chips, cookies, and milk. It seemed like an odd diet, but I supposed it was comfort food for Heather. "Next time I am bringing fruit and vegetables and nothing else. You will either eat nutritious food or starve," I growled.

I was trying to think how I could light a fire under this crazy lady. What did Scott ever see in her? Her red hair was dull, and her hazel eyes looked vacant, like a deer caught in the headlights. It was hard to imagine she was once considered perky and beautiful...a cheerleader and Prom Queen. Now, she looked like an unhealthy-looking waif.

I decided to try another tactic. I can be imposing when I need to be. I am tall, physically strong, and statuesque in some people's opinion. I have street smarts and the ability to protect myself through several different martial arts disciplines.

"Heather, you will either go to see Captain Jones, or I will bring him here. You have no choice in this matter except to run, and just exactly where would you run? Aren't you tired of living like a hermit? Don't you want your life back?... Well, besides that, I am tired of being your delivery person. You are going to do this, or I am going to just let you starve to death. Do you hear me?" I ranted at her.

I knew she would buckle in some way or another, but I wasn't prepared for the complete breakdown that took place in front of me.

Heather ran to the furthest corner of the darkened living room, curled up in a ball, covering her head with her hands and rocked back and forth while whining like a wounded animal. Now, I felt horrible. I went too far.

I ran over and bent down next to her. Pulling her hands away from her head, I spoke softly, "I'm sorry, Heather. I won't abandon you. You can take your own time. I won't push any longer, okay?" I repeated these words or any words I thought might break through to her while she was in this state.

I found myself holding her and rocking back and forth with her in my arms. My mind flashed to days when I would run to my closet, close the door, and stay in the dark, trying to avoid my uncle. I pushed those thoughts aside. Now was not the time for me to feel sorry for myself. Heather needed looking after.

With her being an emotional mess, I couldn't leave her. Fixing comfort food, baked beans, and franks, and turning on an inane television show that captured Heather's attention, I felt it was safe to leave. I explained I would be back tomorrow.

Jumping on to my Harley, I headed for the Jamiesons' office. I knew I was late, but I also knew they would understand. I rode quickly but safely and with the presence of mind to double-check to see if a green truck was in sight.

As I pulled into the office parking lot, I noticed Scott was using the surveillance van and wondered why. Maybe he received a phone call from Patrick saying they would need us to spy on someone.

I entered the office, and Scotty flew to me in a panic. "Tish, are you alright?" he said as he hugged me.

"Well, yes, why wouldn't I be alright?" I asked with some concern.

"When you left this morning, I saw a green truck pull out from a side road, and it was following you. I was sure it was Jack's truck. I ran to the van as fast as I could to follow, but I lost him. It occurred to me you have never told me where you are keeping Heather. Therefore, I did not know how to let you know you might be in danger!" Scott was talking frantically.

"Whoa! Stop! Are you saying you saw Jack in his green truck following me? Or...did you just think you saw someone who looks like Jack in a green truck that happened to be going the same direction?" I wanted clarification since the hairs on the back of my neck were starting to rise.

"I can't say absolutely for sure it was Jack, but I would say it was a huge possibility. After all, how many people have a step-side forest green truck with a logo on the back window that looked like our mascot from high school?" Scotty seemed shaken up.

I did not want to alarm Scotty, but my instincts now told me I was being followed by a green truck, and in all probability, it was Jack. If that was the case, I just led him to where Heather was being hidden.

"I need to phone Captain Jones right now!" I said.

I rushed off before Scotty could stop and ask any questions. As I talked to Captain Jones on the phone, I was aware Scotty was listening to every word I said. When I hung up, the questions started.

"You told Captain Jones you thought you were being followed by a green truck. Did you ever get a look at the driver?" Scott fired at me.

Before I could answer, Scotty said again. "Is Heather in danger? Should we go over right now to make sure she is okay? What did Captain Jones say? Is he sending a patrol car over to watch Heather's house?"

I took a deep breath. Aileen and Patrick were standing and listening to the whole interchange without moving or commenting. Finally, Patrick broke their silence.

"We need to have a plan. Scotty, I think you and Tish should use the van for surveillance. We can give you some time off to keep Heather safe. Aileen and I will be available to spell you whenever you need to leave for classes," Patrick said.

Aileen jumped into the conversation, "I will go to the store right now and get any supplies you might need for several days of surveillance. Give Patrick the address of the safe house, and we will drop by shortly. Park the van where you can see everything yet be as inconspicuous as possible. Do you have blankets, pillows, and is the tank full of water? I can get bottled water if you need some."

I thanked Aileen. I assured her the van had a full tank of water and enough for several flushes as well. There were snacks, but not any real food. There are blankets and a pillow under the bench seat. Scotty and I will take turns sleeping while the other watched.

"I am grateful that our fathers got a chance to update the cameras. We can now use the 360-degree periscopic day and night vision color camera on the roof, hidden by the custom-made equipment/tool rack. A new camera controller tied to the recording system was installed in the console.

Our fathers outfitted a new helmet for Tish with a modified Motorola Astro Sabre 2-way radio. Similar Motorola radios with headsets were placed in special chargers in one of the cabinets. They also provided two Motorola Astro base stations, one for the office and our home.

We can now stay in communications amongst ourselves using the digital voice encryption feature. The only drawback is we all need to study up on amateur radios and pass a 35-question test for the technician license. My dad told me there is an amateur radio club here in Chicago that provides a class and exam proctors. They can give the permit we will need on the same day," Scott told Patrick sounding very technical.

"I hate to interrupt, but I think we should get over to Heather's house. I am going to ride my Harley. I may need to use it while we are doing surveillance. I still need to buy her groceries from time to time until we know for sure Jack isn't a threat," I said.

"Where are you going to park the Harley where it will be out of sight and still keep it safe?" Scotty asked me.

"I have become acquaintances with one neighbor. They have been keeping an eye on Heather's house for me. I am sure they will let me conceal my Harley in their garage," I said.

"Do they know Heather is in hiding?" Scott asked.

I could tell he was starting to resent the fact that I would confide in strangers and not him, so I cut him off before he began to rant.

"It isn't like that, Scotty. These people are friends of Captain Jones. They have been in on this from the beginning. In fact, it is their rental house that Heather is staying in. The man is a retired policeman and a friend of Captain Jones."

I wasn't sure if my answer made Scott feel better or worse. I knew he was thinking about how I should have trusted him from the beginning, but I also knew he was working hard on giving me the benefit of the doubt. He was trying to move on and make a new go of our relationship. I was just sorry there would be things that reminded him of how I had not confided in him, and hurt him. There was little I could do now to stomp out the forest fire, but try to reassure him on how much I loved him and wanted our relationship to work.

I walked over to him and gave him a hug. I intentionally let my breasts rub against his chest. I knew I was cheating, but getting his mind off a sore subject needed a bit of duplicity. I was happy to feel him relax and return my hug with enthusiasm.

When Patrick interrupted us with the clearing of his throat, I knew I might have gone a bit too far. "I hope the two of you remember why you are in the surveillance van...."

I blushed as did Scotty. "Time to go," was Scotty's only response.

"I will bring over the supplies and be as discreet as possible. Should I wait until it is dark?" asked Aileen.

"If you don't mind getting me a double cheeseburger, fries, and a large soft drink, I would be eternally grateful. The snacks will hold us until dark," said Scotty.

"Egad, Scott!" I said. "Do you ever think of anything but your stomach?"

"Well, a few seconds ago, I wouldn't have thought you would ever ask that question." He winked at Patrick as he pushed me out the door.

We talked for a couple of minutes before leaving. I wanted to make sure Scott knew how to get to the address. I also mentioned a side street that might be less noticeable to anyone where he could park. I was going to go straight to the neighbors and tell them what I intended to do and make sure they were alright with my hiding my Harley in their garage. I also wanted to ask whether they saw a green truck make several trips past the house. I knew Captain Jones had a police officer making trips past Heather's house every half hour or so, but Hank, the retired cop, was more likely to notice something amiss.

Scotty found an excellent place to park. He could see most of Heather's safe house from the street. There were a few dead spots that we would need to check out on our own from time to time. Now would have been the perfect time to have disguises and maybe a dog to walk. I made a mental note to add costumes to the closets in the van. The dog was going to need to wait until we found a new house to buy. Our rental agreement did not include a pet clause at present.

After checking with Hank and Eloise, I confirmed Heather was still okay. Before leaving Heathers, I looked carefully up and down the street to make sure no green truck was in view. I then made a quick run to the van and entered the back door.

Scott was busy setting up the equipment. I thought for sure I would find chip bags empty and soda cans all over the van by the time I entered. Disappointed not to be able to chastise him, I found Scotty sitting at the console. His attention was on the cameras and making sure every angle possible was covered.

I kissed him on the neck as I sat down beside him in the other control seat.

"What was that for?" asked Scotty.

"For being the best partner, a girl could ever have," I said as I took my place beside him. I was feeling blessed. The love of my life is my partner; what more could a woman want? True, things were not back to normal, but I knew we would make it through this rough patch.

Back to business, Scotty said, "I can see almost every entrance to Heather's safe house except the back door. I don't think that will be a problem since we would see Jack if he drives anywhere near her house."

I answered. "But what if Jack parks some distance away and uses his military training to sneak to the back door?" I was really concerned about how we were going to handle this situation. I know from experience; I can't leave my partner and sneak off on my own. I learned that the hard way.

"If we had our license, we could use your helmet with the radio, and one of us could wear it and hide in the bushes while the other stays in contact with the radio. The problem is, we don't have our license yet. We will just need to come up with another solution. This time, though, it won't be you hiding in the bushes," Scott said with finality.

I let his comment go for the moment. Time would tell which one of us would be in the bushes if it came to that. In the meantime, I wished we had a way to contact Captain Jones to find out what he knew.

Aileen came a quarter of an hour after it was dark. She was the lifesaver Scotty hoped she would be. I could smell the cheeseburger the minute the back door was opened. Aileen came in quickly.

"I am sure no one saw me enter the van. Here are some goodies for you," she said as she passed the bag with the burger to Scotty. She gave me a few bags with other supplies. I was eternally grateful to pull out a chef's salad along with a box of tea.

"You are the best!" I said to Aileen. "I would make you a cup of tea, but I know you are anxious to get back to Patrick.

"Note the chocolate bars, as well," Aileen said as she watched me pull more items from the bag.

"I am in heaven!" How did you know Godiva is my favorite?" I said as I pulled the candy from the bag.

"It is my favorite…I just hoped you would like it as well," said Aileen. "I need to run. We will be here first thing in the morning to take over. You have time to go home and change. Will that work for you?"

I hugged Aileen and told her how grateful we were for her and Patrick's support. They were like family and not just our mentors. She left as quietly as she arrived.

I turned to Scotty and realized he devoured his cheeseburger and was working on his fries.

"How in the world can you eat so fast and not end up with the worst indigestion imaginable?" I asked with real fascination.

"Hey, we had to eat fast when we were on the bus going or leaving a game," Scotty said, reliving his football days.

"Bullshit!" I said. "Football is no reason to wolf down your food. You need to eat slower and give your stomach a break."

Scotty just stuffed another French fry into his mouth and washed it down with a gulp of soda. I was half expecting him to belch next.

The evening was promising to be very long. I was sorry I did not think to bring along our homework assignments. That will be the first thing to tuck into my bag tomorrow after classes.

As Scotty continued his watch, I recalled the lecture from the morning. I remembered it from memory. I asked Scotty if he wanted me to recant the professor's speech?

"I know I am going to be sorry tomorrow if I say no, but I think I will take the first shift on the bed. Do you mind watching the cameras?" Scotty asked as he tried to stretch all bent over in the van. There was no room for all his 6'3" frame to stand up straight.

I made room for him to get to the couch. He laid straight out on the sofa, but he couldn't turn over well. Luckily for him, he could sleep on his back all night long and never moves. I knew this from experience. I missed sleeping with Scotty, but I knew he was right when he returned to his own bedroom. We moved in together too soon.

"Wake me up around midnight, and I will take over. That way, you can get some sleep as well before Patrick or Aileen relieve us to go to classes. Is this plan okay with you?" Scotty said as he shut his eyes.

I watched the cameras and any movement that seemed suspicious. I tried to think like Jack. How would I kill Heather if I was him? I knew I wouldn't want anyone to know I killed her. I would make it look like an accident, I reasoned. Just how many ways could a person cause death and make it look like an accident?

I decided right then I needed Hank to make a few modifications to Heather's house. Being the landlord and a retired policeman, he was the perfect one to make the changes. The back door and windows needed to be more secure. Unfortunately, we couldn't see any part of the backyard from any angle of the camera. That meant, windows needed to be barred, and the back door locks had to be doubled or tripled with extra-long screws. I was wondering what an alarm system might cost. Would Hank be willing to pay for a full-blown security system? I doubted he could afford it, but I would ask what options he might have.

Hank said he had not seen a green truck driving past the house, but that did not mean he missed it. He went on to say that he can't hear as well as he used to. His wife, on the other hand, seems to listen to every little creak the old house makes. He assured me that he would ask his wife to listen and watch from the front of the house. He also said he would spend more time gardening in the backyard for the next few days to keep a watch. He promised to call the police department immediately if they heard or saw anything that was out of the ordinary.

That conversation gave me some comfort. I wanted to get more neighbors involved, if possible. I knew Heather wouldn't like anyone knowing her circumstances, but if she was right and Jack did want to kill her, we might need every eye and ear on the block watching and listening.

Tomorrow, I would ask Hank and Eloise to talk to neighbors and ask them for help in this matter. Tonight, it was up to me to be the one to watch and listen on my own. The occasional police car cruising by did little to help me feel relaxed. Pins and needles were the expressions used for how I felt.

I was grateful to Gabe and my dad. Without the newly installed periscope camera, I wouldn't have any night vision at all on the fence line or the front and side of the house. Hank lives on the other side of the house and would be on watch with his wife. The only way I could keep watch on the rear of the house would be from hiding in the backyard. Even though my night vision is excellent, I hoped I would not need it.

CHAPTER TWO

I woke Scotty at midnight, as he requested. I was dead tired, but I found it hard to sleep. Unlike Scotty, I am restless at night and need to change my sleeping position often. The small sofa in the van did not allow for much movement. I must have fallen asleep since the next thing I noticed was tickling on my face.

I batted at the offending item and heard Scotty laugh and say. "Wake up, sleepyhead. I suspect Aileen or Patrick, or maybe both will be here before long. Maybe if we are lucky, they will bring coffee and cinnamon rolls."

I yawned and stretched. "Food...again?" I said as I rolled over to get his annoying feather out of my face. I wondered where he got a feather.

I turned back around and sat up. "Where did you get a feather?" I asked. I was curious about that since the pillow was foam.

"I went outside for a stretch, and I found one right beside the van," Scotty said with a grin.

Sometimes he can be such a big goof. When he is acting like a big stupid kid, I wonder what I ever saw in him. I smiled as I remembered what a goof he was growing up, but he was my best friend and always would be.

As Scotty started to tickle me once again with the feather, I realized the bird could have lice. "Get that stupid feather away from my face! There might be lice on it," I pushed Scotty's hand away and stood up.

My 5'10" frame didn't make for standing up in the van any easier than Scotty's brawny size. I hit my head on the roof of the van before I remembered just how low the ceiling was.

"I'm going to duck out of the van for a few minutes. I know Hank is an early riser. I want to talk to him about what he can do to secure the backdoor and the windows we can't see from the camera. In the meantime, use the toilet, if you must, but remember that number two is not allowed."

I left Scotty in the van alone and hoped he wouldn't stink it up too badly with Aileen or Patrick having to be in the van for several hours until we could once again return. I noticed movement at Hank and Eloise's house. When I knocked, Eloise opened the door.

"Hi, my name is Tish, and…" I started to say, but Eloise cut me off by grabbing my hand and pulling me into the house.

"Tish, it is wonderful to meet you. Hank has told me what you are doing for that poor lady next door. I feel just horrible for her. She never comes out, and her drapes are always drawn. She must be in a terrible state," Eloise was talking rapidly, and I was unable to get another word into the conversation.

Eloise pulled me into the small dining area and sat me down at her table. "I will be right back with a cup of coffee for you."

Eloise continued talking from the kitchen, "Hank told me that you and your partner spent the night in a van outside, keeping watch on her house. I bet you hardly got any sleep at all."

Eloise came in with a steaming cup of coffee and a blueberry muffin on a plate in her other hand. As she set the beverage and muffin down in front of me, she continued talking, "It is just a shame what some women must deal with. My Hank has been the best husband in the whole world. I just can't imagine women who put up with an abusive husband. That poor child. She isn't much older than a child, is she? I understand that she lost her baby on top of everything else."

I would have interrupted, but I had a bite of the most delicious blueberry muffin in my mouth. Finally, I managed to say with my mouth partly full, "Did you bake this muffin? It is the best blueberry muffin I have ever tasted." I continued to chew and swallow.

"Oh my, that is kind of you. I did bake it this morning. It is an old family recipe. My mother got the recipe from her mother, and well, you know how that goes. I am glad you are enjoying it. I have more in the kitchen if you would like another or if you would like to take one to your partner," Eloise said with a smile.

I can't say Eloise reminded me of anyone I knew. She was elderly and prim and adorable. I felt comfortable sitting at her table, chatting about recipes, and I could have enjoyed staying all morning, but that was not why I was here.

"I might take you up on a couple more muffins. I'm not sure I would be willing to share them with my partner, though. They are that good.

"I do need to talk to Hank. Is he awake?" I added before Eloise could start on another subject.

"Oh, my, of course. What is wrong with me? You are here to chat with Hank. Silly me. I will call him. He is in the garage now. Just a minute, dear." Eloise disappeared into the kitchen and out the back door. Hank returned with her in less than a minute.

"Tish, what can I do for you?" Hank asked, less chatty than his wife.

"We spent the night in a surveillance van watching Heather's house to make sure Jack does not enter and do her harm. The problem is the backyard. We can see all the windows and the front door, but we can't watch the back. I was wondering whether it would be possible for you to secure the windows and the back door so no one could sneak into them at night? I know an alarm system is too expensive, but maybe nailing the windows closed or something like that would work." I watched him closely to observe how he was taking my suggestion.

"Sure, I would be glad to go over and secure the back windows and install a hardier lock on the back door, but you know Heather won't let me in to do the work. I have knocked on her door several times before, and she pretends she is not at home. I know she is home and I can hear her scurrying around inside like a mouse. Do you think you can talk to her, so she will let me in?" Hank asked in return.

I knew he was right. Heather would not let him in for any reason. I wasn't sure if she would let him in even if I talked to her. It came to me in a flash. I would leave Scotty at Heather's house and go to class without him. I was sure Scotty could convince Heather to let Hank inside, and if he couldn't convince her, Scotty could do the work himself.

I told Hank what I was proposing to do. Hank said he has a hammer, nails, locks, screws, screwdriver, and probably anything else Scotty might need if Heather would allow him into the house.

I thanked him as he went back out the door to gather the tools and equipment needed. I thanked Eloise for the muffins and left to tell Scotty what I needed him to do.

When I quickly entered the van once again, I found Scotty alone in the van. The Jamiesons had not arrived. When Scotty saw the muffins, he made a grab for them.

"Hang on. You can have two muffins if you agree to do something for me," I said as I held the muffins away from Scott's long arms.

"Anything you want. Now, give me the muffins," Scotty said this as if he had not eaten a double hamburger, fries, and a large soft drink last night before going to bed.

"What would you say if I told you I wanted you to skip classes this morning?" His eyebrow raised as I said this to him.

"Why would you want me to skip classes?" He was chewing a muffin, and his question was muffled, but I understood what he said, with some effort.

"I need you to do something for me, and you may not like what I am going to ask you to do." I watched to see what his reaction was as I said these words.

"Go on," he said more muffled than before since he popped a whole muffin into his mouth at once.

"I am not going to tell you one more thing until you chew your mouth full of muffin and swallow it. I don't want you to choke on my account," I said as I sat down on the bench and crossed my arms, feeling squeezed in between Scotty and the wall. I forgot how cramped the van was after sitting at a standard kitchen table.

Scotty chewed and swallowed. "Okay, I am ready. What do you want me to do?"

Now I swallowed. I was not sure Scotty was going to want to spend any time alone with Heather once he saw she was a basket-case. It was hard enough for me to be alone with her, especially when she is acting paranoid and weird.

"I need you to talk to Heather and convince her to let Hank come into her house and secure the back door and windows," I said slowly.

"Is that all. Sure, but why would I need to miss class to do that, and why can't you do it?" Scotty asked.

Again, I talked slower than usual, hoping Scotty would listen carefully, "Heather is not the same person you dated." When he didn't interrupt, I continued, "Heather has become rather...well... weird."

"How do you mean, weird?" Scotty asked. I noticed he was not stuffing the third muffin into his mouth. It was still in the bag. That meant Scotty was listening, and he was concerned.

"Well, Heather is paranoid. I mean, she is acting a bit nutty. No, I mean, she is acting totally nutty." I stopped, hoping I had made my point.

"If she is that nutty, what makes you think she will let me in the house?" Scotty said, and I realized he had a point.

Heather might not let him in. If that were the case, I would need to be the one to fix the door and windows. I was not sure how well I would do with a hammer or screwdriver, but I was going to need to learn fast if it came down to no one or me.

A rap at the back door let us know Aileen arrived. Patrick was nowhere in sight. We let her in.

"Obviously, no one is operating the cameras," Aileen said as she ducked into the van with coffee and muffins.

One look at the bakery bag in Aileen's hand, and Scotty and I laughed.

"What's so funny?" Aileen asked as she set down the hot coffee and bag of muffins.

"Eloise just sent out some muffins, too," I said. "Thank you for your thoughtfulness. I can eat one. Scotty will wolf down the other ones."

Scotty did not defend himself. "I was hungry. Besides, you know I am a growing boy."

Aileen and I just groaned.

"Are you two going to classes this morning, or am I here for nothing?" Aileen asked as she took the command chair.

"We need to go and talk to Heather first. Her back door and windows need to be secured. If she doesn't let Hank secure them, that will mean Scotty will need to stay behind to do the job," I said to Aileen to explain our predicament.

"I will be here anyway, keeping a watch out for Jack. Go ahead and when you are finished, come back and tell me how it went with Heather and securing the rear of the house," Aileen said as she grabbed a muffin to go along with her coffee.

The cameras showed no activity around the neighborhood, so Scotty and I slipped out of the van. Making a bee-line to Heather's front door,

I knocked four times with no answer. I knocked on the door again and again and again. Finally, I heard a muffled voice from inside.

"Go away!" I knew it was Heather since no one else besides myself ever entered the house.

"Heather, it is me. I have Scotty beside me. We need to talk to you," I said through the closed door.

"Go away! I don't want to see Scotty. Make him go away NOW!" She screamed.

I turned to Scotty and asked him to leave. I told him I would meet him back in the van in a couple of minutes once I was able to calm Heather and talk to her.

Scotty whispered, "If she is that crazy, are you safe with her?"

I did not answer him. I just waved him off.

He turned and left the front porch looking rather upset by what just occurred. I knew he would have been even more upset if he saw what Heather looked like these days. His perky, little cheerleader is not to be found anywhere in this house.

I turned back to the door. "Heather, Scotty is gone. It is just me. Let me in."

The latch was heard to unlock, and Heather opened the door the usual small crack. I squeezed through without complaining this time.

"Why did you bring Scotty here?" chided Heather.

"Someone needs to secure your back windows and put on a more reliable lock on your back door. If we are going to protect you from Jack, we need your permission to let someone in to do the work.

So, who is it going to be, Scotty, or Hank, your landlord from next door? Those are your only choices." I was not about to tell her that I would give it the good ole college try if she wasn't going to let either of the men inside the house.

32

Heather sat on the sofa with her face in her hands. She pulled her legs up and curled herself into a ball while still sitting. I waited for her response. I was about to become angry and go ballistic at her when she peeked out from under her fingers and said, "Hank can come in."

I was relieved. I could tell Hank to gather his tools and come on over while Scotty and I had time to go home, shower, change clothes, and still make it to our first class.

I commended Heather for making the right choice. I told her that she was on the road to recovery when she could make good choices. I did not really believe what I was saying, but one should put a positive spin on anything encouraging when dealing with a nut-case like Heather.

I left her house, promising to bring groceries upon my return. I looked at the list and was appalled to see hot dogs and beans on the top of the list. This time I was adding items of my own to her list. Why not, I was paying for all her groceries anyway.

I dropped in on Aileen and told her what was happening. I wanted her to be prepared for Hank to arrive with tools and fix and secure the back door and windows. I described Hank and told Aileen he was the landlord who lives right next door.

I looked at Scotty and said, "Ready, Stud? We have places to go and people to see."

My heart flip-flopped when he smiled at my silly joke. Did I tell you Scotty has the cutest smile? I do miss him in my bed, or have I said that before?

Scotty and I headed towards Hank's garage to retrieve the Harley. "I'm calling shotgun!" Scotty said. He can be incredibly juvenile.

I wished I had two helmets and made a mental note to retrieve my old helmet at home in the garage. I offered my helmet, but there was no way it was going to fit on Scotty's head. I put it on my own head. I started up the machine, and off we went, looking down every side street for a green pickup truck.

CHAPTER THREE

Getting towards the last year of classes, we are finding what we are learning from the Jamiesons to be more valuable than what we are learning in class. We need the certificate at the end of the program, so we can legally become private investigators and buy out the Jamiesons by the time we are 21. I would say we are on the downhill of all things academic and ready for more hands-on. The good news is all our time spent with the Jamieson Detective Agency will apply towards the required preceptorship.

We showered, changed into clean clothes, and gathered our book bags. I knew if we had a pop quiz, I would be fine, but I couldn't guarantee Scotty would do okay. I just hoped the instructor was feeling generous today and would pass on the quiz.

Scotty didn't feel as lucky as the instructor passed out a quiz. I easily aced it. I can draw from my remarkable memory and pass almost any test without studying if I listened to the lecture or read the material. I have a photographic memory, and it comes in handy for these situations.

Scotty must study. I suppose that he wished he had let me recite the lecture verbatim to him last night. If he heard it twice, I think he could have done alright. Instead, his mind was all messed up thinking about Heather's safety.

I took notes when the instructors lectured for today's three classes. I did not need the lecture notes, but I decided to be a buddy and help Scotty. His note-taking is borderline terrible. It isn't that he doesn't know what is essential and what isn't, but he writes so slowly that he misses many vital parts of the lecture.

I caught his eyes to let him know that I had the notes covered, and he could relax and just listen. His smile and relaxing face let me know he understood my sign language. Scotty would do fine in the next couple of quizzes. That would make up for the disaster today.

It was mid-afternoon by the time we were out of classes. Two days we have classroom lectures a bit later than the other three days. I dread those longer days.

We left the Harley at home since we were sure we would be returning home before going back to the van. I wanted to stop at the grocery store and get more items than I can carry on the Harley. Scotty, a willing companion, pushed the cart as we strolled up and down the aisles of the store.

The food was not the only item on Heather's list. There were several items on the feminine products aisle needed. Heather was not specific as to which brand she preferred, or even sizing, so I got her what I used on those days. I threw in a few beauty products as well. It was about time Heather started to take care of her personal hygiene.

If it were not for Patrick and Aileen, I would not be able to do these things for Heather. I more than once sang their praises to Heather when she felt guilty about all the money I was spending to keep her in a house with food, paper products, cleaning supplies, and everything else she needed or wanted.

I explained to Heather once before when she was feeling guilty that the Jamiesons pay us well, and we get bonuses whenever we help them solve a case. We've solved several lately. Subsequently, we have some extra money.

I also explained at that same time that she held stocks in the exact same company that Alumni Class of '92 was invested. I didn't mention that Wally, Tommy, Ray, Rose Lee, as well as, Lucy was killed. I knew that news would send Heather into another freak-out.

I wanted Heather to know if she decided to step forward and tell the police about Jack and what she knew about his involvement in the murders, that she would not be destitute. She, too, had stocks, and they were valuable.

I remember somehow that knowledge scared Heather more than it gave her confidence and reassurance. I just wanted Heather to feel like she was empowered. Instead, the stock made her feel more like a target than ever.

She said at that time, "Jack has all of my paperwork for the stock certificate. If I die, Jack gets that stock. We are married even though I deserted him. If he kills me, he gets it all, and he can just go on with life with his concubine." I remembered this conversation with Heather all too vividly.

I let Scotty help carry the bags to the door, but then I asked him to go and take the car home; bring back the Harley and hide it in Hank's garage. I explained to Scotty that Hank's car took up most of the garage, and the Double Nickel would not fit, and it was too recognizable by Jack. By the time Scotty got back, I would be in the van with Aileen happily on her way home.

Scotty trotted off to the Double Nickel, and Heather let me in as soon as she was sure he was gone. To my surprise, Heather was showered and dressed, and not in her baggy sweatpants.

"You look...good," I said as I entered, handing Heather grocery bags as I retrieved the others on the front porch stoop. "It is nice to see you taking care of yourself again. What made the difference?"

I knew that was rude of me to point out, but I really wanted to know why suddenly Heather was cleaning herself up. I feared that the thought of seeing Scotty was what motivated her. I guess I still had my doubts about whether I would measure up to Heather in Scotty's eyes once Heather was looking her best again.

As we put items away, Heather divulged her reasons, "I think it was some things Hank said to me today that made me realize how stupid I was being." Heather hesitated.

"What did he say?" I wondered. What could a retired policeman who lived next door say to Heather that would make such a profound difference to her? Nothing I ever said sank into Heather's head.

"Hank is a dear man," Heather continued. "I was afraid to let him in to secure the back half of the house. I think I was cowering in the corner. He did not approach me. Instead, he hollered from the back door that he would love a cup of coffee.

I don't think his words even penetrated my consciousness. I was terrified of having a stranger in the house. The next thing I knew, he was handing me a cup of tea."

I said, "So giving you a cup of tea was all it took to make you trust him and come out of your catatonic state?" I knew I was mean again, but something about Heather just brings out the worst in my personality.

"Of course not." Heather didn't miss the fact that I was mean. She continued to talk to me anyway, "No, it wasn't the tea. Hank sat down quietly on the chair across the room after setting down the drink. He knew if he were close, I would withdraw even more.

"After a few minutes of silence, Hank told me I reminded him of his daughter."

"I suppose you could remind Hank of his daughter even though you aren't black. Did he say what it was that reminded you of her?" I went on to say, hardly aware that I was acting catty again.

"Hank told me his daughter lived in a different state but was married to a man who abused her. He said she never told anyone. Her husband kept escalating his behavior until one day, he killed her. Hank said I had the same timid temperament that kept me from going to the police and saving myself. He cried and pleaded with me not to let Jack kill me.

"I don't know, but there was something dear and real about Hank's love for his daughter and the pain he was feeling for not being able to protect her. Even though I never was close to my parents, I did not want to cause them the pain Hank is going through." Heather ended her conversation.

"So, you are willing to go to the police and tell them what you know about Jack?" I asked pointedly.

"I will go first thing tomorrow. I need tonight to gather my thoughts. My brain has been fried, and I don't think I could put two and two together right now. A good night's sleep and I will be ready if you will pick me up.

"Will you take me to see your Captain Jones? I don't want Scott to come?" Heather asked with old fears starting to return to her eyes.

"Sure, I will knock on your door first thing in the morning. We can take the van, and Scott will stay here to watch over your house until we get back. Good enough?" I asked her, trying to reassure all would be well.

"Tish, did you know Hank is letting me stay here for free? Also, did you know he keeps this house as a safe house, so no other parent has to lose their daughter on his watch?"

I could tell Hank influenced Heather a great deal. I did not know Hank well or Eloise, but I liked them both immediately. I, too, was taken back by the story Hank relayed to Heather. I never heard about their daughter being killed. It was sad, but I guess husbands killing their wives happen more often than I really knew even though I teach self-defense to women.

"I added a few personal hygiene items that you will want to use tomorrow. They are in the grocery bags. I should scoot now. I will be out in the van if you need me. You can signal me by either opening and closing your drapes during the day or turning your porch light on and off when it is dark. One of us will see you if you signal, and I will come right over," I said this as I inched my way to the door.

Heather said she needed some time to gather her thoughts. I was also hoping she would make her own meal, and I wouldn't get stuck heating up pork and beans for her again. In fact, I didn't buy pork and beans at all. She would need to eat something healthier or go out and buy the food herself. I did not want to be in the house when Heather discovered I didn't buy her mainstay of comfort foods. I left before she could notice my treachery.

Getting back to the van, I found Scotty in one of the control chairs eating a sandwich. Why the fact that he was eating something annoyed me is beyond even my reasoning, but it did. I snapped at him.

Looking up from the viewing screen, chewing a mouthful of peanut butter and jelly, I could tell he was puzzled, and a bit hurt. I went over to him, hunched over, as I can't stand straight up in the van, and kissed him on the top of his head.

"I'm sorry. That was shitty of me. You didn't deserve my sarcasm," I apologized. "It is just that any time spent with Heather makes me edgy...." I paused for effect, "Heather says she will go to the police tomorrow and make a statement about Jack. Good news, right? This may be our last night of tortured sleep in the van!"

"That is good news. A good night's sleep will do me good after sleeping on that little sofa. I will be glad to sleep in my own bed again. What did you say to get her to cave?" Scotty said, acting as if I had not just been an idiot.

"I didn't say anything to change her mind. It was Hank who did that." I relayed the story Heather told about Hank. I could tell Scott was moved by what Hank and Eloise had been through.

"No wonder Hank is always observing Heather's house," Scott said thoughtfully.

"I never noticed Hank watching Heather's house?" I said, almost defensively. I was usually much more observant than Scott. How was it he noticed this detail when I missed it?

"Oh, come on. Don't tell me that you didn't see Hank gardening more often than anyone else in the neighborhood. Also, don't tell me that you didn't notice that he would walk his little dog so it could relieve itself several times a day when they have a fenced backyard. Also, tell me that you didn't see Eloise and Hank peeking out their drapes one hundred times a day?" Scott questioned me.

I had to admit that I did not put two and two together. I just thought Hank had a routine, and he stuck to it. It never occurred to me that he was also keeping surveillance on Heather. I should have realized Hank's police training wouldn't stop just because he retired, and now that I also know his daughter was killed by her abusive husband, it made sense why Captain Jones picked Hank's house as the safe house. I felt stupid now.

I kissed Scotty again on the head. I was avoiding his mouth due to the sticky jelly on his lips. Otherwise, I would have given him a massive kiss on his lips.

"You are the best partner in the world," I said. "I can count on you to make up for my deficiencies. I guess I overlooked the obvious, didn't I? It makes me feel better to know we are not the only ones looking out for Heather."

Even though Scotty had just eaten a peanut butter and jelly sandwich, he was ready to eat again when I told him I would make dinner. I think Scotty would be content eating a second PB and J sandwich if I had not volunteered to cook something more substantial.

We ate quietly as we continued to watch all the cameras. We concentrated on the periscope as it was getting dark, but it was almost instinctual to check the other camera, just like one checks the side mirrors while driving a car. Neither Scotty or I wanted to be taken by surprise by Jack.

Scotty yawned and announced he was going to take a nap. I told him to go ahead and get some sleep. I wasn't feeling all that tired anyway, and this had become our routine. I took the first watch, and Scotty took the early morning watch.

It was getting close to the time I should wake Scotty. I could get a few hours of sleep, as well. I realized I hadn't phoned Patrick and Aileen to let them know they would not need to make the trip to the van. I was a bit distracted by my irritation with myself and almost missed the shadowy figure moving from the backyard to the front door.

It had to be Jack! I leaped to my feet, hitting my head on the roof of the van; I yelped. Scott stirred but was not totally awake. I told him someone was prowling around Heather's house, and I feared it was Jack.

"I am going, so get up! Go and phone the police at Hank's house, then follow me over," I barked these orders hoping Scotty was awake enough to understand what I just said. I did not wait to see if my words registered. I leaped out the rear door of the van.

I heard Heather scream, and I raced to her front door. Using my key, I came inside as fast as I could, just in time to see Heather crumpled on the floor. Jack was standing over her with a gun.

He pointed it at me as I entered, and I screeched to a halt. I was fast, but not that fast. Jack had his gun locked on me from across the room.

"Welcome, Karate Kid. Just stand there and don't move. Let's wait for Sir Galahad to arrive," Jack said, not moving his eyes from me.

He was right. It wasn't long until my 'Knight in Shining Armor' did arrive…almost on cue. He screeched to a halt when he saw Jack pointing the gun at my chest.

"How are you doing…now, Sir Galahad?" Jack said with a sneer.

"What did you do to Heather?" Scotty asked without a moment's hesitation.

"Ever the caring ex-boyfriend, aren't you?" Jack said, glancing down quickly at the unconscious woman. "Don't worry about Heather. You need to worry about your girlfriend and yourself right now."

"You know the game is up, Jack. Your partners are in jail or dead. It is only a matter of time before you will be in jail as well. There is no Final Alumni contract anymore...why kill anyone else? At this point, there are only conspiracy charges that the police can get you on. If you kill us, you will have three murder charges. You will go to jail and rot," I said, hoping to drive a point into Jack's head and stall until the police arrived.

"There isn't even that...if I kill all three of you. Tran and Riley have no idea I sent Jesse out to kill Wally, Tommy, and Lucy. They can't testify against me since they know nothing. That only leaves the three of you to get rid of, and then I can leave the country permanently. I will have Heather's shares as well as my own. That should be plenty of money for Nicki and myself to live quite happily on a nice island somewhere in the South Pacific," Jack boasted.

"So, Nicki is the name of your whore," Scotty said, with me wishing he wouldn't have antagonized Jack.

I could see Jack turning purple. He was no longer calm and deadly. Now he was angry and fatal.

"Get over there with Heather, both of you and don't try to be the hero, Scott, or Tish gets the first bullet through her face."

As Scotty and I moved slowly to where Heather lay on the floor, I felt Scotty move slightly in front of me and using his finger; he pointed to the knife in the waistband at the back of his jeans. I immediately knew what he wanted me to do.

I quickly grabbed it from the waistband and with one efficient movement, threw the knife at Jack, hitting him in the left shoulder. I was still lecturing myself in my mind that if I took a moment longer to consider, I could have hit him on the right shoulder when Jack grabbed the knife to remove it. I said, "The only thing that is keeping you from bleeding to death is that knife. I hit an artery.

Still standing, with the gun pointed directly at Scott, Jack spat out. "For that, you can watch Scott die first in front of your eyes." His vehemence was blood-chilling.

I saw the intent in Jack's eyes, and this time, consciously, I knew precisely when Jack would pull the trigger. I reacted faster than Jack and pushed Scotty out of the way as the bullet left the gun.

When Jack comprehended what I had done, he leveled the gun towards me, and with the sound of gunfire, he collapsed forward and rolled onto his back...eyes closed. Standing at the front door, was Hank with his service revolver pointing at the now deceased Jack.

CHAPTER FOUR

The sirens could be heard in the distance. Hank kicked Jack's gun to the wall and threw his handcuffs to Scotty and said, "Cuff him."

"Why? Jack is dead, he has a hole the size of a baseball in his chest," was Scotty's reply back to Hank.

"Cuff him anyhow. We don't know if he is dead. Better to be safe than sorry. I've seen a few dead men come back to life and kill officers...especially when the bad guys are on drugs like *crank*. Cuff him!" Hank said with authority.

Hank hurried to Heather's side to inspect the extent of her injuries. He rushed to the kitchen sink and came back with a cold dishrag to place on Heather's swelling face. She was moaning softly, and her eyes were fluttering open and closed. We were pretty sure Heather would be alright.

I met the police officers in the front yard to make sure they stopped at the correct house. I recognized one of the officers immediately from training and waved him over.

Explaining what transpired, we all entered the house. Hank was beside Heather, helping her to sit up.

"She's fine, but I think we should call an ambulance to take her to the emergency room," Hank said with Heather gripping his hand tightly. Hank was almost wincing.

"I won't go unless you come with me," Heather whimpered.

"You are safe now," Hank said, and Heather followed his eyes to Jack's body, lying dead on the floor with blood flowing onto the carpet.

I could see Heather was about to scream. No one needed that now; therefore, I quickly stepped in front of her view of Jack and said, "You are safe!... Stop! ... Breathe!"

I knelt beside Heather, with Hank calmly reiterating what I just said. I could see some of the terror, leaving her eyes.

"You never need to worry about Jack again. Do you understand? You are safe." I observed her face for any sign she really understood and found myself relaxing as I noted she did.

I left Hank consoling Heather and returned to the police officers. I explained the whole situation about this being a safe house and Heather's circumstance as well as explaining Hank's involvement.

"Call Captain Jones if you want more clarification. The captain has been involved from the start with placing Heather in this safe house. He can also verify Hank's connection as well."

I knew Hank retired long before any of these young policemen hired into the force. I did not want any of them to hand-cuff Hank for murder since it was very apparent that Jack was shot in the back.

The ambulance arrived without lights or sirens since Heather's injuries were not life-threatening. Heather needed to be checked out for a concussion. A couple of good night's sleep, and a counselor would do her wonders.

As Heather left for the ambulance with Hank at her side, I could hear Hank telling her she had a home right here if she wanted it. It was heart-warming to hear Hank talking so reassuringly to Heather. I knew Hank had his share of heartbreaks, too. This could be the start of a whole new life for Heather…and Hank and Eloise. I couldn't help it. I had to smile.

CHAPTER FIVE

My dad phoned the next morning, bright and early. It is amazing how quickly news travels out to our small town. Scott received his phone call from his parents the minute I hung up the phone. We both were mildly scolded for putting ourselves in harm's way, but it was said with such pride in their voices, we knew the balance of the scale was tipped in our favor for helping and protecting a classmate as well as ending the chapter in the Final Alumni Standing agreement.

Scotty and I were looking forward to a mundane Fall and Winter. It was going to be a relief to go to classes, take tests, work with the Jamiesons, and instruct my self-defense classes.

Scotty had the police firearms competition coming up soon. He would be down at the shooting range more hours than usual to fine-tune his marksmanship. I would be a bit lonely for a few weeks while he practices each evening.

Captain Jones called us into the department the next day after the shooting. We gave our statements the same night as Jack's death, but Captain Jones still had things he wanted to discuss with us. I imagined that he wanted to make sure Hank would not be charged for shooting Jack in the back. That was only a small part of the conversation. Captain Jones wasn't very concerned about Hank being indicted since he saved three people's lives by shooting when he did.

It seemed what he really wanted to talk to us about, was once again, putting ourselves in danger. We were scolded for not waiting for police back-up before entering the house. Even though I told him Heather's life was in danger, Captain Jones wouldn't budge.

He said, "What if Jack would have shot you the minute you entered the house? You were just fortunate that he wanted to gloat. You could have been killed. That was a bad choice, and you need to be held accountable for bad choices." I am afraid the lecture didn't end there.

It did end with Captain Jones taking us to lunch. I must admit that Scotty and I love him as much as he seems to love us. The captain can be fierce and in one's face, but only when the captain really cares. He must care an awful lot about us judging by the length and how loud the lecture was.

Driving home from our lunch with Captain Jones, I found myself racking my brain, trying to figure out if I had been as rash as Captain Jones said I had been. I talked to Scotty to find out what he would have done if the roles were reversed. He made me feel better when he said he would have reacted the same as I did.

That did not make the decision right, in my estimation. Maybe our parents and the captain were right, and we needed to analyze our actions. We brainstormed on the different scenarios and which one was the correct one. We concluded that neither of us would enter a building or room without the other next time. We would also wait for police back-up if possible. Now, we just hope there would be no next time.

Reaching home, Scotty went down to the basement to work on the computer, and I remained upstairs still in self-reflection mode. I must admit having Jack's gun pointed at my head, and then Scotty's head was terrifying. Even though my training to react consciously to the unconscious details has improved, I know I was lucky. I may not always be able to pick up on the small, hardly noticeable nuances. This time, I could see the little changes in Jack's eyes, his breathing, his stance, facial expression, and his speech that gave me all the clues that I needed to react immediately to push Scotty out of harm's way.

If I die, I am dead...period. If Scotty dies, I would be dead...emotionally. I just couldn't imagine living in a world without Scotty. I realize Scotty has become crucial to my wellbeing. I depend on him.... He makes life livable.... I love him, and my life without him would not really be worth living. I would just be going through the motions.

Just as I was thinking of life without Scotty, I could hear his footfalls on the stairs coming up from the basement.

"What are you doing?" he said, as he reached the landing.

"Reflecting," I answered vaguely.

"How about if we reflect in the kitchen. I am starving." And he headed for the kitchen.

So much for a moment to share my most inner thoughts. With Scotty, it is better to keep things light until I really need to talk. He is a good listener in those situations, but frankly, he is preoccupied most of the time. I still can't help but think of the saying about 'still waters run deep.' I think casual is a better word for Scotty than preoccupied, but he does have depth and perception when it matters.

I joined Scotty in the kitchen. We worked side by side, making bacon, lettuce, and tomato sandwiches. I knew he wanted me to make the bacon since Scotty always burns the bacon. His job was to toast the bread, cut the tomatoes and break up the lettuce. Pouring ice tea and setting the table was the last thing he did before we sat down to eat.

"Do you plan to check on Heather anymore?" Scotty asked matter-of-factly.

"Why do you ask?" I said, wanting clarification on this question. I did not wish Scotty thinking about Heather. It made me feel uneasy.

"I don't think you need to check on her anymore. Heather has Hank and Eloise, money from her stock, and Jack's stock now. She plans to go to college and become a domestic violence counselor. I feel your investment was worthwhile, but babysitting time is completed. You have other people to take care of now," Scotty said, feeling glum.

"Have you been feeling neglected?" I asked, kidding.

"Frankly, yes," was Scotty's reply.

I was taken aback. We spent more time together recently because of Heather, so it never occurred to me that I was neglecting him.

"What do you mean? We have been together day and night," I said defensively of his accusation.

"That's what I mean. We have been together day and night, but our focus was on protecting Heather and stopping Jack. I want our time to be our time again. I want us to have date nights and sit on the sofa and cuddle and the way it was before all this stuff with Heather," Scotty said meaningfully.

"I want that too." I leaned over and kissed him on the lips, not caring about the little mayo in the corner of his mouth.

I continued the conversation after the brief kiss. "It is going to be hard until your competition is over. You know you will be gone every night practicing until then. However, we can set up Saturday night for a date night. What would you like to do?"

Thinking hard, Scott decided dinner and a movie would be great when a flash of genius inspired him. "Unless you would like to try to get tickets to The Second City and watch Steve Carell and Stephen Colbert. I have heard they are hilarious," Scotty said with excitement in his voice.

"Why not. I don't know if we can get in if we are under twenty-one, but let's give it a try. It would be fun, and I would love a night where I laughed so hard my stomach hurt," I said, remembering how intense the last several months had been.

"It's a date. I will leave early and swing by the ticket office on my way to the police shooting range tonight to see if I can get tickets. You have training tonight with a new batch of police rookies, don't you?" Scotty offered.

"That's right, I do. I wonder what this group will be like. I don't mind the Gun-Ho types. I can teach them quickly and put them in their place if they get too full of themselves. It is the timid ones I have trouble training. They must learn, but most of them are afraid of getting hurt. It makes it hard. I feel like I am babysitting with that lot," I said, recalling several in past groups that tested my patience.

It wasn't long before Scotty needed to head out. I had time to shower, get into my workout clothes before it was time to leave.

I pulled into the station and parked. Heading into the building, I was greeted by several ex-students. I was feeling proud of my ex-rookies. They were doing well on the streets. At least, that is what Captain Jones told me.

I went inside the gym, and slowly a group started straggling in as well. I was sitting on the bleachers just watching them as they entered, sizing them up. There were eight in this group. Six were men, and two were young women. Already, I could tell the blond was the favorite of the men. She got a lot of glances and some leers.

I checked her out a bit more. She was small-framed, 5'3" tall, and about 105 pounds. Her slightly olive complexion was exquisite. For being such a small woman, she was busty, but her hips were narrow. She looked like a human Barbie Doll to me.

One of the men stepped out of the group and came forward to greet me. He was taller than average but not over six feet. His red hair and the fact that the other guys called him "Irish" gave away his heritage.

"I'm officer McDowell. You must be Tish Evers, our instructor," he said as he reached out his hand. "The guys call me Irish. You can call me Irish if you like."

I could tell I was going to like this guy when I shook his firm hand. Maybe it was his self-assurance and the good-natured initiative he was taking. There was something special about him that set him apart from the others.

"Would you like me to introduce you to the rest of these lunkheads?" Irish said as he led me over to the assembled group.

"You all know Miss Evers from her reputation as well as from the raves the other rookies voiced; she needs to know our names. How about if everyone steps forward, give her your name and something small about yourself...like a pet peeve or favorite food or something."

"My name is Bart Frank. I like pastrami sandwiches," Bart said with a smile, patting his tummy.

Bart was average height, dark hair, dark eyes with a slight build. I immediately felt he would need any self-defense I could teach him. I also noted he looked as if he was agile, and that would be to his advantage in training.

Next, a large young man stepped forward. "People call me, Swede. I'm only half Swedish. My name is Max Torino. You can guess what the other half is," he laughed a good-natured laugh as he said this.

"And something else about you?" Irish coaxed.

"I love wine and women and not necessarily in that order." Swede continued without stopping his laughter.

I could tell this was going to be a rowdy group. I wasn't sure how much I would be able to teach this clown, but I was going to give it my best shot. I hated to think of this goof-ball dead on the streets because I did not push him.

It was strange to find a big blond man who was half Swedish and half Italian in the neighborhood. I could tell he would try to muscle his way through the class. I mentally noted that he might be useful to partner with Bart Frank. It would be interesting to see how frustrated he might become when he couldn't keep a smaller man down with the techniques I planned to teach. If he were going to get frustrated, I would need to find ways to show him discipline. I figured Swede could get angry when frustrated, and anger would lead to mistakes.

The pretty little blond stepped up next. I couldn't imagine why this blond would want to be a police officer. She wasn't tall enough to be a model, but there were plenty of other jobs she could do that wouldn't get her face punched in.

"My name is Andrea Marchetti. I come from a family of police officers. Don't count me out because of my size. I have five brothers, and I can stand my ground," she said with authority.

Upon closer inspection, I could see Andrea was not a natural blond. Her brown eyes and skin color gave away her heritage, but it was a striking blend. She wasn't going to be the little push over I thought she might be. I was glad I misjudged her.

The second lady in the group decided it was her turn to make her introductions. Trudy was her name. She said her last name was Smith. Trudy Smith wasn't one that stood out in any way. She was very ordinary. Trudy wasn't pretty, but the woman wasn't ugly either. She stood about 5'8". For a woman, that was fairly-tall but not tall in comparison to me. She didn't seem physically strong or athletic. I was hoping I was misjudging her as well.

"Tell us something about you, Trudy. What do you do in your spare time?" I asked.

"I love to read," Trudy answered succinctly.

"Anything else that you would like to add? Did you play any sports in high school?" I prodded.

"I did play tennis," she offered. I watched a smile spread across her face at this admission.

"I guess you were a respectable player," I said, thinking the smile indicated good memories.

"Oh, no! I was horrible. My coach told me I needed to retake the beginner class before he would ever consider passing me on to the intermediate level," Trudy said, smiling again.

I decided she was reliving her tennis memories, and her smile was just part of what she thought was humor…failing beginning tennis. This did not bode well for her in my class, but if I could teach women's self-defense at the dojang, I could at least show this one how to take down a criminal when needed.

Three more introductions and I could start the class. I was anxious to get started, but I gave the last three rookies my full attention as they made their introductions.

I was caught by surprise when Sam Jones introduced himself. "Are you any relation to Captain Jones?" I asked.

"He is my uncle," Sam offered.

"I am delighted to meet you, I am very close to your uncle," I said in the way of starting a relationship.

"Good for you, cuz I can't say that I am close to him," Sam said back with little expression.

"What more would you like to tell me about yourself?" I said, hoping to find some common ground.

"I'm not here to impress you or my uncle. I am here to protect the people of Chicago from gangs and drugs."

"That is admirable," I said and dropped the subject. It was apparent to me that there was more to this story than I was going to get from Sam.

Markus Brown and Chad Masters were the last two in the group. Both were strong, young men. Markus played football, and Chad was a basketball player in high school and college. Chad was taller than Markus, but not by much. I would say both men were just as tall as Scotty. Chad might even be an inch taller.

"Do any of you have a problem with learning self-defense from a woman?" I started the class with these words. I wanted to know right off the bat whether I was going to need to prove I could take down any of them or all of them.

When none of them said anything or indicated they would have trouble being told what to do by a woman, I asked them to create a circle around me. "From this point forward, you will address me as Sensei, and you will bow when you enter and before you leave. Each of you will also bow to your partner before you practice the techniques, I will teach you."

The lesson began. I demonstrated in slow-motion a technique that would protect the police rookies from an attacker approaching from behind. I then partnered them up to give it a try. I walked amongst them, giving them pointers and critiques. When I saw improvement and noted their technique was becoming more exact, I asked them to speed up the exercise. I told them not to speed up so fast that their partner couldn't keep up. "So, pace yourselves accordingly."

When I heard Trudy yelp, I walked over to see what happened. Sam was her partner.

"What's going on?" I asked bluntly.

"I just wasn't ready for how fast he went through the moves," Trudy said meekly.

"Sam, will you partner with me? Trudy can watch one more time, please?" I stepped in and took Trudy's place.

When Sam became overzealous and tried to take me down in one swift movement, I compensated for his speed and used it against him. He went tumbling past me onto the mat, falling face down.

The rest of the group laughed. I did not need for the group to enrage Sam now. It wasn't supposed to be humiliating. I meant it as a teaching moment. Their laughter made it what it wasn't supposed to be. Sam was enraged.

He jumped to his feet, turning purple. I knew I had to nip this in the bud.

"Nice job, Sam. You seem to have the techniques down well enough. I think I will switch you to a different partner at this point.

"Markus, will you partner with Sam. Chad, I think you can slow down the practice enough to show Trudy how to grip for this takedown." Without more words, I turned my back on Sam and continued to walk around the group.

When the two-hour instruction was completed, I turned the group loose. I had no idea Captain Jones was watching until he came into the room after the others left.

"You handled Sam well," Captain Jones remarked. "He is a hothead. I am glad you could defuse him. I am keeping my eye on him. I have some real qualms about him being on the force in the first place. He is just too angry a person to be a good cop at present."

I sat down on the bleachers and patted the seat next to me. "What is his story?" I asked.

Captain Jones began. "Sam is my brother's son. My brother and I were nothing alike. In fact, I spent a good share of my summers with my grandparents in Africa. My brother got so involved in a gang that he never wanted to leave Chicago. He and his buddies ruled the streets and did what they wanted. Unfortunately, my brother married and had kids. Too bad. He wasn't cut out to be either a husband or a father.

Captain Jones continued, "When Sam's father was home, he was high on drugs and abusive. When he wasn't at home, he was either getting in trouble or behind bars.

"Not wanting to be like his dad, Sam became the opposite of his criminal father. I guess he decided the furthest thing from his father would be a cop. The only problem is Sam is an extremely angry young man from those bad experiences at his father's hands."

Taking a brief break to reflect, the captain continued, "I tried to get close to him, but in some strange way, he blames me for not being able to get his dad away from the gang and off drugs. He feels the abuse he suffered from his father was in some way my fault as I did not protect him," Captain Jones stalled again before adding.

Trying to be sympathetic, I said, "I don't pretend to know anything about your family or your relationship with your brother. I do know from other friends that sometimes there is just a bad seed in the family, and there isn't much one can do about it."

"Yes, I suppose my brother was a bad seed. My own dad was a mechanic at a small garage and worked long hard hours. I guess Sam feels I received a magic pass ticket somehow, by following my dad's example and not getting into a gang even with the gang's constant pressure. I suppose Sam felt I should have been around more to help him out when his dad wasn't there. I guess I did use my trips to Africa to escape all the pressure. I told Sam once the only magic to having a good life is deciding you aren't going to go down that wrong path.

"Sam has made the first decision...he isn't going to be in a gang. I just wish I could make his road a bit less rough, but with that chip on his shoulder, I don't know what I can do for him." Captain Jones slumped, and I put my arm around him.

"I won't give up on him. I promise," I said.

Captain Jones walked me to my Harley without saying another word.

CHAPTER SIX

The next morning Scotty and I went to the office. We were pleasantly surprised to hear Aileen and Patrick were taking a short vacation. They told us we were in charge and asked if it would be too much responsibility with classes.

"Heck, no!" Scotty said enthusiastically.

"It sounds like he will be glad to be rid of us," Patrick turned and said to Aileen.

"I think you are right," Aileen replied, "Scotty seems way too happy for us to be gone."

I laughed. "No, we are just happy you two are going to get away for a while. It will be nice for you. You know nothing much will happen while you are away, or you wouldn't be going."

"Such a smart lady," Patrick said. "However, in this business, there is no slow time or busy time. It is just what happens when it happens. We are betting that not much will hit our doorstep in the next couple of weeks."

"If something does come up, we know you will have it covered. Remember, Captain Jones is a good resource; don't get yourselves into anything over your head," Aileen said with a smile and a wink.

Obviously, she and Patrick heard about Captain Jones dressing us down. I should have known he would talk to our mentors to make sure they gave us guidance.

"Where are you going?" Scotty asked with interest.

"Hawaii!" Aileen said enthusiastically. "You sounded as if you had such great fun; you made us feel envious. I don't think we will do everything you two did, but romantic walks on the beach at sunset and an outrigger canoe ride will be exciting enough for us".

"Speak for yourself," interjected Patrick. "I think spearfishing will add some spice to our marriage."

"No way I am getting into the ocean with you having a speargun in your hand. My life insurance policy is paid up," Aileen said suspiciously to Patrick.

He laughed. "You know me better than that. I wouldn't want to train a new wife for all the insurance money in the world. You are perfectly safe with me under the water...as long as you don't look too fishy."

"Speaking of fish, I remember the last time we went snorkeling off Molokini Crater that you took a couple chunks of hard bread with you to feed the fish. A swarm of fish targeted your hand full of bread; you panicked, and you put the bread in your swimming trunks. Big mistake!" Aileen laughed hysterically, having trouble continuing her story. "The guide told you later, that he thought he saw it all until he saw you fighting to get all of the bread out of your trunks, with the largest ball of ravenous fish engulfing you."

"Very funny! You would have panicked, too, if the fish were after you!" Patrick said.

Patrick and Aileen continued to banter back and forth for several minutes with Scotty and me just watching and laughing. Finally, one of them came to their senses and let us know what they expected of us during their absence.

"Just close up the office when you are in classes or running errands. When you come back to the office, check the answering machine to see if anyone has called. You know where to put the mail. If any insurance companies send checks while we are away, put them in the safe. We will divide them when we return," Patrick directed.

It seemed clear-cut enough for us. After promising to phone us daily from Hawaii, probably around 4:00 PM our time, Patrick and Aileen said we could take the afternoon off. They knew we had plans to have a date that night.

I hugged them at the door and told them I expected chocolate covered macadamia nuts when they returned. I was excited for them, but I was also anxious to get home and get dressed for our date. With one last hug and an aloha said, Scotty and I left.

We talked all the way back to the house about our trip to Hawaii. I could imagine Patrick and Aileen sitting on the beach. "Aileen still has a nice figure for a woman her age. She might even do a mean hula for Patrick," I said to Scotty.

He just laughed. I saw him glance over at me and move his eyebrows up and down in that silly way some men try to show admiration for a woman's body. I half expected Scotty to say 'Hubba-Hubba.' Instead, he said, "Aileen can't compare to you in a hula skirt."

"I never wore a hula skirt. Or at least, I don't remember wearing one," I interjected.

"You looked fabulous in your bikini. A hula skirt would only accentuate those swaying hips," Scotty said with a quick glance once again in my direction.

"Watch the road! And I don't have swaying hips…I move like a cat," I said purring.

Imitating a cat's paw clawing in the air, Scotty said, "Meow-Meow."

I had to hit him in the shoulder. He could be such a goof.

We pulled into the driveway, and we both bolted for the door to see who would get to the shower first. I know Scotty let me win. Even though I don't take much time in the bathroom, Scotty was acting gallantly by letting me go first.

We were showered and ready for dinner by 5:00 p.m. "If we go to dinner now, I will order the senior citizen's plate," I said, acting decrepit, holding my back like an old lady. "What can we do for a few hours before we go to dinner. I don't want to waste a minute of our date night. What do most people do this early?"

"They go to a bar and have a drink first before dinner. We can't do that since we aren't legal yet. Let's see…. What could we do for a couple of hours before dinner?" Scotty said, dangling the car keys.

"We can still go for appetizers and drinks, but it doesn't need to be alcoholic. I know. Let's go to Cite' Chicago Restaurant. It is on the 70th floor, and it has a 360-degree view of the whole area. Depending on where we are seated, we could see downtown or Lake Michigan or even Lincoln Park Zoo. It is costly, though," I remarked to Scotty.

"We still have plenty of money from the insurance check. We did not give it all to the Jamiesons. We can afford to stay and eat dinner there if we don't need to wait too long. We don't want to miss our show at The Second City. Let's go. The earlier we put our names in for dinner, the better chance we have of getting a table." Scotty grabbed my arm and started pulling me out the door.

Getting to the parking garage, we parked and headed for the elevator. We were met by the Maître-D and was told we would have an hour wait for a table, but we could sit at the bar and order appetizers. Putting our name on the waiting list, we did just that.

As we talked, we also browsed over the menu. I knew immediately, Scotty would order either the ribeye or the venison. I was glad to see salmon on the menu's list even though I was tempted by the duck breast.

I ordered the chilled seafood platter for Scotty and myself to share, along with a glass of sparkling water, and Scotty ordered a cola. We glanced out the windows and remarked on sailboats seen in the distance. It was still light enough outside that the downtown lights in the skyscrapers were not visible. I was sure it would be lovely later in the evening with lights glittering off the dark lake.

The hour passed quickly, and we were called to a table set for dinner. Since we already knew what we wanted, we put in our orders quickly.

The view was spectacular. I found myself wishing it was a revolving restaurant, so I could see the city from 360-degrees. As it was, we were content to view Lake Michigan and daydream about having a sailboat someday.

The dinner was costly but well worth every penny. Scotty finished the entire rib-eye steak, his potato, and asparagus and even said he had room for dessert. My salmon with couscous and the mixed green salad filled me up. When Scotty ordered a chocolate, hazelnut cake, I told them to bring two spoons. When Scotty eyed me, I said, "I only want one little bite. I'm stuffed from dinner."

"Yeah, right. I know how you are about chocolate. Stuffed or not, you won't stop at one bite, especially when you taste the mousse filling."

I suspected Scotty was right. I am a chocoholic, but I can stop when I want to. When the cake arrived, I knew Scotty was right again this time. I wasn't going to stop at one bite.

Graciously, Scotty shared his dessert, and I practiced as much restraint as I could. Finishing with a cup of coffee, we paid the enormous check, left an appropriate tip, and headed back down the 70 floors.

We had plenty of time to drive the short distance to The Second City. Valet parking was an option. As we drove up to the parking space, the attendant told us to just park right there in front of the club. He was intrigued by the Double Nickel and told us to take the keys. The attendant drooled and said the Double-Nickel could just sit there outside the building, and he would personally watch it all night long.

"That is one Dope car!" the attendant said to Scotty. I wasn't supposed to hear him add in a whisper, "And that is one bangin' chick you are with. You've got it all goin' on."

Scotty gave me his usual goofy look, and said, "If only he knew your real beauty...both inside and out!" Then he told me he loved me! Scotty tipped the attendant ten dollars, and we walked into the lobby of The Second City. I whispered into Scotty's ear, while we were being escorted to our seats, that I loved him more!

We were prepared to relax and laugh away the stresses of the last couple of months. Not disappointed, we did just that. The comics were hysterical.

We were still laughing halfway home. Scotty would repeat something one of the cast members said, and we would both burst out laughing. Some of it wasn't that funny. We just needed to relax. Little did we know that it would be a long time before we got to let loose and have that much fun again.

CHAPTER SEVEN

I knocked on Scotty's door the next morning. I had already showered and was in the process of making breakfast. I knew he was tired, so I let him sleep in. It was the first day of being on our own at the office. I was excited. I was really starting to feel grown-up.

Scott came out, yawning and rubbing his eyes. "Why didn't you wake me up earlier? I could have helped you make breakfast," he said as he stumbled to the table and sat down. A cup of coffee was already at his place.

"I knew you were tired. I woke up early. I think I laughed in my sleep most of the night. That was fun going to The Second City. I want to go again. Maybe next time, we can throw a party and have Tony and his date go along."

Scotty liked Tony as much as I did. We had become even closer ever since Tony started taking private lessons from Grandmaster Kim Yong-Sool. Grandmaster Kim Yong-Sool had told me that Tony was gifted and was progressing remarkably fast. I told him my individual student was doing equally well. I looked at Scotty with pride.

"What?" Scotty said as he noticed the maternal look, I was giving him. "You look just like my mother when I have done something that pleased her. What did I do?"

I sat down the breakfast plate in front of Scotty, and I sat down in my place across from him. I was about to tell him what I thought when I realized Scotty had already forgotten his question. He was knee-deep in his breakfast.

"We have a test on Monday," I said instead of answering his original question. "Are you going to need some tutoring? We must go to the office today, but tomorrow we can spend as much time as you want to prepare for the test."

Scotty took a breath from eating. "That's right. This will be our first day at the office alone. Wouldn't it be exciting if a mysterious lady would walk-in and ask us to help her find the Maltese Falcon?"

I shook my head back and forth. "Scotty, you and your old movies. That is not going to happen. We will be content to have someone come in and ask us to find their lost dog."

Scotty ignored my comment. "This is delicious French Toast. What did you do differently?"

When I scowled at him, Scotty quickly said, "I didn't mean that your normal French Toast is not good. I just meant that this tastes a bit different, and I like it."

I had to laugh at how hard Scotty had to work to keep me from getting angry. Little did he know, I am very even-tempered, and I only act mad at him to keep him off-balance.

"I usually put cinnamon in the egg batter, but this time I squeezed in some orange juice. You like it? I will make a note of that and make it again sometime," I said, putting Scotty at ease.

"You'd best take a shower while I do the breakfast dishes. We need to get our butts in gear. The office is supposed to be open at 9:00 a.m., you know." I grabbed his plate out from under his nose while he took the last sip from his coffee cup.

"I could really go for another cup of coffee," Scotty said.

"So, pour yourself one and take it into the bathroom," I said, making it known that I was not going to be his maid any longer that day. I had babied him enough for one day. "Hurry up. Get a move on."

Scotty left his coffee cup and scrambled into the bathroom. Within a couple of seconds, I heard the shower running. I knew I only had ten minutes to do the dishes and be ready to go out the door. Scotty wasn't one to spend much time in the shower. Military-style showers were what he called them.

Both our fathers served in the military; however, my dad did not insist on us taking military showers. He pampered me. I guess being his only child and a girl child at that, I was spoiled by him. My mother wasn't stern either. They both allowed me a lot of latitudes.

I would have continued to reminisce to myself if Scotty hadn't walked into the kitchen, fully dressed, and ready to go. Part of me wished he had come into the kitchen just with a towel wrapped around his waist. Our relationship had regressed a bit since Scotty found out I helped Heather disappear, intentionally keeping it from him. We were working out our problems nicely. I knew we needed to take things slower.

Grabbing my keys, I locked the door behind us, and we headed to the car. As we drove to the office, Scotty looked at his watch. "We have enough time to stop and get some donuts and coffee. What do you say?"

I groaned. "Scotty, you just ate breakfast. Do you have a tapeworm or something?"

"It isn't that I am hungry. I just want another cup of coffee, and as long as I am going to drink coffee, I might as well have a donut with it," Scotty said as he pulled into the donut shop.

I sat in the car and waited. I did not want to be tempted by the chocolate-covered eclairs with the whipped cream inside. I knew if I saw them, I would order one. I don't tend to gain weight, but my mom is a little on the plump side. That means that I might have a gene for weight gain as well. I will need to have good habits for the rest of my life if I am going to avoid putting on a thick middle.

Scotty opened the door with a donut already in his mouth. "OMG! You are impossible. What are you going to eat with your cup of coffee if you eat your donut now?" I asked with some contempt.

"Don't worry. I have it covered," Scotty said, and he drove away.

When we got to the office, Scotty set down two cups of coffee and revealed a chocolate-covered éclair and two more donuts. "See, I told you I had it covered."

My mind was doing flip-flops. I wanted to resist to make a point, but my evil self-said to take the éclair and eat it before Scotty ate his other two donuts. I listened to my evil self and enjoyed the éclair way too much. I had once heard a saying that went something like this. If you are going to sin, sin boldly.

Scotty was just about to start the computer when the front door opened. A smartly dressed woman in her late forties walked through the door.

Scotty shot me a glance and mouthed the words, 'Are you kidding me…. The Maltese Falcon!'

I shot Scotty a look back and mouthed for him to knock it off. I then stood up to greet the woman entering the office.

"Are you Mr. and Mrs. Jamieson?" she asked.

"No, the Jamiesons are on vacation. I am Tish Evers, and this is my partner, Scotty McFarlan. We are partners of the Jamiesons. Can we help you?" I said by way of introductions.

"I don't know. I was told the Jamiesons are the best in the business. I really wanted to do business with the owners," the lady said with regret.

"I didn't get your name," I said as I held out my hand to her.

"I'm sorry. That was rude of me. My name is Leticia LaPlante. When will the Jamiesons be home from their vacation? Maybe I could come back then."

"Why don't you sit down and tell us what the problem is. If we can't help you before the Jamiesons return, you won't really be out anything, will you?" I said, noting Scotty was remaining very silent.

Mrs. LaPlante sat down on the sofa. I liked the fact the Jamiesons made their front office comfortable and cozy. Ferns softened the room as well as drapes and throw pillows. There were side offices, but Jamiesons avoided using them unless they needed complete confidentiality.

Mrs. LaPlante hesitated. I could tell she wasn't sure how to begin.

"Would you care for a cup of tea?" I asked, knowing that the time it would take to make the tea would give her plenty of time to gather her thoughts.

"I'll make some tea," Scotty said as he took the coffee cups and the empty paper sack into the kitchenette. I heard the water run as he filled the tea kettle.

Mrs. LaPlante asked us what our credentials were. I assured her we were qualified to do most anything the Jamiesons could do, or they would not have picked us to represent their business.

Mrs. LaPlante looked down at her lap, where her hands were tightly grasped around the handle of her purse. "I suppose it can't hurt to tell you what I need from you and the Jamiesons when they return."

Scotty came into the room at that moment carrying three cups of tea on a tray. "Do you take cream or lemon with your tea?" he asked.

I was almost taken aback by how proper Scotty was acting when I realized for the first time that Leticia LaPlante was beautiful for an older woman.

Her hair was blond, natural, and worn in half up fishtail style. With her hair pulled away from her face, her high cheekbones and sky-blue eyes were emphasized. Her figure was perfectly proportioned, and her suit did not hide that fact. Her legs were shapely, and her heels belied the fact that she was petite and barely came to 5'5" without them. No wonder Scotty was on his best behavior.

The tea was too hot to drink, so I indicated that she might begin if she was ready. I thought about taking notes, but it would only be for effect since I had no need for them. If the Jamiesons had questions later, I would be able to tell them the conversation verbatim.

Haltingly, Mrs. LaPlante relayed the details as best she could under the circumstances of not totally trusting us, "I...have a daughter. Recently...she was missing...for a night, and the next day. They found her wandering around Cedar Point County Park near Pentwater, Michigan, the following morning. She did not know where she was or how she got there. In fact, she had no memory of those two days. I want to know what happened to my daughter." Tears started to form in Mrs. LaPlante's eyes as she told her story.

"My daughter is a good girl. She was a nursing student at the top of her class. She doesn't drink or do drugs. She has never had any sort of psychological problems. She has always been well-adjusted and happy. Now she is moody and irritable. She is frightened, and when I ask her what happened, she just says she can't remember anything but shadowy faces."

"Shadowy faces?" Scotty asked.

"Yes, that is all she can remember. Something happened to her. It couldn't have been good. She may not be able to remember what happened, but it has affected her emotionally and physically. She doesn't eat well anymore. She is distracted, and for the first time ever, she started struggling with her nursing classes. In fact, she had to drop out since she is afraid to go out of the house. I need to find out what happened so she can be helped. Can you investigate and find out what happened?" Mrs. LaPlante was pleading with her eyes.

Neither Scotty or I spoke for a moment. Finally, I felt I should be the one to start the conversation.

"We will need to talk to your daughter. Will she be open to talking to us? We don't want to upset her, but we will need to ask personal questions," I said frankly.

"After we talk to your daughter, we will have a much better idea of whether we can continue the investigation. You don't have much to go on," Scotty chimed in.

"We would want to talk to whoever found her at Cedar Point County Park to see if they saw anything strange or suspicious. Do you know who found her?" I asked.

"Yes, it was a ranger from the park. He said she was just sitting on the beach, shivering. She wasn't dressed to be outside on that cold beach…for who knows how long? The ranger phoned me to tell me that my daughter was at the park and had no idea how she got there. He said he would be taking her to the clinic in Pentwater, Michigan, and I could pick her up there. When I got to the clinic, the ranger had already gone back to work. I don't know who he was, but I am sure they know at the clinic," Mrs. LaPlante talked rapidly as she told the rest of her story. It was as if she would forget the few details, herself if she did not say it fast.

"When would be the best time for us to come to your house and talk to your daughter?" Scotty asked professionally.

"You can come this afternoon if it suits your schedule," was the immediate answer. "Constance stays home all the time now, except when she sees her psychiatrist. She said she feels sick to her stomach all the time. I can only imagine since Constance only eats a handful of food a day. She is wasting away before my very eyes…" and the floodgate opened. Mrs. LaPlante sobbed into her hands.

Scotty quickly went to the coffee table to retrieve the box of tissues Aileen always kept there. I found myself scooting over to the sofa and trying to comfort the distressed lady as best as I could. I found myself making promises that I knew we might not be able to keep.

"Don't worry. We will find out what happened to Constance. I promise."

CHAPTER EIGHT

The minute Mrs. LaPlante left after giving us her address and phone number, I asked Scotty whether he was willing to make the long drive to Cedar Point County Park. I knew I was asking a lot of him since it was almost four hours away. I thought if we divided the tasks, we might be more efficient.

"Sure!" Scotty said excitedly. "I would love to see what it is like along the coast of Lake Michigan. Maybe I can find some good fishing spots or a nice port town for us to visit as well. I wish we could go together."

I was about to jump on him and tell him this was business and not a scouting trip for a vacation when I thought better of it. The fact that he had a way of making his work fun was a good thing. Instead, I let my mind sort through my thoughts.

Talking out loud, I said, "I think I have a better chance of finding out any hidden information alone with Constance. If I play my cards right, she might confide things that she wouldn't tell her mother.

"I also think the Park Ranger will be more inclined to tell you things than me. I would love to be able to drive along with you. It does seem like it will be a nice drive, but it is going to take this entire day for you to make the trip and return. I guess you had best get going. Just know I envy you taking the trip."

Quickly I added one more thing, "Do you mind dropping me back at home? I want to get my Harley. I don't relish walking that far or taking a bus." I grabbed my small bag and followed him out the door. Scotty put out the closed sign and locked the office.

"We don't know what the exact dates, time, or anything else when she was found by the ranger. I don't think the clinic in town will give you any information, but I am willing to bet my best boots that you and the ranger will hit it off famously. I just hope the ranger saw something that will help this investigation," I said.

"Oh," I added. "Don't forget to find out if there was anything suspicious that the ranger saw. Maybe someone was lurking about, or a strange car or something in that order as well."

"Give me a break," Scotty said, rubbing his head as if he had a headache. "This isn't my first rodeo. I know how to ask questions and still be subtle."

I leaned on his shoulder. "I'm sorry. You are more than capable. Sometimes I just micromanage. I guess this is one of those times. Forgive me?"

I scooted a little closer to him and laid my head on his shoulder. It felt good to snuggle with him in the car. I knew if I nagged him too much, our relationship would suffer in many ways. It is just too difficult to bite my tongue sometimes. I really was worried Scotty wouldn't get the information we needed. This case was going to be difficult without some leads.

Scotty parked and rushed inside the house. I followed.

"Did you forget something?" I asked, staying close on his heels.

"Money. I don't have enough for gasoline, let alone a couple of meals," Scotty said, racing for his dresser drawer.

He swooped back past me, gave me a peck on the cheek, and headed for the front door. Turning towards me as he pulled the door partially closed, he said, "Don't wait up for me. This is going to be a long day, and I don't know how late I will be. I will phone you this evening to let you know what time I should be home."

I smiled at him as he closed the door, and I whispered, "Take care of yourself."

I heard the Double Nickel roar to life as Scotty put his foot down hard on the gas pedal. He did that way too often just because he liked the way the engine sounded. I found myself thinking it had better not be the last time I heard that rumbling noise.

I don't know why I was feeling negative and morbid. I never could get used to Scotty being away from me, and I found myself feeling afraid. It wasn't fear for myself, but fear that something might happen to Scotty and I might never see him again.

I shook the thought from my head. I was acting silly. Nothing was going to happen to Scotty, and I needed to redirect my thoughts to deal with Constance LaPlante.

I sat down and thought about what I already knew about the case. I realized I knew very little. It was approximately three weeks ago Constance left for her rotation at one of the hospitals. As a nursing student, the programs are set up to give students a chance to become familiar with many aspects of nursing. I gathered she was doing floor nursing this rotation.

Her mother said she did not come home that evening. Her mother went on to say Constance did not come back the next day, either. The following morning the ranger phoned to say Constance had been found, but she was suffering some memory loss and mild hypothermia from being out all night.

Constance was inappropriately dressed for spending a night or maybe even two nights on the beach, but the ranger said it appears Constance had done just that. The park ranger said she had no memory of how she got there.

When we mulled the case over earlier, Scotty mentioned there wasn't a good reason to talk to anyone at the clinic. He felt he would not get any information from the nursing staff. Unless Scotty found a janitor or admission clerk or another non-medical staff member that remembered Constance, Scotty was probably correct. Instead, he was heading straight to the ranger station.

I looked up and realized I had been sitting for over an hour. Looking down at the notes that I had taken, I was surprised to see nothing but doodles. I had no memory of doodling. The doodles were odd. Over and over, I had drawn waves. Nothing but waves.

I got up from the table and went to my room to dress in clothes appropriate for riding on my Harley. I grabbed the keys to the Harley and my small leather backpack, which held the house key. We had a set of keys to the office, but I usually let Scotty carry them in his pocket. I like feeling unencumbered.

Starting up the Harley, I balanced it as I put on my helmet. I knew vaguely where the LaPlante's lived. It was in a nice neighborhood.

Reaching their house, I parked and headed up to the door. I was greeted by Mrs. LaPlante. She was cooking something in the kitchen, so she hurried me inside the house.

"I am cooking Constance's favorite Mexican dish. She loves soft tacos. Can I make one for you as well? The two of you can sit on the patio and talk. Maybe you can encourage her to eat." There seemed to be desperation in Mrs. LaPlante's voice as she said this. I could only imagine how hard it would be for a mother to see her daughter wasting away before her very eyes.

"I will try. Can I talk to Constance alone? I think she will be more honest with me if we are alone." I knew immediately that I had offended Leticia LaPlante. She showed me to the patio. Bristling, Mrs. LaPlante, walked back into the kitchen without introducing me to her daughter.

I walked out the door to the terrace, where I found Constance sitting on a lawn chair gazing into the distance, seemingly at nothing. "Constance, my name is Tish. I am here to ask you a few questions about the night you disappeared. May I sit down?"

I was beginning to think she was catatonic and had not heard a word that I had said when she turned her head towards me and nodded consent. I took a seat by her at the patio table.

Constance was a beautiful little thing with sky-blue eyes and blond hair. She looked much like her mother. Her hair was unkempt now, but I could imagine how sleek it would be brushed and shining. I pictured her with her long blond hair in a ponytail. Her cheekbones were high like her mother's, and her nose was petite. Her lips were quite full in comparison with her small face. Her eyes caught my attention the most. They were large but seemed vacant and haunted.

"Constance, I understand you are a nursing student. Your mother said you had been on the top of your class until three weeks ago. Can you tell me what happened?" I said, not really knowing how to start the conversation. I hoped to jump in would be the right approach.

Constance looked at me for the first time. She studied my face and let her eyes follow the lines of my body down to my boots.

"Do you ride a motorcycle? You seem dressed as if you do," Constance asked.

"Yes, I do when the weather permits. I don't ride when it is icy," I answered in a matter of fact voice, hoping the casual tone would put Constance at ease. "I like the freedom of riding my Harley."

"Maybe you would take me for a long ride. Freedom sounds nice," Constance said, and she looked away, staring at nothing again.

I did not think she was putting on an act, but I decided I needed to shake up the questions a bit to see how she would react.

"Were you with a boyfriend the night you disappeared?" I asked bluntly.

No response.

"Did you stay the night with your boyfriend, and you did not want your mother to find out?" I pushed.

No response.

"Does your mother know you are pregnant?" I asked pointedly.

Tears welled up in Constance's eyes. Her eyes darted to the patio door to make sure her mother was not about to enter the patio with her lunch.

"How do you know I am pregnant? I'm not even sure myself. I missed my period, but that doesn't mean I am pregnant. What made you say that? "Her words were whispered but with intensity. If it were not for the fact that she was afraid her mother would hear, she would have been screaming at me.

I was not 100% sure that Constance was pregnant. Were there signs registering in my unconscious mind, consciously again? It was becoming more second nature for me to do that now. Little things....

I knew I needed to answer her, "You have been protecting your breasts like they are tender. Your mother said you are not eating. You have touched your stomach five times since we started talking. Some women become ill from the moment of conception, and others never get morning sickness. I suspect you are one of the unfortunate ones."

Constance lowered her eyes and hissed. "You can't tell my mother."

"Can you tell me anything about the night you were missing?" I asked, redirecting the conversation back to the reason I was there.

"I don't remember anything. There is no boyfriend. I have no male friends at all. I can't be pregnant unless I was raped...." Constance looked me in the eyes, and I could see the terror in them.

"Why are you afraid?" I asked.

"The shadowy faces scare me," Constance whispered again.

"What shadowy faces?" I pushed.

"I don't know. I don't know. I just know when I close my eyes, I see blurry faces hovering over me, and something about a coffee house," Constance cried softly.

Mrs. LaPlante opened the door and walked out, carrying two plates with soft tacos. When she saw her daughter in tears, her eyes glared in my direction.

"You are upsetting my daughter. I think your questioning should be delayed for another day. This is too much for her!"

"Mom! Stop! Stop treating me like an invalid. I want to talk to Tish. Would you mind leaving and letting us talk, please?" Constance pleaded with her mother.

Mrs. LaPlante set the plates down on the table and said she would be right back with lemonade. Neither of us spoke until she left.

"I'm sorry. My mother is very protective. This whole thing really has her upset," Constance said in defense of her mother. "She can't know I might be pregnant. She couldn't handle it. I can barely handle..." She let the words drop.

I took a bite of the taco. I did not realize I was hungry until that moment. "It's good. Are you going to eat yours?" I almost found myself sounding like Scotty, and I was disgusted with myself.

Constance picked up one taco and nibbled on the softshell. "Thank goodness it is chicken. I think I would vomit if it were beef," she said while chewing the tiny little morsel.

I was afraid to push much more while she was eating. The idea of vomit projecting in my direction suddenly helped me to get my appetite back under control.

"What can you tell me? You said you couldn't remember anything, but there are shadowy faces and a coffee house. Were these shadowy faces at the coffee house? Ah, wait...you say you have never been with a man, but there is a good chance you are pregnant. You said faces...was there more than one man?" I was starting to feel like I was pulling teeth.

"When I was at the clinic," Constance said quietly, "I was aware I hurt...down there. I did not say anything to the doctor who examined me. He asked me if I had been raped, but I couldn't remember anything." She stopped but continued after taking a few calming breaths.

"I heard the doctor tell the nurse I was clean... maybe even too clean. There would be no need for a physical evidence recovery kit (P.E.R.K.) because it was obvious, I bathed recently even though there was evidence of vaginal abrasions," Constance repeated what the doctor said to the nurse.

I looked at Constance closely. "Do you think you were raped?"

"I really think I am pregnant. I have never slept with a man. Yes, I think I was raped, but I can't remember a thing except for shadowy faces," sobs followed those words.

I let her cry. I patted her gently but did not say a word until she was more under control.

"Constance, what is the very last thing you remember that night?" I didn't have a lead, and I needed something.

"The coffee house...after work at the hospital, I was going to join some of the other students at a coffee house near the hospital. I don't know if I ever got there or not...."

"Okay, good. We have something to go on. You were going to meet some of your nursing student friends at what coffee house? Who were these friends? Can I get names from you, and do you know their phone numbers or addresses?" I felt like I had a lead for the first time in this case.

"I do have some of their phone numbers. I will go and get them for you. I will be right back." She pushed her chair away from the patio table and went inside the house. I knew Mrs. LaPlante would be out the minute Constance was no longer in sight.

"What do you know? Did she tell you anything she didn't tell me?" Quizzed Mrs. LaPlante.

"She just remembers she was going to meet some friends at a coffee house. I need to talk to the other nursing students to see if she showed up or not. I also need the coffee house address, so I can ask more questions. At this point, it is my only lead." I told Mrs. LaPlante.

Constance returned with a few names and phone numbers. I thanked her and told her I would be in touch. Mrs. LaPlante walked me to the door, but with Constance following, she was unable to push for more answers.

It was a good thing since I did not have any for her now. I was sure hoping Scotty would have more answers when he got home.

So far, Constance's story made little sense. She did not remember if she got to the coffee house or not. That seemed odd to me. Why would she forget that detail?

Then there was the fact that she is pregnant but denies having a boyfriend or having any relationship with a man or men. She said the doctor did not do a P.E.R.K. exam at the clinic since she was clean. Except for the physical abrasions, the doctor said there would be no evidence from bodily fluids. I wondered if that was standard.

Obviously, if she was pregnant, she had sex at some time during her time away. If she really can't remember, were drugs used to wipe away her memory. It was something else I would need to investigate. What kind of drugs could do that?

CHAPTER NINE

I was getting worried. I knew Scotty said he would be late and not to wait up, but I couldn't sleep with him out of the house. My imagination was starting to run wild again. I kept thinking of the worst-case scenarios. Maybe Scotty had been in a car accident. Perhaps he stumbled onto the bad guys. Maybe, he....

Just then, I heard his car pull into the driveway, and I let out a big sigh. He was home, and I could relax. When he walked through the door, I flew into his arms.

"I am glad you are home safe. You must be tired from the long drive. Are you hungry? Can I make you something?" I knew I was rattling on and on, but I was relieved Scotty was back home.

Scotty returned my kiss, and he said he was a bit hungry but not to go to much work. I wanted to know everything he had learned, but first things first. Together we worked in the kitchen to get Scotty a small meal that would hold him over until breakfast.

As Scotty sat eating his burger and tater tots, I sat across from him, sipping my hot tea. I was having trouble holding my tongue. I wanted him to hurry and give me the details, but I knew his long drive was tiresome, and he deserved a few minutes to relax. The details wouldn't change in the few extra minutes it took for him to eat.

Finally, Scotty was finished. "I need to take a quick shower, and then I will be ready to talk," he said.

I almost bit my tongue in half. Patience is not my middle name. I had very little to go on after my talk with Constance. My hope was Scotty would find out new facts that would lead us to something else. A trail can go cold way too fast, and we were already behind the eight-ball with the three-week delay between Constance's disappearance and Mrs. LaPlante's visit to the office.

I washed up the few dishes and pans while Scotty showered. True to his word, Scotty was in and out of the shower in just minutes. Rubbing his hair dry and wearing his customary towel around his waist, I thought, 'Damn! What a body!' I almost forgot I was chomping at the bit to get his details.

"I am exhausted," Scotty said in a muffled voice as he continued to towel dry his hair.

"I am a bit exhausted myself." It was after 1:00 a.m., and I couldn't fall asleep worrying about Scotty on the road.

"How about if you lay down on my bed with me and you can tell me the details while we relax," I suggested.

"Sounds like a deal to me," Scotty said as he went into his bedroom to put on his pajama bottoms. I went into my room and changed from sweats to my pajamas.

When Scotty came into the room, I was already in bed. He flopped down beside me, and I rested my head on his shoulder.

"Okay, what did you find out?" I asked.

Scotty said, "When I got to the park, I had a bit of trouble locating the ranger. His name is Ranger Larry, and he is a heck of a nice guy. He told me he remembered Constance."

"Yes, go on," I prodded.

Scotty continued. "I asked him to take me to where he found Constance on the beach. He drove me there in his Jeep, and we walked to the spot where he said he found her just sitting and shivering. He said she wasn't dressed to be out in the cold weather."

"Did you ask him if he saw anything unusual?" I interrupted.

"I did ask," tired and grumpy, Scotty grumbled defensively. "Ranger Larry said he has a small cabin nearby where he watches the activity on the lake and in the park. Apparently, it is not unusual for Larry to be outside at night when he can't sleep. He remembered seeing a yacht anchored offshore at about 4:00 a.m. the morning he found Constance on the beach. He mentioned that because it is rare to have a yacht out that early on that part of the lake."

"Could he describe it or give you anything about it that might help us to identify it if necessary?" I asked again.

"Ranger Larry said it was just around 60 feet judging by the anchor lights and the other running lights necessary to be out on the lake at night. He said it was an all-white, very sleek yacht with the bridge and lower saloon enclosed with darkened windows."

"Was that the extent of the conversation?" I asked, sounding disappointed. It seemed most yachts were white; I wasn't sure how much the description would help.

"Give me a chance, will you?" Scotty said as he held me closer.

"I told Ranger Larry that if there were any chance Constance had been aboard the yacht, they would have used a small boat like a skiff to bring her ashore. We decided to check the sand for imprints or disturbances and follow them as best we could. Ranger Larry indicated that the weather over the past three weeks was clear, cold, and calm.

"Surprisingly, we followed what probably was indentations and parallel drag marks from the spot where he found Constance to the shore. The marks became more obscure quickly and finally disappeared as we drew closer to the water's edge. We assumed that a boat could have been drawn ashore, turned around, and pushed back out into the water," Scotty yawned, then continued talking.

"From the deep double rub, still showing in the sand, thanks to the calm and cold weather, the visible marks were most likely a small catamaran-style dingy that brought the girl ashore.

"The disturbances besides the boat impressions, indicated at least two people were on the boat. One imprint was of average size, and the other was a bit smaller. Nothing was obvious since the elapsed time had obscured and shifted most of the impressions. I made sure we captured the scene with our camera...." Scotty yawned and stopped talking. I noticed he had fallen asleep.

"Scotty, wake up. What else did you find out?" I said, lifting my head from his shoulder and peering down at his closed eyes. Not a word. He was deep asleep.

It was going to be a sleepless night for me if I did not get all the information Scotty had obtained, but I was feeling sorry for him and decided the rest of the report could wait until morning. I pulled the blanket over Scotty and laid my head back down on his shoulder.

My brain twisted and turned but not my body. I stayed in one place all night long, not wanting to lose a single moment of Scotty's warmth and the comfort it gave to me by being that close.

I slept fitfully, but Scotty woke refreshed and ready for the day. He was in the kitchen frying bacon when I stumbled out of bed and headed towards the smell of coffee.

Even though coffee was not Scotty's favorite drink, he became accustomed to drinking a cup or two when offered by the Jamiesons. His new caffeine addiction was an advantage for me. He always has the coffee ready for me in the mornings. I gave him a peck on the cheek and headed for my chair at the table. I was not totally awake, but I did manage to ask a question, "What else did you find out?"

"Good morning to you, too," he cracked over his shoulder as he continued to turn the bacon so it would not burn. He was starting to catch on to the best way to cook bacon after only a year of my culinary tutoring.

"You last told me that there were prints in the sand near the drag marks that indicated there were two men. One was averagely built, and the other one was slimmer or smaller or both. What else?" I asked while stifling a yawn.

"Well, there wasn't much more to be discovered at the beach. Ranger Larry told me his sister worked the night shift at the clinic, and he would ask her to find out what she could about Constance. He assured me he would call me or leave a message at the office with any additional information. He did tell me something strange." Scotty paused.

"What did he tell you that was strange?" I prodded. I may not be fully awake, but I certainly catch all the nuances. Strange is a word Scotty uses that could mean almost anything. I was wondering what he intended by strange this time.

"Well," Scotty continued, "it seems Ranger Larry fished another girl off the beach about ten months ago. Ranger Larry said the circumstances were remarkably similar. The girl was confused and wandering around, not sure where she was or how she got there. She was young and pretty and blond, just like Constance."

"Did Ranger Larry call the police the first time or even this time with Constance?" I asked pointedly. Somehow this was strange to me. It may be a coincidence, but I knew deep down that it was not. Someone was using the park as a dumping ground for girls that were abused.

Scotty was talking, and I remembered I had asked him a question, and I wasn't listening. "Ranger Larry said he did not call the police because neither girl wanted him to call. The first girl even resisted being seen at the clinic. She just wanted her mother telephoned so she could go home."

I caught most of what Scotty had just told me. "Did you ask him the name of the first girl and where she lived and all that?" I asked.

Scotty sounded indignant at the question. "Of course, I asked all that information. Ranger Larry said he logged it into his records, but it would take him some time to find it. Clearly, Ranger Larry doesn't keep the best records."

This was a clue we couldn't give up on. We needed the other girl's name and address. Maybe she remembered something about her experience that would help us with Constance.

"Don't let Ranger Larry off the hook. We need that first girl's name and address. In the meantime, I am going to check the newspaper's historical archives. I want to see if there are any articles regarding missing girl articles from the past year or so. While you are practicing for the shooting match, I will do the initial legwork. I suspect you will be done before I am. With two newspapers in town, it is going to be a long day of searching."

While eating breakfast, Scotty asked what I learned from Constance.

I answered, "Constance indicated that the shadowy faces that terrorize her memories were more than one face. The other thing Constance vaguely remembers is that she was either going to a coffee house or she had been to a coffee house with other nursing students. Those details are fuzzy in her memory. I asked her for names, addresses, and phone numbers for the fellow students she hangs with, and I will follow up with them after I check the newspapers."

Scotty suggested I go to the library and use the microfiche reader to scan the microfilm. He said all the newspaper articles should be on microfilm at the Chicago Public Central Library. He thought going to just one place might save me time and wear and tear on my Harley.

I thought it was a good suggestion. Chances are I would not be able to talk to the person who wrote the article anyway, even if I found one.

We dressed and went our separate ways for the day. Scotty said he would go to the office to check the mail and the answering machine. I was itching to know if I could find any other girls with similar stories as Constance's.

The ride to the library went quickly. As I sat down, one of the librarians assisting me in using the reader. I asked if she had any memory of girls missing the last year or so. It was a shot in the dark, but often librarians read almost anything they got their hands on. I was delighted when the mousy young lady said she did remember reading an article. She admitted she remembered because the girl was only a year younger than herself at the time, and she wondered what could have happened to make her forget a whole weekend.

The librarian said, "I suspected she was drinking herself into a stupor or may be using drugs, but the girl in the article looked very nice. I decided maybe she had an accident and was hit on the head, and that is why she couldn't remember where she had been for an entire weekend."

The librarian recollected it was a summer month less than a year ago. She couldn't recall which newspaper ran the short article, but she went off to get the microfilm from each press from the summer months.

I sat and scanned the microfilm she had first set in front of me. It was probably fifteen minutes later when she returned with another microfilm. I thanked her and went back to scanning the news articles.

I was just getting to the point where my eyes were blurring, and my stomach was growling when I happened across a small article indicating that a lost woman was found unharmed. Making a note of the woman's name and Chicago village, I continued my search with renewed vigor forgetting my hunger.

Hours later, I discovered one more article…again small and hidden on the third page. The short newspaper article indicated that a woman was found after being missing for two days. I jotted down her name and village as well.

After hours of reading and scanning, I had only covered two years in the life of Chicago, but from two different newspapers' views. One of the articles about the women was from the Sun-Times, and the other was from the Tribune. Neither of them carried the other woman's story, so I needed to research both newspapers for any other relevant accounts. The Jamiesons counseled us that investigative work would be both time-consuming and tedious.

I thanked the quiet librarian and told her I would probably be back sometime soon. As I left, my stomach rumbled, and I decided I deserved something special to eat. Being on the Harley, there was not much I could carry home safely, but fresh fish from the fish market was an option. I was really in the mood for red snapper or sea bass. I would decide when I got to the fish market. I was sure we had vegetables at home that would complement the fish. Scotty was home when I arrived, fish in hand.

"How's my sharpshooter?" I asked as I carried my prize into the kitchen. "Guess what we are having for dinner tonight?"

"I have no idea. Can I help in the kitchen?" Scotty asked as he got up from the sofa and headed my way.

The next thing I knew, I was embraced from behind. Scotty had his arms wrapped around me and was nuzzling my neck as I unwrapped the fish. "What is that fragrance you are wearing? Eau de Cologne Celeste Jardin? It is intoxicating and reminds me of a rose garden."

"There is a new aroma perfume shop that opened up. I decided we could afford a small bottle of perfume." I said as I continued the preparation for dinner. "Hmmm, your one year of French seems to have paid off," I said, amazed at Scotty's perfect pronunciation.

"We are eating red snapper in olive oil, lemon sauce with fresh cracked pepper for dinner. I skipped lunch…I am starved. If you really want to help, you can clean some red potatoes and get the broccoli out. Tell me about your day while you are doing that," I said, not making any effort to get out from his embrace.

My suggestion to start cooking was enough to get Scotty's mind on food and off romance. It takes a lot to keep him in the mood when he is hungry, and he is always hungry, it seems. The perfume caught his attention, but it didn't keep it. Maybe I should have gone with the one costing $150.00.

Scott started talking as he got out the red potatoes, "I didn't find anything amiss at the office. There were a few notes to jot down from the answering machine, but they were for Aileen. You know the stuff, hair appointment, and someone from an insurance company that said they would call back. Then, I went to the range. Captain Jones was already there practicing. For a moment, I felt guilty like I was slacking for not being there earlier."

I was listening as I worked steadily to get out a pan, turn on the oven, and such, but I had to interject at this point. "You know Captain Jones would not chastise you for not being in at the crack of dawn. He can be stern, but he isn't unrealistic."

Captain Jones has become like a father to both of us. I know how proud he is of Scotty and his shooting abilities. There is a part of me that thinks Captain Jones would love to recruit Scotty for his police force, but luckily, he is content to use both of us in other capacities. That reminded me about the rookie cops' martial arts training that would start in a few hours.

"We better get the food on the table. I almost forgot I have a class this evening. Want to come along?" I asked Scotty.

"Oh! I almost forgot to tell you," I continued. "I found two names of women who also disappeared and then sometime later, they were found. Both had no memory of how they got where they were found and no memory of what happened to them during those missing hours. I will follow up with them tomorrow, but back to my original question. How was shooting practice?"

I was starting to feel the day pressing down on me. My memory is usually good, but today, I am having trouble keeping my thoughts together. Tired and hungry is probably the reason.

"Wow! What a good lead. Do you want me to go along with you tomorrow to talk to the two women?" Scotty asked.

I shook my head to signal no. Once again, I felt it would be best if we divide and conquer.

"Okay," Scotty continued, "I will assume you will give me my marching orders tomorrow. In the meantime, let me tell you more about my shooting practice. The practice went great. I x-ringed all the targets, and my elapsed time was almost a record. Captain Jones said I better do as well at the competition," Scotty chuckled as he said this to me. My heart warmed, hearing him sound self-confident and happy about his abilities.

The table was set, and there were only a few minutes left on the timer. I was feeling grimy from sitting in the library all day. "Be back in a jiffy. I am going to take a quick shower," I said as I ducked into the bathroom. "Take the fish out when the timer rings if I am not back in time."

When I came back out in my workout sweats, the steaming fish, potatoes, and broccoli were on our plates, and candles were lit. I smiled at Scotty and let him push my chair up to the table as if we were on a date. I felt a tad underdressed, but Scotty acted as if I was wearing my finest and treated me like a lady.

We ate quietly but companionably with small talk about the current day's events in more detail. I asked one more time because Scotty hadn't answered the first time, "Are you coming with me to check out the new rookies?"

"Sure, why not. There is nothing on T.V. tonight anyway," Scotty answered. So, this was what marriage would be like, I thought.

CHAPTER TEN

We finished the dishes fast as Scotty washed and I dried. I grabbed the keys to the Double Nickel, and we headed out the door.

"Why do you get to drive?" Scotty said as he tried to wrestle the keys from my hand. I flipped his arm quickly behind his back and lifted it up so he would lose his grip on my arm but was pleasantly surprised when he countered my move instinctually.

"As a reward for being such an astute student, you can drive," I said laughingly. "Did you notice you made that counter-move without even thinking?"

"Hey, I did, didn't I?" Scotty was beaming as I tossed the keys to him.

Time spent in the basement, working on martial arts training has paid off. For a long time, I did not think Scotty was taking the training seriously. He said when I got sucker-punched on one of our cases, and his reaction was to plow in like a football player instead of using martial arts, was the 'aha' moment. He was chastised by Captain Jones and Patrick Jamieson for not thinking. I guess it was an eye-opener.

Getting to the police gym, I was flabbergasted to see the rookie class already assembled and practicing. None of them were due for half an hour.

"Good evening," I said and was greeted in turn by the class as a team. "I am glad to see everyone here early and at practice. Before we start, I want to introduce my business partner, Scotty McFarlan."

The guys came over and shook hands as they introduced themselves to Scotty. Of course, there was small talk about Scotty being the quarterback for the high school State Championship. How guys remember those facts and can't remember their mothers' birthdays is beyond me. I was sure it was Markus who brought up the topic, being a football player himself.

One lady rookie came forward as well and introduced herself. I noted Andrea was standing close to Sam. I wondered how they had become friends so quickly after only a week of training.

Trudy did not bother to introduce herself but stood back a bit from the crowd that surrounded Scotty. I decided to introduce her personally.

"Scotty, the only trainee you have not met, is Trudy. Trudy told us about her athletic abilities in tennis last week." Everyone started to chuckle.

"Tennis. I never got the basics down myself," said Scotty. "It is a good sport. From what I understand, one can play it well past retirement." The group chuckled again.

Scotty looked puzzled until Trudy spoke up for the first time. "The reason everyone is laughing is that I failed beginning tennis." A big smile spread across her face and for the first time. I saw Trudy as pretty, instead of just plain. I was glad she had such a good sense of humor about her own shortcomings. It would serve her well.

"Pair up," I directed. I noted who paired with whom. Trudy and Bart paired up; Andrea and Sam, Irish and Swede, and Markus and Chad. I was glad to see the women did not pair up together but were willing to take on one of the men. I was glad I didn't need to force the issue.

"I am going to use Scotty to teach you a new hold." Scotty stepped up, and with just two words, he knew what I would be teaching the class. He got into position, and as I talked to the group, Scotty did what he needed to do step by step.

With several slowed down motions, we increased the speed until we were performing the hold and counter moves at full speed. I directed the pairs to take it slow at first until each knew the counter move and proceed at a regular pace.

I asked Scotty to watch two groups as I observed and intervened when necessary with the other four. Quickly, the group of rookies caught on to the counter moves to break the hold, and I decided to throw in another technique.

As class ended, the group said they were heading out to a local bar-restaurant for a drink and invited us to join them. I looked to Scotty to see if he was game even though neither of us was old enough to drink yet. It was the first time I realized I was the youngest one in the group.

We accepted the invitation and agreed to meet them at the restaurant in fifteen minutes. I told Scotty tonic water would suit me just fine after the workout, even though I did very little physically that night.

When we entered the bar, I noted beers were the drink of choice amongst the group. Two beers were waiting for Scotty and myself. I was unsure as to how to decline the beer and order the tonic water when Scotty took control of the situation.

"Hey, thanks to whoever ordered us the beer. Sorry, we can't accept the beers. You know, training and all. No beer for your sensei, either. Tish must keep her girlish figure. Who should I thank anyway?"

Andrea laughed. "Sensei, do you let your partner make the decisions as to whether you can have a beer?"

I knew she was directing the question at me. "First off, you don't need to call me sensei in a casual setting, and no, I make my own personal decisions. Scotty is just trying to help me save face. We are both underage, and neither of us is going to jeopardize getting our P.I. License over something like a mug of beer." I decided honesty was still the best route.

"I did not know you were not twenty-one. You are really accomplished for being that young. How long have you been practicing martial arts?" Sam, of all people, asked.

I was really encouraged to see Sam without his usual defiant attitude and wondered what happened during that one week. I answered him directly without looking at the rest of the crowd.

"I have been a serious student from the age of thirteen. At age five, I took one class a week like everyone else. Then at the age of thirteen, I really became immersed in Combat Hapkido and Taekwondo. I spent four and five days per week, two to three hours each time honing my expertise. It has paid off as I am considered a 4th Dan, Sa Dan, black belt."

Though impressed with my credentials, the conversation amongst the rookies gravitated towards inane and silly. Swede and Irish both did impersonations of Trudy's tennis swing while the others, Trudy included, laughed hilariously. Good-natured jibes broke out, giving me the impression that the rookies knew each other very well. Before long, the crowd thinned, and only Sam, Andrea, and Scotty and I were at the table.

Sam asked pointedly, "You said you became a devoted student of martial arts at the age of thirteen. Why?"

I was not wanting to tell Sam or Andrea about being sexually molested. I did not know either of them that well. Scotty sensing my hesitation jumped in.

"I can tell you why." Sam and Andrea both looked at Scotty for the explanation. "As you know, Tish and I have been best friends since, well, since the cradle. Tish was always faster than me, stronger than me and smarter than me until we turned thirteen. I got a big growth spurt, and for the first time, she wasn't stronger than me. She couldn't stand that, therefore, she had to overcompensate."

I laughed. "Scotty is quite sure of himself, isn't he?"

"So, if that isn't the reason, what is?" pushed Sam, looking closely at my face.

"No, that is the reason. Scotty is right," I said and let the topic go. I could tell Sam was not convinced. I wondered why he was interested. Did it have something to do with Captain Jones and my relationship? I speculated if he was feeling a bit jealous regarding it and wanted some ammunition against me.

Andrea changed the conversation, "What are you and Scotty working on right now?"

"We can't give any details like names, but we are working on a very intriguing case. It involves missing women and the fact that they have no recollection of what happened to them during the time they were missing," I said.

"That does sound intriguing. Can't you give us any more details about the case?" Andrea asked.

"This is a case that is just in the infancy of investigation. We have some leads and some strange coincidences, but now, that is all. Hopefully, this week, we will have more information," I hesitated to continue. "However, even when we do have more, we can only tell you a small amount of what we know. Confidentiality and all that, you understand."

"I think it sounds fascinating. If there is anything that I could do to help, just ask. You know I want to be a police detective someday. In fact, Sam and I both are working towards that even though it will take years. Neither of us wants to be a beat cop for long. Sam wants to be an undercover detective," Andrea volunteered.

Sam looked a bit irritated with Andrea. I decided to be bold and ask a question that could cause Sam to ignite. "Are you thinking of going undercover in the drug arena?"

"If you remember, I told you I wanted to protect my community. If it involves going undercover into the gang and drug world, so be it! Do you have a problem with that?" Sam's defiance was flaring up again.

"I think that is admirable," Scotty said. "If I had lost my people I loved due to gangs and drugs, I would want to be on the front line."

"So, what is stopping you? Just because you haven't lost anyone you love doesn't mean that you shouldn't be doing whatever you can to stop it." Sam was becoming agitated.

"You are right," I said. "If there is anything that Scotty and I can do when you are undercover, let us know. We will be there." I hoped this would defuse Sam, and we could regain the camaraderie that began developing earlier.

"Yeah, right," was all Sam offered back.

"Just whistle," Scotty reiterated.

Andrea nipped the conversation and said it was time for her to get going. Sam stood and said he would walk her to her car. The night ended, but maybe not on the note, I hoped it would.

CHAPTER ELEVEN

The ride home left me thoughtful. I couldn't understand Sam and his reactions to us. I did not know if talking to Captain Jones again was a good idea or not. If Sam got wind that I had run to his uncle, I was quite sure my authority would diminish during our training.

"What's your take on Sam, Scotty?" I asked. "I mean, he is defensive. One minute I think he is fine, and I will be able to work with him, and the next, he is angry and surly for no apparent reason."

"I have been around guys like him. Remember, Ty, who ended up moving?" Scotty asked.

"Sure, I remember Ty but not fondly," I responded.

"Well, Ty was a mess. His dad beat him regularly, and he also had to watch his mom get knocked around, and there wasn't a thing he could do about it. I think it made him feel impotent, for lack of a better word. Not having the ability to help his mother made him lash out at everyone. I did not know about his circumstance at the time. I just thought he was a jerk. Anyway, once he moved, one of his neighbors told me what had been happening all those years. I felt guilty for adding to this problem by treating him like a pariah."

Scotty was making me see that I needed to give Sam some space and 'walk a mile in his shoes.' However, when a person is reactive and doesn't explain his actions, it makes it much harder.

Once we got home, I pulled out copies of some of the articles I found regarding our present case in the library. One seemed unrelated, but I couldn't dismiss it. It was about a young woman found drowned two years ago. At the time, no one had come forward to claim the body. The description bothered me. The article said she was young, late teens or early twenties, blond hair, and petite. I searched the newspapers for a follow-up story and never found one.

I concentrated on the other girls' stories. Tomorrow, Scotty and I would be doing follow up work. I told Scotty I was tired and suggested we go to bed.

I looked over at Scotty. He was already asleep on the sofa. I guess I was dull company as I sat and reread the articles.

Touching him softly on his shoulder, I told him to wake up and go to bed. He grumbled something about being fine where he was. I covered him with a blanket and went to my bedroom.

The next morning Scotty was up, showered, dressed, and ready to go. He packed a breakfast picnic to eat on the road. Our day was going to put some miles on the Ford. I grabbed my cup of coffee to go, and we locked the door to the house and left.

The first stop was to swing past the Jamiesons' office. It was part of the routine to check the voice messages and file the mail away for Patrick or Aileen to open later when they returned. It would only be a few more days, and they would be back. I was thrilled since I missed them.

Noting nothing unusual, we decided it would be alright if we both investigated the ladies. Initially, I thought he would be the one phoning the list of students Constance gave to me, but I realized they would be in class. The phone calls to the students would need to wait. Scotty may as well go with me.

I asked Scotty to phone Ranger Larry before we left the office. I wanted him to see if the ranger found the name of the other young woman he found on the beach. Scotty did a lot of 'ah huh,' and 'yes I see' before he hung up.

"Well, did Ranger Larry find the name of the other lady?" I asked.

"No, darn it. Ranger Larry said he must have thrown it away. He said once again what a terrible record keeper he was," Scotty said, sounding disappointed.

"Did he talk to his sister, who works the night shift at the clinic?" I asked, hoping for more information.

"Nothing there either. I guess Ranger Larry is not going to be a resource for us other than what I have already found out. I hoped he might be more helpful." Scotty sounded disappointed.

"Well, we have these two leads. Let's get going and hope they help us with the investigation," I said as we locked the office and headed out.

The first address took us miles across town. We did not have a phone number, or we would have called ahead. A cold call was probably not a good idea, but if we were going to get anywhere, it had to be.

Pulling up in front of a two-story house, I noticed all the drapes were open except one room on the second story. The house was neat, freshly painted, and the lawn was manicured. Bright flowers accentuated the fact that someone loved to garden.

Knocking on the door, I stood side by side with Scotty. I was not sure if the family would be more intimidated by a large, young white man or a tall, black woman. I just hoped we looked clean-cut enough that a door would be opened.

I was relieved when the clicking sound of a door unlocking could be heard. I put on a sincere smile or what I thought would be a proximity of one.

A middle-aged woman opened the door and greeted us. "Can I help you? If you are selling magazines, I am not interested."

I smiled. "No, we aren't selling anything. We actually would like to talk to Brooke if she is here."

A dark cloud seemed to descend upon the sweet woman's face after hearing my request. "My daughter is sleeping right now. Can I ask what this is all about?"

Brooke's mother did not invite us in. I assumed she wanted an answer right now as we stood in the doorway. I decided she would make an assessment and determine if she would talk further with us once she knew our intent.

"I am Tish Evers, and Scotty McFarlan is my partner. Our investigation company is engaged in finding out what happened to our client's daughter during a weekend when she went missing. Her daughter has no memory at all of what happened. I came across a small article in the newspaper about Brooke, and it sounded almost exactly like what happened to my client's daughter. I hope she can tell me something about the time she disappeared that might help us with our investigation. Is there any way we could talk with Brooke?"

"No, you can't talk with Brooke, but you may come in, and I will tell you what I can. My name is Martha. Would you care for some tea?"

"Thank you. That would be very nice," Scotty said for the first time since we arrived.

Martha directed us to her living room and told us to make ourselves comfortable while she put on hot water for tea. "I just made cookies yesterday. They are still pretty fresh if you would like one," Martha called from the kitchen.

"Thank you, Martha, I would love a cookie," Scotty said as he sat down.

I remained standing and found myself walking around the living room, looking at family photos. It seemed Martha and Brooke were the only two who lived in the house aside from a large, fluffy, calico cat. I decided Brooke's father was not living, or maybe Martha had divorced him many years ago. There was no evidence of a man from what I could see.

Martha came in carrying a tray and set it down on the sofa table. She poured three cups of tea and indicated Scotty should help himself to some cookies, which he quickly did.

After taking his first bite, Scotty said, "These are the best chocolate chip cookies I have ever eaten, and my mom makes a mean batch of cookies. What kind of nuts did you put in the cookies? They are delicious."

With a pleased smile on her face, Martha answered, "Macadamia nuts are always the best in chocolate chip cookies even if one has to pay a bit more for them."

Wanting to get down to business since we still had another interview, I changed the subject from cookies to Brooke.

"Martha, what can you tell us about Brooke's disappearance nearly two years ago? Did Brooke ever remember anything? The newspaper article wrote that Brooke had no memory where she had been or what happened to her. It also said Brooke was found wandering aimlessly over a hundred miles from here," I said.

"I can't tell you much more than what was in the article. Brooke was found across the lake in a rather deserted stretch of beach. She wasn't dressed warm enough to be out early in the morning when she was found. She was confused, and when asked why she was at the beach, she said she didn't know. She just repeated she didn't know. The only thing she said when asked about who she was with was shadowy, blurred faces hovering over her." Martha stopped with those words.

After taking a cookie for herself and setting it in her lap on a napkin, she began again. "One of our neighbors thinks Brooke was abducted by aliens. He has been obsessed with his theory; he watches the house constantly. He is a bit strange, but somehow it gives me comfort that someone is watching. Since I have no idea who those shadowy, blurred faces may be, I fear that they might come after Brooke again for some reason. Brooke has become so afraid that she won't leave the house. The doctor prescribed her drugs, and she sleeps more than I like. He says she needs to rest."

Scotty asked the next question. "Can you show me on a map where Brooke was found?"

"Oh, dear, yes. I was phoned by the police to come and get Brooke. I know exactly where she was found. Wait a minute, and I will get the map and show you." Off Martha went hurriedly with the cookie falling to the floor.

I bent over and picked up the cookie, wrapping it in the napkin. I doubt Martha even realized it fell from her lap when she got up; she seemed that upset by our presence and the painful memory coming back to the front of her mind.

Spreading the map out on the dining room table, Martha invited us to join her. Scotty hovered over Martha, as she was a small woman, but still stood straight with impeccable posture. Her hair was graying, but one could see that Martha was a natural blond in her younger years.

"There, right there," Martha said as she pointed to the coastline across the lake from Chicago, but slightly south. "The police from that small town is who phoned me. You can see that it is a small, secluded section of the state where few houses can be found. How Brooke got that far away is beyond me."

I asked what Brooke had been doing before she went missing. Martha remembered the details of the day vividly.

"Brooke is a nursing student...or was. She dropped out shortly after she went missing. Brooke just couldn't concentrate any longer, so we decided a short vacation from school would be best. I remember she phoned to say she was going to a coffee house after leaving the hospital. The girls were on maternity rotation that week. My daughter was excited about being with the mothers who were in labor. Of course, as a student, she had limited duties," Martha stopped and realized she deviated from the question. "I guess what I am trying to convey is that Brooke was excited about her career in nursing and now...her whole life is on hold. It makes me sad beyond words."

Martha paused briefly and then continued, "At any rate, she heard from the fellow nursing students that there was a popular guitarist who would be playing at the coffee house. I, of course, was thrilled she was doing something with friends. Brooke has always been shy, and making friends is not easy for her. That was the last contact I had with her until the police phoned that Sunday morning."

"What hospital was she leaving from, and do you know what coffee house she planned to meet her friends at?" I asked, taking out my notepad to jot down the information even though I would recall every word Martha said from memory.

Martha asked for me to wait one moment while she found Brooke's schedule from her nursing course. Her rotations had her at several clinics as well as two hospitals. All the information would be written down.

As we waited, I looked over at Scotty. He said how it sounded way too familiar to Constance's circumstance. "They are both nursing students, both pretty, blond, and shy. They both went to a coffee house before disappearing, and neither have any memory of what happened other than stating something about blurry or shadowy faces. Starting to sound like a serial abductor, rapist, if you ask me."

Our conversation ended as Martha came in carrying a notebook. It had Brooke's class schedules as well as details about her rotations, such as place, time, supervising nurses, and end dates. I read all the details and committed them to memory but jotted down the names of the hospitals and supervising nurses. I did not know if Constance and Brooke shared similar rotation schedules or supervisors, but it was worth checking these details out further.

We were about to leave when Brooke came stumbling down the stairs. "Mom, are you down here?"

"Yes, honey. I am here in the hallway just saying goodbye to these two lovely young people," Martha answered.

Immediately, a look of panic took over Brooke's vacant facial features she exhibited before hearing about our presence. Quickly, she turned to go back upstairs when I called out to her.

"Brooke, wait, please," I pleaded. "Can I ask you just a couple of questions?"

Martha looked worried and whispered. "Don't upset her, please. She is very unstable right now."

Looking over her shoulder at her mother for reassurance, Brooke slowly turned back around, clinging tightly to the railing. Brooke seemed to be trying to focus her eyes on Scotty and me.

"It will just be a few minutes, I promise," I said, trying to sound comforting.

Brooke descended the stairs and took a seat on the sofa. Scotty sat far away from her so as not to appear threatening in any way. He noticed how skittish she seemed as she passed by him to take a seat. I was impressed with Scotty's sensitivity to the situation.

I softly started my questioning. "Brooke, your mother has told us as much as she can about the weekend you disappeared. I am trying to help another nursing student who has had a similar occurrence as yourself. Is there anything you can remember from the time you were away? Anything at all?"

Brooke sat with a faraway look on her face. She did not answer. She just sat and stared. Finally, she said, "All I remember is shadowy faces looking down at me."

"Like you were coming out from under anesthesia?" I prompted, hoping she would recall something, anything.

Martha interjected at this point, "She has never had any kind of operation; I doubt she would know that feeling. She has never used drugs either."

I knew Martha was trying to protect Brooke from having pressure put on her. I acknowledged her concern and asked one more question.

"Brooke, did you make it to the coffee house that evening, and did you spend time with your friends?" I paused and waited for Brooke to gather her thoughts and answer. Scotty was staying entirely out of the questioning. He knew he would only startle her by asking anything.

"I do remember the coffee house. I did go and meet my friends. I remember the guitar player and how good he was...." Brooke once again stopped talking and just stared.

"Brooke," I said, trying to break through the fog in her brain. "Who were you with at the coffee house, and which coffee house did you go to?"

I knew immediately I made a mistake by asking two questions instead of just one at a time. Brooke became upset and started to shake visibly. "I don't know.... I just don't know!"

Martha rushed to her side and pleadingly asked us to leave with her eyes. Scotty and I both knew there was no sense asking Brooke anything else. We got up, and I bent down and placed our business card quietly saying to Martha to phone us if there is anything more than Brooke remembers, and we quickly went to the door to exit.

"Just one more question," I said before opening the door. Martha now glared at me. I knew I was pressing, but it was necessary. "What street might we find the coffee house?"

Martha said, "There is one coffee house close to the hospital. I met Brooke there once. It is called Urban Legends on W. North Street in Wicker Park. Now leave, please. I need to quiet my daughter down."

We left hearing Martha shushing and whispering to Brooke, "It's okay, darling. It's okay."

The last question, even though insensitive on my part, was great information as this coffee house is a couple of blocks from the hospital on West Division Street where Constance did her clinical work.

I wondered if both girls, Constance and Brooke, did their clinical rotation at the same hospital when they disappeared. I knew I needed to track down the nurses who were students at the same time as Brooke. A lot can happen in two years...I was going to need some luck.

Constance's fellow nursing students would be easier to track since they are still in nursing school. Tracking down the ones who already graduated in Brooke's class was not going to be easy. Most probably have jobs. A few may have entered universities for higher degrees. Many may have even left Chicago to pursue nursing in their own cities. It would be best to start with the ones who were still students...Constance's friends.

Sitting in the car for a moment before starting it, Scotty said sarcastically. "Now that was fun." Referring to Brooke's meltdown. "Geez, what do you think happened to her to cause her to break down like that? That is just awful."

His words brought me back to where we were. I was afraid to tell Scotty some of my theories. They were just too horrifying to put into words. We were going to find out; that is one thing I knew for a fact.

CHAPTER TWELVE

As the car was pulling away from the curb, I asked Scotty if we could stop for lunch before heading to our next destination. We were making another cold stop. I felt it might be beneficial to talk about what we did right at Martha's house and what we had done wrong. I knew for a fact that I pushed too hard with Brooke by asking two questions at once. I did not want to repeat that mistake. I felt Scotty would have some insights that would be valuable. We also needed to check the map for the route to see Josie Randall.

"I'm not very hungry, but if you are ready for lunch, I could eat a hamburger...and maybe drink a milkshake. French fries would be good, too," Scotty said. He laughed as he said those words knowing I would call him a pig. After all, Scotty had eaten four cookies while we were talking to Martha.

One thing about Chicago, there is always a good restaurant close by. We found a small diner with parking in the back. Having to hunt for street parking can be a problem. We did not want to make an afternoon of it.

Settling into a booth, I pulled out the map as the waitress walked up to our table with two glasses of water and menus. We concentrated on finding our route. Since Scotty would be driving, I memorize the map. I would be his navigator this time around.

Our food arrived, and the map was folded up and put aside. As we ate, we talked about the time spent with Martha and Brooke. Scotty reiterated the disturbing similarities between what Leticia had said about Constance's disappearance and what Martha had said about Brooke's. We talked, and Scotty said he felt that he should remain in the background again. It seemed to be working for me to take the lead.

We headed to the second interview. I was hoping the young lady involved would be more coherent than Brooke or Constance. It would be nice to talk to someone who remembered more than shadowy faces.

I was soon disappointed. Josie Randall was no more articulate than the other two. Her mother explained that Josie's doctor, Dr. Kessler, had her heavily medicated. Josie, it seemed, had attempted suicide. Her mother, Melissa Randall, clarified that Josie was diagnosed as paranoid.

We talked about a few facts and found that coincidentally, Josie was a nursing student who is no longer capable of continuing her studies. She dropped out of the program shortly after her experience. The cases were all too alike for me to dismiss. I found my skin crawling as her mother told us she had gone to a coffee house and disappeared.

We both asked the usual questions. Where was Josie found? Did she remember anything? Could Mrs. Randall tell us which hospital was supplying the clinical training? What was the specific rotation at the time of her disappearance? What was the name of the coffee house? Was she alone or with friends that evening? Does she have the name of any of the friends who were also at the coffee house?

Looking at the photo of Mrs. Randall, Josie, her father and brother led us to the fact that Josie looked remarkably like the other two young women. The shadowy face or blurred face was starting to materialize in my mind. It was the face of a predator who liked his women young, blond, and petite. He also wanted them shy and naive. However, I still did not know if he was old, young, large, small, good-looking, ugly, or anything else. I just knew he was a monster.

I wondered how he selected and lured these young women from the coffee house. Where did he take them, and what did he do to them? Why didn't they have any memory of what happened?

As we thanked Mrs. Randall for taking the time to answer our questions, we left her house with more questions than answers, except now we knew the timetable for Josie's disappearance. We also learned it was Ranger Larry that found Josie and who contacted Mrs. Randall. Was it odd that Ranger Larry found two of the three victims? I wanted Scotty's input.

Scotty answered. "The situations aren't a coincidence as far as I am concerned. It seems obvious to me that we are dealing with a serial rapist. I know I am jumping to conclusions because rape hasn't been proven. Whoever the predator is, he makes sure the ladies are cleaned up and dumped where they won't be found for some time. I just want to know what he does to wipe out their memory. How can we find that out?"

I thought for a moment. "Mrs. Randall referred to Dr. Kessler. He is treating Josie. Maybe he would talk to us if we make an appointment. I know he won't talk about Josie, but he might be able to shed some light on why Josie had no memory of what happened to her."

We drove in silence for several moments. I know Scotty was just as upset about what might have happened to the three women. Scotty is a champion of women and has been for as long as I have known him.

I was reflective. "Scotty, remember when we were little, and the kids would call me a pickaninny? You were the only one who would stand up for me. Remember how you punched Doug in the nose for calling me names?"

"What made you think about that right now?" Scotty said as he glanced at me sideways, not taking his eyes off the road for long.

"I was just thinking about how you have always been my champion. You always have my back. It was more than the fact that our fathers served together in the military, and our families were friends. It was more like you cared how I was treated because you thought I was worth something," I said, looking the profile of his face.

Scotty clarified, "Of course, I thought you were worth something. You have always been special to me. When we were little, I almost thought of you as my sister. Later, you became my best friend. Now you are not only my partner but the woman I want to spend the rest of my life with. I wouldn't want to do that if I didn't think you were special."

Turning and looking directly at me, Scotty said, "Is this coming from the fact that you think Josie, Brooke, and Constance were violated, and you are being haunted a bit yourself?" Scotty asked purposely.

I had to admit that Scotty may be right. My abuse at my uncle's hands has molded me into who I am. I studied martial arts to make sure no man could ever violate me again. I hated the thought that those three young women's' lives had been damaged, maybe permanently because of one man's sexually deviant behavior. It sickened me and made me realize that I wanted more than ever to catch this monster.

"Scotty, we need to split up again. Tomorrow, I am going to try to talk to Dr. Kessler. Do you think you would be able to go to the nursing school and find out whether any of the nursing students who were in Constance's class before she dropped out are available to be questioned? I would assume most would want to help with her case. Her mom said that even though she was shy, she was very well-liked by her classmates."

"Sure," Scotty replied. "I will phone first thing in the morning to find out if the students are in clinical training or if they are at the nursing school this week. If they are at the nursing school, I will be there on their lunch break, or if necessary, I will wait until the end of their classes. I will talk to as many as I possibly can. How does that sound?"

I smiled, but I wondered if I was making a mistake to send Scotty out to talk to a bunch of young women. "No flirting, unless it is absolutely necessary to get them to talk, okay?" I said sternly, feeling a bit insecure.

"Back at you. Dr. Kessler could be a young Dr. Kildare, you know. I don't want you to dump me for a successful, good-looking psychiatrist." Scotty winked.

He always knew how to make me smile and put me at ease. We were heading for the Jamiesons' office to check in one more time before heading home. I was tired and ready to relax, but we had some computer work to do first before we could do that.

I really wanted to talk to Aileen and Patrick about this case. I was sure we were doing the footwork necessary to solve the mystery, but I wanted reassurance. Were we missing anything obvious? Patrick would know immediately.

We noted that nothing was amiss, and everything was still in its place when we walked into the office. The phone's answering machine's blinking light was indicating there was a message. As Scotty went to the computer to start work that we had been neglecting, I listened to the message on the machine.

"This is Martha Tully. This message is for Tish Evers and Scotty McFarlan. I just want to apologize for my abrupt dismissal of both of you this morning. I know you are just trying to help your client's daughter. I realize that helping her may answer questions for me as well. What I want to tell you is that I found some names and phone numbers of Brooke's classmates. If you could stop by tomorrow, I will give them to you. It may help with your investigation. At least, you might find some of the girls that went to the coffee house with Brooke. I hope to see you tomorrow. Thank you." The recording ended. I was thrilled to think that another lead in this case, had just fallen into my lap.

I contacted Mrs. Tully to let her know I will be at her home in the morning. Brooke's list of names and numbers could help solve this case. I tempered my excitement, knowing most of these ladies graduated from nursing school two years ago and may no longer have the same phone numbers. It certainly gave me hope that some would still have these old numbers. Tomorrow was going to be a busy day.

I hollered to Scotty. "While you are working on the computer, why don't I go to the store and get something for dinner?" The grocery store close to the office was excellent, and I thought Scotty deserved a nice dinner. I was feeling rather lovingly towards him after our conversation about him being my hero. I wondered what I should cook to show him how much I loved him. Knowing Scotty, I was sure it would need to be beef. What I really wanted to eat was salmon, but beef it would be.

"Sounds good to me. What are you going to get for dinner? I could sure go for a steak," Scotty yelled back.

As I grabbed the keys to the Double Nickel, I couldn't resist teasing him. "You are getting a salad and nothing more." I closed the door of the office behind me and laughed.

That evening after dinner, I snuggled with Scotty on the sofa. I thought that we needed a new one. The black couch that was left in the house when we moved in was lumpy then, and it was worse now.

"Can we afford a new sofa?" I asked Scotty while nestling closer to him. His arm loosened from around my shoulders as he sat forward and bounced up and down on the couch.

"Seems fine to me," he said. Just as he bounced one more time, I heard a crack and knew the frame had just broken. Two hundred and thirty pounds was more than the old sofa could take.

"On second thought, I think we need a new sofa," Scotty added.

"We have way too much to do tomorrow, but maybe the next day, we can check out a few furniture stores nearby. What do you say? In the meantime, try not to move too much," I suggested.

Pulling me closer to him, Scotty said, "No problem. I could stay like this forever."

I laid my head on his shoulder, and he turned his head to kiss me on the forehead. It wasn't passionate, but it was romantic. I knew Scotty wouldn't push for anything more until I was ready.

Finally, I reluctantly said it was time for bed. We hadn't turned on the television that night. We were content to listen to the Whitney Houston 'Bodyguard' Soundtrack Album and just chill in each other's company. Dragging myself off the sofa was difficult. I did not want to end the physical contact with Scotty. I reached down to give him a hand up when he pulled me back down and gave me a long, lingering kiss.

"Do you want to sleep in my bedroom tonight?" I purred.

Picking me up off the sofa, he carried me into my room.

CHAPTER THIRTEEN

The night with Scotty was perfect. I did not have one moment when I thought of my uncle. Tenderly, Scotty held me and kissed me until I suggested more by taking his hand and placing it on my breast. One thing led to another, and I never once wanted Scotty to stop.

As I laid next to Scotty and snuggled back into the curve of his stomach, I cursed the sunlight. I did not want the night to end. I wondered why I resisted making love in the first place. Then my uncle's face came into view, and I remembered. Why did he need to ruin this tender moment for me, I wondered, as I pulled myself to a sitting position?

Scotty was still sound asleep. I grabbed my robe and headed for the shower. It wouldn't have been a smart thing to linger next to Scotty once the beautiful night was intruded upon by ugly memories. I hoped someday my uncle would not be a nasty thought any longer. I prayed my uncle would not be a thought ever again. I wanted Scotty and me to be able to begin our lives together as partners in every way.

I was dressed and making breakfast when Scotty came out of the bedroom. He had a smile on his face that could only be described as a man in love. It warmed my heart and helped to chase away the shadow of my uncle's face. Then it hit me.

"Scotty," I said suddenly, breaking the smile from his face, and immediately, I regretted my abrupt announcement. I hated to see his happy, contented look melt away. I continued anyway, "All three women say shadowy faces...not face. There is more than one man involved in what happened to these women."

Scotty walked into the kitchen and kissed me. "Alright, give it to me." He grabbed a mug of coffee and sat down at the table, giving me his full attention.

"I was thinking about my uncle and how sometimes his face seems like a shadow in the back of my mind, but it is always just one face that haunts me. The ladies all say the same thing...shadowy faces or blurred faces. They don't say a blurred face or a shadowy face. It is always plural. It must be because there was more than one man. Besides, it makes sense in some odd way. Don't ask me why. It just feels right to me."

"You know I have learned to trust your instincts. They are almost always right," Scotty said, giving me credit for the many times I figured things out on a hunch.

"Almost?" I said, starting to laugh. "When have I ever been wrong?"

Scotty was relieved to see a smile cross my face, so he continued the banter. "Once you said you were wrong, and you were actually right. Does that count?"

We kept being playful as we ate breakfast, but after the dishes were done, I reminded Scotty we were going our separate ways today. He grabbed the keys to the van and told me I could take the Ford. It was getting windier as the temperatures were cooling. I knew Scotty was concerned about my riding the Harley. I decided my riding apparel would not be appropriate to wear to talk to the psychiatrist anyway. I nodded in agreement as Scotty went out the door.

I made the phone call to Dr. Kessler's office and was told he could talk to me for about fifteen minutes right after lunch. I told his receptionist I would be at the office no later than 12:30. That gave me plenty of time to run over and pick up the list of nursing students from Mrs. Tully.

Mrs. Tully seemed glad to see me even though I knew my presence only reminded her of the mystery surrounding her daughter's disappearance and mental breakdown. I knew she hoped I would find the answers for my client, and those answers might be the ones she also needed. I couldn't imagine how horrible it must be to watch her daughter become a shell of her original self. Every parent wants the best for their children, or at least the good ones do.

"Tish, thank you very much for returning. I know this is quite a drive for you. I have the list of students who were in classes with Brooke. I sure hope a few of them will be able to tell you something about the night Brooke disappeared. It has been a while, and most are nurses now, and some may have moved to other cities." Mrs. Tully handed me the handwritten paper.

"Did you copy these names and numbers, or is this Brooke's own handwriting?" I asked. I don't know why I felt it was essential to see this information. I guess I thought if Mrs. Tully copied it, there could be mistakes.

"No, this is Brooke's personal list of friends from her class. I found it in her notebook once I took some time to go through her things. I knew you wanted to talk to as many of her classmates as possible, so I took it out. I suppose I should have taken the time to recopy it myself," Mrs. Tully said, now reticent to hand the paper over to me.

"I will make a copy of it at the office, and I promise to mail your original copy back to you immediately. That way, you can put it back into Brooke's notebook just like you found it." Thinking Mrs. Tully might be feeling guilty about snooping around in Brooke's things when she is drugged and sleeping.

She smiled and said, "That would be nice, dear. I have made a plate of cookies for your boyfriend."

"Partner," I corrected her. "Scotty McFarlan is my partner."

Martha Tully smiled, "Of course, your partner. But I would say he feels like he would like to be more than just your partner."

My mind went back to last night and our fantastic lovemaking. "Okay, we are partners in many ways," I admitted and smiled. Having no close girlfriends to confide in, I guess this intimate confession to Martha Tully would need to suffice. I found myself blushing.

"You two are just made for each other. I could see that immediately when you came in and sat down. Your young man could not keep his eyes off you. I think you are a fortunate young woman. He seems to be quite the catch," Martha said in a grandmotherly way.

"I best leave," I said before I became embarrassed by Martha's reference to Scotty's undeniable attraction to me. "I need to stop and talk to Dr. Kessler this afternoon. I have just enough time to make it to his office," I said as I inched my way to the door.

"Dr. Kessler? How did you know Dr. Kessler was Brooke's psychiatrist? I don't remember telling you that information," Martha asked, stunned.

She was stunned! I was dumbfounded. "Dr. Kessler is Brooke's doctor?" I asked.

"Well, yes. I am sorry I did not know that would be relevant," Martha said.

"It seems he is the doctor of choice for young ladies with memory problems," I said. "Can I ask you how it was that you chose Dr. Kessler?

Martha confided. "He came strongly recommended by Brooke's last nursing supervisor, Ms. Lawton. She is the nurse Brooke reported to at her last clinical rotation at the hospital. When Brooke dropped out of the program, Ms. Lawton phoned me to find out why. When I explained what had happened, she recommended Dr. Peter Kessler."

I thanked Mrs. Tully once again for the list of women and their phone numbers, and I left. I had just enough time to make it to Dr. Kessler's office in time for our brief meeting. My mind was whirling with this new information. Again, was it coincidental, or was there more to this strange situation.

I entered Dr. Kessler's office and announced my arrival. I was told to take a seat as Dr. Kessler had not yet returned from his lunch. It gave me a few more minutes to think of the questions I would need to ask. There were some questions I wanted to ask but felt he would become too defensive and ask me to leave. That meant I would need to tread carefully but nudge as hard as I could without getting kicked out.

The assistant opened the door and asked me to follow her to the doctor's office. I entered and found Dr. Peter Kessler to be about forty years of age. He seemed in good physical shape as if he ran or worked out. His eyes, fixed on a paper on his desk, met mine as I walked up. They were piercingly blue. I won't say they were beautiful but more unnerving. It seemed as if he knew more than one would think, but about what, I thought…everything?

I stepped forward. "Dr. Kessler, thank you for meeting with me. I know your day is busy, and I am probably shortening your lunch hour." I extended my hand for a handshake.

He took my hand and gave it a gentle shake and held it a bit too long. Right off the bat, I was feeling uncomfortable and wondered if this was his way to put people off balance or if he thought he was establishing rapport. I gently pulled my hand from his.

"Please, sit down. What can I do for you?" the doctor asked.

"My name is Tish Evers, and I am a private investigator. I am working for a client who has some questions regarding types of drugs that could erase a memory…."

I did not get to finish before Dr. Kessler interrupted, "If this is about any of my patients, I am not at liberty to discuss them or their cases."

"As far as I know, you are not involved with my client. What I do need to ask you is information regarding drugs that could cause a woman not to remember something traumatic that happened to her." I continued but not from where I had left off before his disruption.

"How do you know drugs were involved? Could it be possible the trauma itself caused the loss of memory?" Dr. Kessler asked, looking straight into my eyes.

"At this point in our investigation, I am not drawing any conclusions. I am just investigating all options," I said, not lowering my eyes from Dr. Kessler's intense stare.

"Maybe an anesthesiologist would be a better person to ask. I use drugs to help my patients relax, not to eliminate their memories. My purpose is to help them regain their memories. If that occurs, we talk about what caused their problem in the first place.

"I feel there is nothing more I can add. I don't think I can be of any real help in your investigation." He looked back down to the paper he had been studying when I entered his office. I knew that was my sign to leave.

"Thank you for your time. I appreciate your assistance. Is there any anesthesiologist that you might recommend I talk with?" I said, not liking the way he dismissed me.

"Any phone book will give you plenty of names. If that avenue does not please you, you can talk to a hospital nursing supervisor. They might be able to help you find an anesthesiologist that would know the specific drugs that cause memory loss. Thank you, and good day." He stood to show he was finished with our interview if one could call it that.

I left, feeling a bit angry and wondering if Dr. Kessler was just a jackass or if he was hiding something. I needed to channel my anger into being more logical. Could Dr. Kessler know more about what happened to the women and was trying to cover up by saying he couldn't talk about his patients? Was he covering up for someone else? Or was he just a jackass like my original gut feeling was telling me? I needed to let my mind work on these questions for a while.

I couldn't wait to see Scotty and ask him what his impressions might be. In the meantime, I had a list of women to try to locate. I would need to go back to the Jamiesons' office to make phone calls unless I wanted to get plenty of change and make the calls from a payphone. I opted for the office. May as well be comfortable.

Arriving at the office, I checked the answering machine as usual. Nothing to report, and the mail was routine as well. I settled down to phone the numbers I had been given.

The first three phone numbers were a wash. No one answered the first two, and the third was disconnected. Either the lady had moved or she, at least, changed her number. Since there was no forwarding phone number, I decided she probably had relocated out of the city.

My fourth attempt was successful. I introduced myself to Carly Adams. She was now working the night shift at a local hospital in the emergency room. Luckily, I had not awakened her. I explained who I was and asked if she had time to talk for a few minutes.

"I'd be glad to talk to you," said a kind voice at the other end of the line. "I really liked Brooke and was sorry when she had to drop out of the program. What would you like to know?"

"Carly, by any chance, did you go to the coffee house with Brooke the night she went missing?" I asked.

"No, sorry. I had to scoot home. My boyfriend was taking me out to dinner that evening, and I wanted to shower and get ready," Carly answered.

"Do you know who went to the coffee house that night?" I continued.

"Let me think. It was a long time ago, relatively speaking. Much has happened since then. If I remember correctly, there were three students besides Brooke and our nursing supervisor. I think Maddie went. I also think Terri and Lori went as well, but I may be wrong about Lori," Carly spoke hesitantly as if she was having some trouble remembering.

"You mentioned the nursing supervisor. Do you recall her name?" I asked.

"Sure, it was Sheri Lawton. I remember specifically that Sheri was the one who suggested going out after our rotation that evening. I thought it was a bit odd that she was only asking a few of us. She did not open it up for the whole class," Carly said.

"Why did it seem odd that she was only targeting a few of you?" I asked, using the word 'targeted' specifically. For some reason, my gut was telling me there was something odd about Carly mentioning Sheri Lawton, only asking specific women.

"Oh, I guess Sheri was a bit obvious about having her favorites. Luckily, I was one of her favorites," Carly said as a matter of fact.

I couldn't let this drop. "Was there anything that you had in common with Sheri's other favorites?"

Carly pondered for a moment. "Well, we were all top of our class as far as grades were concerned…." She hesitated a bit longer as she continued to think. "And we were all single. Sheri did not seem to like the married students or the older students very much."

"Was there anything more you had in common with the other favorite students that you can think of, like the same age, same size, or same hair color?" I prompted.

"Now that you mention it, we all do look a bit similar in some ways. In fact, some of the students who were not her favorites referred to us as her blond bimbos," Carly laughed. "That was mean, but sort of funny. We are all blondes, but only one or two of us were natural blondes."

"Are you one of the natural blondes?" I asked, feeling a bit creeped out inside.

"Yes, I am. Brooke was too. I think Terri and Lori get a bit of help from out of a bottle, but that did not keep them from being lumped in with the blond bimbo crowd," Carly said with a hint of a giggle still in her voice.

"One more question, if you don't mind. Do you have Terri and Lori's phone numbers? Lori's number is disconnected, and I have not been able to reach Terri." I felt I had learned about as much as I could from Carly since she had not been at the coffee house that evening.

"I'm sorry," Carly answered. "I don't have either of their numbers. Being engaged, I don't really hang out with them. I do think Lori moved back home, but I couldn't tell you where that may be. As for Terri, all I can say is to keep phoning her number. You may reach her later in the evening." I thanked Carly, and we hung up.

I found myself thinking about what Dr. Kessler said to me. I wondered if he was trying to tell me something without committing himself. Dr. Kessler told me to find the name of an anesthesiologist in the phone book or talk to a hospital nursing supervisor. I wondered why he was specific when he said to speak to the nursing supervisor and non-specific when he told me how to find an anesthesiologist. Was Dr. Kessler directing me to talk with a nursing supervisor for some reason?

I let those thoughts continue to roll around in my brain as I dialed the next phone numbers. I was becoming a bit frustrated by the growing number of known and missing puzzle pieces. I kept telling myself Aileen warned me that most investigative works were tedious. I told myself to dial the last number before going home. I was glad that I did.

Terri answered the phone on the 5th ring. She sounded tired, and I felt horrible that I had awakened her. "Terri, this is Tish Evers. I am a private investigator, and I was wondering if I could ask you a few questions? I think I just woke you up. I do apologize for that."

"It's okay," Terri said with a yawn. "I should be getting up anyway. I have a few errands to run before I start my shift at the hospital. What is this about?"

"I understand that you were with Brooke Tully the night that she went missing. I was wondering if you could tell me some details about that night?" I ventured into the questioning.

"Sure. Go ahead. What would you like to know?" Terri said with more alertness in her voice.

I got to the point. "A fellow student said you, Lori, Brooke and Sheri Lawton went to a coffee house the evening Brooke went missing. Can you tell me if there was anything odd that happened that night?"

I could tell Terri was gathering her thoughts as the phone was silent for a short while. "As I remember, we were sitting in a corner. The guitarist played for about an hour, and he was good. We were having fun. About midnight, Lori said she had to leave. I was about to leave when one of the doctors from the hospital came over with drinks for us. He said he had seen us when he walked in and wanted to show how much he appreciated our hard work. He did not sit down, but passed out our drinks, raised his own glass, and said 'cheers.' I watched him go to his own table, where he was drinking with a few other men about the same age. I did not even drink my drink. I needed to leave."

"So, when you left, Brooke and Sheri Lawton were the only ones remaining at the table, correct?" I asked for clarification.

"That is right. I know Brooke was ready to leave but was going to need to phone home for a ride. I overheard Sheri telling her she would drive her home after she finished her drink. Sheri said she wanted to hear the next performer before leaving if Brooke did not mind staying for another half hour. I left after that. There isn't much more I can tell you." Terri finished her conversation. She excused herself and hung up the receiver.

Now, I knew I would need to talk to Sheri Lawton. As far as I could tell, she was the last one to see Brooke that evening. In fact, it appears she was the one who was to take her home. I wondered what happened to change that.

I locked up the office door, stopped at the market, and headed home. I was anxious to talk to Scotty to see if he found out anything interesting from Constance's schoolmates. I was hoping I would beat him to the house. I wanted to put the meatloaf in the oven. While it baked, Scotty and I could talk without any interruptions.

Scotty was home when I arrived. I walked into the house and was greeted with a hug and a kiss. I can only imagine he missed me a bunch, or he was feeling guilty for the fact he enjoyed himself too much with the nursing students.

I set down the groceries in the kitchen and hid the plate of cookies Martha had sent home for him. If I didn't hide the cookies, I knew Scotty would devour them before dinner.

"Boy, do I have a lot to discuss with you. I hope you are full of information as well. If you help me out in the kitchen, we can sit down with a can of soda and discuss our day while dinner is cooking," I said as I grabbed the necessary pot and pans.

Scotty peeled potatoes as I formed the meatloaf. I figured we could have green beans, and our dinner would be balanced. I worked quickly. I wanted time for us to talk about our day.

Finally, with soda in hand, we sat down on the lumpy sofa to discuss what we had found out. "You go first," I said to Scotty.

"I sat out in the van most of the day. Finally, the students started to file out. I caught the first student and told her who I was and asked her if I could question her about our client, Constance. Before long, I had several of the nursing students around me. It was great to have so many ladies telling me what they remembered about Constance. Four of the students did go to the coffee house that evening. I asked them each to tell me what they remembered." Scotty referred to his notes before he continued.

"Amy and Amberley are twins. I guess they do everything together. They said they went to the coffee house but had to leave early. Neither of them remembered anything unusual. Since Felicity rode with the twins, she left early as well. Val said she and Constance were joined later in the evening by Sheri Lawton, the nursing supervisor, from their clinical rotation. Val went on to say she left earlier than

Constance. She suggested we talk to Sheri Lawton for any further information. That is about the extent of what I found out." Scotty reached for his drink and relaxed on the sofa. "What about your day?"

"Before I start on my day, could you tell me one thing about the students that went to the coffee house with Constance? Were they all blond?" I queried.

"Let me think," Scotty said. Wow, he had to think hard to remember the color of the nurse's hair. This delay and the way he looked made me feel a bit jealous.

I think I said something like that to him, and Scotty replied with, "Give me a break. You know I only have eyes for you. I really do need to think for a minute to remember who was who."

I was starting to feel a bit annoyed. I wasn't sure if Scotty was playing a game with me. He did like to tease a bit more than I wanted to be teased.

"Amy and Amberley are blondes, but more strawberry blond. Val has bleached blond hair judging by her eyebrows. Felicity is a blond but more dishwater blond than Constance. I guess...you could say they are all blond," Scotty finished his assessment.

"Scotty, all the girls who were with Brooke, were blond as well, and another strange coincidence was Sheri Lawton was at the coffee house with Brooke and her friends too. I know one of us should talk to Sheri Lawton. Should we toss a coin?" I said. "This is more than coincidence as far as I am concerned. This is just eerie and a bit frightening. I can't help but wonder how Sheri Lawton fits into the disappearances of the women. I think we need to find out."

Scotty reminded me, "It is really too early to form a theory, but that doesn't mean we can't come up with scenarios. What does your gut tell you right now?"

I thought about it for several minutes. "I really think Sheri Lawton is somehow at the bottom of all this. It is just too coincidental that she was with the groups of ladies both times. Sheri Lawton seems to be the last person seen with either student before their disappearance. I just wonder what kind of a run-around she will give us. Maybe we both should be prepared with a few questions. I think we can get her off-guard if we both fire questions at her. Tomorrow, we will go to the hospital and have ...a little chat with her."

"I suppose we shouldn't include her as one of the villains until we can prove it. I hope she can provide us with some leads if she is not involved in the case." Scotty put his arm around me and pulled me closer to him.

The timer went off for the meatloaf, and I had to jump up. I was just starting to get relaxed next to Scotty, so I resented the disturbance. However, I knew Scotty would be hungry. Some things just don't change. While we ate, we created a plan and a list of questions.

The following morning, we dressed and drove to the hospital. We asked the receptionist where we might find Sheri Lawton. She told us to check at the nursing station on the third floor. It seemed there was a new group of students who would be arriving any minute. We knew we would need to get to the floor if we were going to talk to Sheri Lawton before the end of her shift.

We found her at the nursing station looking at charts to decide which students should be assigned to which patients. I could tell she was irritated by our interruption.

"Sheri Lawton?" I asked.

"Yes, what can I do for you?" She asked curtly.

Scotty asked the next question, "We need to ask you about the nights Constance, and Brooke disappeared. We understand you were with both ladies the night each disappeared from the coffee house. What can you tell us?" Scott tried to look imposing, that wasn't too hard for him to do even with his baby face.

"I don't know what you are talking about, and I don't really have time for a long discussion now. I have fifteen nursing students who are about to arrive, and I need to make assignments for them. Could you make an appointment and come back some other time?"

I spoke up this time, "This is really important. We understand you were to drive Brooke home from the coffee house. Did you do that?"

Ms. Lawton looked startled by the question. "That was two years ago. You want me to remember something that long ago?"

Scotty said again. "I don't think it should be hard for you to remember if you drove her home or not. Either you did, or you didn't."

"I did not," came an exasperated reply from Sheri Lawton. "As I remember now, she wanted to stay a bit longer and listen to the guitarist. She said she would phone her mother to come and get her or take a cab, so I left. If that is all you want, I need to get back to work."

"About Constance, you were also the last person sitting at the table with her at the same coffee house. How often do you go to coffee houses with your students, or should I say, select students?" I was becoming more aggressive with her.

"There is no law about going to a coffee house with students as far as I know. I think you can leave. I have work to do, and if you don't leave, I will ask security to escort you out of the hospital and not let you back in," Sheri said defensively.

"Were you the last person to be with Constance at the coffee house? Did she leave with you? Did you take her home?" Scotty pushed.

Sheri Lawton picked up the phone and dialed a number. She asked for security to come to the third floor and escort two people out. She glared at us when she set the receiver down.

"Did you have something to do with the women's disappearance, Sheri? Is that why you are defensive?" I took up the attack.

Sheri Lawton became visibly upset and left the nursing station just before the security guard came up the stairs. Scotty and I took the elevator down and left the building.

"What do you think, Scotty? Did you feel as if she was telling the truth about Brooke staying and getting a cab to take her home?" I asked once we were in the safety of the Ford.

"I suppose it is possible, but it sure doesn't explain how jumpy and irritated she was acting. If that was the case, she should have remained calm and approachable. It seemed out of character for an innocent person to act the way she did, didn't it?"

I nodded. "You know, Dr. Kessler acted the same way. I felt like he knew something and wasn't wanting to talk about it. I feel like Sheri Lawton knows more as well. I doubt she will talk to us again. I sure hope Aileen and Patrick get back soon. I thought maybe one of them might find a way to get her to talk. They have been at this for a very long time."

"They should be home today from what I understood when they left," Scotty said, probably trying to set my mind at ease a bit. "Are we going to go to the office? I could work on the computer if you had something to do as well." Scotty revved the motor and headed the Double Nickel in the direction of the office.

Opening the door of the office, we were excited to see Patrick and Aileen. "Yay! You are back. How was your trip? We can't wait to hear about it," I said as I gave each of them a hug in turn.

"You will be sick and tired of hearing about our trip once we get the film developed, and we tell you about each picture in detail. I will just say that we had a marvelous time, but right now, we want to find out what you have been doing," Patrick said as he returned my hug and gave Scotty a handshake.

We sat around the table, and I told them about Leticia LaPlante coming into the office discussing her daughter's disappearance. We took turns telling them what we had each discovered up until today. Brooke and Josie, the two other girls who suffered similar mysterious disappearances as Constance, were also discussed as well as our encounters with Dr. Kessler and Sheri Lawton, the clinical nurse. Both Scotty and I talked about possible scenarios, but we explained we needed something more to go on. I asked Scotty to print out a copy of our investigative report for Patrick and Aileen.

Aileen listened attentively. "I think you both have done a remarkable job with this case. The fact that you combed the newspapers and found the other two girls with similar stories and Scotty spent an entire day finding information with the ranger is quite impressive. Following up on leads and talking to the other students, as well as Sheri Lawton and Dr. Kessler, proves you have good instincts for investigative work. At this point, Patrick and I are back and will get involved as well. I have a feeling this case has taken a higher priority over your classwork and your other obligations than it should."

Patrick added, "We know why you got more involved in this case, it is because we were away. We are sorry we put so much on your backs. We know you have many other things that you need to do. At this point, we want you to get caught up on your classwork; get prepared for your shooting competition and Tish, you have a martial arts competition pending as well. I think our timing might have been bad to take a vacation right now. We are impressed, though, as Aileen said with how well you have filled our shoes. Don't think we are taking you off this case because we are not. We are going to step in and do some investigative work now. You can get back to doing what you need to do."

There was a part of me that was relieved. I did have a tournament coming up, and the 4th Dan title was on the line. I needed more time with Grandmaster Kim Yong-Sool before the competition. I know Scotty did very well at his last shooting practice, but Captain Jones has high expectations for him, and the extra practice won't hurt him either. It was also true that we skipped a couple classes while in the heat of the investigation. It would be nice to be able to have our minds on what was necessary at this stage of our lives.

"We will continue to aid in the investigation however we can," I said to the Jamiesons.

"We know you will, dear," Aileen replied. "Right now, it sounds as if I need to talk with Mrs. Jones."

Scotty looked as puzzled as I was feeling. He asked, "Why Mrs. Jones? Is she Captain Jones's wife.?"

"Didn't you know that Mrs. Jones is the Head Nurse at the hospital where most student nurses do their internship? She will know Sheri Lawton well, and I am sure Mrs. Jones will be able to fill in some of the gaps. If she can't, Mrs. Jones has eyes and ears all over the hospital. I know she will be willing to have some of her 'spies' keep an eye out and report back. If Sheri Lawton is involved with the disappearance of these three young nursing students, we will find out."

I wasn't feeling foolish, really. We had just found a possible connection between the student nurses and Sheri Lawton. The fact that Aileen and Patrick know Captain and Mrs. Jones even better than Scotty and I do will benefit us in this investigation. I was feeling pumped up about Aileen talking to Mrs. Jones. I couldn't wait to find out what Aileen might learn.

CHAPTER FOURTEEN

The Jamiesons were home. It was a relief. I felt Scotty, and I had accomplished quite a bit trying to find out what happened to Constance the night she disappeared. However, we were behind in our studies, and we both had significant competitions in front of us. We needed the time away from the case to concentrate on what was ahead for us both. However, the case was always in the back of my mind.

We tried to get back into our regular schedule as best as we could. Back to classes, studying, taking tests, and assisting the Jamiesons during the afternoon was the routine once again. Every evening, I was with the grandmaster, and Scotty was at the shooting range. Time spent together in the evening was minimal, and I was missing cuddling with Scotty.

Scotty was a man obsessed with the upcoming shooting competition. I knew he didn't want to disappoint Captain Jones. We all seemed to know this would-be Scotty's last year on the team. Once we graduated from our course, our time would be consumed by investigations. Scotty could possibly do both, but starting out in business meant double the work. It just wasn't realistic. I, too, would give up my part-time job teaching self-defense at the dojang. It was hard for both of us to think about giving up the things that were now defining us as people.

As I entered Grandmaster Kim Yong-Sool's Dojang, I was still thinking about how I could juggle both a new job and teaching self-defense. I did not want to let my grandmaster down.

Grandmaster Kim Yong-Sool greeted me as I entered. The last students of the day had left. "Aww, Tish, you have a troubled heart."

I smiled. I guess I wasn't doing an excellent job of hiding my feelings.

"Good Evening, Grandmaster Kim Yong-Sool," I said with a bow. The formality would remain in our relationship forever. I respected him that much.

"What is bothering you?" he asked me as he indicated a place to sit.

"I was just thinking how hard it is going to be to work full time as a private investigator and still teach the classes here at the dojang. You know I love my students, and I don't want to let them down, but balancing classes, part-time work with the Jamiesons, and working here is difficult. Starting a business will demand all my attention...." I hesitated, not knowing if I had offended.

"Tish, you know you have an obligation to your students through the end of your eight-week course. You do not have any obligations to me," the grandmaster said with compassion.

In the same gentle voice, the grandmaster continued, "I knew from the very start this would be a temporary arrangement. You have been a superb instructor, and your students have gained valuable experiences in your hands. When it is time for you to move on in your life's journey, you will find that I also must move on. It is the way of life. Life is dynamic. We all learn and grow. You have learned much, but right now, you have a competition in two weeks. You have more to learn, so on your feet."

Without another word, I got to my fighting stance and prepared for the next lesson. I was surprised when I ended up on the floor without the Grandmaster having laid a single hand on me.

"What the heck!" I said instinctively and then realized my words were not appropriate. "Excuse me, Grandmaster Kim Yong-Sool, but what just happened?"

"Your next lesson is something that you must never reveal to anyone, including your friend, Scott. Do you understand?" Grandmaster Kim Yong-Sool looked me straight in the eyes, and I knew immediately, he was about to teach me something sacred.

I left the dojang several hours later. It was dark, but I did not notice how late it was. My mind was consumed with the sacred lessons I was being taught. I reached home, entered the house, and didn't even notice Scotty sitting on the sofa.

"Tish. Hey, Tish. Earth to Tish," Scotty chided me. "What has you that distracted that you don't even notice the Man of Your Dreams?"

I laughed a bit embarrassed and tried to seem nonchalant. Somehow, I had to come up with a plausible explanation for being distracted without telling Scotty the truth.

"I'm sorry, dreamboat. I was just thinking about the case. It is hard to let it go. Aren't you finding it hard to stop thinking about it as well?" I white-lied. It wasn't a total lie because I was having a hard time not thinking about the case.

"Come over here and sit down next to me. Let me give you something else to think about," Scotty said as he patted the space next to him on the dilapidated sofa.

I laughed again and headed to the spot indicated, knowing Scotty would take my mind off things for a while. I let his hands rub my back and neck.

"Wow!" Scotty commented as he massaged my neck. "You are a bundle of knots. You and Grandmaster Kim Yong-Sool must have gone ten rounds. Who won?"

"I never beat the grandmaster, just like you can never beat me." I knew those were fighting words, and I wasn't disappointed when Scotty grabbed me in a bear hug.

"Oh yeah? Get out of this one," Scotty challenged.

I just melted into his arms, and he forgot immediately that we were sparring. Loosening his embrace, he told me to go lay on the bed, and he would give me a massage to help me sleep.

Jumping up, I slipped into shorts and left on my sports bra. Laying on my stomach, Scotty straddled my legs and started his massage. Gentle pressure started at the base of my neck and continued down my spine, sending pulses of electricity throughout my entire body. Scotty began floating his fingers across my feet. Starting from the ankles, his fingers traveled up my calves, my thighs, and across the curve of my bum, he applied soft touch and continued with deeper pressure. Lingering for an extra moment at the dip in the base of my spine, he proceeded slowly up until he tenderly squeezed the back of my neck, sending shivers through my entire being. It was exactly what I needed to take my mind off what was troubling me when I entered the house.

As I woke in the crook of Scotty's arm, my body felt relaxed and rested. Contentment seemed to fill my mind. It was going to be a lovely day.

I wanted to do something special for Scotty. The food was still the reward of choice. I knew I couldn't make pancakes as well as he did, but I was the best with French toast.

I slipped out of bed, grabbed my robe, and headed for the kitchen. Bacon was always the choice of breakfast meat for Scotty, so I put several slabs of it in the frying pan on low. Coffee was something I put on for myself. Scotty would have orange juice as usual unless he decided to join me for a cup of coffee.

I was busy crisping the bacon and seasoning the egg batter for the French toast when I heard Scotty flush the toilet. I knew he would follow his nose and be in the kitchen within a minute. I hurriedly set the table and flipped the French toast to brown on the other side.

On cue, Scotty headed towards the kitchen, where he gave me a deep kiss and said his good mornings. I just pointed to the table where his orange juice was waiting and indicated his breakfast was almost ready.

A smile spread across his face when he realized he was in store for his second favorite breakfast. His smile warmed my heart, and I knew I had made a great choice.

"Why am I getting the King's treatment this morning?' Scotty asked as he picked up a perfectly cooked piece of bacon with his fingers.

"Because you treated me like a Queen last night," I said with a wicked smile on my face.

"Oh, you liked that, did you? I can do even better if you give me a chance." Scotty returned the wicked smile.

"I will give you more chances…that you might like," I teased.

Scotty's smiled broadened. "There is no limit to the chances I might like."

Our cat and mouse game were interrupted by the phone. I headed to the desk to pick up the call.

"Good Morning, Mother. How are you and Dad this fine Saturday morning?" I looked over at Scotty and shrugged. The usual Saturday morning phone call was earlier than usual, and I wondered why.

"Oh, that is wonderful. Both of you and the McFarlan's are planning on coming to Scotty's competition. That will really please Scotty, and I will enjoy the company. It is an all-day event, you know. Are you sure you are up to hearing gunfire for an entire day?" I asked, suddenly realizing the decision to attend the competition was their dad's.

I looked at Scotty to make sure he knew what the conversation was all about. As my mother talked on the other end of the receiver, I held it away from my ear so Scotty could hear the conversation.

"That is great. You have already booked the hotel room for next weekend. Oh, and you booked a room for Scotty and me as well. Oh, two rooms." I rolled my eyes at Scotty, realizing that our parents didn't know we were in an intimate relationship.

Scotty muffled a laugh. I already knew I would be having a late-night visitor unless Scotty conked out watching T.V. the night before the competition, ...which was more likely. Maybe two rooms would be for the best.

We chatted for a few more minutes, and I hung up. "Well, what do you think about that? Your parents and mine will be joining us next weekend. I suspect we won't be paying for a thing. Let's take advantage of them, okay?" I said jokingly.

"Are you going to the shooting range while I teach a couple of classes or what?" I asked, checking on the day's schedule. I knew I had to get dressed and head down to the dojang for my morning lessons.

Scotty said he would probably end up practicing for the shooting competition. "I am getting a bit tired of being down at the range. The guys are giving me a hard time about being the captain's favorite. I know they are kidding, but I will be glad when the competition is over, and things are back to normal."

"Whatever normal is, right?" I commented. Our lives hadn't been ordinary for several years now. It was hard for me to think back and remember when it was normal.

I thought about high school again and our classmates being murdered. That certainly was not normal. Our time here in Chicago hadn't been very routine, either. I wondered what was normal for us?

Scotty grabbed the dishes from the table as I scrambled for the bathroom to get ready for my students' lessons. I loved the fact that Scotty didn't think doing housework was beneath him. Our partnership was based on sharing duties, and he did his share.

After my lessons, I dared to ask the grandmaster a question that could be considered taboo. "Grandmaster Kim Yong-Sool," I proceeded slowly. "I have a favor to ask of you."

My grandmaster said, "What is your request?"

Slowly, I continued. "As you know, Scotty will soon be a black belt, and his shooting competition is next Saturday. He lacks pinpoint focus, even though he is exceptional at visualizing outcomes. I believe what you taught me yesterday would benefit him in more ways than one."

"So, you are asking me if you could teach him what I taught you last night?" Grandmaster Kim Yong-Sool held my eyes with his question.

I blushed. I was sure I had over-stepped our relationship by asking the question. I knew what Grandmaster Kim Yong-Sool was teaching me was beyond sacred. The grandmaster had cautioned that what he was teaching me should never be revealed, and now I was asking permission to reveal the first sacred lesson. I suddenly felt ashamed that I was betraying a trust.

Grandmaster Kim Yong-Sool spoke in a low voice. "I can see you love Scott very much and want the best for him. I will give you permission to teach him the first sacred lesson that I taught you yesterday. You cannot, for any reason, teach him any of the other lessons. Now, we have work to do," with those words, we continued the next lesson.

As I entered the house, I was excited to begin teaching Scotty what had been my first lesson. For Scotty, it would be a lesson that would last the entire week. Without my extensive training abilities, Scotty would not absorb everything as quickly as I had.

"Scotty, it is time for a new lesson, so get your butt down to the basement!" I commanded as I walked into the house to find Scotty sitting on the sofa.

"Oh no! You aren't going to toss me all over the basement again, are you?" Scotty moaned.

Laughing, I said, "Not this time...be still your heart. I know you were looking forward to me wiping the floor with you. No, this lesson is designed for increased focus for your competition on Saturday. I know how much you want to do your best for Captain Jones, and your parents, so, therefore, I am going to help you."

I went to the sofa and held out my hand for Scotty to take so I could lead him down to the basement. He did not make the job easy by leaning forward to help. Instead, he resisted, trying to pull me down into his lap.

"No way! You aren't going to sidetrack me. This is in your best interest." I gave him a jerk, pulling him to his feet.

"If you aren't going to be knocking me around, why can't you teach me the stuff right here on the sofa?" Scotty complained.

"The reason," I stated, "is because the basement is where we train. You need the association with the training area to motivate and keep you on track. Basement...work. Sofa...play. Come on."

When we got to the basement, I first asked Scotty to tense all the muscles in his fingers and hold it. I then asked him to relax his fingers. Next, I asked him to tense the muscles in his forearm and then relax. We worked through his entire body, one part at a time. When he complained, we started over with the fingers. After two hours, I told him we had worked enough for the day, but he was to repeat the exercise tomorrow, and he had best not slack off. I wanted him to work for two hours until he could tense and relax every muscle, in sequence, in his body.

"That's it?" Scotty questioned with puzzlement in his voice. "I do that sometimes to help me sleep when I am really keyed up. At least I didn't pay money for the lesson."

I punched him in the arm. "Don't be a smart-ass. Just do what I told you to do and don't slack off. I will be testing you to make sure you can tense and relax any muscle I call into question. Got it? I am serious about this, and you had best be serious, too."

I know I sounded like I was scolding him, but I did not want him to question my techniques. If the teaching strategy was good enough for the grandmaster, then the same method was good enough for me. Scotty was about to complain again when I gave him a scalding look.

"Look, Scotty, when your coach said to give him fifty push-ups, you never questioned him. If you would have gone into the military service and your Sargent said to dig a ditch with a spoon, you would have done it, with a 'yes, sir.' I know I am your partner and the love of your life. Right now, I am your sensei, and I want you to do what I ask without complaining or questioning what I am teaching. Do you think you can do that? I can promise you that it will pay off."

Scotty glided up to me and put his arms around me, pulling me closer. "I will do what you ask because you are the love of my life. How is that? Good enough?" Just as I was about to say sensei, Scotty stifled my words with a lingering kiss.

Finding myself feeling a bit off-balance from the kiss, I found Scotty's arms stabilizing me very comforting. "You can rock my world, that is for sure, but once again, you have the rooms wrong. Basement...work, sofa...," And my words were muffled again with another even longer kiss.

Later that evening, I was pleased to see Scotty working on his tensing/relaxation techniques. I was about to give him kudos when there was a knock at the door. I opened it to find Tony standing there.

"Come on in, Tony. You look a bit concerned. I suppose from that look, this is not a social call," I said as I ushered him into the living room. Scotty, hearing Tony's name, came in as well.

As Tony sat down, I offered him a can of soda. Getting a drink for Tony, Scotty, and myself, I sat down with Scotty sitting next to me.

Tony started the conversation. "I know that you are close to Grandmaster Kim Yong-Sool. Have you noticed him acting a bit strange?"

"What do you mean, strange?" I asked Tony for clarification.

"Well, Tish, after you left the dojang, the grandmaster called me into the office and said he would be taking extended leave and asked if I would run the dojang for him. He told me that you would not be working at the dojang after you graduate, but there would be another instructor in place to assist him. Did he say anything to you about leaving?" Tony said with genuine concern in his voice.

"Are you afraid that you will not be able to run the dojang without the grandmaster," I asked, "or are you afraid there is something wrong with the grandmaster like he has an illness or something like that?"

"Both!" Tony said.

"First off, you will do a great job at the dojang. Your police training alone will be invaluable, but your time spent with the grandmaster has equipped you to teach. You have moved up the martial arts levels rapidly, and your devotion to martial arts is obvious. Your students love you, and the community is behind you since they know how much you are trying to create a safer place for everyone. As far as the grandmaster being sick, I can't say, but he seems fit to me. There must be some business he has to take care of, or maybe even grandmasters need to do continuing education." I knew when I said the last remark that it was ridiculous. I was sure the grandmaster was not seeking out someone who knew even more than him.

Tony took several sips from his soda can. He was thinking hard, and I did not want to interrupt him. Finally, he said, "Something just doesn't feel right. I can't put my finger on it. I guess I should just be flattered that he thinks that I can run the dojang in his absence. The problem is that when I asked how long he would be gone; he couldn't give me an answer."

"I will talk to him if you would like me to, but I am not sure what good it would do," I volunteered.

"No, Tish. I don't want you to do that. I am here just to find out if you knew something that I should be aware of. I'm sorry if I have caused you concern. You are probably right. The grandmaster is just needing a break or has even more to learn, which I can't imagine. However, I suspect martial arts is a lifetime commitment to learning. That is probably it...." Tony took the last gulp of his drink and said he needed to get going.

"Stay for dinner," Scotty invited. "I am going to barbecue some chicken. I know you will love it because I am the king of the grill!"

I added, "I will make potato salad and coleslaw, and it will be a picnic. What do you say?"

Tony agreed to stay for dinner. The rest of the evening was light-hearted and fun, but I couldn't help but wonder why the grandmaster was leaving.

Scotty's lesson continued over the next couple of days. I explained that he needed to know, subconsciously, which muscles were tensed without having to make an actual physical checklist. We worked on Scotty being able to make different parts of his body heavy and other parts of his body light. We staggered the lesson making his core heavy and his chest and lungs light or his base light while keeping his arms heavy. There were no ends to combinations that I forced upon Scotty's concentration. His competition was on Saturday, and Scotty needed to be able to immediately sense which body parts must be stabilized and purposefully cause this to happen. Being able to check the recoil of his revolver in the competition, or any weapon thrust upon him for self-defense, was imperative to the accuracy he craved to make him the champion of champions.

I wasn't sure why this was important to me, but it was. I wanted Scotty to be all that he could be, and I knew his new-found focus would serve him well. I intensified the training, only allowing him to relax on Friday evening.

"I almost suggested we drive early to the hotel tonight, but I decided you would be more relaxed here at home," I said as I snuggled into the crook of Scotty's arm. "Did you enjoy the dinner I made for you?"

Scotty rubbed his stomach with the free hand that was not occupied with holding me tight. "It was really great. Red meat was what the doctor ordered. I need all the protein I can eat to get through the long day tomorrow. I wish that we did not need to get up early. Thanks for offering to drive so I can relax a bit more."

I just snuggled up closer to him. "We should get to bed early tonight. I am glad our parents understood we would be staying overnight on Saturday to spend time with them on Sunday, but we needed to be home tonight without distractions. I know they were disappointed that we were not taking them up on their generous offer to pay for the hotel rooms for both nights. I think it is funny that they are still going up tonight so they can play around. I am beginning to think our parents coming to the competition was just an excuse for them to take a mini-vacation together."

Scotty stretched and yawned. "Let's go get some sleep. I can use some of your instructions to help me relax before sleeping. Want to join me?" Scotty smiled at the suggestion.

"Not tonight, Champ. You really do need to relax...all of your body parts." With that comment, I jumped to my feet and pulled Scotty to his feet. "Get to sleep. I will wake you up early."

CHAPTER FIFTEEN

The ride to the competition was relaxed, even with the early morning start. Scotty had requested a light breakfast…pancakes, eggs, ham, and juice. I got up early to make it for him, knowing that he would need all the sleep he could get.

We arrived on time and were greeted by our parents. They seemed to be in high spirits. We could check in right away since they had already paid for our room the previous day. Once again, I felt a bit guilty about them paying for two rooms for an extra night that we did not stay, but they did not seem to mind at all. In fact, Scott's mother, Alice, said she took one of the rooms since Gabe had been snoring loudly lately, and she wanted one good night's sleep herself.

"I remember how loudly Dad can snore," Scotty announced when his mother made a comment.

"That's not true! It is your mom who snores that loudly. I always said it was me to keep her from being embarrassed," Gabriel joked.

"So why come out with the truth now, in public?" Scotty retorted.

"One can only be so gallant. I guess my time to be chivalrous has come to an end. My name was being besmirched, and I need to defend my honor," Gabe said.

We laughed, knowing that he was just kidding, but Alice gave him a hard poke in the arm to let him know she wasn't sure he was gallant at all.

"Hey, I need to check-in, but Tish will show you where to sit to be able to see most of the competition the best. I am not sure I will get back to you until lunch. Keep your fingers crossed, okay?" Scotty was off to the registration line.

I led the way to where we would find proper seating in the grandstands. I also pointed out where the restrooms were located as well as where one could purchase a snack.

We reached the grandstand, we sat in a shade-covered area. Even though the weather was sunny, it was not warm. I decided that the shade to protect our eyes from glare was more important than the warmth we might glean from the sun. We wore warm jackets, so I felt I was making a smart decision.

We climbed up to the second row from the top. The top row was already reserved with jackets placed to mark their seats. I was thrilled when Captain Jones's wife came up the stairs and sat right behind us. I had not met Mrs. Jones yet, but I had seen her photo on Captain Jones's desk frequently. Therefore, I would recognize her anywhere.

"Mrs. Jones, my name is Tish Evers. I am the lady who is training the rookies for your husband. I am also working with Patrick and Aileen Jamieson. I would like to introduce my parents and Scotty McFarlan's parents," I said by way of an introduction.

"Tish, it is very nice to meet you finally. My husband speaks highly of you and Scotty. The Jamiesons also rave about you two," Mrs. Jones held out her hand to shake mine as she said these kind words. "I would love to meet your parents and Scotty's parents," she continued as she released my hand, ready to shake the next.

I introduced my parents and Scotty's parents, and Mrs. Jones told each to call her by her first name, Audrey. We sat down but turned so we could talk to her as a group. I found Audrey Jones to be warm and humorous. She laughed readily and put everyone at ease. We were so busy talking and laughing that we did not notice that the competition had started until we heard the first loud gunshot. Putting our earplugs into our ears, we turned to watch the action.

The first round of competitors was quite good. I knew that Scotty would be in the second group. As Scotty came to his first station, I could see he was using his loosening up techniques. He seemed to be swaying and wiggling in place.

"What the hell is my son doing out there? He acts as if he is warming up for a ballet routine instead of a shooting match," Gabe said in a rather loud voice. Chuckles were heard around us as the spectators' gaze turned to Scotty's antics.

I smiled, knowing what Scotty was doing. He was pinpointing which muscles he needed to relax and which muscles he needed to tighten. The fact that Scotty only had one week to learn this technique showed in his comical stance. I knew over time, he would be able to do his warm-up so automatically that no one would be aware of what he was doing, but now, he just looked like a loose goose.

Captain Jones's range master was Scotty's second again this year. He would provide Scotty with the appropriate number of 6 round magazines for each match and stage. Sargent Tomlinson's incredible skills as an armorer would be put to good use again in this year's competition. Scotty often remarked how his weapons never failed to fire or eject the round.

Scotty's first match, Match 8, was 24 shots total from the unsupported standing position. The first stage is 12 shots at 7 yards, and the second stage is 12 shots at 15 yards. Scotty had been given a maximum of 20 seconds for each stage. Each shot in each match was worth a maximum of 10 points. Scotty scored the first place with a perfect score in 15 seconds with all 24 rounds in the x-ring within the bullseye.

Gabriel and Alice were on their feet the whole time. It seemed Gabe was no longer embarrassed by Scotty's technique for getting in the zone.

"That's my boy out there," Gabe said to the crowd.

I noted Scotty's arm did not move at all from the recoil of the shot. He could put each shot into the x-ring with incredible speed since he did not need to reposition his weapon after taking each shot. His arm was utterly steady; even Captain Jones was taking notice.

Match 9 was 18 shots kneeling and standing at 25 yards. The first stage is 6 shots kneeling. The second stage is 6 shots standing left-handed with support, and the last stage is 6 shots right-handed standing with support. There is a total of 90 seconds maximum for all stages. Scott 's experience with shooting with both hands was invaluable.

I recalled when he was 12 years old, he broke his right wrist and practiced shooting left-handed because he could still go hunting with his dad. Scoring another first place with another perfect score in 55 seconds with all 18 rounds in the x-ring, I once more noted that people were taking notice, and I became a bit concerned. I realized Scotty was totally in the zone. People would start to wonder how he could accomplish the task almost perfectly. I knew I needed to interject a bit in the competition and planned my own strategy. I did not want people to question what Scotty was doing for fear that it would somehow come back on the grandmaster. He had been reluctant to allow me to show Scotty even the first lesson he taught me for fear that people might take notice.

I knew Grandmaster Kim Yong-Sool had cautioned me...no, warned me not to let anyone know the techniques the grandmaster was currently teaching me. He had told me this practice was sacred, and that he was taking some risk in instructing it to me, but he felt I was ready to learn this greatest of all lessons. Now, I was afraid I was putting the grandmaster in a predicament.

My thoughts were interrupted by Match 10, the most challenging task for Scotty in last year's competition. It is 24 shots, sitting, prone and standing at 50 yards. 6 shots sitting, six shots prone, and six shots right and left-handed with support. The competitors were given two minutes and 45 seconds to complete the three stages.

Giving my binoculars to Gabriel, I told him he would need them to appreciate this match fully. He gladly accepted them, and I strained my eyes to watch. Not to my surprise, Scotty scored first place with 240 points in one minute and 50 seconds with 18 rounds in the x-ring, with 6 more in the bullseye. Scotty's superb vision once again aided him in this feat.

I excused myself on the pretense of needing to stretch and use the facilities. I headed towards Captain Jones, who was watching from the front lines. I went to his side and told him that he had to somehow distract Scotty from making a perfect score.

"Is there a problem?" he asked. "I can't help but notice that Scott has changed his techniques from even a week ago."

I swallowed and said quietly, "That is the problem. I am afraid that I taught Scotty something that could get Grandmaster Kim Yong-Sool in trouble. Too many people are taking notice that Scotty is about to make a clean sweep of the competition. I don't think that has ever been done before. It is sure to be publicized, and I fear someone will come around wanting to know his secret. That could lead back to the grandmaster, and I already think something is happening to him.

"Tony came over last night and voiced some concerns he has as well. He said something is going on, but he does not know what it is. Do you?"

Captain Jones said he did know a little about what was going on with the grandmaster and agreed it would not do for Scotty to draw too much attention to himself at this point. He said he would go over and have a brief chat with Scotty.

I watched as Captain Jones asked permission to talk to Scott for one moment. The facilitator agreed to a one-minute break. I saw Scotty nod his head in agreement before resuming his station. Captain Jones immediately returned to me and told me that all was well.

Match 11 would have two similar stages of twelve shots, each at 25 yards fired standing and unsupported. 35 seconds was allowed for each stage. Scott finished first place with a total score of 239 points in 52 seconds, but not all 24 rounds were in the x-ring, one shot was in the 9 ring. His perfect record was now broken to my relief.

The final Match 12 is on the National Police Course. There are four stages with a total of 60 shots. Stage one is twelve shots at seven yards standing without support. The time limit is twenty seconds, including the time to reload. Stage two is 18 shots at 25 yards, six each kneeling, and standing right and left-handed with support. The time limit for this stage is 90 seconds. Stage three is 24 shots at 50 yards. Six each sitting, prone, standing left and right-handed with support. The time limit is two minutes and 45 seconds. The fourth stage is six shots standing without support at 25 yards. The time limit is twelve seconds. All four of these stages are completed in one go.

It was astounding how composed Scott seemed. Last year Scotty had been a wreck and showed signs of exhaustion. This year, he was relaxed and composed. When they posted his score, he came in first place again with 593 points in a total of three minutes and five seconds and 45 rounds in the x-ring and only 7 shots outside of the bullseye in the 9 ring.

Scott finished first place overall with a score of 1494 points with only eight shots in the 9-ring. Scotty expertly placed 128 of his 150 shots in the x-ring, just breaking the previous record of 124.

I ran up and kissed him on the mouth without thinking that our parents would be watching. My only hope was that they were looking down at the stairs as they navigated their way towards Scotty.

Our parents arrived with wide grins on their faces. I was not sure if the smiles were for Scotty's amazing accomplishment or for the big kiss, I gave him. I could only wait and see what would be verbalized by our mothers later in the day. Right now, the focus was on Scotty, and he was getting praise and hugs and pats on the back. Captain Jones and Mrs. Jones joined us for lunch before Captain Jones had to compete in the afternoon.

As we sat and ate our sandwiches, I overheard Captain Jones telling Gabriel that he was really going to miss having Scott on the team next year. Gabe said something about Scott being able to juggle work and the team, but Captain Jones indicated that the Jamiesons had already told him they would need both of us full-time.

I wanted to ask Audrey about the case we were working on with the Jamiesons but feared it would not be the best time. Instead, I asked her, "Will you be meeting with Patrick and Aileen anytime soon? I would love to sit in and learn what you have found out."

Mrs. Jones replied that she would be having a briefing next week, and she already asked the Jamiesons to include us as well as Captain Jones. She patted me on the hand and told me to enjoy the day. We would be talking soon enough.

I watched Scotty beaming and knew Audrey was right. This was Scotty's big day, and I did not want to take anything away from it. He was the Champion of Champions at the National Policeman's Shooting Competition as well as in my heart.

We totally enjoyed the rest of the afternoon as well as the evening. Captain Jones and Mrs. Jones spent the night. Last year, Captain Jones had rushed home to help Audrey with the children. This year, Audrey's mom came to stay with the children so that they could have a more relaxed time together. Audrey said how few of the competitions she had been able to attend due to children and work and was pleased when her mother volunteered to stay with them for a long weekend.

We ate dinner together and then went to my parent's room to play cards. Our parents had taught us to play Euchar years ago since it was their favorite card game. Luckily, the Captain and Mrs. Jones knew how to play and were worthy partners.

Our mothers, true to form, packed way too many snacks and soft drinks. We played until the wee hours, and finally, the group broke up to go to their own rooms to sleep. Neither mother had made any comments about my big kiss on Scotty's mouth. I thought we were in the clear until my father offered to walk me to my room.

"Oh, Dad, I am just next door. You don't need to walk me there. Scotty is just down the hall. He can walk me to my door," I said playfully.

"It is a father's duty. Don't make me feel like a bad dad," he said as we went out the door. I looked towards Scotty, who had a big grin on his face.

My dad walked me to the door, and as I opened it, he said. "Tish, you aren't my little girl anymore. Your mother and I know that there is more to you and Scotty than just partners and friends, and we want you to know that we approve of Scotty, but we don't like you two living in sin. We want to know when you plan to marry Scotty?"

My mouth dropped open. I hadn't expected my father to be pressuring me into getting married.

"I'm not pregnant or anything like that, Dad," I blurted out.

"We know that dear, but we come from a very religious background, and we brought you up in those values. Already our friends make comments about the two of you living together. We hadn't pushed before this because we knew you two were just friends, but now we know differently. Being in a relationship means marriage to us. Can you understand where we are coming from?" my father said earnestly.

"I will agree to talk to Scotty tomorrow, but it will sound like I am proposing to him, and that isn't something I intend to do. It has to be Scotty who initiates our engagement." I was starting to feel my dander rise. I rarely argued with my father, but I was beginning to resent being put in this situation.

"Good night, Dad. I love you," I said, trying to make my voice sound less prickly.

"I love you more than you will ever know," my father replied and kissed me on my forehead.

I went into my room, and now I wished that Scotty and I would have headed home right after the competition. I was wondering if Scotty was getting the same lecture from his parents.

I heard a quiet tap at my door. I peeked through the peephole and saw Scotty standing there. I opened the door, and he walked in. I could tell from his face that his parents talked with him about our situation.

"Well, the cat is out of the bag!" Scotty said quietly but with emphasis.

"I'm sorry. It is my fault. I was just extremely excited about you winning that I didn't think what the kiss would mean to our parents when they saw it. I should have just socked you in the arm like I did last year. I goofed," I said as we sat down on my bed to talk.

"I certainly am not opposed to getting married. We could still call our business Evers and McFarlan. We would just be married, though. What do you think? Would you want to marry me? I know you can do better, but I do love you with all my heart. You have been my soulmate since we were just kids. I knew you were something special to me all those years ago; I just did not have a name for it then. Now, I know I have loved you all my life," Scotty said, going to his knees.

I looked straight into his eyes. "Scotty, I do love you with all my heart. I would be honored to be Mrs. Scotty McFarlan, but are you ready to be married?"

I was thinking that we have too much going on in our lives. We have finals, working for the Jamiesons, and working part-time; we are up-to-our-ears! Could we really plan a wedding too?

Scotty stood up abruptly. "Darn it! This is not the way I wanted to propose to you. I wanted to take you up in the Cessna Crusader and fly to some romantic spot to propose to you. I resent our parents for pushing their values on us."

I stood and stroked his face. "Scotty, your way sounds perfect. When you are ready to propose, I will wait and fly off someplace romantic with you. Until then, our parents will need to accept that we are living our lives the way we want to live. We are not children, and we won't be treated like children. We will get engaged when we want to get engaged and not be pushed into it by them, right?"

I was enjoying my defiance. What started out as a gesture to soothe Scotty had become boldness. I was feeling my true self-emerge once again. I was Tish and not my daddy's little girl.

"Tish, we need to handle this carefully. Our parents have been behind us 100%, and there is no sense in slapping them in the face, so to speak. Look how much they have done for us already with the van, car, your Harley...I don't want to alienate them. Do you? I think we can tell them that I proposed and we will marry next December or something like that. It will give them peace of mind, and we can still do things the way we want. What do you say?" Scotty said, being the voice of reason.

I knew he was right. Our parents didn't need to agree to allow us to go to Chicago and move in together. That was a big step for them. Thinking back, I knew our mothers would need to deal with wagging tongues amongst their lady's groups. Selfishly, I did not give it a second thought at the time that we left home. I just wanted to be on my own and feel like an adult. My parent's values were not totally my values, but I had to respect them.

"I guess you are right. We can at least give our parents the peace of mind that we are getting married. I doubt that it will stop the tongues from wagging in their circles, but maybe it will give our mothers something fun to do like, plan our wedding.... Oh great! .... Now they will be planning for our wedding.

"You realize that they are going to want us to come down as often as possible to try on wedding gowns, pick out flowers, decide where to have the reception, and all that. Gosh darn! I don't want to need to deal with all that right now. Any thoughts on how we can get them to give this idea up for a while?" I was feeling exasperated just thinking about a wedding and all it would entail.

"Hey, just give our mothers carte blanc and let them do everything. You can come home one time for the dress fitting, and they can do everything else," Scott ventured.

"Oh, no! They are not picking out my wedding dress. I would end up looking like a poodle. They can come to Chicago, and I will pick out my own wedding dress. I won't concede in that detail. They can plan everything else, including my bridesmaid dresses.

Oh dear, who would I have as my maid of honor for that matter? I really don't have anyone that I am that close to." I was feeling tense and irritable just thinking about a wedding.

"I know you aren't going to like my suggestion, but why does it need to be someone your own age. Why couldn't it be someone like Aileen Jamieson or even one of the rookies you are training. If you are desperate, you could even ask Heather. You two became close while she was hiding out from Jack." Scotty stopped talking. I think he knew he had said enough, but some of what he said had merit.

I kissed him good night and shoved him out the door. "I think we have had enough excitement for one day. Go get some sleep."

We had agreed to tell our parents that we were engaged and planned to marry next December if that would work for their schedules. Our news was greeted with hugs and tears and our mothers already with their heads together planning our wedding. I swallowed my irritations and told myself it was a small price to pay for their happiness and peace of mind.

Captain and Mrs. Jones had left before breakfast. Our good news would be told to them later. My plan was not to tell anyone anything until I absolutely had to do so. Scotty agreed. He said we needed to take things step-by-step and just let our mothers have fun.

It was a good thing that I was not like other girls who planned their wedding day from age five on. I had never thought about a fairy book wedding, so not being involved with the plans was fine with me if I got to find my own dress. Maybe I would shock everyone and get married in a pantsuit, or better yet, leather pants and a leather jacket. The thought amused me to no end. I let my imaginary wedding play out in my head to still the idea of what was really ahead for me.

We left on cordial terms with our parents and headed once more back to Chicago with Scotty sporting his trophy and metals. I was incredibly proud of his accomplishments and told him so.

"Aww, come on. I couldn't have done it without your Qi Gong (Chee Kong) calming techniques. If you remember, I was a basket case last year," he said pleased I was gushing over him.

"Even if that was the case," I affirmed, "you also did well last year. I knew you had it in you. It was just a matter of you letting yourself experience what you need to feel and then build on that."

I wasn't sure if Scotty had any idea of what I was saying. I wasn't actually sure myself. The things that the grandmaster was trying to teach me was near impossible, yet, he claimed it was all very possible. I had my competition in two weeks, and I needed to spend every minute with my training.

Grandmaster Kim Yong-Sool said I was his diamond in the rough. I did not want to disappoint him by not doing well in the competition. He was hosting the event in his dojang. I knew it was important to him. I wanted to do him proud. Tony would be competing as well, but for some reason, the grandmaster was not tutoring Tony. I wondered if he thought I needed more practice. Maybe he felt I had the acuity to succeed in some manner that Tony did not.

I let my mind wander. I couldn't help but think what Captain Jones and Tony had said about Grandmaster Kim Yong-Sool. Could he be in some trouble? I thought I was perceptive, but maybe when I am totally absorbed in other things like Scotty and the abduction case, I am not as aware as I should be of my surroundings. I would need to work on that. A private investigator can't allow themselves to become oblivious to their surroundings. Unaware isn't a word I would use to describe myself usually, but my mind was on Scotty more than it should be.

"Scotty, do you think I have let myself become oblivious?" I asked him, and it must have seemed out of the clear blue sky to him.

"What are you talking about?" was Scotty's response. "Were you not prepared for how our parents would react when they found out our relationship was more than just friends?"

"No, actually, well maybe, but I was thinking more that I am not as observant as I use to be. Maybe oblivious isn't the word I am looking for. Maybe less vigilant is what I mean. Both Captain Jones and Tony remarked they feel something is wrong with Grandmaster Kim Yong-Sool, and I haven't noticed anything different. I must be too preoccupied with myself and what is happening in my life."

"Wow!" Scotty exclaimed. "If you are unaware, I must be as dense as a rock. You always see everything before I do. I think you are too hard on yourself. If you didn't notice anything wrong with the grandmaster, there is probably nothing wrong, and the other two are just seeing things that aren't there. I would say the grandmaster lets his guard down around you more than anyone else."

"Hmmm," I mused and said nothing more on the subject. I probably was making more of the whole thing than I needed.

"Want to stop and get a burger before we get home?" Scotty asked. "I see a sign ahead for burgers, fries, and milkshakes. I really don't want to cook dinner when we get home. Do you?"

We hadn't eaten since breakfast with our parents, and I think the new pressure from them made both of us lose our appetite. "I think a burger or fish sandwich sounds like a good idea. In fact, I could really go for a fish sandwich. I hope one is on the menu," I said as Scotty took the turn off the highway to head for the restaurant.

While munching my order of fish and chips, I told Scotty about the short conversation with Mrs. Jones. I really was busy with Scotty's competition and our parents coming down on us that I forgot to tell Scotty before now that Mrs. Jones was going to have a meeting with the Jamiesons, Captain Jones, and ourselves. My interest was now peaked. I wondered what she might have found out about Shari Lawton. I just had a feeling the meeting had to be about her.

Scotty asked, "When is this meeting going to take place?"

"Sometime this week. Aileen will probably call to let us know when and where to meet. I would assume she would make sure that the meeting wouldn't conflict with our classes. She is quite protective of our study time," I answered.

"Do you have any idea what the meeting is going to be about?" Scotty continued with questions. "Are you thinking she has been watching Shari Lawton, and she has some interesting information about her involvement in the case? Or maybe she needs us to go undercover."

At first, I was going to tell Scotty he was a dope, but once I thought about it, I wasn't going to rule out Scotty's thought as a possibility. I wasn't exactly sure what we could do at a hospital to be undercover when Shari Lawton had just kicked us out.

"I somehow doubt that Mrs. Jones would ask us to go undercover. If you remember, Shari Lawton sicked the security guards after us. She would spot us immediately. No, I doubt that is what she wants to talk to us about. I guess we will just need to wait and see what she says." Even though I wanted to know more about what the meeting is going to be about, I was right when I told Scotty we would just need to wait and see. Patience is not necessarily my best trait, but I am trying to be more patient.

The rest of the trip was spent talking about the competition and how *in the zone* Scotty was. He told me that Captain Jones had asked him whether he would be willing to teach the other members of the team the same techniques he used.

At first, I was concerned the focus on Scotty's success would create a trail through me to the grandmaster. Once I gave it more thought, there was nothing sacred about what I taught Scotty. It was a simple relaxation of some muscles and consciously tightening others. The fact that Scotty could go a step beyond and get into the zone was nothing I taught him. If he could show his team members to do the same, I was sure I was not breaking any rules. I would ask the grandmaster tomorrow, but if that was the case, why had I become alarmed that Scotty might ace the competition and his miracle would be traced back to the grandmaster. There seemed to be a line that was a bit fuzzy to me. Did I cross it? I couldn't see how I had.

It was nice to turn into the driveway and know we were home and would be sleeping in our own bed. I did not realize until just that moment how much I missed sleeping in Scotty's arms last night. I was tired, and I figured Scotty would be as well. Early to bed sounded good to me. After all, we didn't need to cook dinner, wash dishes, or any of the regular routine. Then I remembered we had a test in the morning. Darn! I knew Scotty was not prepared. Now our supposed early bedtime would be…late-night studying.

After the exam and our other classes, we ventured over to the office to check in with Aileen and Patrick. I knew Scotty was a bit behind entering data into the computer. I was sure I could help him in some way if Aileen didn't have anything better for me to do. I also wanted to stop in at the dojang and talk to the grandmaster. It was nice that he allowed me to take Saturday off to attend Scotty's competition.

Patrick was in the office. He said Aileen was having her hair done, consequently, working with Scotty would be okay with him. There was data that would be easy enough for me to enter while Scotty worked on the more complex stuff. I finished the easy things quickly enough to duck out and go to the dojang.

Tony was covering the office. He had two classes that evening for two different ages of teens. At the beginning stages, Tony did not like to allow the younger teens to learn with the older boys for fear that younger ones might get hurt. Stressing fair play, honor, and all the super values did not always stop boys from being boys and being too rough. Tony felt there was no sense in putting anyone at risk.

"Hi, Tony. Is Grandmaster Kim Yong-Sool here?" I asked as I entered the dojang.

I noticed Tony's eyes light up as I entered. I knew he would have liked for our relationship to have taken on more permanent status, but with Captain Jones nixing the dating, as well as Scotty, becoming my main squeeze, Tony stepped back good-naturedly. It didn't keep him from flirting a bit.

"Hi, Gorgeous," Tony greeted me. "No, the grandmaster stepped out for a bit. I am sure he will be back in a few minutes. Got time to spar with me? I need a bit of work before our tournament. I am excited about moving from a brown belt to a black belt."

Tony was studying karate. My training was different, but I could stay with him on the mat. I took off my jacket, shoes, and socks, and agreed to give him a target or not.

Tony was flexible and had become accomplished with his roundhouse kicks. Unfortunately, for him, I could tell instantly when he planned to attack. I could move away without getting tagged. It didn't really frustrate him since he did not want to hurt me, but he was intrigued that I was able to detect the signals he gave off. He stopped and asked me what he was doing wrong.

I couldn't possibly explain how I could see the intent in his eyes, the small changes in his breathing, or the smallest tightening of muscles, which clued me into his next move.

"I can see it in your eyes, and I don't know how to explain what I see," I answered directly, but I could see his disappointment. He had hoped I could tell him exactly what he was doing, which would alert his opponent during the meet.

"That is it? You can see it in my eyes?" Tony asked bewildered.

"Well, I can see you take in a breath and hold it. I can see certain muscle groups tighten. I don't know how to explain it better. I just can tell you are about to kick. Maybe the grandmaster can explain it better than I can," and as I said those words, the grandmaster entered and applauded.

"Nicely done. Your round-house kick was technically perfect," the grandmaster said to encourage Tony. "Aww, Tish. How did the competition go for Scott?"

I bowed to Tony and turned to the grandmaster. He motioned to me to follow him into the office. We sat facing each other.

"Scotty did wonderfully. In fact, if I had not asked Captain Jones to distract him, he would have shot a perfect score. I was afraid the publicity Scotty would receive for doing the impossible could have consequences for you. Was I right?" I asked, frankly.

"I do not think there would be any consequences for me if Scott managed a perfect score, but I appreciate your wanting to protect me. What you taught Scotty is not inappropriate, but what I am teaching you has serious repercussions and must never be taught to anyone else," the grandmaster reminded me in a quiet voice.

"Then, it would be okay for Scotty to teach what I have taught him to his teammates on the pistol competition team?" I asked. "Captain Jones was impressed with Scotty's ability to fire with no perceptible recoil due to what I taught him. Captain Jones would like Scotty to teach the skills he learned to the others. I told him to wait until I talked to you before he committed to doing it," I said.

"You do not need my permission. Scotty is free to pass on the techniques you taught. Captain Jones would not ask him if he thought that it was a revered technique. Grandmaster Jones understands much of what we know. Are you ready for another lesson?" He dismissed the subject, and we went to prepare for the next lesson he would teach me.

When I returned home, I was feeling giddy. The grandmaster was accelerating our lessons. I felt as though I was becoming one with my innermost being and learning new senses I never knew existed. I felt things I never felt before. I could sense changes in heat, sounds, smells, and currents of air that allow me to anticipate every movement the grandmaster made, even with my eyes closed. After each lesson, I felt both totally exhilarated and totally exhausted. Somehow, the two balanced each other out, so I seemed relatively ordinary to Scotty when I entered the house.

"Hi, darlin'. Guess what? I am cooking Pork Chops a L'Orange. Are you impressed?" Scotty greeted me with a kiss, as well as these words.

"Yes! I am totally impressed, but I don't know why. You have become an incredible cook. It smells delicious. Do I have time for a shower before dinner?" I asked as I started to strip.

Barely into the shower, I heard the door open and close. The curtains were drawn apart, and Scotty stepped in.

"I think the pork chops need to cook a bit longer," Scotty said as he grabbed the bar of soap and made lather. His hands slid down my back as I enjoyed his gentle touch. In my ecstasy, I wondered how such a big man could be so caring.

CHAPTER SIXTEEN

The next two weeks flew by as I immersed myself in the grandmaster's lessons. Giddy was no longer the word I used after each session. Awesome, in the overwhelming sense of the word, was more my internal feeling as I took each task in hand.

Our criminal justice classes were always easy for me, but now I felt invincible. I could ace every test with no studying at all. However, Scotty still needed my tutoring; mechanically, I would quiz him on each chapter that was in my memory word for word.

The individual first-place trophy Scotty won sat in a glass display case for everyone to see at the police station beside the overall International Tournament Champion's trophy the team took home. Captain Jones marveled at the team's accomplishments and gave Scotty credit for his astounding achievement.

Scotty was enjoying teaching his newly learned techniques to his fellow pistol competition team. Captain Jones sat in on the methods Scotty was training the team members, thinking he was never too old to learn.

Arriving at my martial arts rookie training class, Captain Jones commented on the fact, the police rookies were learning twice as fast as the previous rookie class. The captain noted I was teaching the same techniques to them as I had to Scotty. After watching from the bleachers in the police gym, Captain Jones took me aside as the rookies gathered their belongings, pushing and shoving each other in comradery.

"Tish, I just want to commend you on a superb job training these rookies in self-defense. I am especially impressed with how much calmer Sam has become. I think I owe you a debt of thanks for helping him to mature. I don't feel the same hostile vibes from him as before," the Captain said.

"I can't take all the credit for his change of attitude, Captain. If you notice, he is smitten with Andrea Marchetti. I suspect his change of attitude has more to do with her than it does with my training," I remarked as I watched Sam picking up Andrea's duffle bag to carry to her car.

"That leads me to a second question. How capable would Sam and Andrea be undercover? Do you think Sam has changed enough that he could act inconspicuous?" Captain Jones queried.

I answered with a question, "What exactly are you asking? I can't answer if I don't know what the circumstances would be."

"You are aware that our meeting with my wife is taking place tomorrow at an early dinner with the Jamiesons. She has some major suspicions, but she wants some surveillance done before any of us can act. The surveillance would best be done by someone invisible at the hospital. That means a temporary janitor to fill a job for three weeks while the real janitor is on vacation. The fact that Audrey has a spot to fill was more than serendipitous. Could Sam do the job without becoming volatile? You know how defensive and argumentative he has been in the past," Captain Jones watched Sam and Andrea leave together as he said these words to me.

I thought for a moment and replied, "If we can convince Sam he is an actor playing a part, and he is not to get personally involved with anything other than the job and spying, he might be alright. However, he would need to buy into this plan for him to stay level-headed. Asking a young black man to be a janitor would trigger his anger if it is not presented correctly. He needs to feel in charge and feel like it was his idea if you catch my drift."

Captain Jones continued his scenario, "I think there is a way we could get him to volunteer since the second part of my wife's plan is to have one of the rookies go undercover as a student nurse. The only one who could fit that bill is Andrea. She is petite, blond, and exactly matches the other three victim's physical attributes. She is the perfect match for the job. I suspect if Andrea is willing to go undercover, there will be no stopping Sam from joining the efforts. Agreed?"

I chuckled a bit. "You have a point. Sam is very protective of Andrea; he would do anything to keep her safe. Pretending to be a janitor would not be insulting under those circumstances. Are they going to attend the meeting tomorrow with your wife as well?" I asked.

"No, not yet. We must sit down and work out all the logistics to this plan. Of course, if either Sam or Andrea declines our offer to work as investigators, we will be back to square one. Obviously, you and Scott can't fill their shoes. You made yourselves quite well known to Shari Lawton. You two will need to be on the sidelines of this investigation at this point. If things heat up, I will need both of your skills to pull this off," Captain Jones looked very serious as he told me briefly about the plan.

As we parted to go to our homes, Captain Jones had one last parting word, "Tish, if you are correct, and the first blond girl found floating in the lake has anything to do with the other three girls' disappearance, we could be dealing with murderers. I hate to get you and Scott involved. You are, after all, citizens and not police officers. My job would be on the line if anything happened to either of you."

I reminded Captain Jones that Scotty and I had been involved with murderers before as citizens. "We both can handle ourselves in bad situations. You, of all people, know that we have had our lives threatened more than once. We know the risks. We will sign waivers or whatever we must do to work this case. In fact, this is our case, we investigated the case from the beginning. It is personal to both of us.

The three girls' lives are on hold because of whoever these monsters are. We want to stop him or them."

Captain Jones patted my hand as he turned to leave the gym. I watched him go out of the doors. I gathered my own belongings, checked to make sure I had the keys to lock up, and followed suit. My Harley was waiting for me to start it up.

Scotty was at the door, waiting for me as I pulled into the garage and headed for the back door. Pulling me into his arms, I was greeted with a warm, soothing kiss. We went into the house and sat at the table. I told him about my conversation with Captain Jones.

"Of course, I would sign a waiver if that was necessary. I intend to see this case through to the end. I am totally with you on this. We are going to catch the monster who did this to these girls. Do I need to sign a paper saying I won't beat the pervert to a bloody pulp?" I could see Scotty was serious.

I answered him, "If we are required to do that, we will just be perjuring ourselves. I won't say I won't kick the shit out of him either. In fact, a beating is too good for him. I hope he gets life in prison."

We both were feeling exhilarated about the case. "I think we are jumping the gun here. We will find out more tomorrow at dinner. I don't know what our role will be in this investigation at this point. I hope the Jamiesons let us have an active role. I suspect that means that we both should act cool. No threats or shows of anger or Captain Jones will sit us out. Can you do that? I mean, can you act indifferent?" I watched Scotty's eyes change immediately. I saw a cold resolve, and I knew he would be perfectly calm.

"I can get into the zone whenever I need to now, thanks to you. I will be able to sit at the table and have my blood pressure so low that the Jamiesons will think that I am asleep," Scotty said in a long, drawn-out voice.

I laughed. "Come on, Scotty. Either extreme will get us kicked off the job. If they think you are going to fall asleep on the job, we won't get invited to the game either."

Getting back to our routine for the evening stopped the discussion. Dinner needed to be prepared, dishes done, homework finished, or in Scotty's case, started. I was glad Scotty knew calming techniques...we would both get a good night's sleep before starting another new day.

Sunrise came, as we knew, was inevitable. Neither of us wanted to leave the warm, comfortable bed to go to classes, but we could only linger a short time before we had to get up. Rushing to get to class on time meant peanut butter and jelly on toast for breakfast. Scotty was happy enough with the quick breakfast if he got two PPJ sandwiches.

We headed to classes and talked about the dinner meeting with the Jamiesons and the Joneses. The day could not go fast enough for either of us. We were excited to be on this case again. It had been hard to give up any of the investigations once the Aileen and Patrick arrived back home from their vacation. We knew Leticia LaPlante was relieved to have the Jamiesons on the case. Their reputation inspired confidence that Mrs. LaPlante would finally have her answers to what happened to her daughter, Constance.

As the hour approached, we headed toward Aileen and Patrick's home. Captain and Mrs. Jones were already there. We entered and were greeted by both couples warmly as if their children had just arrived. It made me feel good to know that both couples cared deeply for Scotty and myself. Chicago is a large city, and one can feel very alone without the support of good people. We just happened to have the support of four of the best people in town.

"Pour yourself a glass of wine if you want. You are twenty-one by now, aren't you?" Aileen offered.

I declined. I was almost twenty-one, and Scotty was only two months younger than me, so I wondered if we were being tested. I nudged Scotty as he started towards the counter to pour himself a glass of wine.

"Scotty, pour me an iced-tea, too, will you?" I said to redirect his gaze to the iced tea pitcher. He immediately understood that he was to pour two glasses of iced tea and join me.

Aileen had chips, dips, cheese, crackers, olives, and other assorted snacks on the counter. Seeing Scotty fill, a plate made me realize that we had not had lunch. I ambled over to the countertop and filled a small plate for myself. I knew dinner would be soon, but I did not want my rumbling stomach to give me away. I suppose a few crackers with cheese would not spoil my appetite. I took my glass of iced tea from Scotty to leave his hands free for his large plate of snacks.

Small talk ensued mainly about our studies and the fact that our time at the community college was coming to an end. Aileen interjected how happy she is to have us on board full time. That way, she and Patrick could wean themselves out of their business.

Small talk continued about trips that she and Patrick would like to take. I remembered that we did not look at the photos taken in Hawaii with more than a cursory glance. Patrick retrieved the albums so I could look at them longer and closer while we chatted.

Before long, Aileen called us to the dinner table. She had declined my offer to help. In fact, I was a bit embarrassed that I had not even offered to bring something to contribute to the dinner when I realized Audrey had brought along a tossed garden salad.

"I am sorry, Aileen. It just never occurred to me to offer to bring something tonight. I feel really foolish and very impolite," I said to admonish myself.

"Don't be silly, Sweetie. I would have asked you to bring something if I wanted you to do so. We both know you and Scotty have your hands full right now with teaching classes as well as completing your coursework. The meal is simple, and really, there was nothing you could have contributed anyway," Aileen offered to comfort my guilt.

We sat down to a large dish of lasagna, the tossed salad, and French bread. Patrick dished up the lasagna to each of us, and the salad and bread were passed around.

Audrey started the conversation immediately. "I definitely agree Shari Lawton is somehow involved in these cases. I was becoming increasingly alarmed when I realized that each girl who had gone missing were students who interned at my hospital. That put me on alert. When my dear husband told me that Tish and Scotty had been recruited by one of the mothers, my interest was piqued even more. When Barry sat down and talked to Aileen and Patrick, a plan started to unfold. My assistance was required, and this is the plan.

We think Andrea would be the perfect lure to set the trap. We know each victim was similar in size, age, hair color, and personality. Even though Andrea is less than shy, we feel she will be a talented enough actress to play the part. Mothers willing, Andrea can spend time with the victims. This should help her to get into character.

Sam, if he is willing, will fill the shoes of the janitor who is going on vacation. His job will be to snoop around and watch Shari Lawton closely as well as keep an eye on Andrea." Audrey paused for a breath.

"What will our role be?" I asked directly to Audrey.

Audrey looked to the Jamiesons to reply.

Patrick picked up the baton. "There will be a point, if all goes as before, where Andrea will be at the coffee house. Somehow, the girls were lured away or drugged or something. We will need eyes at the coffee shop. Since Shari knows you, disguises will help. Scotty, could you start growing a beard and let your hair grow, for instance? Tish, you will be more difficult. You are quite striking. It will be hard to disguise you."

"Hey, wait a minute. Are you saying I am not striking?" Scotty said, offended.

Patrick laughed. "Of course, you are striking. Big guys like you are hard to forget, but if we get you looking grungy enough and dress you like a biker, you might go unnoticed."

Aileen was thinking. "Tish, on the other hand, looks like a biker now. To get her to look different, we might need to go with a long wig, and maybe a dress, but she will still stand out. We will need to think about Tish's disguise for a while."

I just sat and looked smugly at Scotty. "See, I am striking, and you aren't."

Scotty laughed. "You don't need to tell me that. I have noticed how striking you are since you were thirteen."

I couldn't help but blush. Audrey saved me by continuing her plan.

"We need to find out if Andrea and Sam are capable of working undercover."

Scotty's face lit up. "I have an idea that will test if all of us are ready."

Captain Jones looked at Scotty. "Well, out with it."

Scotty continued. "I noticed when I was making entries into the computer from Patrick and Aileen's cases, that there were many stolen cars and most of them are Honda Civics and Toyota Camrys. We should interview the victims of the stolen cars to find out where they were just before their cars were stolen and what they were doing. We might just discover a way to catch the thieves."

"Go on," Patrick encouraged.

"I thought that we could rent a Civic or Camry and use it as bait. But first, we need to talk to the victims to see if there is something, they all have in common other than the car models. With your permission, we could get Sam and Andrea to help us canvas the list of owners and find out. What do you say?"

Captain Jones thought for a moment and said, "Sure. I will call them into my office tomorrow and enlist them. You can be there to set up the particulars and run with it."

The rest of the evening was spent talking about the Jamiesons' vacations, how the Jones and Jamiesons met, and a bit more teasing me about how they could possibly disguise me for the coffee house caper.

The next day we met in Captain Jones's office to present our case to Sam and Andrea. Captain Jones had given the details of the hospital case to them before our arrival. There was no mention that the car theft case was a test to see if Sam and Andrea could work undercover, however, neither were stupid and as we talked, it was apparent they understood the importance of aiding us in the investigation.

"So, when do we start?" Sam asked pointedly.

"Yes, I am anxious to show the captain that I am capable of going undercover. You all know that I want to be the youngest female officer to make a detective. That is no secret to anyone who knows me," Andrea offered.

"We can start now if you want. The sooner, the better, is what I say," I interjected.

We decided it would be better to work as two teams. Keeping Sam and Andrea together and Scotty and myself seemed like a no-brainer. Another thought was a black couple may have fewer doors open for them than a mixed couple. Captain Jones agreed even though he tried to take the race card out of the equation.

We divided the list of car owners. My thought was that Andrea and Sam would get doors to open quicker by using their badges than Scotty, and I would with our P.I. Business cards, but one never knows how people are going to react.

We set a time to meet back at the Jamiesons' office to compare notes and findings. We left Captain Jones's office, noting that Andrea and Sam seemed confident and cocky.

With a long day under our belts, we returned to Aileen and Patrick's office to find an extra-large pizza and soft drinks waiting for us. Andrea and Sam pulled in just minutes after we arrived. Stuffing our mouths with pizza, we sat down at the table with Patrick and Aileen waiting to hear what we had found out.

I started by flipping open my notepad. "We interviewed six different people. What we found out...that they had in common...was 1990-1993, light-colored Honda Civics or Toyota Camrys. It was split equally between the two makes. All the people said they had been to the mall the day their car was stolen. Each said the car was stolen from their driveway during the night while they slept. They each said that no neighbor heard a thing. Whoever stole their cars did it quietly."

Scotty offered, "I know the car companies only make a certain number of door lock types for each year, and the thieves may have access to the master keys for those door locks. That could be a significant number of keys. I am not sure the bad guys would take the time to hunt for the right key."

Sam jumped in, "Andrea and I also interviewed 6 people. The statistics are about the same, except there were four Hondas and two Camrys. They all said the same as your car owners. They had been to the mall, and the car was stolen at night with no witnesses. The thieves are very quiet. No theory from me as to how they get the cars away quietly and unnoticed."

"Hauling a car away would be noisy, wouldn't it?" Andrea asked.

Sam suggested, "It would seem to me that the thieves are probably masters at picking locks, or they use a bump key."

"Makes sense to me, Sam," Patrick said.

Aileen was the next to talk. Her plate had a piece of pizza on it that was untouched. "I have already rented a Toyota Camry. I said it had to be light-colored. Of course, the rental companies only rent new cars, but I doubt that will put off the car thieves. I will pick it up tomorrow if the rest of you can come up with a plan."

"No problem," Scotty said. "If you remember, I worked for mall security, so they know me there. I am sure I can get permission to do some surveillance work, and they will help any way possible."

"What are you thinking?" I asked. I knew Scotty had some plan initiating in his brain.

"Well, I thought that you and Andrea would go to the mall in the rented Camry. Sam and I would have inconspicuous jobs that would allow us to watch without being taken seriously. You know, sweeping the walks, gathering shopping carts, or the likes. It has to be jobs that we can come and go as we please."

"I already know who is going to be pushing the broom or picking up cigarette butts," Sam said grumpily. "I may as well get some practice if I am going to be the janitor at the hospital for the next several weeks."

"The two of you will be scouting around the outside of the mall in the parking lot to see if you see any conspicuous people lurking, correct?" Patrick asked.

"Right, and if we see someone checking out cars, we will use our walkie-talkie to tell Andrea and Tish where to park. My thought is two good looking women driving a Camry is sure to get the thieves' attention. Hey, those two women would get the thieves' attention even if they were not driving a Camry," Scotty said as he laughed.

Andrea and I both ignored Scotty's comment. We were both used to guys checking us out. His explanation was obvious. Of course, men would look at the two of us together.

Aileen asked, "Just how many days do you think I will need to rent the Camry? Will a week be long enough for this scheme to work?"

Sam laughed now. "Are you kidding. Didn't you hear Scott? It will probably take one trip to the mall to get the thieves' attention if Scott and I do our work correctly."

"May as well get this plan off right away. Excuse me while I phone my friends at the mall security office." Scotty grabbed another piece of pizza and headed for the phone.

While Scotty was on the phone, Aileen, Andrea, and I talked about what we should wear. My leather pants would get attention, but Aileen suggested short skirts. She felt nothing caught a man's eye faster than short skirts. Andrea had several, but I would need to make a trip to the mall yet today to find one for myself.

Andrea grabbed her purse. "Come on, Tish. Let's go find the right one now. Aileen, want to come along and give your opinion?"

"Thanks, but I need to make sure the rental is all lined up for tomorrow. You two have fun. Meet back here in a couple of hours, and we will finalize everything," Aileen said as she finally took the first bite out of her pizza.

That evening I modeled the skirt Andrea, and I had found at the mall. I twirled around to see what Scotty would say.

"That is short...black and short!" was all Scotty offered.

"You said short twice," I shot back.

"Well, that skirt is...very short. What are you planning on wearing under it? May I suggest bloomers," Scotty said not taking his eyes off my legs.

"Bloomers! What the heck are bloomers?" I asked, thinking Scotty was acting like a moron.

"You know, those long, loose underwear the women used to wear back when our mothers were young," Scotty retorted.

"My mother never wore bloomers. Did your mother?" I questioned. I couldn't imagine Alice wearing bloomers ever. I knew Scotty had no idea what he was talking about.

"Maybe in the 1890s or something like that era women might have worn bloomers. I don't think one could find bloomers outside of a museum, and even if one could, I wouldn't be caught wearing them," I said indignantly.

"What are you going to wear under that skirt then?" Scotty asked nervously.

"I was thinking of wearing my thong!" I looked at Scotty to get his reaction and noticed his jaw-dropping wide open. I couldn't help but laugh.

"Do you need to wear that skirt? I think your leather pants would get enough reaction. I am not comfortable with you wearing that in public. How am I going to be able to watch for car thieves if I need to keep both eyes on you?" Scotty said seriously.

"I promise not to bend over. Also, we don't plan to be in the mall long if you and Sam find the thieves. It will just be a matter of parking, getting their attention, and coming back out in a few minutes with a shopping bag. I mean, we need to be somewhat convincing, don't you think?"

Scotty nodded and dropped his car keys, he looked at me with a wicked grin and asked if I would pick them up for him. Laughing, I bent over to retrieve his keys, watching him watch me the whole time.

Scotty suggested we go into the bedroom. "No way am I getting my skirt wrinkled. I need to wear it tomorrow," I said coyly.

"So, take it off," Scotty said as he moved in and gave me a hug.

CHAPTER SEVENTEEN

The next morning, we all met at the office again. Aileen had the Camry parked outside. She commented that Captain Jones made sure the license plate holder did not have the car rental agency name. He wanted to make sure the car seemed ordinary in every way.

Andrea and Tish were dressed to kill. I could see that Sam was every bit as uneasy about Andrea's short skirt as Scotty had seemed the previous night. I couldn't help but make matters worse by telling Andrea that we should plan a girl's night out and wear the skirts.

"Not funny!" Sam and Scotty said in unison.

"Okay, give us a chance to get in place and check out the mall before you head our way. Maybe an hour or so will be enough time for us to get into uniforms and scout around. Park nearby so you can hear us over the walkie-talkie. Try to find a parking place as close to the entrance as possible. We want you to be very noticeable," Scotty said professionally.

Once again, I couldn't resist, "Noticeable, you say. Like we should drop our keys on the way into the mall?"

This time I just got a glare from Scotty, "Not funny!"

Aileen and Patrick joined Andrea and me in laughter as Sam and Scotty stomped out of the office. Somehow, the two guys did not seem to have a sense of humor today.

We talked with Aileen and Patrick for about an hour. It was planned for Andrea and me to take the Camry to the safe house the Jamiesons had allowed us to use once before when we were investigating a jewelry theft. It was a lovely house, and I was excited to get to stay there overnight.

The plan was for us to drive home from the mall and park in the driveway, where it would be easier for thieves to access. Andrea and I would go into the house and stay the evening waiting for Scotty and Sam to let us know if anything suspicious was happening. While we would be warm and cozy, Sam and Scotty would be in the surveillance van watching the Camry.

Captain Jones would have two officers available within a few blocks, also waiting for a call. When Scotty alerted us to anything suspicious, we were to phone Captain Jones, who would inform the officers to be ready.

Patrick and Aileen insisted they would also be spending the night at the safe house with us. The Jamiesons have had this safe house for years. It has served them well. Now, once again, we would be using it to keep the thieves from knowing where we lived. The thought of undesirables knowing where we lived caused me to shudder. I was glad Patrick and Aileen would be with us. With years of experience, they were rock solid and never made amateurish mistakes. It made me feel confident, knowing they would not let us do anything stupid.

It was time for Andrea and me to get into position. We took along some soft drinks and snacks. We had no idea how long we would be sitting before we got the call to park at the mall. Oddly enough, we did not even have time to open one drink before the walkie-talkie clicked on.

"Ladies, do you hear me?" Scotty said over his hand-held set.

"Yes, Scotty, we can hear you loud and clear," I answered back. "Are you ready for us to come to the mall, and where should we park?"

The clicking could be heard again as Scotty told us which store entrance to head for. We acknowledged receiving his message and started the car.

I knew precisely where Scotty wanted us to park. I drove down the aisle heading straight for the mall with Andrea looking for an open parking place close to the entrance. As luck would have it, a lady pulled out of the closest parking spot just as we were approaching. I spotted three men loitering near the entrance and figured these were the men Scotty and Sam were watching.

One was smoking a cigarette while the other two were watching the parking lot casually. Most people would not have paid any attention to them except to give them room. All three of them looked rough around the edges, and hardly someone, especially a woman, would stop to hold a conversation.

We pulled into the parking spot and decided to make ourselves conspicuous by laughing, loudly, as we departed the car as if we were sharing a hilarious joke. We knew our looks alone would probably catch their attention, but why leave anything to chance.

I saw Sam a distance from the entrance pushing his broom along the sidewalk. I didn't see Scotty. I figured he was going for the surveillance van. I knew the guys planned to tail the three men if they followed us when we left the mall.

Andrea and I continued acting silly and walked slower than most people would to the mall entrance. I glanced quickly to see if the men were watching us, and we're not surprised to see all six eyes on us. So far, so good.

We went to the mall. It was hard to pretend to be shopping since we were excited about the plan to catch the thieves. Andrea reminded me that we needed to walk out with a shopping bag in hand. We need to buy something. The closest store was a baby store.

We headed to the store. Andrea grabbed the first thing she saw, which was a stuffed bear. I followed suit and grabbed some diapers. We went to the register and paid for the items noticing the rude look we were receiving from the matronly clerk who obviously disapproved of our short skirts.

Smiling, we waved goodbye to her and left the store. Andrea looked at her watch.

"That only took three minutes. We should stay away longer than that. For two women to go inside a mall and out again in three minutes is unheard of. We should stay for at least 30 minutes."

I groaned. I hated shopping, and I hated malls. I like to get in, get what I need, and get out. Now, pretending was starting to annoy me.

"Let's go get an Orange Julius if we need to stay here longer," I said to Andrea.

"I'm not in the mood for Orange Julius. Can't we find something else to drink? There is a donut shop not far from here," Andrea persuaded.

We headed for the donut shop, and Andrea bought several donuts. "These are for Sam. He loves donuts. I know you thought they were for me since I am a cop, but I haven't gotten that brainwashed...yet."

I laughed at her joke about donuts and cops. I knew some cops ate donuts since there were few places open early in the morning, but I also knew that the poked fun was overstated. Scotty, on the other hand, would be considered the stereotypical cop...if he was a cop. He would have eaten the bag as well. I decided to buy a few donuts for him.

We drank our coffee, checked our watches, and decided we could leave the mall. Oddly enough, the three men were nowhere in sight when we left. Puzzled, I pulled out of the parking spot. I wondered whether to head to the safe house or back to the office when I noticed a black Dodge Charger pulling in behind us. Without being obvious, I looked behind me and saw three men. I knew it was the same thugs Scotty and Sam were watching.

I drove slowly back towards the safe house, not wanting to lose them, but I realized I didn't need to go slow. These guys were good at shadowing us. They stayed just far enough behind that I knew they were there, but only because I had made them back at the mall.

The click from the walkie-talkie was heard, and I watched Andrea answer without putting the two-way radio to her ear. I realized she was smart. She knew if she put it up to her ear, there was a good chance the guys following would see her.

"Andrea, this is Sam. You guys need to be more animated. Put on the radio, sing along, and act like you are having fun. The guys tailing you are good. They will become suspicious if you don't act more casual. Try varying your speed, acting less in control, like you're preoccupied with having fun."

"Got it. Will do," Andrea answered back.

"We think we have been made...we are turning at the next corner. Let us know if anything weird happens; otherwise, we will be driving parallel to you," Sam said and doubled clicked off.

Turning on the radio, singing at the top of our lungs while waving our arms in the air like maniacs, we couldn't help but be noticed. I was sure the men stalking us would think we were just crazy girls trying to have fun and not suspect we were bait.

We pulled into the driveway and turned the car off, locking it as we walked away. Aileen greeted us from the kitchen.

"Hi, ladies. Come on in. I have some dinner cooking. Why don't you go change your clothes, and we can eat, watch some T.V. and relax? Patrick is in the garage. Two police officers are a couple of blocks away waiting for the Captain's call, and we have nothing more to do but chill."

"Hey, wait. What do you mean? Are we off the case now? We lured them in, and now we do nothing more?" I did not like the idea. I wanted to be there to make sure nothing happened to Scotty, and I was sure Andrea felt just as protective about Sam.

"Ladies, ladies, ladies...I didn't say we would be doing nothing, but we must continue the charade. We are being watched by now. If you don't act normally, you will cause them to rabbit," Aileen said, and I realized her experience was showing.

"Gotcha! I'm sorry. You are right. We will change and be right back down." Andrea and I went upstairs to change our clothes.

"You want to keep those guys interested?" Andrea asked.

"What are you getting at now?" I asked.

"How about teasing them a little and changing our clothes next to the open curtains?" Andrea giggled.

"Andrea, you are bad!" I exclaimed. "My father drilled into my head that curtains are drawn the minute it starts to get dark. I would never dream of changing my clothes in front of an open window. Were you raised in a bordello?" I asked kiddingly.

Andrea laughed. "You don't need to join in. It only takes one of us to keep their attention. You might be shocked to learn I was an exotic dancer before I joined the police academy." She wiggled out of her tight little skirt and threw her top off over her head.

I could only imagine what the guys were doing in the black Dodge Charger parked across the street. For being professionals, they were acting rather dumb.

Shortly, I could hear the car as it drove away. I knew they would be back as soon as it was dark. Maybe if for no other reason than to catch the second half of the peep show.

We came down the stairs giggling, and Aileen asked us what was so funny. I decided that sharing Andrea's little strip tease adventure was up to her. When she did not say anything, I tried to cover by talking about the stuffed bear and diapers that we purchased at the mall. Aileen seemed to buy the story since it really was ridiculous for us to have spent money on something neither of us would need for years to come.

"You can donate them to the women's shelter, you know. Or if you want your money back, you can return them. You haven't opened the diapers yet, have you?" Aileen said with a wink.

I began to wonder if she bought my cover story or not. If she drilled me later when Andrea was not around, I would know she had not.

Dinner was on the table. Aileen said the chances are the criminals would not be back until late at night. She was feeling bad for the guys. They had the job of staying in cramped quarters with no food or very little food since the van was stocked only with snacks. Patrick had a thermos of coffee and a sandwich while we were eating crab salads and chocolate mousse for dessert.

"Wowee! You made chocolate mousse?" I asked. "I love chocolate, and chocolate mousse is one of my favorites." I totally forgot about the guys at that moment.

"It is easier than a person thinks," Aileen admitted. "Come on, let's eat and relax. We have a long night ahead of us. We will be sitting quietly in the dark in case we are needed. I already have the phone and a flashlight inside the closet. That way, I can make the call without any lights being turned on in the house. We don't want to give away the fact that we aren't in bed sound asleep."

We ate, did the dishes, and turned on the television. It was too early to pretend to be asleep. When 11:00 p.m. came around, Aileen yawned and told us it was time to go to bed. We doubted the carjackers were watching, but it was best to keep to the plan just in case one was assigned to watch.

We undress, Andrea in front of the window once again. I was beginning to think she missed her life on stage. I drew the shades, turned off the lights, and dressed back into my dark clothes ready for action. Andrea followed suit and put on dark jeans, a dark turtleneck sweater, and running shoes. I had on my boots.

We carefully descended the stairs in the dark. Aileen whispered from the den. It was pitch-black in the house, but our eyes adjusted enough to navigate around without bumping into furniture. Now it was time for us just to sit and wait.

The clock struck midnight, and nothing happened. Andrea was getting drowsy. I felt her head drop on my shoulder. My first impulse was to shrug her off, but I stopped myself and let her sleep. Aileen breathed a sigh near me. She was still awake.

Aileen opened one window a crack, near the driveway. It would not be noticed by the crooks, but it gave us a way to listen for noises outside.

Two o'clock chimed. Aileen hushed us as I gently woke Andrea. We thought we heard a shuffling noise in the driveway. I wanted to crawl to the window to look, but as I started to head that direction, Aileen put her hand on mine to stop me. I stopped.

We sat quietly, listening for any more sounds. A metal scraping and a muted thwacking sound could barely be heard. My hunch was it was the sound of the bump key being used to open the Camry's door.

From the garage, I heard Patrick's thermos hitting the floor. I looked at Aileen, whose eyes were wide open. She was crawling towards the closet as fast as she could without making any noise.

I crawled the opposite way to the window. I saw there were four men by the Camry, but one was heading towards the garage. I knew Patrick was in trouble when I caught the glint of a wrench in the moonlight.

Everything happened quickly after that. The Camry's engine was started. I saw Sam jump out of the back of the van. Scotty, who had backed in and parked in the neighbor's driveway, started the van.

Just as the Camry was being backed out, Scotty drove the van in front of Jamiesons' driveway blocking the Camry's escape. The doors of the Camry flew open, and three of the men jumped out, running in all directions.

I grabbed Andrea, and we bolted out the door to follow the perp who ran past the back-garage door, heading for the alley. Andrea was fast, and she out-ran me by a few feet. Closing the distance between herself and the stocky man we were following, I forced myself to pump my legs faster. I did not want Andrea to reach the man alone.

Turning to face Andrea, the man raised his fist to sucker punch her just as I dove and tackled Andrea. His closed fist missed her face as she went down, and I rolled, knocking the man off his feet. The three of us were a tangle of arms and legs until I could get a hold of his arm and force it behind his back.

Andrea grabbed her handcuffs from the jeans back waistband and slapped them on the wrist I had contained. Grabbing the other arm, she twisted it behind his back to apply the second cuff. We dragged him back to the driveway to find the other three men subdued as well.

Sam quickly came to Andrea's side to inspect her. The bruises she sported were from me, but I doubt Andrea would squeal. Andrea would have received worse if the brute of a man smashed in her jaw.

I glanced at her with an apologetic look, and she grinned. She knew I had just saved her from a fractured jaw.

The police car sirens were heard coming to our address. Aileen made her call to Captain Jones, and the dispatcher did her job. The officers questioned the men in custody to find out where the man who drove the Dodge Charger had gone. All of them were quiet until I stepped behind the guy Andrea and I had cuffed. I found his thumb, and none too gently pulled it out of its socket.

He screamed, quickly telling the officer the name and address of the chop shop where they would find the driver of the Dodge Charger. He received several attempted kicks from his comrades until we could pull them away from the stool pigeon.

One officer radioed into the department requesting officers to go to the address to see if the Dodge Charger was at the chop shop. The handcuffed perps were taken to the police cars to be booked. Once again, we were told to follow to make our statements. Andrea and Sam would have paperwork to fill out.

Before heading to the police department, we took a minute to find out what each experienced. Patrick told how embarrassed he had been to knock the thermos off his car. "It was just plain clumsiness," he said. He went on to say that when he opened the garage door, he was about to be clubbed to death, but Sam sprang out of nowhere and took the criminal down.

Shouting for Patrick to chase the fleeing man who was heading for his neighbor's fenced backyard, Patrick took pursuit. He did not need to run far, as the man was older and more cumbersome and couldn't quite make it over the fence. Patrick said all he had to do was pull the man down by his legs and draw his gun.

Scotty said his man headed for the street. Jumping out, just as the van stopped, Scotty recalled how fast the man was running. He was the younger, fitter, and faster car thief.

"I knew I was in for a battle," Scotty said melodramatically. "Luckily, I still jog most days to keep in shape. I kicked myself into high gear and ran him down. He was zig-zagging, thinking he could outmaneuver me. Little did he know he was dealing with the State Champion Quarterback!"

I interrupted Scotty at this point in his story. "Yeah, yeah, yeah. We get the idea. You tackled him, right?"

"Excuse me. I was not a tackle. I just ran the thief into a street lamp pole. The stupid idiot was so busy looking back at me that he knocked himself out. Easiest arrest I have ever made," Scotty said with a big toothy grin.

Hugging him, I let Andrea tell how we caught the fourth guy. She did not even leave out my tackle to save her from a broken jaw. I was impressed with her truthfulness when I was giving her an out.

Aileen asked if we had time for some coffee before we needed to head to the police department. It was late, but we were not tired. We were all running on pure adrenalin. We were about to decline until

Andrea remembered the donuts she and I had bought. We all filed into the house.

Once at the police department, we were pleased to see the police officers brought in the chop shop owner and the driver of the black Dodge Charger. Two officers were joking and laughing with Sam and Andrea. I recognized them from a previous rookie training class and went over to say hi.

"You should have been there, Tish," laughed Paul. "The owner is so stupid; he actually kept every license plate from every car the group stole. He had them nailed up on the walls of the bathroom in the back of the storage area. How incriminating is that?"

I couldn't believe it either, that anyone would be that dumb as to keep something that would tie them to the stolen cars. Laughing, I said, "Good thing for us that these criminals were dumb. Can you imagine how the scenario would have played out if they were smart?"

Sam stopped laughing. "You are right. Andrea would have been hurt; Patrick would be dead, and who knows about the rest of us."

"Well, it ended just the way we hoped, but it should give you some pause. Undercover work is not always as easy as this." I left my next comment, unsaid. I was about to ask him if he and Andrea really wanted to go undercover to catch the rapists. I feel confident this next undercover case will be far more dangerous.

Captain Jones came out of his office and motioned for all of us to join him. The only one missing from the team was Aileen.

"First off, Patrick, please tell Aileen how much I appreciated the fact that she kept me informed. Without her telling me the address of the chop shop, I couldn't have gotten the search warrant to the officers as quickly as we needed to keep them from bolting. I know she was making calls in the dark from the closet at times.

Secondly, great teamwork. You managed to catch the criminals red-handed, and no one was hurt. Surprising, since Tish and Scotty were involved," Captain Jones smiled as he said this.

"Andrea and Sam, you proved to be quite valuable to the team. You both kept cool heads and Sam; you kept Patrick from having his skull caved in. Good police work, both of you."

I was impressed by how well Sam took the compliment from his uncle. It seemed as if their relationship was improving. If Sam continued like he was heading, he was going to be an asset when he went undercover in the hospital. I wished I could be there to watch him in action.

Captain Jones continued, interrupting my thoughts. "Andrea and Sam, you know after your assignment undercover in the hospital that you will be beat-cops for quite a while. I see good things in your future, but there are valuable things to be learned on the streets. Sam, I know you want to get to the heart of the drug rings in our old neighborhood. I won't be able to assign you to those streets as a beat-cop if you are serious about going undercover sometime soon."

Sam said, "I understand completely, Captain. I will accept whatever assignment is given until the time that I can do the undercover work that I need to do to make our neighborhood safe."

Once again, I was impressed with Sam's new-found maturity. He called his uncle, Captain. That was a good step forward for him. I was really beginning to like this guy.

CHAPTER EIGHTEEN

Scotty reminded me that my tournament was starting in two days and asked me if I was ready? We were finally home after a very long but rewarding night catching thieves. Snuggling on the couch, I looked up at him and said, "I am sure a good night's sleep and one last session with the grandmaster is all I will need to be ready."

It might sound cocky to anyone else. Scotty knew how hard I worked every day to be as good as I am in the many forms of martial arts that I can perform. Of course, I would not be near as good without Grandmaster Kim Yong-Sool. I still marvel at how much he has taught me. The fact that I know things that I can't share with Scotty gives me some anxiety. We are in a relationship that is based on openness and honesty.

We almost broke up when I kept the fact from him that Heather was alive and not dead. I promised never to keep anything from him again, and here I am with a secret I can never reveal. But a promise is a promise. I swore to the grandmaster never to disclose to anyone what he is teaching me.

I guess I was too deep in thought, that I did not even realize Scotty had scooped me up to take me into the bedroom. "Boy, you must be tired. You didn't even resist one little bit when I picked you up. You usually start to scream something about me dropping you," Scotty said as he entered the bedroom.

"I am tired. Aren't you?" I asked to deflect another question.

Yawning, Scotty admitted that he was exhausted. He said something about not being comfortable in the cramped van with Sam. I was only listening with one ear. I was still trying to convince myself that not telling Scotty was not really lying. That same logic had backfired once before.

"Are you going to take a nap with me?" I asked as I pulled Scotty towards me on the bed.

"Is this an invitation, or are you really talking about sleep?" Scotty asked.

"Sleep, first," I said as I snuggled into Scotty's waiting arms. I was tired enough that I fell asleep almost instantly.

Awaking slowly, I looked at the clock. I knew I needed to get up and moving if I was going to get to the dojang on time. All classes were canceled so Tony and the grandmaster could prepare the dojang for the tournament. I knew any offer of help would be much appreciated. I wanted to get there early enough to lend a helping hand before Tony left, and my lesson began.

Scotty said he had a few things that he needed to get done. I figured he would go to the grocery store and make dinner, knowing I would be occupied for the afternoon and into the early evening. It is nice to know that I do not need to ask for help; Scotty is always there for me.

Kissing him on the lips, I slipped out of bed and changed clothes. I had napped in the same clothes I had worn last night. I put on loose-fitting clothes and kicked my tight jeans under the bed. I smiled when I thought about how Scotty was becoming a neat freak, and I was now the sloppy one. I knew when he woke up and saw my black jeans sticking out from under the bed that I would be in for a scolding when I got home. It was now just part of our game.

I locked the door behind me and headed for the garage. The night would be chilly, but right now, I could ride my Harley and not worry about my leather jacket. I still tucked my jacket neatly into the saddlebags, knowing I would be glad to have it on the way home.

I arrived at the dojang in about five minutes. Entering the door, I could see relief flood across Tony's face. "Great! Reinforcements."

I smiled at Tony and asked what I needed to do to help. He indicated paperwork on a long table. All the entries required to be arranged in levels for the competitions. Medals, certificates, as well as belts, needed to be organized. Not everyone would advance, and that was part of the problem. It was essential Tony would know who was competing for a higher belt and who was just competing to compete for the experience. The one with the most accumulated points would be the Champion of Champions. The title was one the grandmaster came up with for this tournament. I don't remember competing before where there was one person set apart from the others.

Grandmaster Kim Yong-Sool entered with another gentleman as Tony and I were busy doing our separate tasks. Tony was laying out mats and setting up chairs for spectators as I continued with organizing the competitor lists.

"Tony, Tish, I want you to meet Chung Moo-Hung Sa Bom Nim. While I am gone, he will be the master here." Turning to Sa Bom Nim, the grandmaster continued talking directly to him. "Tish will no longer be instructing here after the tournament. She has been my pupil, and I am pleased with her abilities. Tony will continue under your care. He will be Shihan Dai to you and will help to run the classes."

Sa Bom Nim bowed to both students. His eyes went to the office, and Grandmaster Kim Yong-Sool led the way and closed the door.

Tony quietly said, "Do you think he speaks English? The fact the grandmaster introduced him using the Korean word for a 4th Dan or higher as his title makes me suspicious that I may need to learn Korean in the grandmaster's absence."

I said, "You may have a point. I guess we won't know until Chung Sa Bom Nim decides to speak to you directly. I think it would be impolite to ask Grandmaster Kim Yong-Sool anything very personal. I do know that Chung Sa Bom Nim is a 6th Dan from the markings on his belt. We had better get back to work. We have a ton of setup to do before tomorrow."

Tony still had some concerns. "I guess the grandmaster really is leaving. I was hoping he would change his mind. Do you think he is ill?"

"He will tell us what he wants us to know and nothing more. Just how chatty has he ever been?" I left it at that and went back to the table, sorting the medals and belts.

Glancing towards the window of the office, I noted Chung Sa Bom Nim was medium height, bald and stocky. It was apparent he was muscled under his monk's gray robe. His eyes gave no hint into his soul. Often, I can tell from the eyes if a person is good-humored or ill-tempered. I had no idea what kind of person Tony would be dealing with. For Tony's sake, I hoped, at least, he is kind.

About an hour later, as I was finishing my tasks and felt that things were organized enough that Tony would have little trouble with registration in the morning, I got up from my chair. The door opened from the office, and the two grandmasters entered the dojang.

"Tony," Grandmaster Kim Yong-Sool said, directing the conversation to him, "I will be taking Chung Sa Bom Nim to my home. He will live in my house while I am gone. Tomorrow, Chung Sa Bom Nim will be one of the judges alongside me. I know you have asked two ladies to do the registration and to help hand out certificates. Chung Sa Bom Nim and I will present medals and belts. You will stand beside us and hand them to us as we need them." No other words were exchanged. Tony bowed to the grandmasters as did I as they left the dojang.

"You may be right, Tony. If Chung Sa Bom Nim does not speak English, what will you do? It won't be easy to take a crash course in Korean. I know I would be in trouble if I was staying. If you don't have anything else that needs my attention, I think I will head back home. I promised myself a good night's sleep. I want to be ready for the tournament tomorrow," I said as I began heading towards the door.

"Tish," Tony said, stopping me from opening the door, "I have studied martial arts for three years now. During the past year, I put in more hours than I can count. I tested out at a high enough level to make the grandmaster comfortable with my being a full instructor here. If I prove myself, I will be a 1st Gup Red Belt with Black Stripe. You are testing for your 4th Dan Black Belt. You are a couple of years younger than I am. How have you gotten so far in Hapkido at your age? Have you really been studying for fifteen years?"

I answered Tony with as brief a run-down as possible. I wanted to get home and relax as well as spend some time with Scotty.

"I have been studying intensely since I was eleven. Before that, I was just interested in martial arts and took classes more casually. Once I realized how valuable Hapkido was, I just threw myself into the work. I went to classes daily instead of just two days a week for all those years. I progressed rapidly through the belts until I got to your stage. I am actually on-schedule if you take into consideration that I have studied several other forms of martial arts besides Hapkido." Smiling, I waved and went out of the building.

I could see Tony trying to figure out the years and where I should be at the belt level. I decided it was a great brain exercise for him. Tony would never figure out how I did it without knowing the number of hours I put in.

I remember my mother complaining that she never got to see her little girl. My father would drop me off after school and pick me up after all the other students had left. I am not sure how much they paid for all the individual instructions I received. There is so much that I will never be able to repay my parents.

I pulled out my jacket, put it on to fend off the lake wind chill, and rode home to Scotty. As I pulled into the driveway and on into the garage, I was once again pleased to see Scotty standing at the back door. He had a cup of hot tea in his hand and placed it in mine as I walked inside.

"Thanks, I am going to enjoy this tea." Handing it back to him while I slipped out of my jacket, I turned and took it back from him. I kissed him gently on the lips, and we went into the kitchen. Lifting the lid from a pot, I saw Scotty made a mouth-watering beef stew.

"Not too heavy and not too light is what I was thinking. It has carrots, potatoes, celery, and of course, beef. I made a salad. You might just want a small bowl of stew and a salad. That way, you won't feel weighed down for tomorrow. I think you will do well with yogurt and fresh fruit for breakfast, but I can make you pancakes if you need to carb-up before the tournament. What do you say?" Scotty was asking for my opinion and my approval.

"I think the stew is going to be perfect. I also like your idea of yogurt and fresh fruit. If I am hungry, I might eat one piece of cinnamon toast. Pancakes might be a bit much. Often, fighters don't eat hardly anything for weeks before a fight to make sure they are at the right weight. Combat Hapkido is boxing, you know. I mean, we can box, but it isn't the same as being in the ring with Evander Holyfield or anything like that."

Leading the way to the set table, Scotty pulled the chair out for me to be seated. "Dinner will be served in one minute. Are you good with hot tea and a glass of water, or would you like iced tea?"

I indicated I was good with the hot tea and water and waiting patiently while Scotty dished up the dinner. I never know what Scotty will decide to cook when he is left to his own devices. I just love the fact that he tries hard to please me.

We sat and talked about Chung Sa Bom Nim as we ate. "You mean he wears the traditional fighting monk's robes and has a shaved head?" Scotty asked excitedly.

I knew Scotty was thinking about all the Bruce Lee movies he had ever seen. In fact, if I had not introduced Scotty to Hapkido, he would think the only martial art was Jeet Kune Do (The Way of the Intercepting Fist).

"I don't even know if Chung Sa Bom Nim speaks English or not. He did not say a word to Tony or me. I am feeling a little sorry for Tony if Chung Sa Bom Nim does not speak any English. I suppose he will get across what he wants one way or another.

"What really bothers me is the fact that Grandmaster Kim Yong-Sool is really leaving, and no one knows why or for how long," I said sadly.

"You really don't know why he is leaving?" Scotty said as he looked straight into my eyes.

For a second, I could see the doubt in Scotty's eyes. He knew, from the past, I can keep things from him. I was relieved when I saw trust restored in them again.

"Both Captain Jones and Tony have mentioned something being wrong. We have never talked since my lessons are difficult and hard work. With the amount of intensity each lesson takes, I think neither one of us has anything left for small talk. If Tony thinks the grandmaster is ill, I sure don't see any obvious signs of it. I just don't know...."

I told Scotty how Chung Sa Bom Nim would be one of the judges tomorrow. "You will be able to watch and see for yourself whether he will be an asset to the dojang. I don't suppose the grandmaster would bring in just anyone to be the sensei while he is away. I get the sense that Chung Sa Bom Nim may be disappointed with the commitment levels of the present students at the dojang. Few can match Tony's determination at this point. I am hoping more of the police rookies will want to further their skills by taking classes at the dojang. They would be a higher, more dedicated caliber of students for Tony to teach. A grandmaster wants a Shihan Dai to excel under his tutelage, developing worthy Hapkido students that the grandmaster can instruct."

"I will do the dishes. Why don't you take a nice, long bath and relax? I think it will help you get to sleep. A night of good long sleep will do both of us a lot of good. Leave some hot water, and I might join you in the bath."

I laughed. "The last time you tried to take a bath with me, your legs had to hang out of the tub. You know that the tub is not built for a man of your height. There is barely room in it for me to slip down under the bubbles and relax. If you crawl in, I will need to curl up into a small ball. The water displacement alone would probably pop me into the air, and I would bounce around the room.". I was hoping the bath would relax me enough to feel like rubber.

"Okay, no bath, but I could give you a massage after your bath, so your muscles are nice and supple and ready for all the rough stuff you are in for tomorrow," Scotty offered.

"I will definitely take you up on that offer," I said as I closed the door to the bathroom.

The next morning was supposed to be an early start. The alarm was set, but I did not need it. I was up way before the alarm went off. I left Scotty sleeping, and I went downstairs to work on my ground flow. It was optional for the requirements, but I did not know Chung Sa Bom Nim, and I had no idea if he would expect the technique to be demonstrated or not.

Hearing Scotty in the kitchen, I went upstairs for a quick shower and a change of clothes. Scotty had a nutritious breakfast waiting, but not a large one. He knew I did not want to be loaded down with carbohydrates even though he thought it was the way to go.

We ate quietly. Scotty had the good sense to let me take the time to center myself. I believe his shooting competition helped much for him to understand my needs. It was just another reason I loved him as much as I do.

We drove separately. I was on my Harley, and Scotty drove the Double-Nickel. I told him I would need to stay longer to help clean up. Even though Scotty volunteered to stay and help, I knew I would want to talk to Grandmaster Kim Yong-Sool alone. If my hunch were correct, he would be leaving right after the tournament. There was a lot I wanted to ask him if he was open to the conversation.

We entered the dojang to a crowd already forming. Students of Tony's were handling the registration table. I felt I had everything organized well enough that they would have no trouble registering the candidates.

Folding chairs lined three walls of the dojang. Mats covered the floor, and a line formed at the registration table. I was happy to see some of my students in the line even though; I knew they would be there. I was proud of my younger students. Many showed great promise. I was feeling conflicted by giving up my teaching job when I graduated. Part of me felt like I was abandoning them even though I knew Tony would do a great job with them.

Technically, Tony did not have a full teaching certificate, but his abilities allowed him to assist by instructing the younger students. Chung Sa Bom Nim will be teaching all advanced classes.

Entering the dojang, was the Grandmaster Kim Yong-Sool and Chung Sa Bom Nim. Tony immediately called the students to attention, and all bowed to the teachers. The judges took their place at the judging table and sat quietly. It was time to start; Tony clapped his hands once. All students gathered and faced Tony, I included. Tony commanded aloud:

"Do Rha!" We turned and faced the flags,

"Kyung Yet!" We bowed to the flags,

"Doe Rha!" We turned and faced our sensei,

"Kyung Yet!" We bowed to the sensei,

"An Jo!" We all sat down cross-legged.

The younger students started first. Each was called forward to demonstrate the traditional Kicho Hyeong form. The judges look at energy, speed, precision, and control as each student demonstrated long stances, low blocks, middle punches, and front kicks. Belts were awarded immediately, and I swelled with pride watching my newest class turn in their little white belts with yellow stripes for their yellow belts. The students I taught when I first arrived at the dojang, we're adding a red stripe to their blue belt. I could hardly believe I was with some of these students for just over two years now.

The older students went next, and the forms became more creative and acrobatic as they demonstrated their abilities. Students came from surrounding dojangs as well as our own.

I marveled when Tony was called forth. He had gained a lot of knowledge since Grandmaster Kim Yong-Sool took him on as his protege. Watching for calmness under pressure, Tony excelled as he sparred with multiple attackers. I saw no fear or anger as he completed his tasks. Going from brown belt to red belt would not allow Tony to have his instructors license. It would be years yet before Tony could have his own dojang, but I could see he had the right stuff to make it.

I was almost startled to hear my name called along with two other students from a different dojang. We would be asked to demonstrate our forms before we would be asked to spar two times for two minutes each. One would be against multiple opponents.

A young man named Gerard was the first to perform his Jee Pahng Ee. His technique with the cane was proper but not fluid. He obviously, was concentrating on power and energy over precision and control. I noted his form, knowing he would be one of my sparring partners.

Tyler was the next one on the mat. He also lacked control with many of his kicks, but his punches were fast and precise. I focused my studies on his movements carefully. Knowledge was power, my teacher said.

I was called in as a second with Tyler. Gerard was also called upon to be part of the two-person opponents sparring. Tyler started his sparring as expected, but halfway through, Tyler allowed his anger to take charge. He became unnecessarily rough with the takedowns he was to demonstrate. His cane landed brutally upon both of us as he used the cane to knock us off our feet or pin us to the ground by our throats.

I looked to the judges to see if they would intervene. I realized I needed to defend myself even though this was Tyler, who was being judged.

Doing the best that I could to follow protocol during the sparring match, I deflected the cane from landing any more blows, frustrating Tyler. His anger was mounting, and his strikes were now being aimed only at one of the opponents...me.

The judges called the match. Reluctantly, Tyler stopped, turned to the masters, and bowed. As he bowed to me, his eyes tried to bore holes into my soul. I knew I was up next, and I was in for trouble.

I demonstrated my forms with efficiency and fluidity. I floated through the exercises, but the energy was noticeable when it was needed. I added creativity, especially with many of the kicks. I held kicks longer and higher to show my balance and poise. I felt I had demonstrated my abilities superbly and was satisfied with what I demonstrated.

The signal was given, and my single opponent sparring was next. Gerard came forward. We bowed, and he approached as was required with punches, kicks, attempted takedowns, and holds. Maneuvering and out-maneuvering him allowed me to block each attempt he made. When holds were necessary to prove I could get out of them, I did so swiftly and with little effort. The two minutes flew by, and time was called.

Gerard was now joined by Tyler. With canes in hand, the signal was given, and the sparring began. Tyler immediately charged at me with his cane held in both hands, like a sword, high above his head. He struck down with a swift and strong force. He became irritated when I nimbly side-stepped his cane. In a single move forward, I used my cane to slam behind his knees, bringing him to the ground. I side-stepped, quickly again, this time to avoid the cane wheeled by Gerard. He seemed just as frustrated as Tyler. Side-twirling in a 360, I slap-kicked Gerard in the head and knocked him to the ground.

I was hoping the masters noted that I needed to protect myself from my opponent's aggressive and harmful moves with their canes. I tried to block each attack with finesse and control. I did not show concern that my opponents were not conducting themselves in a manner associated with our training.

My defense escalated as the attacks became more and more fierce. Out of the side of my eye, I saw the signal from Grandmaster Kim Yong-Sool to finish the sparring. With rapid blocks and kicks, I disarmed each opponent of their cane and quickly turned to face each without my cane.

Gerard charged foolishly, and I used his force against him, letting him rush by as I did a backflip side-kicking him to the ground. Without a milli-second to gather my wits, Tyler launched upon me, slamming into my backside with his head and shoulder, knocking me to the mats. I rolled quickly away from his body. I used my long legs to wrap under his arm and around his neck while holding his left arm in an armlock until he tapped-out to be released.

The sparring was over, but I knew I made two enemies. I knew the grandmaster judges would complain to the masters of their dojang's for their unsportsmanlike conduct. Unfortunately, martial arts can attract the wrong type of person.

Before the belts were awarded, I learned I would also be the Champion of Champions.

The grandmasters agreed that Gerard would get his next level, but Tyler was disgraced. Grandmaster Kim Yong-Sool said with dignity, that Tyler lacked self-control and did not show he was ready for the next level. I was now a 4th Dan, and I could hardly contain my excitement.

Bowing, two of us accepted our belts and medals, while one stood seething in anger and hatred. Once I received the Champion of Champions medal, Tyler, without bowing, turned and exited the dojang. Gerard exited soon behind him.

My students surrounded me, and I felt immersed in love and admiration. I could see Scotty beaming on the outskirts of the crowd, waiting for his turn to congratulate me and give me a well-deserved hug and kiss.

I, in turn, told each of my students how proud I was of them and their personal accomplishments that day. I would still be teaching at the dojang for a few more months; there was no need to dampen the excitement by telling them that I would no longer be their instructor. There was plenty of time for that announcement.

Parents came forward next to congratulate and thank me for what I had done for their children. Many told quick stories about how martial arts was changing their child for the better. Words like confidence, improved study habits, weight loss for one of my chubbier little students, and respectfulness were used. I think the parents were most surprised by how humble their children had become.

Slowly, the crowd thinned, and I got my hug and kiss from Scotty. He stayed to help put away the folding chairs, tables, and mats. When Grandmaster Kim Yong-Sool and Chung Sa Bom Nim came out of the office, each bowed to the other, and then Chung Sa Bom Nim left the dojang. My grandmaster called me into his office.

"You are the only student I have called by the first name, Tish. From the very first day we met, I knew you would be special. That is one of the reasons I have over-stepped my boundaries and have taught you sacred techniques. I know I have asked you never to reveal these techniques or to teach them to anyone under any circumstances. I now must request a solemn promise again, on your part never to do so," my grandmaster said.

I looked him in the eyes and said, "I swear, with all my heart, that I will never reveal or teach anyone what you have taught me."

"It is because I fear for your life that I ask this of you," he said.

I looked at him questioningly but knew not to ask. If the grandmaster wanted to tell me more, he would. A part of me was afraid to find out why he felt my life would be at risk.

"I can see from your eyes that you would like to ask questions. I can also see from your eyes that you have concerns. I must ask for your forgiveness for putting you at risk. I was a foolish old man who felt no one would ever find out."

Now, I was genuinely puzzled and even more concerned than before. I started to open my mouth but stopped myself. I knew I should let the grandmaster proceed at his own pace and on his own terms.

He said, "I was once a Guardian of Sacred Rituals at the monastery. It was my job to enforce the laws. One law was the mystical martial arts could not be passed on without the permission of the Council. Doing so could be punishable by death. As a younger man, I was one of the enforcers. I have followed the rules and doled out punishment when needed. When I became too old to be an effective guardian, I came to America to open my own dojang. I have obeyed all the rules until the night you were attacked by your student's abusive husband. His intention to kill you stirred my protective instincts for you. I now confess that the man did not just die at the police station. I was responsible for his death."

As the grandmaster hesitated, I recalled the incident where the abusive husband attacked me with a knife on the sidewalk outside of the dojang. I subdued him, and the grandmaster asked me to phone the police. I remember the grandmaster telling me that the man tried to attack him as well, and he stopped him with a kick to the chest. The next day, the man's heart stopped, and he died. I never put two and two together before.

I was deep in thought when the Grandmaster Kim Yong-Sool continued, "I did not think the Guardians would ever find out about the incident. They are in South Korea, and I am here. I felt I was safe, and no one would need to know what I did. My own shame made me confess, and now I must go to South Korea and place myself in their hands. I do not know whether I shall return or not. It is up to the Council to decide my fate. I will leave tomorrow morning.

"I want you to stay in contact with Tony. He will need your friendship. Chung Sa Bam Nim is very skilled, but he is not always friendly. Tony will learn much, but he will need words of encouragement from you. He will get only a few from his teacher. That is one reason I was not unhappy to learn that you would no longer be instructing at the dojang when I leave. You act tough, but you are easily wounded by unkind words and deeds."

I was still processing the fact that Grandmaster Kim Yong-Sool killed a man he thought was a threat to me. I asked him why he did not feel that I could handle the man.

"This man was evil. He would have been let out of jail in a short time. I could tell he was intent on killing you. He would have kept trying until he succeeded. I was not willing for you to live the rest of your life, looking over your shoulder. Sooner or later, he would have killed you. You are too precious to many people to allow that to happen. I know American law would find me guilty of murder if they understood what I did, but it was not unlawful by our standards."

I was wondering what the grandmaster meant by our standards. Was he referring to him and me, or was he referring to the Guardians of Sacred Rituals? They may very well have their own codes and laws. It seemed that way to me. Maybe when he went before the Council, they would find him innocent. I was clinging to that hope.

"Tish, it is late. Scotty will want to celebrate your excellence. I will say goodbye to you now and leave in the morning. If I return to the dojang, I will contact you. If I do not, know that you are the best student I have ever had the pleasure to teach." The grandmaster gave me an uncharacteristic hug and held me at arm's length. "Now, go and don't spend energy worrying about me." Releasing me, I turned and left the office.

I headed out of the dojang's door and quietly closed it behind me. I wondered how the grandmaster expected me not to worry. The grandmaster just told me he killed someone to protect me, and it may be punishable by his own death. Walking towards my Harley, I did not see the two men, but I could feel their presence. My senses picked up their body heat and their rapid breathing. I prepared myself for the possibility of being assaulted and was not taken by surprise when one of the men threw a punch directly towards my face.

I turned, ducked, and blocked the blow with little effort. I moved slowly and gracefully, anticipating which opponent would make the next move. I recognized the two men when they stepped from the shadows into the street light. Gerard and Tyler were holding weapons. Gerard had his cane, and Tyler was brandishing nunchakus. Gerard looked scared, but Tyler had a wicked smile on his face.

No words were exchanged. No insults were flung, just a slow, menacing walk towards me, hoping to trap me in the alley. I was in my fighting stance, and my senses were sharpened as Qi Gong training was second nature to me now. Finding the center of my being, I was balanced and needed a minimal movement to disarm Gerard and send him to the ground writhing in pain. His cane was lying broken and useless as Gerard wailed and cradled a similar compound break in his arm.

Tyler hesitated for only a moment. At that moment, Grandmaster Kim Yong-Sool appeared at the entrance to the alley. Tyler approached me, demonstrating his expert knowledge of the nunchaku. Swinging the weapon under his arm, around his neck, he tried to intimidate me. I saw the grandmaster raise his arms waist high with his palm and fingers point straight up to the sky. This signal gave me permission to use the mystical martial arts technique he taught me. I remember the grandmaster telling me that this technique is always forbidden where it could be viewed by the public, and now he was giving me permission.

I mimicked his movements, and with my arms extended towards Tyler, focused and centered, I released my pent-up energies and watched Tyler fly into the brick wall without my having touched him. He slammed tremendously hard into the wall. He was utterly dazed. His partner in crime, Gerard, was in too much pain to notice that I had just used the mystical martial arts technique for the first time with the permission of my teacher.

As Tyler started to regain consciousness, he slowly got to his feet. "How the hell did you do that? You slammed me against the wall without even touching me!"

For a moment, I was afraid. I really was not supposed to use this technique in public. Did it count if my opponent realized I just did something mystical?

The grandmaster stepped forward and touched Tyler's forehead using his extended right index finger. In an instant, Tyler looked totally confused. The grandmaster then shouted, "Hey, monkey breath! Get your buddy out of here now, and we won't press charges!"

Tyler scurried towards his pal, who was sobbing in pain. He grabbed him and pulled him into the street, looking back continually.

"Monkey breath?" I questioned my grandmaster.

Chuckling, he said, "It was the quickest insult I could think of under the circumstances. I do not believe we will need to deal with them again on this issue. I am quite sure Tyler will come up with a benign scenario to explain what just happened."

The grandmaster continued to chuckle as he walked back to the dojang. I followed along, not sure if I had miscued or not.

We got inside, and I had to ask, "Grandmaster Kim Yong-Sool, did I do what I was supposed to do. I thought you were giving me permission to use Qi Gong on my attackers."

Composed and solemn once again, the grandmaster said, "You were right. I wanted to see if you could put into practice what I have taught you. You know there is a great responsibility for what you have been taught. Normally, I would not advise you to use it when there are witnesses, but Gerard was too preoccupied with his broken arm to notice anything. Tyler needed to know that you could hurt him without ever touching him. He will never bother you again, and he won't tell anyone what happened for fear they will think he is a liar. You are safe if you follow the teachings."

I was flabbergasted. I just used the mystical martial arts…something forbidden. Something I promised I would not do in front of anyone.

I stopped Tyler without touching him. I was in awe of the power and, at the same time, fearful of what I could do. The responsibility of tempering myself was overwhelming. I wondered whether I could stop myself from using this incredible skill the next time I felt endangered. Depending on my acquired 4th Dan skills seemed primitive and inefficient now for some reason.

"You must use your judgment. You must be wise. You know what you can do. You need to learn there is a time and place when you may use your mystical power. Most of all, you must use your judgment wisely," I heard the grandmaster say, getting through my heightened and exhilarated brain.

Use my judgment on when and where…. Use my powers wisely…. I knew I needed to do some soul-searching to figure out what all this meant in the real world, but right now, I was mentally, emotionally, and physically exhausted. All I wanted was to go home to Scotty.

"I am saddened by the fact that I won't see you tomorrow, grandmaster. I promise to use my mystical martial arts well. I will not disgrace you or bring shame to your teachings. I promise…." I said nothing more, as nothing more was expected. I gave the grandmaster a kiss on his cheek, knowing I may be crossing boundaries, but cared little that I was. I had grown to love him, and the thought I may never see him again stabbed me in the heart.

CHAPTER NINETEEN

Scotty asked me why it took so long for me to get home. "I was beginning to get concerned about you. I thought when I left that you would be right on my tail."

I brushed off his comment and told him I wanted to ask the grandmaster some questions before he left, and it took longer than expected. I was relieved when Scotty accepted what I said.

"It is going to be strange for you to finish up your classes with Chung Sa Bom Nim supervising. How are you going to continue your own training now that you passed your final 4th Dan Midterm? How many years until you test for the 5th Dan?"

I wasn't really listening to what Scotty said. I did not want to think about on-going training without Grandmaster Kim Yong-Sool. I had much more I could learn from him, and Hung Sa Bom Nim could only keep my attained skills sharpened.

"You aren't really listening to what I am asking, are you? Maybe you are just so hungry you can't concentrate. You did expend a lot of energy. How about if I fix you something to eat?" Scotty asked, feeling a bit worried.

That last question did register. "Thank you. That would be sweet of you, but don't go to a lot of effort. A salad would be fine with me."

As Scotty chopped up vegetables and hard-boiled eggs along with ham and cheese, I knew what kind of salad I would be eating. If Scotty had an excellent Balsamic dressing, I would be happy, but I knew I would need to watch him closely. If not, he would flood my salad with bleu cheese dressing...his favorite.

I poured each of us a drink. Scotty had milk, and I poured iced tea for myself. I really wanted hot tea, but I just didn't have the energy to heat the water.

I was exhausted both mentally and physically from the day. I thought about the two men from the alley and whether the grandmaster was correct when he said neither would tell anyone what happened. I was sure he was right about the one whose arm I broke. He didn't seem to see anything once I broke his arm.

Tyler was still a threat, as far as I was concerned. Once he got over his bafflement as to what occurred, I feared he might start to talk to his own dojang teacher. Grandmaster Kim Yong-Sool was sure he would be too embarrassed to admit he was beaten again by me, but I just wasn't as convinced.

Scotty put the plate of salad before me. I was pleased to see there was no bleu cheese dressing on it. I had been lost in thought and had forgotten to watch him in the kitchen.

"It looks perfect," I said to Scotty as I looked up at him.

Placing his salad next to mine, Scotty offered bread and butter or crackers. Passing on the carbohydrates, I dug into the dinner salad and enjoyed each crispy bite of lettuce.

"Things sure have gone well for us for the last two weeks. Both our competitions could not have turned out better. I am proud of both of us. We are going to be a team to reckon with," Scotty said between bites of buttered bread.

I thought we would need all our skills in the future to tackle whatever came our way. So far, our cases had been manageable, but that might not always be the case. If Sam really went undercover in the drug and gang world, and he asked for our help, we could have more on our plates than we could handle. Right now, I did not want to think about that.

"First things, first," I said out loud without realizing I had spoken my thoughts.

"What first things are you talking about?" Scotty asked. "Do you mean first we eat our salads and then have dessert, or first we concentrate on the abduction cases?"

"I guess I mean both. We can only do one thing at a time. Right now, we need to eat."

Our time together soothed me. I needed just to relax and be in Scotty's company. I couldn't tell him what was bothering me or what I had done to Tyler, but we could watch TV, relax and pretend there was no tomorrow. That is what I needed right now.

We woke the next morning and realized we had a day off. We did not have any plans.

"What would my Princess like to do today?" Scotty asked. "We have the whole day off. We can go to a museum, or out to eat or whatever you want to do."

I thought for a moment and said, "How about if you take me flying? We can phone ahead. I know your dad will arrange for us to fly for an hour or so. We could have an early dinner with them and still get home at a decent hour. What do you say? You need some time in the air to keep your license current, isn't that right?"

"Well, yeah, I am game. I would love to fly. I always love to fly. I will phone Dad right now to see if he can arrange it. I know they will be disappointed we can't stay overnight, but I am sure any time spent with their favorite children will be what they want. I need to admit I was a bit surprised they did not come to your competition," Scotty said.

"I didn't tell them about it," I said in return.

"Why not? I would think they would want to be there to watch you get your 4th Dan," Scotty said with some question in his voice.

"Do you know how many hours, upon hours, my folks had to sit in a dojang all these years? At this point, I don't even think they know where I am in my training. My dad is proud as can be, but my mother would have preferred I become a ballerina."

Scotty laughed. "You would have been a kick-ass ballerina. I can picture you knocking your partner out cold as you performed your Grand-battement."

"I can't believe you know ballet terms…oh, that's right, Heather took ballet." The amusement left my voice.

I really was no longer jealous of Heather and Scotty's relationship, but I did resent those years lost with Scotty. I knew I was acting silly. Our relationship needed those years as best-friend to develop into what we have now, but I couldn't help but feel just a little jealous of the petite redheaded girl who stole Scotty's heart for several years.

Scotty immediately knew why my mood changed, and he changed the subject. "I am going to phone my dad right now. Why don't you get showered? We can leave as soon as you are ready to go."

I took his suggestion and headed to the bathroom. I was awfully tired last night; I did not even bother to shower. It would feel great to let the hot water run over my shoulders and back. Even though my training teaches me to use my opponent's energy against them, and I am not expending vast amounts of energy, I think the fight in the alley has me tensed. My muscles seem knotted today.

I took longer than I usually do just to let the water beat on my neck and back. I felt more relaxed as I left the bathroom and put on what I would wear for the day. Scotty was true to his word. He arranged everything with his father and was dressed and ready to go when I came out.

The drive was pleasant. Scotty put on the radio station, and he sang along with most of the songs. He kept trying to get me to sing along as well until I finally succumbed and did so. I felt rather light-hearted when we arrived at the airport.

Scotty's dad was already there. He had everything arranged. We greeted him warmly. Scotty, with a simple handshake and me with a hug and kiss. There was little small talk as he guided us to Scotty's favorite airplane.

"Are you going up with us, Dad?" Scotty asked.

"Only if three is not a crowd," Gabe replied.

Hugging him again, I added, "We would love it if you came up with us."

"You probably need to do your six-month instrument currency check flight. So, we should plan a flight for at least three hours and make three approaches going down and coming back," Scotty's dad said.

"Where is a good restaurant on our planned flight route?" Scotty said without hesitation. I got the feeling he and his dad had done these many times in the past.

"I thought we could head for the Flying Pink Pig Restaurant in Seymour, Indiana. We can pick up the barbeque for our dinner. That way, the women won't need to cook, and there will be almost no clean-up. What do you say?" Gabe suggested.

"I will phone in our flight plan," Scotty said.

"I will phone the Flying Pink Pig and ask them to have our order delivered to the ramp at the Freeman Municipal Airport," I offered.

Scotty and I both headed to phones to make our calls while Gabe stayed with the Crusader. He would do a pre-flight inspection before Scotty did as well. I knew Gabe would be checking up on his son to make sure he did not make any mistakes.

We got back, and Scotty did his pre-flight inspection to Gabe's satisfaction. Scotty took out the Jeppesen approach plates he needed for the flight plan and clipped them to the pilot's control yoke before we took off. He also placed the IFR aeronautical chart on his kneeboard, showing the airports and his flight route.

We took off, and Scotty contacted Air Traffic Control (ATC) for clearance to proceed with his IFR currency flight plan. Once he received clearance information, Gabe put an IFR hood on Scotty to make sure he only saw the instruments. I, on the other hand, got to look out the windows to see the landmarks. I knew Scotty wasn't missing out on much. We had flown this terrain a few times, visually, in the past. It was just another beautiful day with Scotty flying in and out of the clouds.

Gabe told Scotty, "Your first approach will be an ILS approach coming up soon."

I did not have my instrument license yet. Wanting to learn more, I paid close attention to what Scotty was doing. This approach was not straightforward; it included a few precise turns as we descended. The ride was smooth as Scotty nailed the approach. We did not land, Scotty called in a missed approach and continued his flight plan to the next airport for the VOR, (variable omnirange) approach. Air Traffic Control placed us in an IFR holding pattern to allow for other air traffic in the area before providing him with the intercept radial to the VOR approach. Again, Scotty flew this approach with precision to the minimums before calling a missed approach again.

The third approach would be an NDB (non-directional beacon) approach to Freeman Municipal Airport. Again, ATC placed Scotty in an IFR hold before guiding him onto the NDB course. This time Scotty was a bit high and slightly right of his course before he reached the minimum altitude to peek at the airport runway. Looking out from under his hood, Scotty said oops! Asking ATC for a missed approach and vectors to the NDB. ATC provided Scotty with left turns back to the NDB course. This time he aced the approach, and we landed.

I grabbed my small purse and told the guys I would meet them back at the plane after retrieving our food. Gabe grabbed my arm and stuffed a wad of bills into my hand.

"Dinner is on me," he smiled as I looked down at the bills in my hand.

Scotty said, "Don't bother to argue, Tish. He isn't going to take back a single dime."

I gave Gabe another hug and took off to the ramp. We were on schedule. I was hoping the restaurant would not keep us waiting too long. I knew Scotty needed to repeat the two landings on the way home. It took longer than just flying over the airports. I was already hungry, so I did not want to wait long.

I ordered lunch for us and dinner for both families. I figured Scotty and Gabe would be happy with the grilled tenderloin sandwiches, and I order the signature sandwich for myself. We would eat our sandwiches on the ground before Scotty was in the air. Once in the air, he would be occupied with the instruments and the radio.

Dinner was going to be a feast. I ordered two whole barbecued chickens, beef brisket, coleslaw, green beans with sausage, purple potato medley, and a five-cheese mac. I was already feeling myself swell with all the salt.

Finally, I saw the catering truck pull up to the ramp. I was standing there waiting, signaling the driver to pull over. I paid him and gave him a generous tip since Gabe would not take any of the money back. Smiling, he handed me two large bags full of boxed meals.

After eating lunch, it was back on the plane. Scotty was comfortable with the return flight, and I was feeling chatty until Gabe reminded me what was in store for me when we got home.

"You know, Alice and your mother have had their heads together planning your wedding for hour upon hour. I think you will be pleasantly surprised by all the details. I and your father, try to stay away from them when they are planning, but what I have over-heard sounds very nice…if you like a lot of pinks," Gabe said as he watched me closely.

I guess I did not disappoint him when I scrunched up my face and let my mouth drop open because Gabe roared with laughter.

Scotty said, "Hey! I'm flying blind here. What did I miss? What is the big joke?"

Gabe turned to Scotty, "You should have seen Tish's face when I told her your mother and Dorothy were planning a pink wedding. It was priceless!"

"That wasn't funny," I said when I realized Gabe was teasing me. He knew I didn't like pink at all. I did not have a stitch of clothing that was pink.

"I am serious. Your mothers have had their heads together since they arrived home from Scotty's shooting competition. You are going to need to listen to all their ideas at dinner," Gabe concluded.

He and Scotty did some 'shop talk' about the instrument panel, and I let myself digest more than my lunch. I had forgotten about the wedding. We really hadn't wanted to get married this young, but it seemed plans were being made and we couldn't stop the wedding now unless we eloped. Eloping would break our mothers' hearts, so that was out. Besides, it was the chicken way out.

I thought to myself, 'What does my mother have planned for me?' I already told them they couldn't pick out my dress. They could plan all the rest, but I was not going to wear anything princess. I let my mind drift to frilly dresses with puffy sleeves and started feeling nauseous.

My day-dream shifted to seeing myself wearing a long, skin-tight black leather skirt with a black vest...studs and spikes on my long elbow-length leather gloves. I would carry a skull vase with black ribbons and dark red roses as my bouquet. I giggled quietly to myself as I pictured the audience's faces as I walked down the aisle.

We landed back at our home airport. Scotty and Gabe shut everything down, complete the post-flight checklist, and tied the Crusader down. Gabe signed Scotty's logbook, approving his 6-month instrument currency requirements.

I knew it was only a matter of time now until I found out what real horrors waited for me at my wedding. I passed the bags with the boxes of food down to Gabe, and we drove to my parents' house.

Entering, we were greeted with kisses and hugs and comments about how skinny I had become. I knew I had lost five pounds at most, but my mom loves to stuff people with food. She was overjoyed to see what was in the boxes.

"Alice, you are going to love what we are having for dinner. There is way too much of everything! I have a feeling no one will have room for the pies we made for dessert."

Scotty immediately shouted out, "Hey, speak for yourself. I am going to have room to eat a piece of both pies. What kind of pies do I get to have?"

"Oh Scotty, you know we made your favorites. We have peach and strawberry-rhubarb. We also made an extra pie for you to take home. That one is a cherry pie," Alice said to her smiling boy.

"You are a saint!" Scotty said.

I thought we would need to fast for days just to shed the pounds we would put on today. It is a good thing we live in Chicago and not in the same town as our parents, or we would both be extremely over-weight.

The chicken and brisket were put in the oven to warm, and our mothers pulled me into the sewing room. I saw multiple Bride's magazines lying open. There were sample menus and pieces of material resting on a table. Everywhere I looked, I saw signs of my upcoming wedding, and I almost panicked and ran out of the room. If Alice had not been standing in the doorway, I might have made an escape.

"Come over here and look," my mother said. "We think your bridesmaids should all wear burgundy-colored dresses."

I visibly relaxed. That was a good sign. I could live with burgundy colored dresses. "No pink trim, right? I can't handle pink on anything," I said as I stepped closer to see what style dresses they might be looking at. The elegant A-line dress caught my eye. It was one I felt Aileen would look very sophisticated wearing. Not knowing who else would be an attendant, I concentrated on Aileen and how she would look.

"I really like that one," I said as I pointed to the A-line. "Don't you think Aileen would look nice in it?"

"Oh, yes. My, you are right. Aileen would look very pretty wearing that dress. Maybe you and Aileen can go to the shop in Chicago and try it on. If it fits her, we can order it for her," my mom said.

"Mom, the bridesmaid pays for her own dress. You won't need to pay for it." I was a bit surprised my mother thought they would need to pay for the bridesmaid's dress. I wondered what else they felt they would need to buy.

"Mom, we want to keep the wedding simple. Scotty and I want to help pay for the wedding as well. I know tradition has the bride's parents paying for the wedding and groom's parents paying for the honeymoon, but none of that is what Scotty and I want. We really want only a few guests, a nice restaurant for dinner, and a weekend away."

I watched both mothers' faces sadden. I couldn't help but wonder what they had envisioned. I was hoping it was not going to be the whole congregation invited, a sit-down dinner at a hall with a band and champagne toasts abounding. I knew our parents were doing well with their new business, but there was no reason for them to go into any debt for a wedding.

From the kitchen, I heard Cliff shouting, "It smells like dinner is ready. Come on, you three. The kids still have a long drive ahead of them."

I was relieved to get to leave the sewing room and all the wedding decisions behind. I wasn't starving, but I sure was wanting anything else to occupy my mind.

The meal was good, but I was saturated with barbecue from lunch. I ate mainly the side dishes and ate a small piece of the strawberry-rhubarb pie. I knew I would probably get one small portion of the cherry pie in the next day or two, but not more than one.

On the way home, I suggested we take the cherry pie to the meeting scheduled at the Jamiesons' office the next day. I figured we could cut it into eight pieces, and there would be a piece for Aileen, Patrick, Audrey, Sam, Andrea, Scotty, and myself and one leftover. Scotty immediately nixed the idea.

"I think we should stop and get donuts for everyone. The pie should be kept for us," Scotty said as he patted the box next to him on the seat where the pie was being transported.

"Scotty McFarlan! You are acting selfishly. My mom makes the best pies, and everyone would enjoy a piece." I knew I was losing the battle, but I wanted Scotty to feel a bit ashamed of himself.

"You are right. Your mom does make the best pies in this world, and I am not sharing. I don't feel ashamed at all. I only get a piece of pie a couple of times a year, and I am not sharing," Scotty said emphatically.

I laughed. I knew Scotty would not share. I also knew I was right about only getting one piece of cherry pie, and that is if I was lucky.

We talked a little about what the next meeting might entail as we drove back to Chicago. Being preoccupied with our competitions and schoolwork, neither of us was aware of where the investigation was going. I was excited to see how we were going to be plugged into it.

"I sure hope we get to do something more exciting than just sitting in the van doing surveillance. I sort of feel like this case is our baby. After all, we did do most of the legwork," I said this, feeling a bit peevish.

"No, you're right," Scotty commented. "We did start the investigation, and we did all the preliminary work. I must admit that a part of me was resentful when the Jamiesons took it over. I mean, I understand that Mrs. LaPlante came to the office to hire the Jamiesons, and once they returned, it was understandable she would want them to take over, but darn! We did some good work."

"I know the Jamiesons did not mean to hurt our feelings. Truly, they really were thinking we needed to pull back because we had too many irons in the fire, but I feel so invested. I want to bring down the scum who did those awful things to those girls!" I was starting to feel riled up and angry again.

Scotty glanced over at me as he drove. "You know we might not ever find out what happened to the girls. Whatever Audrey and Captain Jones have planned could fall through. Aileen once said more investigations go south than north."

"I won't accept anything short of finding out what happened to those girls and bringing down the creature who hurt them terribly. I will continue to work this case even if the police say it is a dead-end." I muttered this under my breath.

Scotty said nothing more. He turned on the radio, and we drove the rest of the way home without another comment on the investigation. We would need to wait until tomorrow to see what was planned.

CHAPTER TWENTY

The skin on the back of my neck rose. I could feel the presence of someone in my bedroom. A hand pressed tightly over my mouth as the man's other hand slid under my top. I screamed, but no one could hear me. I kicked and fought as hard as I could, but the weight of the man's body held me down. Tears formed in my eyes as I realized there was no escaping what was about to happen.

"Tish, wake up! You are having a nightmare." I could hear Scotty's voice, but it sounded far away. I tossed and turned until Scotty's voice sounded more frantic. I woke up.

"What were you dreaming? It must have been a horrible nightmare!" Scotty said as he pulled me closer into his arms.

"It was horrible," I said, but I did not want to go into details. I knew thinking about the three young ladies whose lives had been ruined caused my brain to tap into my own demons. I had not had a rape dream for many years, and I was feeling sick with the real emotion of the nightmare.

"Can you talk about it?" Scotty asked sympathetically.

"I would rather not right now. I think a shower will help to clear my head. How about making me breakfast? An omelet with Lox and cream cheese sounds nice right now," I said, but I did not make any effort to pull myself out of the safety of Scotty's arms.

Scotty shifted his weight onto his elbow and turned onto his side. He looked down into my face. "You know, I will never let anyone hurt you for as long as I live, right? I would kill anyone who tried to do you harm."

I let my hand caress his face. "I know you would. This was just a bad dream from my past. I know I am safe with you," I said, trying to sound reassuring. As much as I loved Scotty and he loved me, I knew there were no guarantees with life. I did not want Scotty to think that I doubted him. It was important for him to feel that he could protect me.

"We have things to do today. We better get started. I promise I won't take long in the shower." I pulled myself to a sitting position and turned to look at Scotty, "I love you."

Scotty smiled. "I love you more." He watched me as I made my way to the bathroom. I could see the concern in his eyes, and I felt terrible that I had put it there.

We did not talk about my dream at breakfast or on the way to the donut shop. Instead, we talked about what our roles might be in the next week. We still had finals and graduation in front of us. The Jamiesons would try to protect our time so we could concentrate on those two things. I wanted to be involved in the case as much as possible, but I knew that would not happen.

We arrived at the office. Audrey was sitting at the table. She told us Sam and Andrea would be along in a short time. The meeting was scheduled for 10:00 AM, and they had best be punctual. She also told us Captain Jones would be joining us as well since Sam and Andrea would be representing the police force in this investigation.

"My husband will actually be leading this investigation. Sam uncovered a few things that make it a police matter. He will tell us more when he gets here. In the meantime, Aileen is making coffee, and Patrick is running one quick errand."

Setting the donuts on the table, I went in search of a plate on which to place the donuts. Aileen smiled as I entered.

"Good Morning, Tish. The coffee is almost finished. I also made a pot of hot chocolate for Scotty and whoever might prefer it to coffee. Did you have a nice time visiting with your parents?"

We chatted a few minutes while the coffee perked. I told Aileen about Scotty having some instrument flying time in the Crusader with his father. I also told her that there was a cherry pie available, but Scotty would not share. I was hoping she would bring it up and embarrass Scotty at the table.

We heard more voices from the meeting room and knew more of the group had arrived. Aileen poured the coffee into a carafe. She asked me to bring sugar and cream as well as the plate for the donuts. Aileen had two carafes in her hands, as well as napkins and stirring rods as she followed behind me.

Everyone was assembled, including Captain Jones, who winked at me as I entered the room. I smiled a greeting in return and greeted Sam and Andrea as well as Patrick.

"Everyone come on in and take a seat," Captain Jones said in his friendly but commanding voice.

As we gathered around the table, cups were filled with coffee or hot chocolate. The donuts were passed around, and everyone looked at Captain Jones to begin.

"As all of you know, Sam has been undercover as the temporary custodian at the hospital. Andrea was placed on the new nursing student roster and has been coached by my lovely wife so she could present well as a nursing student. They have been in place at the hospital for the past week. In that week, Sam discreetly has been watching Sheri Lawton closely. It has come to his attention and to mine that Sheri Lawton has a suspicious relationship with a pharmaceutical representative. Sam is quite sure that Sheri Lawton has a drug addiction and has been hiding that fact for several years.

Andrea reports that Sheri Lawton has taken an interest in her more than the other students. Andrea has been playing to that fact and is establishing a rapport with the nursing instructor. Andrea also told us that Sheri Lawton had approached her and a couple other nursing students about going to a coffee house this Friday night.

We are at a point in the investigation where we feel a stake-out might be advantageous. Scotty, Tish, would you be available this Friday to be stationed at the coffee house along with Sam to keep an eye on Andrea?" The captain's question needed answering, but he continued before I could say a word.

"We intend to have another undercover officer at the coffee house as well and a uniformed officer within a few blocks of the coffee house waiting to assist if needed. There should be little risk for the two of you. It is more for Sam to have people sitting at the table with him, helping to watch all the strangers in the room for any suspicious activity. You will need to be in disguise since Sheri Lawton knows you." Captain Jones stopped talking, and I realized that was our cue to answer his question.

"Of course, we will be available. Not too sure about a disguise for Scotty, though. Would you suggest a wig or something? He has been trying to grow his hair and beard, but not with much luck. As you can see, it hasn't changed his looks at all," I said as I reached over and rubbed his whiskers.

"Hey! Don't rub that hard. Those whiskers are barely rooted," Scotty said good-naturedly.

Sam joined in the fun, "How about dreadlocks? He would look great and fit into the coffee house ambiance very well."

I started thinking. I would need to abandon my biker chick look for something less eye-catching. Maybe if I had to give up leather, Scotty could wear leather instead. His size would lend himself to looking like a biker easily. I started to suggest it when Scotty opened his mouth.

"No, Tish. I am not going to dress like a biker."

I could not believe Scotty read my mind, but he must have. "It would be hard to find a pair of leather pants that would fit you any way," I said.

Stopping our banter, Captain Jones added, "I'm sure you two will find convincing costumes to wear. Sam will need to try to blend in as well. Probably Sheri Lawton has noticed him, but a custodian stopping for coffee would not seem as strange as the two of you being there. One officer will be at the coffee shop before you all arrive. I doubt you will be able to spot the officer, so don't spend time trying to figure out who it is. I just want the three of you to be in a position where you can keep a very close eye on Andrea."

We stayed around after Audrey and Captain Jones left. We talked to Sam and Andrea about how things were going at the hospital.

Andrea confided that she hated being in the hospital, "All those sick people. Yuck. I don't think I would make a good nurse. It is too hard for me to pretend I care when they start whining. Most of the time, they want a back rub or some special attention. Even though I am just a make-believe nursing student, it is hard for me to pretend."

Sam laughed. "I'm the one who has to clean up the vomit; why are you complaining?"

Andrea was quick to answer. "Some of those people who want back rubs are men with hairy backs. It is awful. I would rather clean up vomit. Do you know your hands go numb when you need to rub all that back hair?"

Now I had to laugh. The fact that Andrea was complaining about back hair just seemed too ridiculous for words.

"What about the case?" I asked.

"Sheri Lawton took a special interest in me the very first day. She also gathered up a few other blonds for her group. I noticed that Sheri is weeding out some of the students. If they are married or in a relationship, she drops them from her 'favorite list'. The fact that after only a couple of weeks of being on the floor, Sheri suggesting the coffee house is great for the investigation. I am hoping I won't need to stay undercover as a nursing student much longer. It really does suck!" Andrea said as she curled up her lip.

Sam added, "You know that I managed to watch Sheri Lawton with the pharmaceutical representative several times. I have no doubts that he passed her drugs. I would testify to that fact under oath in court. I just am not sure what she is hooked on. I suspect the pharmaceutical rep may just be our guy."

"So, if he comes into the coffee house, you will know him on sight and let us know, right?" Scotty asked. "It is hard to know who we are supposed to be watching out for when our assignment is this vague. Keeping an eye on Andrea is crystal-clear."

I spoke up, "That is all we can do for now. If we watch anyone who comes near the table, we will need to decide if one of us will tail that person or just stay and wait for Andrea to get ready to go home. I mean, do we suspect waitresses and everyone?"

Scotty thought for a moment and then spoke up, "You know, we have no idea why any of the girls left with Sheri or even if they did leave with her. The fact that they can't remember anything but shadowy faces doesn't help much. It is even possible that a waitress or bartender could be involved with the kidnapping of the women. The bartender could slip something into a drink and tells the waitress to give it to one of the girls? If that is the case, someone should be watching the bar. We may need to arrange our seating so one can watch Andrea and her table constantly, while another can watch the bartender and waitresses. Yet, a third-person watches for anyone acting unusual in the rest of the coffee house. I wish we knew who the fourth undercover officer might be. It might be good to be able to talk with him."

I finally added my two cents, "I just can't imagine there would be that many people involved in Sheri Lawton and the pharmaceutical rep's scheme. It just seems the more people involved, the more that things could go wrong. It is more likely the pharmaceutical rep gives

Sheri Lawton something to slip into the woman's drink, and then once she is woozy, he comes to help escort the young lady out. He probably has a car outside close by, and the two of them walk her to the car, put her inside, and drive away. If my scenario is right, we must have our vehicles really close by so that we can follow them or stop them."

"I say, the minute Andrea looks unsteady on her feet, we intervene immediately!" Sam bluntly said.

"No, Sam. We can't do that. If you rush in just because I am unsteadied on my feet, we don't have a case, and we have blown our cover," Andrea argued. "We need to wait to see where they take me and if anyone else is involved. As much as you want to protect me, you should be patient, or this isn't going to work. Remember, this is police work, and we are cops."

Sam looked uneasy. I could see he did not like Andrea being the bait one bit. It is evident to me that Sam had fallen in love with her. I also knew if anything happened to Andrea, Sam would explode, and all the gains I had seen in him the last several months would be undone, and he would be the angry young man I first met. I did not want to see that happen. I was really enjoying this new Sam.

Scotty spoke again, "Tish is right. The Double Nickel and Tish's Harley will be parked close by the coffee shop. Sam, what is your ride?"

I spoke up before Sam could say anything, "If we tail their car, the van would be less conspicuous than the Ford. Maybe you should consider driving it instead. Besides, it has all the surveillance equipment, and it could come in handy."

Scotty shrugged but did not comment. I knew he needed time to process my suggestion. The Ford was faster and more maneuverable. Scotty did have a point.

Sam finally said, "My Dodge Daytona is older, but it is in good shape. I think I could keep track of their car if I follow them closely.

The trick is limited street parking. I get off at 4:00 p.m. I will come straight here and circle the block until I get a close parking place."

"Good thinking, Sam. Tish and I will be able to get here early as well. If I bring the van, Tish can park her Harley and jump in with me to put on her disguise. Whatever she wears will probably not be what she would want to ride on her Harley," Scotty said.

"Speaking of disguises, how about you and I go shopping and see what we can come up with?" Andrea suggested looking at me.

"Like right now?" I asked.

"Sure, I don't have anything I need to do for the rest of the day. Captain Jones gave me the day off. This is a day set aside for the nursing students to be in class and not at the hospital. I am exempt. Let's go," Andrea said with some excitement in her voice.

"See you at home, Scotty. I suggest you study for our exam tomorrow. I will quiz you this evening." I gave Scotty a quick kiss as Andrea did the same to Sam, and we were out the door.

We drove to a used clothing store. I did not want to spend much on an outfit that I would wear one time. I was thinking about what I would need. It had to be ordinary and boring, so no one would look twice at me. It also needed to be comfortable and something I could move in if I had to act quickly. Jeans, of course, was what I wanted to wear. Not my usual tight black jeans, but blue jeans were so…blue. I thought about going 'hip-hop' and wearing baggy jeans, a baseball jacket, and a baseball cap. The more I thought about it, the more I liked the idea. It would fit for what I needed. I could wear my Nike running shoes

My hair was going to be something of a problem. I would be wearing a ball cap, but did I need a wig? I wear my hair short, so maybe a longer wig would help to disguise my looks. I did not think I could find a wig at a second-hand store. I was not sure I would want to wear it if I did find one. Somehow, I imagined lice or other crawly things.

As we walked around the store, I told Andrea the basics of the character that I wanted. She immediately got into shopper mode and was looking through racks like crazy.

"Baggy jeans, baggy jeans…what size do you wear? Are you like a size 6?" Andrea said, not taking her eyes off the rack of clothes as she checked each quickly.

"Wow! You are right on. How could you tell?" I asked in wonderment.

"Your height is the factor. You are thin but tall. Looking at your waist, I decided you were a size four or six. I went with size 6 because of your height. You would be a string bean if you were a size 4. Hey, I think I have a pair of baggy jeans that might fit if they aren't too short. Try these on while I look for more." Andrea threw the jeans over the rack at me to try on.

I went into the changing room and gave them a try. I was happy to say the jeans fit. However, the jeans could be a bit longer to please me. Hopefully, I would only wear them this one time. The problem was going to be finding a decent sports team jacket.

I came out of the dressing room and gave Andrea thumbs-up, and she halted her search for baggy jeans and went to another rack. I was amazed how quickly Andrea could fling through hangers of clothing at full speed. A big smile spread across her face as she held up a sleeveless Chicago city shirt.

"Now, all we need to do is find you a baggy sports jacket and a long wig, and you will be all set." Andrea came towards me with her new find.

I had to admit the shirt would be perfect. Scotty had more ball caps than anyone I knew. I was sure I could borrow one of his and make it fit. We made one more pass through the racks of clothing before leaving.

"I think I should buy Scotty a Chicago Cubs jacket, and maybe he would let me borrow it. It would be nice to buy something, one of us would wear again. Got time to make two more stops? One to a wig shop and one to a sporting goods store?" I asked Andrea, not wanting to assume she had a whole afternoon to waste.

"If you have time, why not stop for lunch as well? It has been several hours since we ate donuts. I could use some real food. There is a fun Mexican restaurant around the corner." Andrea seemed to be having fun with the project.

"My treat. You have been really helpful. I would still be in the store looking for baggy jeans if it wasn't for you," I said, laughing.

It wasn't long before our stomachs were full, I had a new shoulder-length wig, and Scotty had a new jacket. I was thrilled with what we accomplished.

When I arrived home, Scotty greeted me at the door. "Change of plans. Captain Jones phoned and told me that I would be assigned to the surveillance van along with a police officer. Since Andrea will be wired, he feels we need to be in the van."

"Well, darn! I was really excited about finding you a perfect disguise," I said. "Oh well, I guess he is right, even though I am sure the police have surveillance vans."

"I know. I was looking forward to trying to blend in," Scotty said with a wink. I knew he did not want to be stuffed into leather pants and a leather jacket.

Scotty continued, "The Jamiesons are going to be paying for the use of the van and our time since it helps the police department budget. I can see where Captain Jones would jump at the suggestion. I only wish you were wearing a wire too. I could communicate with you while I am sitting out in the cold van with a stranger."

"Come on. It isn't going to be that bad unless nothing happens this particular trip to the coffee house, and we must stage the whole thing again. That would be a bummer for you. I, at least, will have a nice warm place to sit with a steaming cup of coffee and Sam to keep me company."

"Right now, we have other things to worry about. We have that final tomorrow, and I need some serious tutoring. How about cracking the books with me?" Scotty suggested.

"Not until we put in quality time sparing downstairs. We have skipped a couple of days now, and you need the time in on the mat. I also need to get back to limbering up and keeping my skill set sharp. With the grandmaster gone, and if you don't try to make an effort, I will only have Tony to spar with. Neither of us can afford to get sloppy, you know," I said this as I took off my jacket and headed to the bedroom to change into comfortable workout clothing. Scotty was already in sweats. He would be ready to work out immediately.

We returned upstairs, sweaty and happy. I liked having an opponent that outweighed me by a useful one hundred pounds. Using Scotty's weight against him was not the problem. Now that Scotty was improving, it was good practice for me to be able to get out from under the extra weight. I purposefully allowed Scotty some take-downs just so I would need to make some real effort to get the advantage.

"How about a shower? We can make a small snack and hit the books afterward," I said as I headed towards our bathroom. Scotty was throwing his stinky sweats in the direction of the washing machine. I didn't even blink an eye or scream at him. It was his turn to do the laundry. I wouldn't need to be the one to bend down and retrieve his dirty clothes. In fact, I decided to join him, and I threw my dirty sweats down on the ground beside his stinky clothes.

"Hey!" Scotty blurted out. "Your dirty clothes belong in the laundry hamper and not on the floor."

We both laughed. I knew Scotty was throwing my words back in my face. I have often scolded him about his sloppy behaviors, and now he was getting even with me.

Refreshed from the shower and with cheese and crackers, olives, and pickles in our stomachs, we cracked open the book. I pushed the book in front of Scotty. I already knew the material word for word. My job was to make sure Scotty knew the main ideas well enough to pass the test.

Today, I would be happy if Scotty got a passing grade. We had way too much else on our minds for me to get out the whip and crack it over his head. My mind was thinking about Andrea and what dangers might be ahead for her.

CHAPTER TWENTY-ONE

To my surprise, I was able to put Friday out of my mind. The fact that we had final tests might have had something to do with that. I bullied Scotty into studying and kept him on task. When we were not studying, we were working out on the mat. I was impressed with how well Scotty was doing with his Hapkido training. I felt a bit guilty I was not spending near as much time at the shooting range with Scotty as he did on the mat with me. I let my guilt subside when I stopped to think how far away the drive to the gun range was in comparison to how close our mats were down in the basement.

Scotty was enjoying his ability to get the better of me from time to time. I was not about to let him know that I was letting him do so. I wanted the practice of getting out from under a man almost twice my weight, but I did not want him to know that was what I was doing. I just told him how well he was doing and watched his chest puff with pride. He was getting better anyway, so why burst his bubble with the truth.

Patrick phoned and asked us to come in earlier than usual if we could. It seemed Andrea and Sam had another new insight they wanted to run past the team. Scotty assured Patrick we would be there early, especially when Patrick asked Scotty what deli sandwich he should order for him.

"Pastrami on rye with Swiss cheese for me," I overheard Scotty reply. "Hey, Tish, what do you want from the deli?" Scotty shouted in my direction.

I answered and waited anxiously to find out why we were having another meeting this soon after our last one. I did not expect another meeting until Thursday when we finalized our plan.

"What was that about?" I asked Scotty once he hung up the phone.

"Don't know. We will need to go and find out. Can you be ready in ten minutes?" Scotty asked.

I laughed. "Scotty, getting there early won't make the deli sandwich arrive any quicker. Get yourself a snack if you are hungry. I will be ready in an hour since we don't need to be there until noon anyway."

Scotty grumbled as he headed for the kitchen. I heard the refrigerator open and then close. A cupboard opened next, and finally, I listened to the bread wrapper being opened along with the lid of the peanut butter jar. Scotty's old standby...peanut butter and jelly.

I went into my room and changed my clothes. I could have kept on the same clothes I wore to class, but I knew Andrea would be wearing something smashing. I did not want to look like a total slob next to her.

I walked out of the bedroom wearing my new studded boots, tight pants tucked into the boots, and to Scotty's surprise, something other than black. I had on a gray top with my black vest.

"Wow! I like that top. When did you buy it?" Scotty asked. "I did not know you owned anything that wasn't black."

I sneered at him. "I own things that aren't black," I said defensively. "I just don't wear them often because I don't like them."

"The only things you own that aren't black are things your mother bought for you at Christmas," Scotty laughed.

"And I don't like them...I don't wear those items." Glaring at Scotty, I dared him to say one more thing about my fashion sense. "I'm ready. Let's go if you are finished with your sandwich."

Scotty seemed insulted now. "I finished that sandwich over forty minutes ago; I have been waiting forever for you to change clothes.

You could have showered and tried on your whole wardrobe in that amount of time. What took so long?"

As we walked down the hallway, heading to the front door, Scotty glanced into the bedroom. "What tornado hit that room? There are clothes strewn all over the place. You did try on everything in your wardrobe. Why?"

I grabbed Scotty by his arm. "Let's go." I was not about to go into details about wanting to find the perfect outfit for the meeting when I knew Andrea would look like a Barbie Doll.

We entered the office and saw all the team was assembled except Captain Jones. We sat at the table after greeting everyone, and Scotty immediately reached for his pastrami sandwich. I elbowed him in the stomach.

Everyone followed suit, and before long, mouths were full, and no one was talking. I couldn't stand the suspense one more minute.

"Why are we meeting?" I asked as my sandwich sat in front of me, only half-eaten.

Sam was the first to speak. "Remember how I told you at the first meeting that I saw Sheri Lawton accept drugs from the pharmaceutical rep? Well, today, guess who she was sequestered in the nurse's office?"

"I don't really want to play guessing games, Sam. Can you just tell us and let us know what this is all about?" I asked, a bit annoyed.

Sam did not seem offended in the least bit. Instead, he grinned and said, "Dr. Kessler. You know, *the* Dr. Kessler you talked with that wouldn't give you any information about the ladies he is treating."

"I know who Dr. Kessler is. What were they talking about? Did you manage to overhear something, and you have more to share?" I was hopeful we might have something on Dr. Kessler. I was suspicious of him from the minute I left his office.

"Sorry," Sam said. "I couldn't hear a thing they were saying. Sheri Lawton broke down and was crying when they were talking. That should mean something. Why would Dr. Kessler be visiting the student nursing supervisor? There doesn't seem to be any other reason for him to be in the office with Sheri Lawton unless he is involved."

Audrey Jones spoke next, "Sam has a point. Dr. Kessler is one of our doctors on staff, and he only deals with psychiatric patients. I had no idea he even knew Sheri Lawton. There would be no reason for them ever to meet. Our student nurses never work on the psychiatric floor. While I am certain he wouldn't know Sheri Lawton from a professional point of view, he may know her socially. I am leaning towards Sam's theory that he is involved in this somehow."

I spoke up again, "The fact that Constance, Brook, and Josie are all three patients of his, does not bode well for him. He was very defensive when I asked about drugs that could make a person forget memories. In fact, he was more than defensive; he was downright rude at that point in our conversation."

Patrick and Aileen were sitting silent from the start of the conversation. I glanced at them to see if they might have something to add.

Aileen took my glance at her as a signal to speak, "I talked to each of the mothers of the ladies in question, and they all have nothing but good things to say about Dr. Kessler. If he is the villain, in this case, he is good at convincing the mothers that he is not."

"What puzzles me is that none of the ladies have improved under his care," Scotty said.

Andrea joined in, "That is something I have been thinking too. Why aren't any of the young women doing any better? Some have been under his care for over a year. I would think they would remember something other than shadowy faces if Dr. Kessler is not keeping their memories fogged. I think we need to keep an eye on him as well on Friday."

Audrey Jones added, "My husband couldn't be here today. When I get home later, I will ask him if he can put a patrolman at Dr. Kessler's office and have an officer follow him. If he is involved, he won't go home. He will go wherever they might take Andrea."

My stomach turned at hearing Audrey's statement. Andrea was putting herself on the line. If anything went wrong, Andrea could be one of Dr. Kessler's patients who can't remember anything but the shadowy faces. I was determined Andrea would not be harmed on my watch.

I looked over at Andrea and knew she was thinking the same thing as me. Her eyes were downcast, and her hands were wringing slightly under the table. Sam noticed as well, and he put a protective arm around her shoulders.

When the rest of the group left, Scotty and I stayed to do some computer work for the Jamiesons. We had been putting their files in order and onto the computer for quite some time now. Often, Patrick would request input into recent cases. This was one of those days. I had little to do to help Scott, so I went upstairs to talk to Aileen. Something was troubling me.

"Aileen, can I run something past you. I have this odd nagging feeling that I am missing something about our case," I said as we sat down with a cup of tea.

"What is on your mind, Tish?" Aileen asked and waited for me to answer.

I sat my cup down on the table. "It is this thing with Dr. Kessler. You know that I went to his office when Martha told me Dr. Kessler was Brooke's psychiatrist. Now that I think of it, what Martha said was Dr. Kessler came strongly recommended by Brooke's last nursing supervisor, Mrs. Lawton. Shari Lawton was the nurse Brooke reported to at her last rotation at the hospital." I stopped for a second to let my statement sink in.

"Okay. You think it is odd that Sheri Lawton was the one to recommend Dr. Kessler if they are both in on this crime together. I think it would be perfect to have her partner in crime be the one to make sure the victim never talks, don't you?" Aileen questioned.

"Yes, but that isn't all of what is bothering me," I said. Continuing, I added, "When I went to ask Dr. Kessler, trying to find out what drug might cause a person to lose their memory, he told me that I should speak to an anesthesiologist. He said his job is to help his patients regain their memory...not to eliminate it. When I asked him if he could recommend an anesthesiologist to talk with, he told me to check the phone book, or if that avenue did not please me, I could talk with the nursing supervisor, and she might help me to find one."

"That doesn't seem too odd to me. Why is that conversation bothering you?" Aileen asked.

"It is just that I wonder why he would point me towards the nursing supervisor. If just seems odd to me," I said, furrowing my brow in deep thought.

"Dear, he pointed you towards an anesthesiologist first. Maybe he just meant that you should talk with Audrey Jones. Were you thinking he was steering you towards Sheri Lawton?" Aileen prodded.

"I don't know. It is just something that is nagging at me for some reason. You are probably right. I am just reading something into the conversation that wasn't really there." I chit-chatted with Aileen about other things for a while until Scotty came out of the office.

"Ladies, I hope I am not interrupting anything meaningful. I can't do much more damage to the computer right now. I think you and I had best get back home, Tish. The test tomorrow isn't one I am looking forward to. I need a bit more tutoring."

I knew that was my sign to wrap up the conversation and leave with Scotty. He was right. He did need a bit more tutoring.

We were both looking forward to graduating and working full time as investigators. I was not concerned about the final exams right now. It was a hurdle yet to be overcome.

Aileen smiled and winked at me, knowing I had some work ahead of me with Scotty. Scotty would pass even if I didn't tutor him. Scotty knew he would never live it down if he didn't ace the test. Living with a perfectionist was not easy for him. He once told me it was a small price to pay to live with the most beautiful woman in the world.

We left and drove home to crack the books. I needed to concentrate on Scotty, so I let that troublesome thought that Dr. Kessler was somehow more involved in these cases than he should be lapse to my subconsciousness. I knew I could make my mind rest, knowing an officer would be assigned to watch him on Friday. That knowledge would stop me from doing something careless, like returning to his office to confront him.

When we got home, I allowed Scotty some time to relax while I started dinner. Since we would be studying a good share of the evening, I decided Scotty needed some comfort food. I knew that meant a roast, mashed potatoes, and vegetables. I wasn't in the mood to try to make a pie. Ice cream would just need to do for dessert. Since the meat would need a bit of time to cook, I knew I had to get into the kitchen soon.

From the kitchen, I could tell Scotty was watching 'The Jerry Springer Show' on television. Momentarily, I was irritated. I found the show to be absurd. However, the sound of Scotty's laughter soothed my exasperated mood. I smiled. Sometimes, I found Scotty to be such a boy. This was one of those times. I was almost surprised he wasn't watching *Rugrats*.

After scraping the carrots and peeling potatoes, popping the roast into the oven, I was ready to interfere with Scotty's fun. I walked into the living room and turned off the television to Scotty's surprise and frustration.

"Hey, I was just about to find out which man was really the father of that child!" Pointing at the darkened TV, Scotty whined a bit annoyed with me.

"Sorry, Scotty," I said, not really meaning it. "Time to study. Dinner is in the oven, and I want to get started now. After dinner, it will be too late. We have other things to do this evening."

"What's so pressing this evening that we can't study then?" Scotty asked with real curiosity. "I didn't know we had anything else on the agenda tonight."

I smiled a wicked smile at Scotty. Then with my left hand, I slipped my blouse off my right shoulder, baring my soft skin.

"Alright!" Scotty said. "Let's get our studying done and eat quickly. How could I forget our evening plans?"

Distracted from television, he jumped to his feet and came to the table. The books were opened, and my notes were laid out in front of the seat Scotty would take. The long tutoring session was beginning. I only hoped he had enough incentive to work hard.

Hours later, dinner was eaten, dishes were done, and Scotty went over my notes one last time. Closing the books, he announced, "I am going to ace this test. Now, it is time for your reward for getting me through this course."

He jumped to his feet, swept me up into his arms, and carried me towards the bedroom. When he put me down, I slipped his arm behind his back and forced him down on the bed.

"First, you get a back rub. I am sure your muscles are all tense from hunching over the notes all evening." I straddled his back, pulled his shirt off, and let my fingers ply the knots I found. I knew he would return the favor….

I awoke early. I wasn't thinking about the upcoming tests or graduation. I was thinking about Andrea and what danger she might encounter with her undercover assignment. I didn't doubt Captain Jones's decision to put two rookies undercover. Ever since we first met at the rookie martial arts training, I feel quite close to Sam and Andrea, and I just didn't want either of them to get hurt. Whoever we were dealing with was a terrible person. I was sure he would not hesitate to kill either Andrea or Sam if he felt cornered, and that was what this surveillance plan was supposed to do...corner him.

We were sure Sheri Lawton was involved in the crime. She probably was the procurer to the pervert we were after. Thanks to Sam's undercover efforts, we know Sheri is using drugs, and she gets them from the pharmaceutical representative that Captain Jones has a detective doing background checks and surveillance. How Dr. Kessler fits into all this is still puzzling me.

I admit that I don't like Dr. Kessler. I did not want that to cloud my thinking. It keeps running through my mind that it is an odd coincidence that he is the psychiatrist treating Constance as well as Brooke and Josie.

I felt Scotty's arm enfold me and pull me close. I didn't resist but snuggled into his chest.

"Good morning, Beautiful," Scotty whispered into my ear.

"Good morning, My Love," I cooed back. "Whose turn to make breakfast?" I knew the answer. It was my turn, but I was hoping Scotty would forget and offer to make breakfast while I took a shower.

Chuckling, Scotty said. "Oh, no, you don't. You can't trick me. I know you think my mind is clouded with all those facts you have shoved down my throat for the test today, but my mind is still clear enough to know I made breakfast yesterday."

"And it was such a good breakfast, that I would love for you to make it for me again today." I snuggled even closer to Scotty as I said this. If I could have batted my eyelashes, I would have done so, but I refuse to play *that* coy for any reason.

"No! It is your turn to make breakfast, and I want fried potatoes or hash browns, your choice, and eggs, sunny side up. I also want ham or bacon and toast. If you are really feeling generous, you might also make me some pancakes. After all, I need all the energy I can muster to make it through three tests in one day," Scotty countered.

He had a point. It was going to take all his energy to complete those tests. I gave in and pushed myself to a sitting position on the side of the bed.

"You win. You made a good point. These tests will be a breeze for me. I could do them with one piece of toast for breakfast, but you will need every advantage possible to pass all of the tests. I'm up. I will make you a king-size breakfast. You should probably go over the notes one more time while I cook."

I knew that would cause Scotty to grumble, and I was not disappointed. Not only did he complain, but he pulled the covers over his head and disappeared. I could only imagine what kind of face he was making at me as I pulled on my robe and headed for the kitchen.

Peeling potatoes and slicing them thin enough to fry, I listened to hear if Scotty was out of bed yet. I feared that he had fallen back to sleep and was not going over the notes for the first test this morning.

I tip-toed to the door of the bedroom, and I could hear snores from under the covers. Springing into action, I leaped upon the hulk under the covers and gave a banshee scream. I should have anticipated the reaction I would get. I found myself on the floor, looking up at Scotty's startled face.

"What the hell?" Scotty said with surprise, still registering on his face.

"You aren't studying! Here I am slaving in the kitchen, and you are sleeping," I said as I picked myself up off the floor.

Smelling something burning in the kitchen, I fled from the room with a backward comment. "If the bacon is burned, you better not complain. Get up right now, or I will be back with a vengeance!"

I was relieved to find the bacon and potatoes frying but not burnt. As I turned the bacon, I smiled, remembering the startled look on Scotty's face. I found myself laughing out loud.

"What's so funny?" Scotty said as he stumbled out of the bedroom.

"I just recalled the look on your face when I pounced on you," I said as I laughed again.

"You just wait. *Revenge is a dish best served cold*," Scotty said with a pout on his face.

I laughed even harder. "You have about ten minutes before I dish up breakfast. Do you want orange juice or apple juice?' I asked as Scotty turned to leave the kitchen.

"Orange juice, I guess. No, apple juice," Scotty replied.

I loved how decisive Scotty could be, was my thought as I turned my attention back to the sizzling bacon and potatoes. I also found myself thinking about how much I loved this man.

Watching Scotty shoveling the breakfast into his mouth as I ate my one piece of toast, I wondered how he kept from gaining weight. He hadn't gained a single pound since high school. I was always stepping on the scale and fighting against gaining five pounds and then dieting to lose the pounds. I was envious of Scotty's metabolism.

Gabriel, Scotty's dad, was the same way. He was still as trim as he was when he was a Navy Seal. Alice, on the other hand, was a little on the chubby side. How fortunate Scotty inherited his dad's genes. My parents were both a little overweight. I guess I would have this battle for the rest of my life.

"I want to take a shower before we head to classes. Will you do the dishes? I didn't really make too much of a mess," I asked as I got up to head to the bathroom.

Scotty, chewing his last bite of toast, just nodded in agreement. I was happy he wasn't complaining, but I guess with his stomach full, he was a happy man.

As we walked to classes, I remarked about how quickly the last couple of years had flown by. "I can't believe we will actually be finished with all our courses and be working full time within days. I won't really miss classes, though, will you?"

"Heck, no! I will be glad not to need to study. Of course, we will still have other things to concentrate on that may be harder than our studies or, at least, more tedious. I don't relish all the time we may spend in the Hall of Records, tracking down information."

I just nodded. Aileen had warned us that most of our time as private investigators would be monotonous. Surveillance had already proved to be that. Soured from the many hours and days spent in the rear of the van the last two years, neither of us wanted to get back into the cramped quarters.

"I think we deserve a little vacation before we start working full time. Do you think Patrick and Aileen will be okay with us taking a week off to do something fun after Friday night?" I asked earnestly.

"They just got back from a vacation not that long ago. I think Jamiesons won't begrudge us a week. What do you have in mind? We can't really afford anything big like going to Hawaii again."

"How about camping?" I asked Scotty. "You love camping and fishing. I remember enjoying fishing with you and our dads. In fact, maybe we could make it a big family event. All of us could go to a lake out of state. What do you think?"

"I like the idea as long as you don't get stuck back at camp with our mothers, but you can go out fishing with us men," Scotty said.

"Scotty, you know our mothers like to fish. There is no way they are going to sit on the beach and watch the rest of us dangling our poles. In fact, my mother holds the record for the largest fish caught by any of us. She isn't about to let us fish without defending her title."

The walk was brief, and before we knew it, we were walking into the classroom to take the first of three tests we had that day. I was relaxed, but I noticed Scotty's forehead developing a bit of sweat. He wasn't feeling quite as sure as I was.

CHAPTER TWENTY-TWO

The exams were over. The results would be posted in a few days, but mainly, classes were over, and we would be graduating in a week. It was strange for this part of our journey to be coming to an end, but I relished the freedom from classes and exams. I could only imagine how ecstatic Scotty must be feeling.

Scotty must have been reading my mind. "Wow! We are finished with all the classwork. We will be able to work full time from here on out, I mean, once we get our license."

I wasn't worried. We had the Jamiesons to guide us through the licensing process. We were on our way to the office as we spoke.

Entering the office, we found balloons and a cake waiting for us. "Surprise!" Patrick and Aileen yelled in unison.

Scotty, quick to respond, said, "Your surprise is we made it through all of the classes?"

I laughed. I figured that was what the Jamiesons meant when it came to Scotty. I went over to the cake and was excited to see it was chocolate.

"Of course not," Aileen said. "We just wanted to celebrate another milestone on your road to success. We also have a little present for you both."

That got my attention. I always had trouble with receiving gifts. I think it is that indebtedness factor that I don't enjoy. However, I was interested in what they might have gotten us. I swallowed my pride and asked what it might be.

"We know you were thinking about taking a little vacation before starting full-time. We wanted to make your vacation time special, so we rented rooms for you and your parents. We will give you the details later, but we wanted you to know that you can look forward to a break soon."

"How did you know we wanted to take a trip with our parents?" I asked curiously.

"Scotty, of course, mentioned the two of you were hoping to take some time off soon, and he went on to say you thought it would be fun to spend time with your parents as well. In fact, he even told Patrick about fishing on a lake. It wasn't hard to put two and two together," Aileen confessed.

I looked over at Scotty, who was looking at the cake. "Scotty, you just say anything that pops into your mind, don't you?" I scolded.

"Hey, I didn't do anything wrong. I was just telling Patrick about our future, or our hopes for a short vacation. I wasn't hinting that he and Aileen pay for it," Scotty said defiantly.

"Come on, Tish, give Scotty a break. It was harmless. We know he was not in any way hinting for us to pay for the trip. We just want to do it for you. Patrick and I agree that you could use a break before going full-steam into the business with us. It would be our pleasure if you would allow us to do this for you," Aileen said sweetly.

I was feeling foolish. I felt as though I was about to burst the Jamiesons' bubble if I disagreed with anything said. I did not want to feel indebted. But I also did not wish for Aileen and Patrick to feel I was ungrateful. I knew I needed to be gracious and just thank the couple with a big smile. It was obviously forced.

Aileen came to my side and gave me a big hug. "I know getting any kind of a gift is hard for you. Please don't feel that you owe us anything for giving you this trip. You and Scotty have done more for Patrick and me than you know. We want to do this for you, okay?"

I relaxed into her embrace. "Thank you. You and Patrick have been good to us. I guess I just feel like we are taking advantage of you."

Aileen squeezed me hard and then released me. Holding me at arm's length, she looked me in the eyes. "I want you to get that notion out of your head. If anyone has taken advantage here, it is Patrick and me. You have done all the grunt work we did not want to do or know how to do. You also have protected our backs and proved yourselves valuable allies. In fact, I can't imagine doing this job anymore without your help."

It was settled. Scotty and I would be getting a week away with our parents, and it wouldn't cost us a cent. The only thing left to do was to eat the cake.

Scotty went to the computer, taking a second piece of cake with him. Aileen and I took the plates and forks to the kitchenette. I had a few questions I wanted to ask about the case. Since Aileen and Patrick were now taking the lead on the Constance LaPlante case, I had not had as much contact with the three ladies involved.

"Aileen, have there been any changes with any of Dr. Kessler's patients as far as you know?" I asked.

"Funny you would ask that," Aileen said. "I was just about to ask you to make a trip to each of the women's houses to talk with their mothers to see if there had been any significant changes. I know you are suspicious of Dr. Kessler. For that reason, I can't let you talk to him. We don't want to arouse his suspicions since Captain Jones has him under surveillance. However, I would like to know if any of the young women have seen him this week. Here are my notes from my discussions with the girls or their mothers."

I was excited to have the assignment. Reading through Aileen's notes did not reveal anything new. I wanted nothing more than to check up on Constance, Brooke, and Josie. I kept hoping one or all of them would have a breakthrough before Andrea was put into a compromising situation on Friday night. If any of the women could shed some light on who had abducted them, that might save Andrea from the danger of going undercover. My gut was in a knot just thinking about Andrea and what might happen to her if anything went wrong.

"We can take Scotty home when he finishes his computer work if you want to take the Ford. I have already phoned all three mothers to let them know you would be stopping by," Aileen informed me.

"Great. I will let Scotty know that I am taking the Double Nickel, and I will be off," I said with a bounce in my step. I was feeling hopeful that one of the women might remember something.

I drove to Constance's house first. Since the incident was fresher with her, I was hoping she did not bury her memory as deeply as the other two seemed to have done. I knocked on her door and was greeted by Leticia LaPlante.

"Good afternoon, Tish. Aileen phoned to say you would be dropping by today. Come in. I have tea and some cookies if you would like to sit down with Constance on the patio. She is in a good mood today...so please don't upset her."

Leticia LaPlante has been cold to me since the first day I entered her house and questioned Constance. I knew she thought I knew more than I did and was keeping things from her.

As I walked to the patio, I saw Constance sitting in the sun facing the sliding door. Both hands were held relaxed on her lap. I noticed instantly that she was showing no signs of being pregnant. I walked over and sat down next to her on her right side.

"Hi, Tish," Constance greeted me with a smile.

"You miscarried?" I asked instead of greeting her politely as I was brought up to do.

Constance glanced in the direction of the door to make sure her mother was not listening. "Yes, I did miscarry. I am not the least bit sad about it either. I was relieved when the cramping started. Carrying a baby to term, under those circumstances, would have been unbearable."

"So, you never told anyone...not even Dr. Kessler?" I asked.

"I didn't see any reason to tell anyone. I did not tell Dr. Kessler out of fear he would tell my mother. You are the only one who knows, and I can count on you not to say anything," Constance said in a hushed but warning whisper.

I looked up and saw Leticia LaPlante coming through the doorway with the tea and cookies. I could tell she noticed Constance talking to me in a whisper and was on high-alert.

Setting the tray down on the table, she started to pull up a chair to join us when Constance said rudely, "Mother, don't sit down. I am talking to Tish, and I want to be alone."

Leticia looked at me long and hard, but turned without a word and left. She closed the patio door behind her but gave another backward glance in my direction. I pretended not to notice.

"I have your word. Right!" Constance repeated.

"Yes, you have my word," I said without hesitation. If I was going to establish a relationship based on truth and trust with Constance, I knew I had to make the promise and stick to it.

"Constance, have you had any other memories from the night you went missing other than the blurry faces?" I asked in a quiet voice. I had no idea if Mrs. LaPlante was listening from an open window that looked out on the patio.

"I wish I had something more to tell you. I just don't. The blurry faces still haunt my dreams, but they stay blurred. I don't recognize anyone," Constance answered.

"There are definitely faces. Not just one blurry face but several?" I asked.

Constance sat silent for a minute in thought. "Yes, there are multiple blurry faces. I know this because one is larger and looms more than the other two, but I am sure there are three and maybe four different shapes."

I felt like this was a breakthrough. Constance knew there was more than one assailant. One assailant was larger than the others. "And the larger blurry face seems to be the more menacing one?" I asked.

"It is the one that scares me the most, but the others seem to fade in and out. The one larger face stays constant even when the others fade away. What do you suppose that means?" Constance asked me.

"Have you talked about this with Dr. Kessler? If so, what does he say?" I prodded.

"I have told Dr. Kessler about the blurry faces and how one seems to loom more than the others. I have also told him it is the larger blurry face that scares me the most. He said to give it time. That is what he always says. *'Give it more time.'*"

I found myself wanting to scream. This poor woman's life is on hold. How much time is she supposed to give up? She needed her life back, as did Josie and Brooke.

When it was evident that Constance had nothing else to tell me, I gave her a hug and left her house, but not before Leticia cornered me. She had an icy reserve about her as she asked me, "What are the two of you keeping from me? I have a right to know. I am Constance's mother, and I want the best for her. If you know something that I should know, I want you to tell me right now!"

"Mother! You leave Tish alone right this minute!" Constance said as she walked around the corner of the room.

I used this moment to slip out the front door as Constance and Mrs. LaPlante continued to have words. I could hear Mrs. LaPlante's voice begin to quiver, but I wasn't going to stay around any longer to intervene. This was not a fight I needed to be involved in.

I drove to Brooke Tully's house next and found Martha at the door. I decided she was waiting for me.

"Good Afternoon, Martha. How has Brooke been?" I asked as she let me into the living room.

"Brooke hasn't left the house in months, but she isn't sleeping all day and then all night as well. We have sat and watched television together many times in the evening. Her appetite is better, but she is still skittish. Brooke leaves the minute anyone comes to the door. She is up in her room with the door locked right now," Martha said as she indicated where I should sit.

I noticed her famous macadamia, chocolate chip cookies on a plate with a glass of milk sitting beside it. It was clear the refreshments were for me. "Please help yourself to some cookies and milk while we talk," Martha said, always the gracious hostess.

"I don't mind if I do. I remember thinking your cookies were the best I have ever eaten." I hoped she wouldn't think I was flattering her just to get answers to questions but knew I was sincere.

"That is very sweet of you, dear. I have a bag made up for your boyfriend. I remember he really loved my cookies, too." Martha indicated a small brown bag on the table next to my glass of milk.

"Martha, is there any chance Brooke has remembered anything more lately? I know it is hard for her to talk to strangers, but I really need some answers. Would she talk to me?" I asked meekly. I did not want to seem pushy in any way since I knew how protective Martha could be towards Brooke.

"I will call up the stairs and invite her down. If she doesn't come down, I won't push. You understand that the small gains she has made are still fragile. I am enjoying the fact that she will sit with me in the evenings. I don't want to do anything that will jeopardize our new companionship." Martha got to her feet and walked to the base of the stairs.

Standing at the foot of the stairs and leaning over the banister, Martha called up the stairs, "Brooke, that nice young private investigator would like to speak with you. Do you want to come down and talk with her for a few minutes?"

Martha stood at the bottom of the stairs, listening to hear if Brooke was moving around in her room. After a couple of minutes without hearing any sounds, Martha returned to the living room. "I don't think she is coming. Maybe you can ask me a few questions, and I will answer the best that I can."

I was sure this was not going to be a helpful visit. I doubted Brooke would have talked to her mother about the shadowy faces. Brooke was just too afraid. I asked the question anyway.

"Has Brooke ever said whether there was more than one face that looms up at her from her nightmares, or is there just one blurry face?" I asked, hoping Martha might shed some light on the subject.

"No, dear. Brooke never talks to me about her nightmares. I run to her room when she screams out, but she never wants to talk about bad dreams. Dr. Kessler said not to push her, so I don't. I just sit and hold her and whisper how she is safe now that she is at home. I don't know what else to do for her." Martha looked down at her hands in her lap. Her face looked so sorrowful that my stomach tightened.

"Martha, there is another one of Dr. Kessler's patients who recalled to me three distinct blurred faces. One she said was very large and imposing, and the other two were smaller faces that faded away from her mind quickly, but the large one is the one that haunts her the most. Has Brooke mentioned one, large looming presence to you?" I asked, hoping the question would jar Martha's memory.

A spark seemed to cross Martha's eyes. "Why yes, Brooke did say the shadowy face was large and looming. She couldn't describe any features or details at all, but I just thought the whole incident was scary and exaggerated in her mind. How awful to have the blurred face loomed in her imagination like a boogeyman. It never occurred to me that the person could really be a large man. Odd, I never thought of that before...." Martha's mind seemed to be whirling.

"Do you know if Brooke spoke to Dr. Kessler about there being a large man?" I asked.

"Do you think my Brooke was attacked by a big man?" Martha asked, ignoring my question about Dr. Kessler.

"It is possible. It is also possible there was more than one person involved in her abduction. We are working hard to get to the bottom of what happened to her and the other victims. I am trying to figure out the similarities in their cases. The circumstances seem too similar not to suspect that the crimes were committed by the same person or persons. I was hoping Brooke might be able to give me more details. However, it doesn't seem like she is going to come down. I will leave now, so she does not stay locked in her room for much longer. I am thrilled she is making some progress."

"Don't forget the cookies for your boyfriend," Martha said as she retrieved the bag from the coffee table and put it in my hand.

I thanked her and told her how happy Scotty would be to receive the cookies and left, not knowing much more than I had when I first arrived. I wondered if Josie would be able to tell me more.

The last time I had stopped at the Randall house to talk with Josie, I was not allowed to speak with her since Josie was heavily medicated due to a suicide attempt. I wondered what I might be walking into this time. I must admit that I was afraid I would be greeted by Melissa Randall wearing black and saying Josie had succeeded in her attempt to kill herself. I was comforted to see Josie sitting in the living room when her mother opened the door.

"Please, come in, Tish. Josie is waiting to chat with you," Mrs. Randall said as she closed the door behind me.

I thought it was odd that Mrs. Randall was acting as if this was just a social visit. She did know that I was here to bring up a disturbing subject.

I walked over to Josie and held out my hand to offer her friendship and reassurance that I was not there to upset her. She smiled and shook my hand. She patted the sofa pillow next to her, and I sat where she indicated.

"I am sorry that I did not get to talk to you when you were here before. It is nice of you to return. I know you are very busy," Josie said to me as an opening. Her pretty, petite face looked so like Constance's that I was visibly startled. The dark circles under her eyes indicated Josie still was not sleeping well.

"I am really pleased to see you looking well," I lied. "I have thought about you many times in the past weeks. Are you feeling up to talking with me for a few minutes?" I asked.

"Of course, ask any question you want. I really am fine," Josie said with a weak smile.

I had this unsettled feeling that Josie was not as okay as she said. I knew I needed to be careful in how I framed my questions, but being subtle does not come naturally to me.

"Josie, do you have any new memories from the time you went missing about a year ago?" I asked, hoping this was a safe lead-in question.

"No...I am sorry. I really don't remember anything from that time," Josie said too casually.

"I think your mother said that you only remember shadowy faces and nothing else. Is that true?" I asked, pushing just a bit more.

"That is true. That is all I remember," Josie recited mechanically.

"Josie, when you recall the shadowy face, is there more than one or only one face. I mean, is there several, and one face is larger than the others, or is there just one blurred face?" I pressured.

"Did you recently visit with Dr. Kessler, and did you speak to him about these faces?" I asked.

"Yes, I told him in the past that there were many blurred faces, ...not just one. Sometimes one of them seems very large, pressing closer into my mind. I don't know if the others are smaller or if they just stay further back. I really can't tell you," Josie started to squirm a bit on the sofa as she said these last words.

Melissa Randall also noticed Josie was beginning to become unsettled. She interrupted the questioning. "Josie, would you mind going up to your room and laying down for a little bit. You are starting to look tired, and I think you could use a rest."

I was feeling irritated with Mrs. Randall, but I couldn't say anything. I did not have children, so I couldn't understand how fearful she might be feeling that her daughter could become unhinged again. I could sense her anxiety and respected the fact that she wanted to limit my questioning.

"I'm alright, Mother. I want to talk to Tish. I just don't think there is anything else I can tell her," Josie said to her mother but looking straight at me.

I decided to push just a little further before Mrs. Randall insisted Josie leave the living room again. "Josie, how many blurred figures do you see?"

"There are three," came Josie's immediate answer. "I see three blurred faces. One is close to me in my nightmares, and the other two stay further away."

"Three..." I said with some excitement in my voice. I immediately tried to calm my voice. I did not want Josie to become unsettled.

"Does three mean something to you, Tish?" Mrs. Randall asked.

"One of the other victims said something that made me feel she sees three blurred faces as well. I feel this is important to the investigation," I said and offered no more.

"I am tired," Josie said. "I think you were right, Mother. I am going to go upstairs and rest a bit."

I rose to leave. If Melissa Randall had anything more to add to the conversation, I knew she would detain me, but she didn't. I thanked her at the door and left.

I was pretty sure we were looking at three villains and not just one. At this point, we had to go ahead with the surveillance on Friday night even though I did not want to put Andrea in that amount of danger.

I stopped to talk with Captain Jones on the way home from Randall's house. He greeted me affectionately and led me into his office.

"Okay, spill it. What is on your mind," Captain Jones said knowing I would not interrupt his day if I did not have something important on my mind.

"I just talked with Josie Randall, Constance LaPlante, and Martha Tully, since Brooke Tully wouldn't talk with me. I think we are dealing with three criminals, maybe more," I said after taking my seat in the chair.

"Three criminals, you say," was all Captain Jones said after my announcement.

"Two of the girls definitely said there are three shadowy faces; two that are more in the background, but one is large and is looming. However, there is still no definition or facial feature details," I said, leaning forward with enthusiasm.

"That still doesn't give us a lead," Captain Jones said.

"I know it doesn't, but we now need to think about Andrea. We will be watching her at the coffee house, but if there are three different people involved, how are we going to keep tabs on her. I am terrified for her," I said, looking intently.

"Andrea is a policewoman. She knows the risks. We are also taking every precaution to make sure Andrea is safe. However, to get evidence on the criminals, she will need to be in some danger. All we can do is have her wired; watch her like a hawk, and have police standing by to follow her if needed." Captain Jones sat back in his chair. I knew he had been through stake-out situations a thousand times, but this was a first for me.

"Andrea and Sam are just kids," I said, knowing it was a lame statement since Andrea and Sam were older than I was, and Captain Jones knew that.

"Tish, I know you feel responsible for both. I understand they are your students, and you probably don't feel they are completely ready to be in the situation they may find themselves in. But they are trained police officers, and they did volunteer. I did not force them into taking the assignment. Partially, they are doing this for you. They know one of the ladies is your client," the captain said, knowing his statement was not making me feel better.

"That makes it worse. If anything happens to Andrea or Sam, I will never forgive myself," I said softly.

"Buck up, Tish. What can happen? You, Sam and Scotty, will be on the job. Besides yourselves, there will be undercover officers and uniform police ready to join in on a second's notice. It is going to be alright. Just go home, relax, and get some rest. I expect you and Scotty to be alert and ready for action, ...but not too much action. After all, you two are not officers. You are private investigators, and your role is surveillance only. Got it?" Captain Jones said sternly.

I nodded, but both of us knew that if I needed to do more than just watch, I would. I could tell from Captain Jones's eyes that he knew what I was thinking.

I got up, thanked him for his time, and left his office. His eyes were felt on my back as I walked away.

My next stop was back to the office to fill in Aileen on my discussions with the victims and their mothers. Grateful for my legwork, Aileen did not keep me longer, knowing that I had much on my mind and wanted to get back home to Scotty.

Getting home was a relief. Scotty could sense my tension as I walked through the door. We sat, and I told him about my day and about my talk with Captain Jones.

"Tomorrow night is going to be a big day for us. Captain Jones is right that we need to get as much sleep and rest as possible. We both will need to be vigilant. We can't let anything happen to Andrea, but we can't make any mistakes that will allow the criminals to slip through our fingers, either. That means we are going to need to let Andrea be in more danger than we like if we are going to get evidence on those creeps.

I have the van ready, and we will leave early enough to have a parking place. You will have your Harley at the back door. Sam has his car, and he said he was going to go straight from work to get a parking place out front as well. You and Sam will be wired, Andrea will also be wired, and I will be listening to all of you. I think a uniform officer will be in the van with me. Having some company will keep me awake if the hour gets late. It is going to go just the way we planned," Scotty said as he held me tightly.

CHAPTER TWENTY-THREE

Thursday night found me tossing and turning. Scotty was sleeping like a log. I kept wondering how he did that…I mean, let nothing interfere with his sleep. He could sleep anywhere and in any position at the drop of a hat. I envied him. All I could think was what Andrea might encounter on Friday night if we failed in our attempts to keep her safe.

I would be going over early Friday morning before Andrea left for her assignment at the hospital. Andrea asked me to come over to pick the right clothes for the coffee house. She planned to change her student nursing uniform to a different outfit to wear out. We both knew it had to be sexy enough to lure the perverts, but loose enough to hide her wire. We also wanted enough spandex to allow her to move freely to fight if necessary.

I got up out of bed. It was midnight, and I wasn't the least bit sleepy. I looked in the medicine cabinet. I found some antihistamines. Reluctantly, I took two. I needed sleep, and I knew I wouldn't get any at this rate.

Waking in the morning, I felt sluggish and wondered whether my decision to take a sleep aid was a good one. I might have been better off being tired than slow. I dragged myself into the kitchen and started the coffee. I knew I would be drinking quite a bit of it today.

Scotty must have smelled the coffee. Even though he does not drink it regularly as I do, from time to time, he will join me in a cup. This morning seemed to be one of those days where he would be happy for me to pour a cup. Knowing that I reached into the cupboard for sugar and then I went to the refrigerator for cream. Scotty did not take his coffee black. In that regard, he was a wimp!

"Are you going over to Andrea's place this morning as planned?" Scotty asked as he reached for his mug of coffee.

"I need to get a move on, don't I? I know Andrea will be at the hospital by 9:00 a.m. I just have time for this mug of coffee and a piece of toast. I need to leave. I will meet you at Aileen and Patrick's office for last-minute updates to the plan. Captain Jones will probably stop by. I know Sam intends to be there."

Scotty grunted something. I was sure he was mumbling about breakfast and not having my company, but I couldn't be sure. I did not ask for clarification. To me, grunts aren't worth the time to make clear.

I dressed quickly and grabbed my helmet and keys. Scotty was at the door for a kiss, and I was on my way. I was lucky that the traffic was light, and I had no obstacles, like road work, to hinder my travel. I arrived at Andrea's within fifteen minutes of leaving our house.

Andrea opened the door in her student nursing uniform. I had not seen her in the nurse's uniform before and was surprised at how comfortable she seemed to be wearing it.

"You look like a real nurse," I said as a way of greeting.

"Don't I," Andrea laughed as she smoothed down a wrinkle she found in her dress. "A real Florence Nightingale, right?"

I laughed now, too, because I knew how much she hated floor nursing. Remembering her comment about how hairy backs make her fingers get numb and how she would rather clean up vomit than give a back rub, I knew she was not meant to be a nurse.

"Well, buck up. If all goes right tonight, this will be the last time you need to wear that uniform. You will be able to burn it if you like," I said this as I stepped into Andrea's house.

Andrea had a small house. It wasn't any larger than what Scotty and I shared. The floor plan was similar, but the decorating was totally different. Whereas Scotty's and my house were based on the colors black, gray, and burgundy, Andrea leaned towards the cool spring colors like green, yellow, and soft orange. I liked her style even though it was unlike what I felt natural with.

She led me into her dining room. The wallpaper was leaves in multiple colors of green. Small dainty tangerine flowers seemed to peek out from the leaves. It was clean and cheery, and I liked it.

We sat at her rattan table and chairs. I felt as though I had just entered a garden. Cut flowers adorned the table, and even the placemats were floral. A cup of coffee and pastry was waiting for me.

"Andrea, I actually like what you have done with your place. Have you thought about becoming an interior decorator instead of a cop? It sure would be less dangerous," I said genuinely. I was concerned for her well-being, and I was wanting her to say she was stepping away from the undercover gig tonight.

"Don't be silly. Interior design is not safe. Have you ever dealt with the rich and famous? Do one thing wrong, and you might be missing body parts," Andrea laughed again. She laughed easily.

I did not want to bring up how dangerous her situation could be this evening. There was no sense in making her more afraid than what she must already be. Instead, I turned the conversation to clothing.

"Have you decided what you are going to change into before meeting at the coffee house?" I asked.

Andrea got up and motioned for me to stay put. "I will bring out what I am going to wear," she said as she entered a side room that had to be her bedroom.

I don't know why I had assumed that she and Sam were living together. I was surprised to see that her room was without any of Sam's belongings. Andrea came out carrying several items.

"I decided that these skin-tight spandex pants might be sexy enough to draw in the perp, but my top is just loose enough that I can hide a wire in my bra. What do you think? I am trying for a disco look. I can move really well in the spandex, but I could actually hide a small-caliber handgun under this top." Andrea pulled out a Smith and Wesson snub-nosed 38 special caliber revolver from under her pile of clothing.

Visibly relaxing, I reminded myself that Andrea was a trained policewoman. She knew some martial arts now. I don't know why I had been acting like she was a sheep about to be sheared.

"Andrea, I think you have the perfect outfit picked out. Will you change at the hospital, or are you going to want me to take the stuff and put it in the van? I know an officer will be in the van. What did Captain Jones tell you to do to get wired?"

Andrea replied. "Yes, you are going to take all this with you. I will leave the hospital in my nursing uniform and slip away before Sheri can stop me. I will tell her early in the day that I have an errand but that I will meet her at the coffee house at 7:00 p.m. The idea is that we will have a light dinner, listen to music, and relax. I did not want her trying to babysit me from when we got off at 5:00 p.m. until 7:00 p.m. Originally, that was her suggestion. She wanted me to tag along with her, but I nipped that in the bud, so she shouldn't be suspicious when I slip away."

I interrupted, "I will drive in early to make sure I have a good spot by the door of the coffee house for my Harley. Sam and Scotty also plan on circling the street until they get the perfect spot. They won't need to worry about a parking ticket either if they stay in the spot for hours. I am sure Captain Jones has all those details covered. At any rate, when you get there, just knock on the back door of the van and slip in quickly. Your clothes, revolver, and the officer who will wire you and be listening in will already be there with Scotty. They are using our van because it doesn't smack of police. I will be there, too. I think Sam will get a table where we can watch you without being too conspicuous. I will join him after you are changed and wired. Sound good to you?"

Andrea grabbed a tote and put all her clothing inside. The revolver was on the bottom with her boots.

"Andrea, if you end up on a yacht as we suspect, I think those boots will be slippery on the deck. What else do you have?" I questioned.

Andrea dug the boots out of the tote and turned them bottom side up. "I took the time to put rubber soles on the bottoms of my boots. I remembered the yacht part and decided sexy looking still needed to be functional. I hope this rubber will do the job of keeping me on my feet if the water gets rough. What do you think?"

"I think you have thought of everything. I am impressed. I wish there was time for sparring in the gym. Our last session was a week ago. I sure hope you and Sam practiced everything that I am teaching you. It has to be second nature," I spoke like a teacher.

Andrea smiled. She sat down and patted my hand. "Sam and I do practice. I won't ever be as good as you, but I am working hard. I know how much time you put into our sessions and how much you worry about each of us. You know that even though you are younger than any of us rookies, and you are our sensei, we call you with respect, *Mother Hen*."

From the puzzled look that passed my face, Andrea guessed I never ever heard any of my students calling me Mother Hen. "I guess it could be a lot worse. Mother Hen isn't so bad. In fact, I sort of like it. I guess I make a fuss over all of you. Do I dare ask what you call Captain Jones?"

Andrea quickly said, "We call him, Sir."

We both laughed.

I gathered up her tote bag and walked to the door. I gave Andrea a hug. "I will see you after your last shift as a student nurse. Make it count. You give the best-damned back rub you can give." I winked and walked out of her front door.

Riding over to the Jamiesons' office, I was glad to see everyone was assembled. When offered donuts and coffee, I passed on the donuts. The pastry at Andrea's house was sitting heavy in my stomach. I knew I wouldn't pass on coffee, even once during the day. I wanted to be fully awake and alert through every minute.

Sam was visibly nervous. I knew he cared about Andrea and would blame himself if anything happened to her. I sat down next to him and gave his hand a squeeze.

"You and I will have her back, no matter what," I said with a smile.

His dark eyes bore into mine. "We've just got to," Sam said with little humor.

Sam was powerfully built. He wasn't as tall as Scotty, but he could hold his own on a football field, of that I was sure. It occurred to me that I knew very little about Sam. I wondered if he played sports in school? Was he a good student? I just did not know much of anything except that he was Captain Jones's nephew and that drugs were a problem with his family members. The issues that drugs played around his life made him a bitter young man. Andrea had smoothed his rough edges and made him a happier person. We both knew Andrea needed to be protected. We had a shared purpose for this day.

"I talked to Andrea this morning. I have her change of clothes; her revolver and I suppose you know who will be the officer in the van with Scotty who will wire Andrea? Am I right?" I asked.

"Yeah, I know the officer. Her name is Jamey Wright. She is very technical. I am sure she will do a great job in the van. She has been an officer for over ten years; she should know her stuff." Sam didn't seem pleased when he said these words.

"If she is competent, why do you seem upset?" I asked.

"She has no real field experience. If something goes wrong, she won't be any help at all. She is just eyes and ears and nothing else," Sam growled.

I patted his hand. "Sam, we don't need her to be anything but eyes and ears. You, Scotty, and I, as well as the undercover officer, has it covered. We are a force in ourselves. Anyone who is not afraid of us should be," I said this flippantly, trying to defuse some of the intensity that I was feeling coming from Sam.

He looked at me squarely in the eyes. "You know it. We are badasses!"

"You've got that right. Nothing is going to happen to Andrea. I know you will put yourself between her and a bullet, and so will Scotty and myself. Nothing, I repeat, nothing is going to happen to her."

I wasn't feeling as confident as I sounded, but I knew I needed to defuse Sam before he exploded. He could be a walking time-bomb on his best day. I hated to see what he would become if his fears got the best of him.

Audrey was in the room, chatting with Aileen and Patrick. She walked over to us.

"How does it feel not to be a janitor anymore? I bet you are thrilled to have that assignment lifted off your back. I was glad when Jon came back from his vacation so you could get out of the hospital. I did not want Sheri to take too much notice of you. You did great work and got us valuable information about Sheri Lawton, the pharmaceutical rep, as well as that odd encounter Sheri had with Dr. Kessler. Good work."

Patrick and Aileen sat down at the table with the rest of us. Scotty joined us earlier with a plate of donuts, passing them around. Sam made no reply comment to Mrs. Jones. He smiled a charming smile, which put the conversation to bed.

Captain Jones walked through the door, which saved Sam further. Sam did not seem to be in a chatty mood, and it was apparent he wasn't going to comment on the completed janitor undercover assignment. Captain Jones gave Sam a pat on the back as he walked around the table to find his seat.

"I am glad everyone is here on time. I only have a few minutes to spare; I will make this quick. Sam and Tish will be inside, as I said before, watching Andrea. You should be in place before she arrives with Sheri Lawton. I am assuming you have that covered."

Sam and I both nodded affirmatively. Captain Jones's eyes moved to Scotty. "Scotty, you will be parked in front of the coffee house early. Officer Wright will join you by 6:00 p.m. with the wire needed for Sam, Tish, and Andrea. That means all three of you will need to be in the van shortly after that. Audrey will tell Andrea when she goes to the hospital soon.

"Officer Wright will also make modifications to your van's com gear, Scotty. This will allow us to hear all three participants as well as track Andrea when she leaves the coffee house. I instructed Officer Wright to be at your house at noon to make the needed adjustments to your van's equipment. We should be finished here in plenty of time for you and Tish to get home by noon."

Captain Jones shifted his gaze towards me when he spoke next, "Tish, you are not an officer. I don't need to remind you of that fact, do I? Your job is to help Sam observe. I don't expect you to be involved in any of the police work after that. We will have an officer waiting near his patrol car as well as an undercover officer in place at the coffee house. Between Sam, Andrea, and the other two officers, I expect the bases will be covered."

Captain Jones's eyes bore into mine. It was all too obvious that he was telling me to stay out of the way. I knew he was concerned about civilians being harmed, and I was a civilian. I knew he was waiting for me to nod my head in agreement, but I just couldn't do it. If Andrea were in trouble, I would help her any way that I could.

Scotty's words tore the captain's eyes off mine. I was thankful for Scotty getting me out of a situation. Lying did not come naturally to me, and if I nodded my head in agreement to Captain Jones's demands, I would be lying.

"Captain Jones, will my van follow in pursuit if Andrea is lured into an automobile?" Scotty asked.

"Yes, Scotty, I will want you to follow the police car. Officer Wright will be in constant contact with the other officers. She will be the one tracking Andrea; therefore, it will be important that you follow as best as you can while driving safely. There will be no need for you to speed or go through red lights. The equipment Officer Wright will install in your van can pick up the tracking device on Andrea's wire from quite a few miles away. I don't want any traffic accidents or anyone harmed."

Aileen spoke next, "Don't think that Patrick and I will be left out either. We plan to be at the coffee house as extra eyes and ears as well. We are making this look like a date night, but we will be seriously watching the rest of you."

I chuckled at this. I knew Aileen and Patrick regularly had date nights. I hoped they could keep their eyes on the crowd. For an old married couple, they were totally into each other.

"I might make a trip to your table if I think you aren't watching the crowd well enough," I added to the conversation as a way of a joke. "I have noticed the way you two get lost in each other's eyes."

Aileen blushed, and I was satisfied that I had done my job. Smiling, I winked at her.

Captain Jones stood. Audrey did as well. "Both of us need to get back to work. If there is anything that we overlooked or if something changes for any of you, let me know immediately. Otherwise, I hope to hear that our criminals are caught, and every one of you are safe." The couple went out of the door with that remark.

The rest of us stayed a few minutes longer to finalize our timetables. I asked Sam if he would like to come to our house for lunch and check out what Officer Wright would do to the van. He declined and left. I was disappointed since I felt that Sam could use some company now.

His mood did not improve much from when he first arrived, and I was concerned for him.

Scotty nudged me and suggested that we head home. He said he wanted to clean the van a bit. He did not realize the officer was going to be a woman. I knew that meant that the toilet was probably used and not cleaned. I stood up and hugged Aileen and Patrick and told them I would see them at the coffee house.

"Don't really come over to our table. We aren't supposed to know you, remember?" Aileen said.

I guess she was afraid that I meant what I had said earlier. I just smiled and said I would stay in my seat. I wouldn't even nod or laugh at them. That seemed to make her relax.

Scotty went straight to the van when we got home. I had all of Andrea's clothing and revolver to stash inside as well, but I decided to wait until Scotty had the van smelling a bit better. I placed her bag of clothing on the table and went into the kitchen to make a cup of tea.

Scotty came in about thirty minutes later and asked what we had for lunch. He was afraid that if he did not eat before, Officer Wright arrived that he might forget to eat afterward.

"There is no way you would forget that you hadn't had lunch. However, I will make you a grilled cheese sandwich if that would suit you," I said as I made my way to the kitchen.

Scotty sat at the table and watched me prepare his lunch. "I hope everything goes well tonight. I am not exactly sure what to expect. Do you think Andrea will be asked to go someplace, and at that point, they kidnap her, or do you think they might drug her? It would make a difference as to how we would handle things, don't you think?"

I flipped the cheese sandwich over so the bread could grill on the other side. I walked to the refrigerator to get out some grapes to put on his plate.

"When Andrea comes to the van to change and get wired, I think we should ask her to give us some sort of sign if she is leaving with them willingly and on her own volition. If she is drugged, she probably won't remember that there is a sign. If she doesn't respond, we will know for a fact that she is drugged. What do you think about that suggestion?" I asked.

"I think that is a good idea. What could be a sign? It should be something that isn't obvious. What about if she flips her hair behind her ears or something like that?" Scotty added.

"Sure," I said, "as long as it is something, we all know to watch for. I think putting Andrea's hair behind her ears would work just fine. Let's make certain that the rest of the group knows what her sign will be and what it will mean. I will call Aileen and Patrick. I will see Sam so that only means letting Captain Jones know. He can tell his undercover officer to watch for the sign as well. If she doesn't give us the sign, we will know she is drugged. That will make the rest of the evening much more complicated and dangerous."

I put Scotty's sandwich on a plate along with his grapes. I poured a glass of milk and set his lunch on the table in front of him. "Aren't you going to have lunch?" Scotty asked as he picked up his sandwich to take his first bite.

"Not yet. I want to make those phone calls, and then I might just lay down for a few minutes. I have a feeling it could be a long night, and I want to be rested. I will get something to eat when I wake up. It might not hurt for you to take a nap after Officer Wright leaves. You know how tedious surveillance can be."

I gave Scotty a kiss on his forehead and went to the phone to make those calls. I was thinking how much I hoped to see Andrea slip her blond hair behind her ears before she left the coffee house.

CHAPTER TWENTY-FOUR

It was time for me to change into the disguise I would be wearing. I would put the wig on after getting to the van. Scotty had already left to find a perfect parking spot in front of the coffee house.

I found the baggy jeans in my closet, slipped on the t-shirt and the jacket I bought for Scotty. My studded boots would need to go. I thought about wearing them as I rode on my Harley to the coffee house and switching shoes once I got there, but I decided it was too likely I would forget to change.

My makeup would need to change, as well. I would probably keep my sunglasses on as a fashion statement, so with the wig, most of my face would be hidden. I did not really think Sheri Lawton studied my face all that well the one time we made contact. Especially with my hunky Scotty by my side, I was probably just a glance anyway. However, to be safe, Captain Jones felt I should change my look as much as possible.

I studied myself in the mirror and didn't mind what I saw. Maybe I should consider a new look. My biker style was getting old. The baggy jeans didn't do much for my figure, but I would be able to move freely.

Taking one more glance at myself, I grabbed the bag with my wig and cap and headed to the front door to retrieve my helmet and keys. It was early, but I wanted to be totally ready for what may lie ahead. I was wondering how Andrea was fairing. I would be on pins and needles if I were her.

The van was parked in a convenient parking spot. It was not right in front of the coffee house, which was better. Andrea needed to slip in and out without arousing suspicion. No one had said whether Andrea should be in place before Sheri or if she should follow her in. I guess that was something that would be played by ear.

Finding a spot to park my Harley was easy. It took little space compared to most vehicles. I knew the traffic cops knew not to ticket it no matter where I parked it.

Noticing Sam's car already parked out front, I assumed Sam was in the van with Scotty and Officer Wright. I knocked softly and opened the door. I was sure it was too early for Sheri Lawton to be prowling around, but no one knew who her accomplice might be. Possibly, he may be lurking around surveying the situation. That thought made me uncomfortable. It was hard to be undercover when anyone on the street could be the person we were seeking.

"Hi everyone," I said, as I entered the van, "room for one more?"

Scotty moved off the sofa and went to the other console chair to make room for me. "Come on in, honey. We are just getting the last of the changes made. Everything should be in working order in a moment. You and Sam will need to be wired after Officer Wright gets this last adjustment made."

All eyes turned towards Officer Wright. She turned and smiled a greeting at me. "Just a moment, Tish. I will have both of you set up, and you can be on your way. I would like for you to go to the coffee house to make sure you can hear me, and I can hear you."

"No problem," I said. I looked towards Sam, who was fidgeting with his fingernails. I gently touched his hand and gave him a reassuring smile when he looked up.

"Are you ready for action?" I asked Sam, knowing that the statement would trigger the cop inside of his head.

Instantly, Sam stopped fidgeting and looked me straight in the eyes. "I'm as ready as I will ever be."

"We have this covered, Sam. Nothing is going to happen to Andrea when we are around," I said as confidently as I could.

"Hey!" Scotty interjected. "I hope you include me in the 'we' statement. Officer Wright and I have your backs covered."

Both Sam and I smiled at Scotty. Scotty was in his usual attire. Luckily, Scotty did not need to wear the disguise I had planned for him to wear tonight if he was going to be in the coffee house. He told me earlier that day that the only saving grace for being exiled to the surveillance van was that he could wear his comfortable clothes. Remembering his statement made me smile even broader.

"That does it," said Officer Wright. "Let's get the two of you wired. We need to make some room in this van. Andrea will need to change quickly as well as get wired, so we will need the room. Besides, Captain Jones said you should be in place in the coffee house before Andrea and Sheri Lawton arrives. It will give you time to study the individuals who are already at tables."

Officer Wright started with Sam. Once Sam was wired, she booted him outside. With Sam out of the van, she could have me remove my top to wire me. I regretted wearing the t-shirt at this point. It would have been easier to unbutton a few buttons than to remove my pull-over top. Scotty just studied the console so as not to make Officer Wright uncomfortable.

Once I had my shirt and jacket back on, I went to the mirror and fitted my shoulder-length wig and cap. My sunglasses were the last touch.

"Ahem," I cleared my throat to get Scotty's attention. "How do I look?"

"Wowzah!" was all Scotty said.

I stepped out of the van and met up with Sam. We will need to order a meal if we plan to stay. It was a bit early to eat, but that would mean I could play with my food for quite some time.

Looking over the menu, we decided to stretch the time by ordering an appetizer first. While we sat, Officer Wright contacted us through our concealed earpieces. She asked us to talk sociably with each other to make sure the microphones were working correctly.

Making small talk was not easy for Sam or me. Our relationship had been purely instructor/student to this point. "What do you think of the Cubs?" I started the conversation.

When Officer Wright let us know she could hear us fine, Sam and I settled down to watch the people in the coffee house. I noticed Sam was giving each person as much scrutiny as I was.

The two couples at the furthest table from the door did not seem suspicious in any way. They were talking and laughing. It seemed to me that the pair were old friends. The guys were talking sports, and the two women were checking out clothes that other women were wearing in the coffee house. I pretended not to hear them as they talked about my outfit. I think I looked too ghetto chic for their tastes. I wondered what they would have said about my standard biker-chick look.

Scanning the room, I noted two guys at the bar. Both were drinking espressos. I decided they were college guys on the prowl, looking for dates. Both were wearing Dockers and Madras shirts. They were clean-cut and rather dull looking. It was difficult to imagine them as sexual predators. I kept telling myself that anyone in the room could be a suspect. I needed to keep that in mind and not dismiss anyone out of hand.

Casually glancing around the room as I tried to make small talk with Sam, I located a man I had not seen before. He was older than most of the people who were hanging out at the coffee house. I whispered to Sam to check him out. I wanted to know if Sam recognized him from the hospital.

The older guy seemed like a professional person to me. He was tall, well-groomed with a goatee. His sandy brown hair was cut short, and he appeared to be watching the door.

"Do you know him from the hospital?" I asked Sam behind my hand, which was blocking my mouth from view.

"Don't recognize him at all. He isn't the pharmaceutical rep if that is what you are asking," Sam said in a hushed tone.

I had to admit to myself that I figured the pharmaceutical rep would be our villain. I already decided he would be able to come up with the drug used to knock the young women out. I kept telling myself that I should leave my mind open to any scenario. I didn't want to cloud my thinking.

"Tish, the couple sitting by the back door, do you recognize them?" Sam asked.

"Silly, that's the Jamiesons'. Great disguise," I responded.

Hearing laughing coming from the entrance, I was both excited and anxious to see Sheri Lawton arriving with three of her nursing students, including Andrea. I would never have thought that Andrea was uncomfortable with how well she was joining in with the laughter. I marveled at her acting abilities. She was one cool cookie.

Andrea looked great, maybe too great, since Sam could not take his eyes off her. I nudged him to remind him that we were undercover, and he should not draw too much attention to Andrea or us, for that matter. I could understand, though, why his eyes were drawn to her. Andrea looked stunning in her spandex pants and top that she put on for the occasion.

I noted the man with the goatee was also watching the party enter the room. I kept my eyes on him to see if his eyes stayed on one girl more than another. All three of the girls were blonde and pretty, but Andrea was the most striking of the three. I was relieved to see that he was drawn to the honey-blonde girl with the larger busts. Figures, I thought.

I let my eyes wander around the room to see if anyone else was too interested in the ladies as they took chairs at a table. I did see the two women checking out the girl's outfits and making comments, but no one else seemed particularly interested. No one else had entered since we had arrived. That made it easy to scan the action.

The guitarist was setting up. He was bearded and rather shabby looking, but he had rave reviews in the newspaper. It seemed he could play about anything, but liked to concentrate on his own original work. His music could be considered bluegrass or country. I noted he had several instruments in cases. I guessed he played banjo as well as guitar. I wasn't sure what the other case held. I was afraid I would find out eventually and rather dreaded the evening of music.

I have never been a country-western music lover, and bluegrass was not up my alley either. I like drums and a beat, not hee-haw or ya'll. I guess my bias was showing. I suspected Sam would say the same thing, but we were not here for the music.

The waitress was at Andrea's table. She was taking drink orders. I heard her say she would be right back with the drinks, and then she would take the food order.

Sam and I were picking at our appetizers, but it would not be long before the waitress would be at our table again, expecting us to order something more. I let my eyes drop to the menu so I would be ready when she returned. If there was a decent salad, I knew I would order it. I suggested to Sam that he also look at the menu just so he would get his eyes off, Andrea.

The guitarist announced something about playing a Ricky Skaggs song, and I quit listening. I wouldn't recognize it no matter what he played. The strumming began, and I tuned the music out.

It wasn't long, and the cheery waitress did descend upon us. I asked Sam to consider ordering something that would take a long time to eat, but at a coffee house, the menu does not lend itself to such meals. Sam ordered the turkey sandwich, and I ordered the cranberry, walnut, goat cheese salad. I could toy with mine, but I couldn't see Sam nibbling at his sandwich. I hoped there were some excellent dessert choices for him after he gobbled down his turkey sandwich. Luckily, there was an endless list of coffee drinks we could order and sip away.

A few more people filed into the coffee house. I suppose some were lured by the music on the outside speakers. Judging by the excited looks on their face and the toe-tapping, they were going to stay awhile. I looked them over quickly and hoped Sam would say he recognized one of them, but he didn't.

Two women and a man sat at a table close to the guitarist who stopped playing and was nodding appreciably to the group applauding like maniacs. I was upset to see the musician grab his banjo. I knew I was not going to like the next choice.

"You might know this number made famous by Sam Bush. For those of you who don't know it, it is called 'Leather Britches,'" the banjo player announced.

I must admit that the name of the song caught my attention. I thought the song would be great with a name like 'Leather Britches,' but I was soon disappointed. I thought the song would be about a motorcyclist, but was I wrong. It was something about his daddy kicking him out of bed because he had his britches on. It was just plain odd to me.

I noticed Sheri Lawton was not clapping along to the song like the three young ladies. She seemed preoccupied and kept glancing at the door. From time to time, I noticed Sheri checking her watch.

The food arrived for their table, and the three blondes were eating and listening to music. Sheri was picking at her food. I wondered if Officer Wright was listening to all the chewing and swallowing as well as getting a free concert. If Scotty was listening to all the chewing, he was probably complaining about being hungry and wishing he was at the table with Sam and me.

It seemed like hours had gone by since we arrived. Sam ordered two desserts, more coffee, and I was still picking at my salad when two of the blondes announced they had to leave. I immediately became more alert. I knew this could be the start of the real undercover work. Up until now, we had just been watching the audience eating and watching the guitarist. No one new had entered the room of late.

Blond #1 and blond #2 grabbed their purses and said their goodbyes to the other ladies. Andrea, the buxom blonde, and Sheri settled back into listening to the guitarist and quietly chatting between songs. The two ladies paid their bills at the counter and left together.

I watched closely to see if the third blond would announce that she also needed to go. I knew Sheri told Andrea she would take her home. Officer Wright quietly told us the conversation at Andrea's table. We knew the plan was for Andrea to say she did not have a car and would need to leave to catch the bus. Sheri was right on cue to say she would drive her home, leaving Andrea no excuse not to stay.

People were now shuffling in and out. The guitarist was taking a break but promised to be back in ten minutes. In the meantime, the two couples left. The man with the goatee was still watching the honey-blond haired girl sitting next to Andrea. My suspicions started to peak. I was wondering if he knew the honey-blond girl would not be leaving with the other two women and was waiting for her to go so he could make his move on her. Suddenly, he became more interesting to me, and I watched him more closely.

When he got up and left, I relaxed, dismissing him from the plot. I was becoming more uptight as the evening went along. We had all planned for this evening. We were sure this would be the night the criminals made their move. If we were right in suspecting Sheri Lawton as the procurer, it only made sense that this would be the night. It would be too hard to set up this scenario again. Surely, Sheri would notice Sam if we had to re-stage the evening another time.

Several more people entered the coffee house. Some went to the counter and ordered a beverage to go. Two men were amongst the ones who went to the bar, and I observed them. I wasn't sure if I had really caught a look between Sheri Lawton and one of them or not.

I quietly told Sam that I wasn't sure, but I thought Sheri Lawton had made eye contact with one of the men when the two entered. I asked him if he knew either of them from the hospital.

Sam studied them carefully. "You know, I am not sure, but I think the taller of the two men might work in surgery. I never got to know all the staff, but he does look familiar."

I observed the two men. They had their backs turned to the tables and were murmuring with each other. Neither seemed nervous or on edge in any way.

I started to squirm. I drank way too much coffee over the time we had been sitting in the coffee house. My bladder was making me terribly uncomfortable.

"Sam, I need to go to the ladies' room. I won't be long," I said as I started to push my chair from the table.

"You better turn off your mic if you don't want everyone in the van listening to you," Sam laughed as he said this to me.

"I hadn't thought about that. Thanks for reminding me," I said as I walked away.

I did not think that I took that long in the ladies' room, but when I returned to the table, Sam was gone. I looked up at Andrea's table and discovered they were gone as well. My mic was still off, and there was no way to find out what happened in my short absence. The Jamiesons came to my side and said everything happened quickly, and they would cover our check…go now!

I ran out of the coffee house to see if I could see any of them. What I saw was Sam's car pulling away from the curb very fast.

CHAPTER TWENTY-FIVE

I raced to my Harley and started it up just as our van pulled away from the curb. Reaching for the button on the mic, I spoke excitedly, "What the hell is going on?"

Officer Wright responded. "Where have you been? Why did you turn off your wire?"

"I was in the ladies' room," I hollered as my Harley roared into action following Sam's car and cutting off the van. "Now, what did I miss?"

It was hard to hear with my Harley's engine roaring in complaint. I could make out most of the words as Officer Wright brought me up to speed. "Sam said a tall man came over with drinks for the women, and it seemed he knew Sheri. He passed out the drinks and sat down at the table just as the one other student dismissed herself and said goodbye. Sam said Andrea quickly started acting woozy, and the man offered to help Sheri get her to her car."

"I was only in the ladies' room for a couple of minutes. Boy, did things happen fast," I shouted as I maneuvered my way between traffic.

I was on Sam's bumper now and slowed down. I was trying to see which car Sam was tailing. As a blue minivan changed lanes to make a turn, Sam signaled his intentions to do the same. I stayed close on his bumper, and Scotty in the surveillance van made the corner as well.

Coming to an intersection, the light went from yellow to red. The blue minivan went through the red light, leaving Sam hitting his brakes to avoid hitting a car entering the intersection. I swerved out from behind Sam's car and revved my Harley sliding around three vehicles in the intersection just as they crashed.

"Tish! Don't be crazy!" Scotty yelled through my earpiece.

"I'm not letting them get away!" I yelled back. Sam was right behind me in his car. "They just turned on the street leading to the harbor. I am slowing down to make sure they don't get suspicious of me."

The minivan pulled into a parking space close to a white yacht, I knew this was what we were waiting for all evening. I prayed Andrea was okay.

I turned into a parking space up the hill from the docks and told Sam to pull into the side street with his lights off and join me. As I waited for Sam, I watched as two men came from the yacht and talked to the tall man Sam described. Sheri got out of the back seat of the minivan. I couldn't hear a word they were saying.

As Sam came quietly to my side, I filled him in on what had just happened. "Where are the police and Scotty's van?" I asked.

"I am afraid they got stuck behind an accident. It seemed when the minivan ran the red light, it caused a fender bender involving three cars. We both skirted around the vehicles, so I suspect Scotty and the police should be here in a couple of minutes.

We continued to watch crouched down behind parked cars, slowly making our way closer and closer. I wanted to hear what was being said.

"Get the girl on board. We are going to take off now," a large, heavy-set man yelled from the back of the yacht.

Sheri reached in and pulled Andrea to the door. It was evident that Andrea was drugged since she made no effort to pull away or to assist. The taller man came around and helped Sheri pull Andrea to her feet.

They half dragged Andrea towards the gang-plank with Andrea's head lulling from side to side.

We heard the engine of the yacht starting up and looked behind us to see if the police were in sight. When we saw nothing, Sam and I looked at each other.

"They are going to get away with her if we don't do something," Sam whispered harshly.

We saw the gang-plank being pulled up onto the yacht, and I sprinted towards it with Sam on my heels. Staying in the shadows, we got into a hiding place behind some barrels that were sitting on the dock.

The yacht pulled away from the pier slowly. I sprang into action and landed quietly on the swim platform when Sam, in tow, landed on my left side. We clambered onto the rear deck and scampered downstairs to the crew cabin. While en-route to a hiding place, we observed Sheri Lawton, the two men, with Andrea slumped on a couch in the main cabin.

The larger man was obviously the one at the helm as someone had to be operating the 70-foot yacht, and he was the only one not visible. I decided he must be the owner of the boat and the largest blurred figure that scared my client to death.

"What are we going to do now?" Sam whispered. "We must do something to save Andrea."

"Right now, we are going to be quiet and listen," I responded. "Remember, Andrea is wired, and anything that they say could be what would be needed to put them away. We need to give them time to talk and see what their intentions are going to be. Right now, we could have them for kidnapping Andrea, but that would be all. We need to find out if they are the ones who kidnapped and stole the lives of my client and the other two young ladies. Try to stay calm for a few minutes. We have another problem as well since the police probably don't know where we are."

"I thought they could track Andrea?" Sam said gruffly. "Do you mean they may not know we are on this yacht?"

"I don't know what they know. I have not heard anything from Officer Wright or Scotty since we got to the harbor."

Just on cue, a crackling was heard from my earpiece. I strained to hear if I could make out words. "Where...r...u?" Officer Wright's voice popped in and out.

"We followed kidnappers who have Andrea...we jumped aboard. We need backup. Call Harbor Patrol to intercept the large white yacht." I whispered, hoping Officer Wright would hear me and the yachtsmen would not.

Officer Wright responded, "We won't be able to hear... after... get... from shore. I... contact... Patrol. We are...harbor now. I think I see ... navigation ... in the distance. I will... helicopter ...distance, out of sight. They can ... radio repeater."

I could barely make out what Officer Wright said and was glad Sam was listening as well, so there was no sense making any extra noise to tell him anything else. We both knew it would take many minutes before the helicopter would be in the air. In the meantime, we were on our own.

We sat quietly on the top of the stairs that descended to the crew's cabins. We hoped there would be no one using this cabin since there was no apparent crew. I was thinking they were probably planning on dumping Andrea across the lake on some deserted beach as they did in the past. Sam and I both knew it was not going to happen this time.

Straining our ears to hear what was being said, voices suddenly became louder, and we could distinguish one voice from another. We were trying to put a face to a voice.

"You got us a real cutie, Sheri. I think she might be the sexiest one yet," one voice said. I did not think he was the tall one or the heavy-set man. I suspected he was the smaller of the three.

Sheri Lawton made no comment back. She remained totally silent. I looked at Sam and whispered, "I hope they are getting all of this back at the harbor."

The boat was slowing now, and a rather deep, gruff voice became clearer as the big man obviously was joining the others. "What's your pleasure, men?"

I wasn't sure if he was offering them a drink or if he was looking at Andrea. My skin crawled when I thought of Andrea as being the object of their pleasure.

The taller man's voice was crystal-clear when he spoke, "I'm tired of drugged women. I want my pleasure to be awake and fighting. I can't get the image of the first blonde we took aboard this boat. I want a bit of that action again. It's no fun having my way with a limp dishrag, no matter how good looking she is. We've had enough drugged girls to last me a lifetime back at the frat house."

"The problem is that we need to throw her over if we give her the antidote. You know that from the first little darling," the gruff voice boomed.

"We got away with it. No one ever suspected that the first girl was anything but a drowning. I say, let's do it again. I want some real fun," the tall man droned.

I could feel Sam becoming tense, and I put out a hand to calm him. Listening to the men talk about Andrea, the way they were discussing her was making him crazy. I feared I would not be able to contain him in the stairway for long.

The third man's voice stated, "I have the antidote with me. I'm just a little concerned about killing another woman."

Finally, Sheri Lawton spoke in a halting, shaky voice, "She's a nice girl. I don't want to be involved in her murder."

"Shut up, Sheri. You have no say in any of this. Your job is just to find the right girl and bring her to us. If you don't, your career is at an end when they find out about your addiction. Besides, you are already up to your tight-ass in this. You were the one who procured the last four pieces of ass for us. We go down; you go down," the big man said threateningly.

I could feel my stomach tense. I was trying to decide how to get Andrea out of this mess. We were miles from shore and no place to go. I had no idea if any of the men had guns. I did not know a thing about any of them except they were evil.

The gruff voice commanded, "Sheri, take her down to get her changed, then give her the antidote. I think I would like to see her in the Brazilian beach bikini. Make sure she has plenty showing before you bring her back for our approval. I think she will be just about ready to give old Freddy here, the fight he wants by then.

There was silence, and then one could hear Andrea start to mumble. "Josh, help her to her feet and down to the cabin. It is time for Sheri to get her into the costume."

We could hear the shuffling of feet as the two of them took Andrea below.

"Why do you always get to pick the costume?" Freddy whined again.

"It's my boat, well, my daddy's boat. Big Daddy is the one who pays for all this. It is my decision as to what our little darlings wear. Do you have a problem with that? You always were a whiner. To tell you the truth, I am not sure why Josh and I hang with you anymore," the big man said.

"You know exactly why you hang with me. My dad owns a pharmaceutical company that makes this all happen. If it wasn't for my dad's rep finding out Sheri Lawton was a junkie, we wouldn't have Sheri under our thumb. Then where would we get our little playmates?"

"Keep irritating me, and I will find another source. It wouldn't be that hard to pick up some girls at a bar. Most girls are impressed when I tell them I have a yacht."

"Yeah, but those girls all have families. Sheri always hand-picks ones who only have a weak mother at home. How do you think we have gotten away with all this so far? Besides, you need my special drugs to keep their memories wonked. You can't do this without me, and you know it, so bluster away. I'm not afraid of you."

Steps could be heard as the third man came back. "It shouldn't be too long now. She was stirring when I left. I think Sheri found the little bikini you requested. In a few minutes, we can start the party. Anyone want a drink while we are waiting?"

We listened to the clanking of glasses. Even more disgusting talk was heard, and I spent my time reassuring Sam that nothing was going to happen to Andrea.

We got our first word from the helicopter. The voice was Scotty's, and my heart skipped a beat. I was wondering how Scotty managed to get on the helicopter, but there was no time to ask questions. We were assured the helicopter had the yacht in view. Scotty said they were getting everything on tape, and they were standing by.

Just in case they did not catch everything, we told them what we could about the conversations being held by the three men. Captain Jones came on to say we were to sit tight and do nothing. The Harbor Patrol would be pulling alongside the yacht in less than ten minutes. He repeated, "Do nothing. Do you understand?"

We both said we would stay put. It was dark in the stairwell, but I could hear Sam breathing hard. He was enraged and ready for action. I could understand how he felt. I felt like I would like to kick the big guy in the gut myself.

Hearing more footsteps nearby, Sheri's voice sounded strained and panicked, "She's wearing a wire. My gosh! She's a cop. They are onto us."

"What are you saying?" the taller man said in astonishment. "If you are right, we need to get rid of her now. If they are onto us, there will be a boat here soon. Let's throw her overboard now while she is still woozy. She will drown, and they will never find her out here."

"No! You can't kill her," Sheri shouted.

"Shut up, Sheri. I am warning you. We will throw you overboard as well." The words were menacing, and not another word was heard from Sheri.

"Go get her now!" commanded the large man.

"Don't we get to play with her before we throw her into the lake? If we are just going to kill her anyway, I want my turn with her," Freddy said.

"Will you shut up, Freddy? Don't you have any idea what this could mean if they pull up alongside us, and we have her on the yacht with us? What makes you think they have not heard everything we have said if she is wired?" Josh said.

"For one thing, we are too far out from shore. They can't hear anything. The only proof that we kidnapped her...is her. If we get rid of her...like weigh her down and throw her over, there will be no evidence. We will just be three guys and a gal out for a ride. No law against that," Freddy shouted back at Josh.

Sam was straining against my arms. I held him as tight as I could. "Wait," I said.

"I'm not waiting for them to throw her overboard. I won't let them hurt her. Are you going to come with me or not?" Sam hissed through his teeth.

I sighed. "Of course, I will fight with you to make sure Andrea is safe. Let's go, but quietly. We need the element of surprise. We still don't know if they have guns or not."

Sliding the hatch open, we both stayed low and in the shadows. We slowly made our way closer to the voices.

Sheri brought Andrea to the waiting men. Andrea looked confused but no longer totally drugged.

"We have a surprise for you, cop," Josh said, trying to sound mean.

Andrea looked down at her outfit. She noted the ridiculous skimpy costume. "What in the world am I doing in this thing, and where are my boots?"

It sounded odd to me that Andrea would be worried about what she was wearing now, but I realized Andrea didn't even know where she was. She had been drugged from the moment she left the coffee house if not actually in the coffee house. I was only hoping her senses would return quickly. We could use the extra hands if this came to a fight.

"Tie her up and find something heavy to weigh her down," the big guy snapped.

As Josh went to find a rope and weight, Sam could no longer endure seeing his love being poorly treated. He sprang from his cover and ran to the open cabin door to her defense.

I could only groan. Sam's timing was not the best. We did not have the advantage in our favor as I had hoped to have. All we had was the element of surprise, but I had hoped for more.

The big man was surprisingly quick on his feet. He ran to the back of the cabin just as Sam was coming in. The large man kicked Sam back out the door to the aft deck and yelled for Freddy to help.

Andrea, recognizing Sam's voice, shook her head to clear it. As Josh came towards her with the rope, Andrea moved awkwardly behind the sofa chair, staying out of his reach. As Sheri reached to stop her from moving away from Josh, Andrea let her fist hit Sheri square in the nose. Blood gushed from Sheri's nose as she crumbled to the main cabin deck. Josh continued his pursuit of Andrea as her wits slowly seemed to come back to her.

The big man had Sam down on the deck and was hammering him with his fist. I kicked the big man in his ribs to move him off Sam.

Seemingly unaffected by the kick, the man came at me menacing as Freddy scampered across the main cabin, waving a gun. My biggest fear was realized. They did have a gun. It was Andrea's gun that was hidden in her boot.

"Back off, right now," Freddy threatened me as I was preparing for another launch at the big guy.

Freddy waved the gun at Sam as well and told us to get over beside Andrea, who was still eluding Josh. When she saw the gun pointed at her, she stood still.

The three of us were herded against the wall. Freddy kept the gun pointed at us as they escorted us out to the railing of the side deck.

"What do we do now, Kip?" Josh asked.

So now I finally had the big guys name, Kip. It did not fit.

"Well, they are all going to need to go for a swim. That means more rope and more weights. I guess we could shoot them first to make it easier, but I don't want blood on my yacht if the patrol does come aboard. No, Josh, you are just going to need to tie them up. We have them covered. Go get more rope," Kip ordered.

"We don't have much time, Kip. I see lights on the water. I think the Harbor Patrol is on its way. We need to hurry."

With Josh coming with rope and weights, and Freddy with a gun pointed at us, I had no choice but to use my Qi-Gong. Grandmaster Kim Yong-Sool warned me to never use the mystical powers when there were witnesses, but I had no other choice. The Harbor Patrol would not get here in time, and neither would Scotty and the helicopter.

I closed my eyes and allowed myself to draw all my powers within my body. I focused my energies and lifted my hands towards Freddy, with Kip standing next to him. The gun was the first thing I needed to disable. I let loose a wave of energy, knocking Freddy and Kip to the deck. The gun went sliding down the stairs to the swimming platform below.

Standing now, shocked for a moment, Kip soon got his wits about him and raced towards me. Using his bulk, I flipped him onto his back while twisting his arm until it snapped. This time, with all my might, I kicked him in the side of his chest. I heard all his wind escaping his lungs as he bellowed.

Josh, with Andrea between him and myself, came rushing like an enraged bull, knocking an unsteady Andrea over the rail and into the water. Sam, hearing her screams, raced to the railing, and dived in to save her. I found myself on my own to confront the two remaining men.

Into a fighting stance, I raised my hands for self-defense and for killing blows if necessary. I had never killed anyone with a kick or punch. If it came to that, I knew where to aim.

Josh stopped his rush and stood still, unsure of what he should do next. Kip, winded from broken ribs and possibly a punctured lung, rasped out at Freddy and Josh to finish the bitch. Telling Freddy to move to my left side, he instructed Josh to be prepared to rush me from the right side of my body. Kip laid on the deck in pain.

I was relieved to hear the 'womp womp womp' of the blades of the helicopter. The lights from the patrol boat were growing brighter with the spotlight directed straight on the deck where we all stood. Sheri had never gotten up off the cabin deck from the blow she received from Andrea.

As Freddy advanced, Josh picked up a boat hook off the outside of the cabin to stab me. I was circling away from Freddy and coming within range of Josh's hook when I saw a flash of light from a rifle in the helicopter. Blood was gushing from Josh's ear, and the boat hook was lying on the deck.

A bullhorn sounded from the boat, "Step away from the woman and put your hands in the air."

Freddy looking over his shoulder saw a rifle aimed at him. Looking up, I saw Scotty in the doorway of the helicopter proudly holding the gun that took Josh's ear off. He gave me a wave.

Not being totally stupid, Freddy and Josh raised their hands over their heads and waited for the Harbor Patrol to board the vessel. Sheri and Kip were incapacitated and no longer a threat to anyone.

I rushed to throw a lifeline to Sam, who was treading water while holding Andrea's head above the waves. I was relieved to see Sam and Andrea were alright.

I stood shaking and told myself to breathe long and deep. The adrenalin was taking its toll on my body. One can't perform Qi-Gong without some adverse effects. I only hoped the three, who were being taken into custody, would not tell what I had done. I could deal with what Sam and Andrea saw after this was over.

CHAPTER TWENTY-SIX

I strained my eyes to see if Scotty was amongst the crowd waiting for us at the dock. One of the Harbor Patrol officers had taken control of the helm and was docking the yacht while the three men apprehended were aboard the Harbor Patrol's boat. I could see two of them being led to an ambulance, and the third was being led into a waiting police car as we approached the dock, but I did not see Scotty. I was anxious to find out how he had gotten aboard the helicopter.

Captain Jones was waiting to talk with Sam and Andrea, huddled in blankets, and me. I was sure we would be taken to his office as soon as we left the yacht. I knew he would want every detail. Some of the events were recorded by Officer Wright, but there were many minutes of missing tapes, and the good captain would want to be filled in.

I was right. As soon as we set foot on land, Captain Jones ushered us into his car. We drove away from the harbor with me, scanning the crowd to see Scotty.

"Where is Scotty?" I asked with anxiety ringing in my voice.

"Don't worry, Tish. He will meet us at the station. His helicopter landed, and he is on his way in another squad car."

I watched as Sam cuddled Andrea protectively into the crook of his arm. The drug had worn off, the cold water helped, and I could see relief in both of their eyes. No one wanted to talk at this point. We all just sat and replayed the events of the evening in our minds.

I saw Scotty inside the captain's office. My heart skipped a beat. It wasn't until that moment that I realized I could have been killed and dumped into the lake, never to see Scotty again. I found myself fighting back the tears, and I raced into his arms and clung tightly to him. He returned my hug ferociously, like a protective bear.

As Captain Jones came into the office, I forced myself to let go of Scotty, but Scotty took more time to release his hold on me. When the captain told us all to take our seats, Scotty finally released me but refused to let go of my hand as we sat side-by-side. I noticed Sam and Andrea were doing the same.

"I will need each of your individual statements. I want you to know I understand that it has been many long and dangerous hours. I don't know whether I should scold you or give you each a medal. At present, I think you all need to go home and get some rest. Sheri Lawton is giving us all the information we need to put the other three away forever. I know you will be able to collaborate with some of her stories."

Sam became animated and jumped to his feet. "They were going to kill Andrea!"

I was aware Sam was pent-up with anger, and he didn't know how to deal with it. There was murder in his eyes. If any of the three men were in this room right now, there is no question in my mind that Sam would not be able to stop himself from beating each one to death. To be honest, I am not sure I wouldn't have joined him myself.

Captain Jones remained in his seat and said calmly, "But they didn't kill her, Sam. You were there to keep that from happening."

"But what if Tish and I had not been able to jump aboard the yacht? What if...." Sam's words trailed.

"But you did, Sam. You and Tish saved the day, and the department is proud of both of you.

"I can't promise you that Andrea will never be in danger again. I know that is what you want to hear from me. You are both police officers and mighty fine ones, but the risk is just part of the job. I will understand if you both want to resign."

"No," Andrea spoke for the first time. "I knew what I was getting into when I accepted the assignment to go undercover. Someone had to stop these criminals, and I am proud that I... I mean we...could do that. This is what I want to do with my life. I want to make a difference."

I watched Sam start to defuse. He looked at Andrea, and I could see the love and pride he had for her. He took his seat next to her and reached for her hand once more.

"I don't like that any of you were in danger. I am particularly concerned that Tish was as involved as she was since she is a civilian and not a police officer. I may find myself being criticized for allowing her to be entangled in the apprehension." Captain Jones hesitated, and Sam took the opportunity to speak once again.

"None of us would be alive if Tish had not been on that boat. I don't know how she did it, but she disarmed the men and gave me the opening to dive into the lake to save Andrea. Whatever criticism you find yourself in for allowing Tish and Scott to be involved, be aware of how all this would have ended without them. Tish is the real hero here, and I think you should make sure the world knows it."

I panicked. "Gosh! No! I don't want anyone to know, let alone the world." I was suddenly aware that everyone would want to know how I disarmed and kept three men at bay. I couldn't let anyone know about Qi-Gong. My grandmaster had warned me how dangerous it would be if anyone knew.

I tried to calm myself, knowing that all eyes were on me. Scotty was patting my hand, attempting to relax me.

"I think Tish is right," Captain Jones said knowingly. "We need to downplay her role in the apprehension of these criminals. When I talk to the newspapers, I will come up with a storyline that will minimize her actions on the yacht. In fact, we all need to say the same thing, so let's come up with a scenario right now before any of you leave this room." Captain Jones was taking the lead.

It was decided that Andrea did not get knocked overboard until the three men were subdued, and the Harbor Patrol was already moored alongside the yacht. "Andrea was still woozy from being drugged, and she lost her balance, right?" Captain Jones rehearsed.

I could feel myself relax as I realized my secret would probably not be revealed. I kept reminding myself that I had to be more careful. I could not let myself be in this situation ever again. I dodged a bullet this time, I hoped.

Captain Jones finally told us to go home and get some sleep. He said he would want us back in the morning. He directed Andrea to get checked out medically at the hospital for a blood test and hair follicles to provide evidence of the drugs the criminals used. Sheri Lawton would corroborate the use of the drugs and the provider.

Andrea was lucky on many levels. If they decided to rape her and drug her the way the other three women had been used, Andrea would have no memory at present. It was odd the way things turned out. As horrible as it was, it could be a whole lot worse.

Someone had brought the van and my Harley to the police station. Relieved to have a quiet ride home since I wasn't ready to explain anything about the events to Scotty. I let the wind whip against my face. I knew I would be scolded by Scotty when he saw I was riding without my helmet. I knew it was stupid, but I wanted to feel life…and every aspect of it. The cold, the biting wind, and the rush of speed as I rode faster than the speed limit, weaving in and out of traffic made me feel alive and exhilarated. I slowed down when I realized the danger Scotty was putting himself in trying to keep up with me. I only hoped Scotty wouldn't be mad when we got home. I didn't want to be scolded tonight.

When we got back home, Scotty didn't mention my recklessness. He just grabbed me and held me close again. We let our lips touch, and I melted into his arms. Finally, releasing me, we headed to the sofa.

"I saw what you did from the helicopter, Tish, but I won't ask you any questions. I know there are things you can't tell me or anyone, but I wanted you to know that I know, so you understand I am on your side forever, one-hundred percent. I will never ask you about what you did, how you did it, or even mention it again. I am just glad you could do what you did." Scotty started to go on, but I hushed him by kissing him on the lips.

"No more talking," I said. "I just want to be next to you for the rest of our lives."

Scotty scooped me up and carried me to the bedroom.

In the morning, I woke up early. Thoughts were spinning through my head, and I just couldn't sleep in as I had planned. Scotty stirred beside me. Opening one eye, he pulled me closer to him.

"Want to tell me how you got on that helicopter? I sure was happy to see you up there. You probably saved my life," I said as I snuggled closer to Scotty.

Scotty yawned. "I'm sure I saved your life. You owe me. I think you should make breakfast for the next year to repay me."

I dug my nails into his ribs. "Yeah, right. You think my life is only worth one year of breakfasts?"

"Okay, you make breakfasts for the next ten years, and we will be even," Scotty joked back.

"Seriously, how did you end up on the helicopter?" I asked as I settled my head on Scotty's shoulder. "Tell me what happened from your point of view."

"There isn't that much to tell. After we got caught up in the traffic jam, Captain Jones radioed to say the yacht had launched, and you and Sam had sneaked aboard. Captain Jones asked the Harbor Patrol to pick me up at the dock in their helicopter since I was the best shot available right then. The captain just thought we should have every angle covered. See, not much of a story." Scotty nipped my ear after telling me these words.

"Ouch! That hurt," I complained. "Just because I owe you my life doesn't mean that you get to be mean to me."

Laughing, Scotty nipped my earlobe again. He was ready for a wrestling match, and I obliged. Rolling out from under his arm, I jumped astride him and leaned down and bit his nose.

"There, now we are even," I said as I rolled off his chest. "I think your story should have been embellished a bit to make it more exciting. You didn't even mention hanging out of the door of the helicopter as you took that shot. Were you aiming at his ear, or did you miss your mark?"

Scotty laughed. "Oh, yea, that! Of course, I missed my mark. I was really aiming for his other ear! But the story sounds better if I say I hit what I was aiming at, doesn't it? Can you imagine hitting a small target like an ear from a hovering, vibrating helicopter?"

"What if you missed him completely and had hit me?" I said out loud.

Scotty laughed even harder. "There is no way I could miss my mark that badly. Give me a break."

"I guess you are right," I remarked. "You are pretty darned good with a rifle, even hanging out of a door, five stories in the air."

"Five stories? It was more like twenty stories," Scotty exaggerated.

"Get up! I'm hungry, and I want my breakfast. I want pancakes, eggs, and orange juice...freshly squeezed." Scotty laid back on his pillow with a smirk on his face.

I reached for my pillow and smacked Scotty on the head as I rolled out of bed to start making breakfast. "I am going to need to save your life soon, or this stuff is going to get old very fast."

We were back at Captain Jones's office before 9:00 a.m. Andrea and Sam were already seated as we entered. Captain Jones was looking at the newspaper.

"The article in the newspaper is pretty good. Tish, you are barely mentioned; avoid the press at all costs. Sam, you are going to need to stay clear of them as well. Hopefully, the press will be more interested in the court hearings, and the police officers will take a back seat." Captain Jones laid the newspaper down on his desk.

"What do you know about the case, Sir?" I asked.

Replaying the past events in my head, I knew the culprit's first names and basically what they had been doing. I did not know who the men really were and how long they had been kidnapping women and ruining their lives. I knew the men would be in jail forever since they admitted to murdering the first woman. I just didn't know why. I guess no matter what their motive was, I would never understand the inhumanity. It was just horrible and unthinkable.

Captain Jones filled us in with the information he received on Sheri Lawton's statement. "It seems that Fredrick Jorgenson's father owns a big pharmaceutical company. Freddy, as he likes to be called, went to a costly college where he roomed with Joshua Morgenstern and Gustaf 'Kip' Vandermint. All three were wealthy, privileged boys whose fathers covered for them when they got in trouble. From what I gathered, they got in trouble a lot. It seems they avoided trials by paying off the young women they violated. Even back in college, Freddy got drugs from his father and used them to drug the coeds and date rape them. Kip master-minded these crimes, and Josh went along with them.

At any rate, their sexual appetites did not diminish as they matured. Once Freddy's father's pharmaceutical representative caught Sheri stealing from the medicine cabinet, he found a good source of extra money by telling Freddy about her. Kip is the one who came up with the scheme. Once they had Sheri blackmailed into doing their bidding, it was easy to keep her silent and working for them."

"I thought for sure we would find Dr. Kessler involved in this case," I said to Captain Jones.

"My wife talked to Dr. Kessler," Captain Jones said. "It seems he was suspicious of what was going on. Sheri Lawton felt guilty and remorseful for her students and the part she played in the ruination of their lives. She was the one who would recommend Dr. Kessler to the women's mothers. At first, Dr. Kessler just thought she was concerned about her former students, but when three young women presented with similar histories and diagnoses, he became suspicious of Sheri Lawton. He talked to her once, and Sam overheard their heated discussion. From what I gather, Dr. Kessler is innocent of any wrong-doing and is just a good psychiatrist trying to help his patients."

"I guess I owe him an apology," I said. "Arrogance does not mean guilt. I will need to remember that in the future."

Scotty asked, "So, Kip's father owned the yacht, and all three men liked to use it to party. I don't understand how they got away with this for so long and were there more women than the four we know about?"

"I don't know how long the three men have been drugging women and raping them. If they used the drugs from Freddy Jorgenson's father's company, there could be other women. We might never know.

"I imagine they started out with the date rape pills for any of their previous crimes. Probably any of those women were drugged, raped, and left to sleep it off. They would suspect that something happened to them but did not report it. Many young women feel they were somehow responsible for what happened because they were in a bar alone or at a party drinking.

"The three women, in our case, were a different set of circumstances from the usual date rape scene. I suspect that they used stronger, memory-altering drugs because they kept the last three women for longer periods. It is probably a blessing they don't remember what all happened to them," Captain Jones said the last sentence under his breath.

"We will be starting another investigation into the fathers of these three offenders to see if they are part of the conspiracy," Captain Jones added. "The fact that Freddy got drugs from his father's company puts his father at the top of the list for the investigation."

Andrea spoke up with some vehemence in her voice, "This time, those creeps' fathers won't be able to cover up for them. They are going to jail for what they did. I hope they rot in jail!"

No one was going to argue with Andrea. We all knew how close she came to being another victim and how angry she must feel. The fact that she had remained calm for this long was a testimony to her training.

It sickened me to think about how many girls had been their victims in college and for years afterward. I wondered how the fathers of these men could live with themselves. Why did they think they were somehow above the law just because they were rich? I figured some of what their fathers did was to cover-up to protect their jobs, reputation, and lifestyles. It was just immoral as far as I was concerned.

Scotty's words shook me from my contemplations. "Boys will be boys...right?" Scotty's voice dripped with sarcasm. "Someone should castrate all three of them!"

I found myself musing what might happen to these three in jail, and I hoped for the worst. I couldn't find any mercy in my heart for them. My thoughts turned dark as I thought about my own experience being molested as a child and how I wished my uncle would have gone to jail for what he did. I felt cheated by his death.

The next morning, I grabbed the newspaper and sat down with a cup of coffee. The headlines were about the heroic policeman and policewoman who assisted the Harbor Patrol in the capture of the three men who had been victimizing young women. Andrea and Sam were highlighted, and good to his word, mine and Scotty's part was downplayed. We were barely mentioned. I was thankful to Captain Jones for making sure we were kept in the background. I knew he did it as much for the police department as he did for us, but I also knew he was protecting us.

Aileen and Patrick phoned to say they would like us to meet them for lunch. We had much to talk about.

Scotty was dressed casually as was I, we walked out the door to the Double Nickel. As I slid into the passenger's seat, I was taken back to all the fun days we had in high school driving around in Big Red. I guess I needed to be transported back in time when I felt more light-hearted. This case made me feel like I needed a bath. Being around such filthy men still made my skin crawl.

I knew I would be asking Aileen about Constance LaPlante. The case was solved, and there would be justice, but would Constance ever lead a healthy life again. While there was more to Constance's case, she seemed more stable than Brooke and Josie. I secretly had high hopes for her recovery.

Reaching the office, we found the table set and the Jamiesons ready to eat. Corned beef sandwiches were on the table, and I saw Scotty's reaction out of the corner of my eye.

"Wow! I haven't had a corned beef sandwich in ages. I almost forgot how wonderful they taste," Scotty said as he guided me to the table. We sat down, and I munched on a potato chip as Aileen poured iced tea into our glasses.

As she poured, she said, "We saw the newspaper article in this morning's paper. I asked Captain Jones to keep your names out of the paper if possible. It seems he could do only so much. You two were only mentioned as private investigators assisting the police department in this case. Don't get me wrong, the free advertisement for the firm would have been nice, but not at the expense of putting you two in jeopardy. We need your anonymity for future cases. The more well-known you become in the community, the less effective you will be during surveillance. I hope you don't mind. We know you deserve the credit owed. After all, this case would not have come to such a tidy ending without the two of you."

As Aileen sat down to join the rest of us, Scotty said after swallowing a big bite of his sandwich, "Gosh, no, we don't mind. Tish and I like being able to move around without being recognized. I don't always love the hours of surveillance in the van, but being undercover is exciting. Also, if it keeps Tish out of danger by not being recognized, I hope we never get famous."

I smiled inwardly. I knew what Scotty was trying to say. "I agree we will be more effective if we aren't known. I do have a question about Constance, Aileen. You have been to her house on several occasions. Do you think she will be alright eventually? I would like to think solving this case will give her some peace of mind, and maybe, she will be able to re-start her nursing career."

Patrick looked at Aileen to see how she would answer the question. I noted that Aileen let her eyes lock on Patrick's momentarily. I feared what was going to be said next. I hoped and prayed Aileen would not tell me Constance took her own life. I waited with a chip in my hand.

"I talked to Dr. Kessler. I was asked by Captain Jones to see if he felt the women involved would be able to identify their kidnappers and rapists. He said not now and maybe never. Captain Jones knew it would make his case stronger if any of the ladies were able to identify any or all the men. However, Sheri Lawton's statements will probably be enough to put them away for a very long time. Andrea's and Sam's testimony will also help strengthen the case against them. As far as to whether Constance will be able to work anytime soon, the answer is no. She is doing better than Brooke or Josie, but she is very fragile. The best Dr. Kessler could say was perhaps in a few years."

I sighed a big sigh of relief. "I was so afraid you were going to tell us Constance had committed suicide. Hearing Constance may be able to hold down a job in a couple of years is actually good news to me."

We continued to talk about the abduction case for another hour, and then Patrick switched topics. "We have everything lined up for your weeks' vacation at the lake with your parents. I know you are going to have a great time relaxing, and when you get home, we have possibly two new cases we would like your help with. Do you think you will be ready to go again in a week? I know a week isn't very long, but we can't put this case off."

Both of our interests were sparked. Scotty asked first. "What are the cases we will be working on when we come back. If you need us to postpone our trip to the lake, we can, right, Tish?"

Before I could answer, Patrick said it would not be necessary for us to postpone the vacation. "You need it, and you are entitled to it," were his words. "Besides, your parents would never forgive us if we postponed. Your mother, Tish, phoned us yesterday to thank us for such a lovely gift. I think her heart would be broken if we delayed. She was talking about how she had to catch the largest fish. Something about some competition."

I laughed. "I don't remember who was the last one to hold the honor of best fisherman in that group, but my mother is as competitive as the rest. It may have been her, but if I get my way, I will be the one with the biggest fish this year."

"Oh no, you won't!" Scotty butted in. "I have a new lure that hasn't even been used yet. I am locked in for getting the biggest fish this year."

For a moment, the new cases were forgotten, as we laughed at Scotty. "What are the new cases?" I asked as I picked up our plates to take to the office kitchen.

Scotty jumped up to gather the rest of the glasses, condiments, and leftovers. "Will it require lots of hours in the van?"

"Of course, it will," said Patrick as he pushed his chair back to stretch out.

"In a way, this first case is much like the last one. I hate to put you two on these cases so soon after having to deal with the scum of the earth, but frankly, that is what you must get used to as private detectives. Our jobs have us dealing with the worst elements of society way too often." Patrick sat back straight and out of his relaxed position as he continued talking.

I was listening and dreading what the next case would be. I had been hoping for another fraud case or something involving research in the archives or something equally as dull. I had a feeling that was not going to be the case.

Patrick pulled out a file folder. "Captain Jones gave us countless runaway and missing children's files for a possible case. Most are young girls between the ages of twelve and sixteen. Captain Jones fears there is a human trafficking gang in the city. He needs some extra eyes and ears on the street, and he came to us. The city has agreed to pay for our detective services. He feels you two could blend into the streets better than most of his officers. Once again, you will be working closely with Andrea and Sam. I believe a few more of your rookie trainees will be on the streets as well, Tish. I am not exactly sure which ones he has assigned to this case, but you will find out when you return from your trip.

Captain Jones also gave us a lead to a possible serial robbery case. We can't tell you much more at present, so we think you two should go home and pack your fishing gear. We will talk more when you return.

Leticia LaPlante is giving us a generous check for solving the previous case. She is thankful the men who harmed her daughter have been taken off the streets. In fact, she added a bonus check just for the two of you. You will find your checks ready to be cashed when you return from your vacation."

With hugs and kisses, we thanked the Jamiesons for the best corned-beef sandwiches in the world and left to pack our bags. We had plenty of time to pack and drive to the lake should help us to unwind. Our parents...and the fish would be waiting for us.

Carole Walker Carter

Starting life in a small town in Nebraska, Carole and her family moved from the Mid-West to the West Coast. Carole continued traveling from California to Texas, Ohio, back to Nebraska and finally settling in the Pacific Northwest with her husband, Don, her childhood sweetheart and partner, their dogs, and a few fish.

Carole's career involved working with children from pre-school through high school, dealing with special needs, and "at-risk'" children as an Occupational Therapy Assistant and Educational Assistant.

Meeting unique people throughout her life, fascinating characters formed in Carole's mind. These individuals shaped the basis for real and imagined characters found in her various forms of storytelling from Science Fiction, Detective, to her Children's Books.

Find her books on Amazon, Kindle, Nook, Apple Books, and Barnes & Noble Now by searching for *Carole Walker Carter*!

Aztara, The Mastel Kingdom
By
Carole Walker Carter

Aztara, The Mastel Kingdom, tells the background story of the majestic mastel creatures that roamed the rugged mountains and the fertile valleys of Aztara. The setting for this book is two generations before the plague that killed all the Aztarian women during Volume I, *Surtees, Science Rules*.

Idyllic as the lush lavender summer pastures might seem, the mastels are forced to be nomadic, dependent upon the weather and growing cycles for their diet. Equipped with spiraling horns and clawed feet, the stallions are always at the ready to protect the herd against terrifying river monsters and voracious tree-dwelling beasts.

The newly established bond between the cave-dwelling griswells and the mastels seems destined to fail, until Morsian, an inventor from the eastern factory villages, creates a symbiotic relationship that will change everything on Aztara...forever.

Explore the early world of Aztara and enjoy the Mastel's unique story.

Find this book on Amazon, Kindle, Nook, and Barnes & Noble Now!

Surtees, Science Rules
By
Carole Walker Carter

Surtees, Science Rules, is Volume I in the *Aztarian Series.*

In *Surtees, Science Rules,* we discover how ruthless a dystopian society can be when the ruler is a despotic scientist determined to achieve longevity to remain in power forever.

Ananaya brutally seizes power from his father, Ryndor, who set up several senior scientists as the leaders of scientific research centers. Under fear from retaliation, the scientists carry out the plans of Ananaya, which in turn, causes destruction to the air, water, and food supplies for the citizens of Surtees. As the Surtarians' lives crumble under the oppressive rule of Ananaya, two unlikely young females, Tawtanya and Myana, rise from champions of the Surtees Zrymir Games to become heroes of the planet.

Find this book on Amazon, Kindle, Nook, and Barnes & Noble Now!

AZTARA, A Galactic Love Story
By
Carole Walker Carter

AZTARA, A Galactic Love Story, Volume II in the *Aztarian Series,* centers on two main characters from two different planets whose lives are turned upside down by the ruthless scientist, Ananaya.

Shayla, an Earth woman, grieving for the loss of her only child and deceived and abandoned by his father, is close to suicide. A unique bond with fantastical creatures on her new home of Aztara helps Shayla to return to a balanced life in a strange new world.

Ty, having lived through a plague killing all the females on Aztara, finds refuge in his work, mining the mineral, phyrium, instrumental to all aspects of life on Aztara, including telepathy, longevity, and levitation.

Ananaya, the Chief Scientist from Surtees, leaves a dying planet to relocate on Aztara to seize control of the mineral phyrium for his own benefit. In his attempt to rebuild his army of Enforcers, he abducts Earth women who carry a specific gene, the warrior gene, to mate with the Aztarian men. This momentous event brings our two main characters together to face the seemingly insurmountable challenges of an intergalactic romance.

The story is about finding internal strength, trust, and love. Intrigue and thrilling moments prevail while the two main characters come to grips with a situation, not of their own choosing.

Find this book on Amazon, Kindle, Nook, and Barnes & Noble Now!

AZTARA, Secrets Revealed
By
Carole Walker Carter

AZTARA, Secrets Revealed, Volume III in the *Aztarian Series,* is the culmination of Ananaya's ultimate plan. The offspring of the intergalactic mating produce some surprises for the peaceful Aztarian men. Shayla's and Ty's love produced twins.

Nayela is the only interspecies girl on Aztara that bonds telepathically with a mastel. Kestle, jealous of his sister's abilities, has his hands full with being a gang member.

A tragic event occurs, changing everything for Kestle. Self-banished to the Wildlands leaves Kestle alone to deal with situations for which he was unprepared. Going deeper into the Wildlands brings Kestle to the dreaded Orange River, where dangerous monsters lurk. Saving a young runaway girl, Sinaka, from certain death. He discovers, however, there is more to this young girl than he first thought.

Sinaka finds it is her turn to save Kestle when a monster wounds him. With unexpected help from a beautiful creature and Sinaka's psychic and empathic powers, Kestle finds healing.

The Surtarian Chief Scientist, Ananaya, accelerates his plan to genetically modify the Aztarian/Earthling boys' Warrior Genes. Ananaya's plot is to create a daunting army of new Enforcers. All hell breaks loose when the usually passive Aztarians decide to fight to get their boys back.

Find this book on Amazon, Kindle, Nook, and Barnes & Noble Now!

Final Alumni
By
Carole Walker Carter

The Final Alumni is Volume I in the *Evers and McFarlan Detective Series*. This series follows two high school best friends who join forces to start careers as private investigators. Tish, haunted by a childhood experience, enables herself mastering many disciplines of martial arts, while Scotty falls back on his expert firearms training and physical prowess as a football quarterback.

Out of high school, the two go to Chicago, Illinois, to pursue their career through education and on-the-job training. Mentored by a well-respected couple who owns The Jamieson Detective Agency, Tish and Scotty are enlisted to assist Aileen and Patrick Jamieson in solving cases in Chicago while pursuing a series of unsolved murders in their own hometown as well.

Find this book on Amazon, Kindle, Nook, and Barnes & Noble Now!

Shadowy Faces
By
Carole Walker Carter

Shadowy Faces is Volume II in *the Evers and McFarlan Detective Series*. In *Shadowy Faces*, Tish and Scotty are confronted with the lives of three young women who have been ruined. Each young woman deals with lost weekends where all they can recall are vague faces tormenting them. The shadowy faces become the focus of the investigative team of Evers and McFarlan along with the Jamiesons and the Chicago Police department. The team works methodically to discover what happened to each of the women to bring the criminals to justice.

Tish needed to lean on a secret discipline her Grand-Master taught her even with the warning of what could happen to her if anyone should learn of her new martial arts fighting technique. Scotty also faces the threat of losing the love of his life

Find this book on Amazon, Kindle, Nook, and Barnes & Noble Now!

Nine Points of a Circle
By
Carole Walker Carter

Nine Points of a Circle is Volume III in the *Evers & McFarlan Detective Series.* In *Nine Points of a Circle*, Tish and Scotty are fully licensed detectives in The Jamieson Detective Agency. Even though the Jamiesons' are preparing to retire, they continue to mentor, advise, and direct Scotty and Tish on new cases.

Nine Points of a Circle

Evers and McFarlan Detective Series

Captain Jones tries to block Tish and Scotty from getting involved in what appears to be an intelligent yet spine-chilling serial killer. Three homeless girls were murdered over the past five days, and their bodies were dumped on different streets in greater Chicago. At the same time, Tish and Scotty are assigned to a serial robbery case and are approached by a well-known Chicago business executive regarding his missing daughter.

All three of the cases challenge Scotty's mathematical and technical expertise and Tish's detective and martial arts skills to solve. Follow Tish, Scotty, and Duma, their tracking canine, as they plunge themselves into the plight of the homeless on the dark and perilous Chicago night streets.

Find this book on Amazon, Kindle, Nook, and Barnes & Noble Now!

The Child Rowanda, Little Dragon
By
Carole Walker Carter

The Child Rowanda, Little Dragon Volume I, Twelve-year-old Rowanda lives with her mother and grandmother, an elder sorceress, in the lush garden planet of Neslora. Seemingly an idyllic world with endlessly blooming flowers, buzzing bees, and birds chirping...until.

A tyrannical king's guards abducted and transport several women of Neslora to the desert world of Arolsen, where they are being kept as slaves.

Rowanda and her friends discover, with horror, the abduction of their mothers. Armed only with four talismans, chosen by mystical means, Rowanda goes through a portal to Arolsen where her fate is intermingled with two desert dwellers. Together they join forces to brave the scorching desert days and frigid desert nights to rescue Rowanda's and her friend's mothers. Rowanda learns to use her magic to defend against nomads, desert serpents, sand dragons, and vicious felines.

The Palace City of Arolsen reveals the true identities of Rowanda's traveling companions and the reasons they accompanied her on her quest.

Find this book on Amazon, Kindle, Nook, and Barnes & Noble Now!

The Child Rowanda, Return to Arolsen
By
Carole Walker Carter

The Child Rowanda, Return to Arolsen, Volume II, Alarm spreads through Neslora as unexplained destruction occurs to the bountiful planet. The Elder Sorceress discovers the evil king, Nashua from Arolsen is using charms Rowanda left for her friend Boultori to use to turn their barren desert into an oasis.

Now, Rowanda, with the help from her father, her grandmother, and best friend, must right the wrong by retrieving Rowanda's talisman and exchange them for charms that Boultori might use to overthrow his evil brother's rule of Arolsen.

Two new talismans, chosen by magic, assist Rowanda as she learns to control the most feared, yet fascinating creatures on Arolsen. These creatures aide Rowanda on her quest for justice.

Magic abounds in this second book of the Child Rowanda series as good battles evil to rescue a world from slavery and hardship and to keep Neslora from the same predicament.

Find this book on Amazon, Kindle, Nook, and Barnes & Noble Now!

The Child Rowanda, Underworld
By
Carole Walker Carter

The Child Rowanda, Underworld, Volume III, Rowanda, attempts to rid the world of Neslora of the evil wizard, Nashua, Rowanda finds herself dragged into the Underworld with the evil sorcerer.

Navigating the terrifying darkness of this new world, Rowanda finds a mysterious and mystical guide who reveals that Rowanda can only exit the Underworld the same way she came in, with the evil sorcerer at her side. However, Nashua must be truly repentant of his depravities before he is allowed to leave, which means Rowanda cannot depart the Underworld if Nashua does not repent.

Trying to find Nashua in the darkness and convince him to repent, becomes a complicated and dangerous process. Making matters worse are the demons, intent on making both Nashua and Rowanda one of them, meaning living an eternity in the Underworld in agony.

Find this book on Amazon, Kindle, Nook, and Barnes & Noble Now!

Khaos, Lord of the Thunder Dragons
By
Carole Walker Carter

Khaos, Lord of the Thunder Dragons, is the prequel for *The Child Rowanda, Dragon Princess* book. Dragons have been depicted as monsters, devils, or even good-luck symbols throughout history. Dragons have been the focus of many stories throughout fictional and fantasy literature.

This is Khaos' story. Created by a mythological goddess, he is cast down with the lesser dragons to a world below. In this desert world, the dragons are thought of as either flesh-eating demons or good-luck omens. Differing labels are placed on these creatures, depending on the experiences of the nomads. Terms used include abductor, greedy hoarder, devourer, custodian of wisdom, guardian of the tree of life, chaos, as well as being symbols of good and evil.

You will find stories of brave young men, wanting to prove themselves and protect their villages, traveling to meet the monsters in battle, while others are rescued by the dragons and hold them in high reverence. Whatever men call Khaos, he remains, above all, the Lord of the Thunder Dragons.

The history of the dragon Khaos continues with many stories in these pages culminating in an encounter with Rowanda, the Dragon Princess. Here this story ends, but with more to be told by the many who will continue to encounter *Khaos, Lord of the Thunder Dragons.*

The Child Rowanda, Dragon Princess
By
Carole Walker Carter

The Child Rowanda, Dragon Princess, Volume IV. Leaving the Underworld through another portal, Rowanda finds she has not returned to her home-world of Neslora but finds herself on another parallel world with the devious Nashua. Here Rowanda is elevated to a princess.

Friends and members of her family are in this world, but they are not as they should be. They are doubles with a different personality and...no recollection of Rowanda.

Rowanda finds herself at odds with her look-alike parents, the king, and queen of Soleran.

Rowanda's magical talent of charming animals allows Rowanda to help the enslaved citizens of this world by joining the rebel army in opposition to the king and queen.

Wanting nothing more than to return to her own world, Rowanda seeks the aid of an ancient fire-breathing dragon.

Find this book on Amazon, Kindle, Nook, and Barnes & Noble Now!

Childhood Stories My Dad Told Me
By
Carole Walker Carter

Childhood Stories My Dad Told Me, is about growing up on a farm in Nebraska during the Great Depression. It was difficult, but for two young boys, life on the farm was also filled with fun and adventures.

This book is based on stories my dad told me about the amusing antics that he, his siblings, and friends found themselves in during these hard times.

The stories, filled with insights about rural schools, country social events, and harvest time, as well as the day-to-day chores of a working farm, are informative as well as enchanting.

Find this book on Amazon, Kindle, Nook, and Barnes & Noble Now!

www.ingramcontent.com/pod-product-compliance
Lightning Source LLC
Chambersburg PA
CBHW070808180626
46818CB00001B/162